THE GUARD

The Guard Trilogy Book 1

N. L. Westaway

Original Cover Photo by Gregory Morit
Cover designed by Beach House Press

This book is a work of fiction. Names, characters, places, and incidents either are products of the author's imagination or are used fictitiously. Any resemblance to actual persons, living or dead, events, or locales is entirely coincidental.

N. L. Westaway
Visit my website at www.NLWestaway.com
ISBN: 978-1-7339442-3-6
Printed in the United States of America

December 2018 Limited Edition Print Copies – Not for Resale.
First Publication: May 2019 Beach House Press

The Guard Trilogy

The Guard

The Unseen

The Believer

This book is dedicated to my mother, Sarah (Sally) Elizabeth Westaway, who was a voracious reader and who would never have guessed I would ever write a book.

It is also dedicated to all those who have fought against an illness, those who have witnessed a loved one struggle with an illness, and to those of you who have lost someone they love due to illness.

~ Strength to you all.

"The relationship between modern daughters – especially grown-up daughters – and their mothers never ceases to fascinate me.
It is warm and close, and loving. It is also frank and terse, and ruthless. It ranges over every conceivable topic, from their inmost dreads, and from the strength of their sauces to the colour of their handbags.
Mothers and daughters, in my experience, no longer have secrets from each other worth talking about. All is grist to the never-ending mill." ~ Godfrey Smith

Anagram - An anagram is a type of word play, the result of rearranging the letters of a word or phrase to produce a new word or phrase, using all the original letters exactly once. *www.en.wikipedia.org*

The eyes = They see
Salvaged soul = God save us all
Listen = Silent

Chapter 1

They called it the *Summer of Love*, a social phenomenon, though with the constant news of race riots filling the airways, it sounded more like the summer of never-ending hate. In contrast, that summer, famed civil rights attorney, Thurgood Marshall, made history when he became the first African-American confirmed to serve on the U.S. Supreme Court. It was also the same summer the Beatles found their way to peace and relaxation with a two-month pilgrimage through India, their single *All you need is love* hit #1 on the charts, at the same time the United States were sending 45,000 soldiers over to Vietnam. The summer ended with the Labor Day Telethon broadcasting on one station, WNEW-TV in New York City, and hosted by Jerry Lewis, who raised $1,126,846 for Muscular Dystrophy.

The universe has an interesting yet terrifying way to balance the dark and the light, the happy and the sad, and the good and the evil— it's Yin and Yang. While wars are being fought far across the ocean, here in North America as children head back to school, a peaceful gathering is about to take place.

* * *

Parliament Hill - September 1st, 1967, Ottawa, Ontario Canada

The four stood together on the walkway between the Queen's Gates and the Peace Tower facing the Eternal Flame. They spoke openly as regular men would if merely on a lunch break from some office job nearby, but it wasn't as if anyone could see this host gather.

"Prime Minister Pearson is supposed to light the flame this coming New Year's Eve. Wonderful job on the stylized maple leaf logo," one exclaimed.

"Canadian Centennial, the 100-year celebration," Uriel said. "Did any of you attend the Expo in Montreal this past summer?"

"Do we have just cause to celebrate?" Michael asked.

"Why, is something worrying you about your Charge?" Uriel said back.

"Mine? No. She'll be 10 years old at the end of the month. Well, she's not my Charge yet, but she will be. She's a strong girl, constantly seeking knowledge, always full of questions—though she may exhaust her mother before she turns 12." He laughed. "My current Charge, her mother, is the youngest of that generation, but her daughter is the eldest with two younger brothers to contend with. She's quite the rebel already. She'll make a fine Linguist like her mother and grandmother before her." Michael turned to face Raphael. "And what about yours?"

Raphael stood with his hands behind his back, rocking on his heels. With raised eyebrows, he glanced towards the question, then turned to answer Michael's inquiry. "The nurse, yes—she is well. She has suspended her nursing career since the birth of her daughter, and similar to Michael's *pending* Charge, she's the eldest with two younger brothers. Her daughter, only 2 years and 9 months at present, will be my next Charge. She was born on the same day as Michael's current Charge in fact—clearly not the same year." He chuckled. "The child's grandmother—*she* too the eldest, but of three sisters, works for a doctor in Napanee. The young-one's line of women is strong, and I am told she has a baby sister arriving next month. I have no doubt my new Charge will be a fine Healer like her mother," he said, gloating. "Uriel, you seem concerned. Where do things stand with your Charge?"

Uriel stood still as if pondering how he might answer. He looked to Michael on his left, then back to Raphael on his right. Leaning forward he spied Vretil's nervous face peek from around the other side of Raphael. Then he spoke, "Mine... she... well... she is the youngest with one brother older. Her mother also has a brother, and four sisters. Another strong female line. Being of Irish descent, these women passed... uhm... *recipes* verbally, but she possesses the book—the one handed down from her mother. She is a natural with the herbs, perceptive to the elements, a true Mother to the earth, and she has become an accomplished conjurer. At present, she has a son who is the eldest, a daughter born between yet another son. Although, I'm told this daughter is not the one." Uriel took a deep breath. "Fortunately, she is pregnant again, and I have been assured a daughter will be born in March of next year. She will be the youngest like her mother, and my new Charge." Finishing, he moved to stand by his brethren, Vretil, who's expression held a deep concern. "Why so worried my friend? Does your Charge not already have a daughter?"

Vretil ran his hand down his face as if trying to free himself of negative thoughts. He straightened to face his dear friend, and said, "Yes, my Charge has a daughter. She is 5 years old and I'm told also— this daughter is *not* the one. The child's father is no longer in the picture, as they say."

"Does she know yet?" Uriel asked, pushing for more.

"That she's The Scribe? No—not yet. Another who watches over, tells me there will be no other children born from this line. Interesting enough though, thanks to the family dog, the daughter had found a new companion for her mother, and this December they will have been happily married for 3 years." His face beamed, and his voice lifted in sharing the news. "Soon things will be revealed by the grandmother to her mother, but in the meantime, all I can do is observe and wait." He paused. "Awareness of the role too soon... could influence the mother's decision to have or not have more children. But I am confident she will make an excellent Scribe like her mother. I was especially pleased after seeing her skills with the bridal etiquette book she wrote last year, and she adapts quite swiftly with her life's career changes and challenges. She has a younger brother, and is the middle of three sisters, also from a strong female line. However, I still worry... we still only have three of four so far—there must always be four." He grimaced, the pain of his concern returning to his expression.

The four stood in silence reflecting on the problem.

Gabriel, who was also of their brethren, appeared next to the four. "Bad news!" he exclaimed, his words causing the others to scatter like startled birds. "The Arab summit conference in Khartoum is over. It is written; the Arab states appeared to have slammed the door on any progress towards peace."

"Shouldn't Shamsiel be watching after Haj Amin al-Husseini?" Rafael blurted. "He assured Hitler that the Arabs were Germany's natural friends because they had the same enemies. He spent the rest of World War II as Hitler's special guest in Berlin. Shamsiel had to watch over the two of them." Raphael panned the faces of the others.

There was a collective sigh. They knew *watching over* was one thing, but involvement or interference was all-together another.

"Gabriel—what are you doing here?" Michael roared, fury flooding his face.

"Don't tell us you're checking up on our little venture, now are you?" Uriel asked next, taking a step forward.

"We've gotten everything under control down here," Raphael said, once again looking to the others.

Vretil didn't say a word. Instead, he pretended to examine the hem of his sport coat, waiting to hear what Gabriel had to add.

In a slow turn, Gabriel looked at each of them, only to stop at Vretil, watching him as he fiddled with his jacket. "You think the balance is maintained, do you?" Gabriel questioned. "You all think this is so simple. A daughter is born and oh, all is well in the world. Wrong!" Gabriel said, his voice rising as he spoke. "While you were busy attending the Expo and now waiting for yet another New Year's Eve celebration, the world continues to sway out of balance. This past decade is a clear indication." Gabriel crossed his arms over his broad chest.

The mouths of the others gaped, and their faces flushed.

Vretil kept his eyes down, staring at the hem of his jacket like a scorned child. "It's not all bad, Gabriel," Vretil said. He still didn't glance up. "Martin Luther King Jr. made his speech, *I have a Dream* in 1963. You know the impact that had."

"John F. Kennedy was assassinated in 1963," Gabriel said, rebuffing, his tone mournful.

Vretil took a breath. "Again in 1963, John Glenn was the first American to orbit the Earth. How about that?" Vretil responded. "The first Civil Rights bill was passed to stop racial discrimination in 1964. The surgeon general determined finally that smoking was a health hazard, and in 1965 required cigarette manufacturers to place warnings on all packages and advertisements."

"Vretil, people still smoke," Gabriel disputed, shaking his head. "Look at this year so far; January 27th, the Apollo 1 spaceship fire killed those three astronauts Grissom, White and Chaffee. February 23rd, US troops began the largest offensive of the Vietnam War. What about on April 3rd when the 113 East Europeans who attended the World Amateur hockey championships in Vienna, all asked for political asylum? Does that look or sound like balance to you?" Gabriel paced as he continued. "June 4th, the Stockport Air Disaster; if you don't recall, was the British Midland flight G-ALHG which crashed in Hopes Carr, Stockport, killing 72 passengers and crew. Happy day, right? Then there was June 8th, when Israel attacked the USS Liberty in the Mediterranean, killing 34 US crewmen."

Michael opened his mouth to speak, but Gabriel lifted his hand stalling his dispute. Index finger pointed up, he shook it at each one of them. "Let's not forget about the race riots this past summer, Tampa, Cincinnati, Buffalo—Detroit was the worst. The police confrontations with patrons and observers on the street evolved into one of the deadliest and most destructive riots in this continent's history. It surpassed the violence and property destruction of Detroit's 1943 race riot. And don't even get me started about the natural disasters." Gabriel turned to face the Peace Tower, letting out a long-exhausted breath.

The others said nothing. Vretil dropped his head again and let out a little sigh, returning to fidget with his coat hem.

Gabriel turned again to meet the faces of his friends. "Yes, Vretil— it is not all bad, but there are no signs of things improving." He paused. "I am told that *He* is not confident the balance will be upheld." Taking a deep breath, he readied himself for more. "Over the centuries, I have continued to support all of you in the choices you have made. I have stood back while you did what you thought would ensure *He* was happy, and that those choices would prove humanity was not affected by those who *fell*." He glanced at each of them. "Long ago, you convinced Him," he said, pointing up, "that only four would be needed to keep the balance. That the *four* would continue to be born throughout the generations and that the sacrifices of the mother for the daughter would prove humanity was worthy of His love. And in turn, avoiding humanity's potential destruction. You have also shown Him that those who have fallen... that *not* all are evil. But as the population rises, so does that evil," he finished, glowering at them.

"What makes you so sure our four won't continue? Just because Vretil's Charge does not yet show signs another daughter will be born, does not mean one won't be born in time," Uriel said.

"I have seen the worry in our friend Vretil's face for some time now," Gabriel responded. He stepped closer to Vretil.

The others turned to observe their worried friend.

Gabriel took another deep breath. "Concerned for the plight of my friend, I sought council with those who oversee matters concerning childbirth. I shared my concern over the lack of another birth regarding Vretil's Charge."

"And?" Michael questioned.

"Their response came as two-fold." Gabriel took another pause when Vretil glanced up. "Be assured my friend, Vretil, there will be another birth. With it—a daughter, and she will be your new Charge. There *will* be four as it has always been." Gabriel stopped, but his face revealed there was more.

"So, what is the problem?" Vretil asked, piping up and ending his childish pouting.

"The overseers worry too much about the children," Michael stated. "My Charge shows great promise even at 10 years old and she has only begun her journey."

"The problem is not the new daughters under your watch, the problem is... not all the daughters—will have daughters themselves!" he shouted. "Herein lies the problem, don't you agree?" Gabriel let out the breath he'd been holding, yet his expression revealed he still had more to say. He took in another yet calmer breath.

"What can we do to ensure the four continue?" Raphael questioned. "We are not permitted to get involved. We cannot interfere with fate or their free will."

"You won't have to," Gabriel breathed out. "I have already set things in motion. I have ensured the balance will be upheld, four... will now become... *five*."

Michael gasped and grabbed Gabriel by the arm. "My brother — what have you done?"

Gabriel folded a hand over Michael's in a gesture for forgiveness. Closing his eyes, he slowly bowed his head.

Chapter 2

September 15th, 2009, Current Day, Ottawa, Canada

Thunder clapped, and gloomy clouds blanketed the sky in shades of deep blue and grey. Rain tapped against the glass windows like tiny clear pebbles. The room within was long and narrow, the ceilings high were edged in squat windows reminiscent of an old-fashioned schoolhouse, and wooden benches for seating filled most of the space. Near the front awaited a raised area with steps like a small stage.

After listening to each of my brothers speak, it was now my turn. I stood, and my knees gave a little. I caught myself before anyone noticed my weakness. I moved through the small space, squeezing by my eldest brother as I edged out into the aisle. I turned and paused, facing down the steps leading to the podium.

I'd agonized the night before over what I should say. I hadn't thought the need to write these words would have come so soon nor had I ever pictured myself saying them. But I had rewritten the speech until I'd had it just right. Even if my brothers and cousins still saw me as the youngest, I was no longer a child. I was all grown up now. Maybe it wouldn't be what everyone would expect or hope to hear, but I had written what I wanted to say. It would not be the story of a whole lifetime, but instead a story dear to me of how *we'd* first met.

Wearing a dress—which was rare for me, though it was the right choice for the occasion, I climbed the steps in my all too unfamiliar high heels. My girlfriends had helped me pick out the dress a few days prior and with try-on after try-on, we'd known it was the one. Shopping was one thing of those typical girly-girl things which most women loved to do—just not me. My girlfriends knew how difficult a chore it would be for me, and knowing my aversion to shopping, they'd happily assisted in the hunt for the perfect dress. I loved new clothes, it was the process of getting them I found unpleasant. So, here I was, in my dress and high heels, my hair just so, and a vintage butterfly pin fastened over my heart. It was one of my mother's many butterfly pins and it finished the outfit with both style and sentiment.

My mother loved butterflies. They had become a real passion of hers over the past 10 years. The fascination started when her friend's mother had passed away and the friend had given my mother the opportunity to choose a piece of jewelry from the woman's collection. Mom had always been fond of a butterfly brooch the elderly woman often wore and picked it even when she could have chosen something from the more expensive items. Mom treasured it and kept its use for only special occasions. Over time, the piece became fragile, the clasp weak, and much to her dismay, the butterfly must have lost its grip and the brooch was lost. Her grief over losing it was tremendous and the sense of guilt for not fixing the clasp lingered. Ever since, she had made it a point to search for the piece, hoping for it to turn up in some little boutique for her and it to reunite. She had painfully recalled the story and had told me how she now felt the need to have butterflies around her. She has received numerous gifts with the butterfly theme, but nothing could replace that special piece. Over the years she must have purchased a dozen butterfly brooches and various other items in butterfly form, but she never found the lost pin.

Today, the piece I wore was of similar antique quality, with muted colours of bronze and earth tones unlike the traditional colours and appearance of other crafted butterflies. Still, with my new tailored black dress, the vintage piece made for the perfect finishing touch.

Standing at the podium now, I took a deep breath in and out to calm my nerves. At the far end of the room, right in front of the doors, stood the bagpiper in his formal outfit, dark blazer, a tartan kilt, and bagpipes. He nodded at me, and I unfolded my speech.

I glimpsed the first line of words, then glanced up and over the heads of my family in the first row to review the faces of the others waiting for me to speak. My cousins were with their families, and my Uncle, who a month earlier had stood in my place to make a similar speech, watched me patiently. Familiar faces from the years gone by filled the seats: family, friends and neighbors. Near the middle, I could see the waiting faces of my girlfriends. Some were with their children, some with spouses, and others with their mothers.

I looked back down at my speech and took in another deep breath. Clearing my throat first to avoid any squeaks, I read aloud. "Thank you all for being here with us. Thank you to Mom's neighbors, who have been so good to us and to Mom. Without them, we would not have been able to get through the past year and certainly not the past few weeks." I paused and glanced around the room again. I swallowed hard and then continued. "It was only a few weeks ago we gathered in this same place to say goodbye to my mother's sister, my Aunt Kay. For my aunt's service, my Uncle Mick brilliantly told the story of her life. For those of you who knew both women, they were two halves of a whole, and now they are whole once again." I took another quick glance up. The torn expressions on my girlfriends stared back at me, watching the tears that now rolled down my face.

"We were...," I continued, but my voice cracked in my attempt and I lost the air to speak. I paused and took another shuddered deep breath to push forward. "We were all part of her life and we all have stories and memories from her life to share and cherish. I'm here not to tell you the story of my mother's life, but to tell you about her life... with me." I smiled through my tears. "My favorite things about my mother were her humor and the stories she would tell me about her life before I was born. The best ones were stories from her teen years and those during her time as a nurse. Stories about old boyfriends and the memorable patients she encountered through her nursing career. But my most favorite story has always been the story about how Mom... met me."

I knew with confidence that the next part I was about to share would help ease the pain in those faces. I stood up straighter and once again took in a deep breath. Letting out the cleansing breath, I began my story. "For those of you who don't already know, I have three older brothers, James, Robert and Scott. When Mom would get frustrated with me, she would yell '*Ja-Ro-Sco-Lynn!*' And with that label, I realized they each had frustrated her equally at some point before me."

I glanced up again. All the faces and along with my brothers were nodding in recognition. I smiled out at them and continued. "My mother always wanted to add a girl to the mix, but since my Aunt Kay also had boys—four, her chances didn't look good. So, the Westlake family decided they would adopt one. Yes, I'm adopted, but I prefer to say I'm *The Chosen One*," I added, with a little laugh, and continued again. "Anyway, Mom finally got her girl—but what she hadn't realized, with her little girl being surrounded by all those boys, the big impact it would have." I grinned. "From a young age it had started. It was a fight to get me into a dress. I was determined to be like the boys or a tomboy as she called me. But there have been a few times over the years I have given in. I wore a dress for my wedding, and again here for her today." This time I smiled directly at my girlfriends.

"The story of how Mom and I met is not a long one, but I used to get her to retell it to me all the time—simply because I loved how *she* told it. Each time she would add another facet to it, perhaps something one of my brothers had said, or maybe a comment from Aunt Kay— who I considered my second mom."

I looked around again. The faces weren't so sad now and it made it easier to go on. "I started out my life at the Civic Hospital and it was a short three months later when I went home with the Westlakes. That part of the story I'd known for quite a while, but it was of recent—about a year ago, when Mom had added the latest piece to the story." I grinned again because I loved this part. "We were talking about how I was born exactly three months before her birthday, how I was a birthday present. She hadn't realized what she was getting." I smiled bigger, and those who understood laughed. "She mentioned—being a nurse herself, that when babies were in the hospital nursery under similar circumstances, the nurses would often give the babies temporary names. It was usually something like Hope, or Joy or something equally inspiring. So, I asked Mom, *'Do you remember if the nurses gave me a name?'* She had taken a minute to think about it while I waited to hear the *something inspiring.*" I paused again, both for effect and for another calming breath. "Now if you know my mother's humor, she—without missing a beat and with a straight face, said, *'Yes, they called you... Little Baby... oooover to the left'.* Silly me, I asked, *'Really?'* which she'd promptly responded, *'No, I just made it up'.* And we both laughed hard at her comical response."

What I hoped would happen—happened, and I paused to take it all in. Laughter had escaped from the mournful faces, especially from those who truly knew my mother and her humor. Some snorted back tears, as did I, while others smiled big and dabbed their eyes. My oldest brother smiled and nodded with pride because he knew Mom would have loved that everyone was laughing. I gave him back a knowing grin and continued on to finish my speech. "We all have our stories about Sally and all of us are her life story. Continue to tell the stories and laugh aloud because laughing was another one of her favorite things. Please share your stories with everyone so we can continue to be a part of her life. They—whoever they are, say it's the journey and not the destination. So as *The Chosen One*, otherwise known as *Little Baby Over to the Left,* I'd like to wish my mother a wonderful journey. Thank you."

I folded my speech, left the podium, and stepped away from the altar. I'd given my speech standing next to a beautiful wooden oak box embellished with carved butterflies. The box contained my mother's ashes.

As everyone quieted, I again squeezed by my eldest brother and took my seat. He tapped my leg and said, "Good job," the way a big brother would if you'd gotten the word right at a spelling bee. A hand from behind, came over my left shoulder. It was my cousin Thomas, my Aunt Kay's eldest. He said no words, only squeezed my shoulder.

My tears came again, and it was the hand of my husband that moved to cover both of mine, which were mashed together still holding a wad of damp tissue. William didn't care my hands were clammy or that the tissues were wet. He knew any gesture greater would have caused a breakdown of my strength, ending in a pool of ugly tears.

After the minister spoke, and the service ended, the funeral director gathered up the beautiful butterfly box and stood at the end of the row to which we all sat. We all rose from our seats and turned to move to the pew's opening.

Joining my brothers in the aisle, I followed the slow gentle walk of the funeral director as she carried my mother towards the open double doors at the end of the room. At the start of the service, we had entered this small chapel on the grounds of the funeral home led by the son of one of my mother's best friends. The bagpiper. He had played as he led us in and now once again as he led us out.

In the days before the funeral at the wake, we had had many visitors. There were so many faces I had not expected to see, and so many emotions I had not expected to feel. Now, as we stood in the hallway, family, friends, and a few strangers addressed each of us with sympathies and blessings. I hugged many of them. I was surprised at how seeing all of them now brought a smile to my face. It was good — good to feel some happiness at such a sad reunion. I wasn't sure you were supposed to smile, but I did. With the formal part done, we all piled into cars and headed to my cousins to gather for food, drinks, and conversation.

Everyone chatted, ate, and drank, but I sat alone, watching through the kitchen door to the living room. I spied my old neighbor Karen sitting on the couch with her 5-year-old son. As I watched them, my thoughts drifted off to a summer afternoon, when she and I had sat in her backyard watching as her husband fiddled with the barbeque. I recalled looking over at an open area of their yard when the words just came out.

"*That would be a great place for a swing-set,*" I'd said, baffled by my comment, but still pointing a hand to that area in the yard. She'd given me a puzzled expression and shot a glance over to her husband whose head had popped up due to my words.

"*Why did you just say that?*" she'd asked.

"*Weird, eh? Don't know what it means,*" I'd told her.

"*I do,*" she'd said, "*I'm pregnant — how did you know?*"

"*I didn't—I just felt the need to say the words.*" I'd winked and given her my knowing Lynnie grin. She'd been 40 years old at the time and by no means had I known she was even considering having a baby. She never mentioned she was trying, but that *feeling* about the yard, premonition—or whatever, had been strong and had felt natural to say the words. I didn't know *what* I knew, just that it was *something*. Later during her pregnancy, she'd asked me if I knew the sex of the baby, hoping for another one of my *feelings*. She'd asked because she'd not been able to see on the ultrasound. I'd *felt* it was a boy. I'd told a friend what I knew but told them not to say anything. When a baby boy arrived two days shy of Christmas, she'd said, "*You knew didn't you, but you wouldn't tell me?*" I'd smiled and hugged her. However, I had told her I didn't see or *feel* anything bad around the birth nor in the home, because sometimes—just *sometimes,* I can reach out and sense things.

The memory faded and my head and heart wandered off to a different *feeling,* about another special someone who was not there, one who was much too far away to travel for this occasion. *Alison.* She and her husband Ken Kiely live out West in Canada, in the cowboy land of Calgary Alberta. And because Alison was that person who always knew the right thing to say, I had called her the night prior. She had lost her mother in the spring and understood what I was going through. Like many conversations before, they all started with the exchange of our shared nickname, Spooky, which sounded more like *Spewkay* when we say it, and had nothing to do with the real meaning of the word, and we often went with *Spook* for short. For whatever reason, neither of us can remember why we use it, but we've referred to each other by that name for what seemed like forever. The exchange always made us laugh, and Alison with her infectious giggle—made me giggle more and she'd giggle right back, causing us to erupt into our usual giggle-fest. On the call last night, I'd told her, "*I have that old photo of us from when I visited you in Calgary. We're standing outside your old apartment building hugging each other, squishing our faces together.*"

She'd replied saying, "*Oh I love that photo! That's sweet, Spook. How ya do'n?*"

"*Not sure how I'm doing,*" I'd told her.

She'd told me it was okay and had said, *"Now it's going to feel like a movie tomorrow. Just like scenes you've watched in movies, where people will say things you've seen in every funeral piece. They will have that expression as if they're in pain for you and for themselves. It will feel like one big cliché. You'll respond with the same phrases, as actors do in those same movies. It's the way it is—gonna feel surreal and familiar at the same time—but almost therapeutic."* And it was. It had been as she had said. She had also told me, *"It's ironic, but an anagram for 'funeral' are the words 'real fun'—not that you'd ever hear the words spoken together without the word 'not' thrown in there."* But, the gathering after a funeral, had been a form of therapy I hadn't expected. It was a strange therapy perhaps but exceptional just the same.

Before my mother's funeral, when I had arrived in Ottawa alone, I had stayed with Olivia and her family, but when my husband Will arrived a few days after, we'd gone to stay at his father's place. And as par for the course when staying with his father, we often visited with close family friends and neighbors, Andre and Louise. They're not much older than my husband and I, and we'd become good friends during the years since Will and I had gotten together. They'd even hosted our wedding rehearsal dinner at their home, making all the food and providing all the drinks and the beautiful scenery of their back garden. Andre is a master gardener, an artist with plants and flowers. My aunt—who also had a green thumb, her gardens often the talk of the town, together with my mother had continued to talk and brag about his garden after seeing it at the rehearsal dinner.

Long before Will's mom Joan had passed, she and Louise had been great friends. Now Louise and Andre watch over Will's dad, and he in his way watches over them. It had been at our wedding, after Louise had heard the speeches, that she approached me with an interesting comment. She'd told me she and Joan would go for bike rides and sit in the park down the way, and that Joan would often mention *'Will's friend, Lynn'*. Louise had said, *"It was only after the last speech—your speech about how you and Will met and the part about Joan helping to keep you in touch, that it all came full circle... you're that Lynn."*

It had been the best things she could have shared with me in that moment because Joan had been the key facilitator in the continued communication of Will's and my prolonged friendship over the years since high school. Staying in touch had been difficult because Will travelled for a living and we had no email back in those days to close the distance. She always made sure my mail got to wherever he was or would pass along messages he was coming home to visit. After a time, I'd stopped trying to keep in touch, because I'd felt like a nuisance. But now I knew she cared, and she remembered who I was and had even talked fondly of her son's friendship with me. I wished she'd known how much her efforts meant to me — to us. It pained me that Joan hadn't been there at the wedding. It had poured rain before the ceremony, but at 4:00 pm when the wedding was to start, the rain had stopped, and the sun had come out allowing us to have the wedding outside as we'd planned. Will and I had both agreed it was Joan bringing the sun for us, just in time. My mother had been there for our wedding but both women were gone now.

My mother, until the year of her 74th birthday, had worked as a real estate agent. Before that, she had been a nurse for twenty-plus years and had also owned her own business with my aunt. Mixed with those jobs, she'd also worked in retail. In her later years, she'd gone back to school to become a real estate agent. She was a natural with selling, great with people and had been a successful agent. She had figured she'd work until she was 75 and then retire. Though as fate would have it, she'd gotten sick shortly before her 74th birthday, and within a few weeks, cancer was the diagnosis.

She had originally believed treatment was not for her but had reconsidered after meeting the team of doctors who would guide her through the battle. After several sessions with chemotherapy to shrink the tumor, surgery to remove her bladder and surrounding lady parts, they followed up with a horrendous adventure in radiation. In May of this year I'd gone home to celebrate Mother's Day with her and take her shopping for new clothes. Cancer and treatments take a toll on a person's body, and hers had gone from a size 10 to a size 4, and she'd been in desperate need of new clothes. I'd spent a week back home with her. Even though she appeared weak and as skinny as a rail, I'd believed the worst was behind us, or I'd tried to convince myself it was. It had been nine months since the original diagnosis, and she had appeared to be cancer free. Then two months later, after she'd had her last MRI to check that her *new plumbing* was working, I'd gotten a call from her.

The only reason I knew it was her, was because of the personalized ring I had assigned to her number. But as I'd grabbed the phone, a tingle of foreboding had shuddered across my skin like cold prickling icicles. When I'd answered, Mom had given me her usual, *"helleew,"* pretending to sound chipper, but I'd known what was coming. *"I have some bad news,"* she'd begun, *"The cancer is back. It's gone into my lymph nodes and it's spreading fast."*

Foolishly, I asked, *"Are you sure?"* Then I'd sucked in a breath at the reality. In fact, she'd acted as if she'd expected it, like finding a cavity in a tooth rather than finding her body infested with cancer. She'd explained how the doctors had not expected to see what they did, but she'd known—had felt it, but she hadn't wanted to say anything until she knew for sure. When she'd paused in the conversation, I'd known again what was next. *"It's too much...,"* she'd told me, *"This past year has been hell... they say I could have a year, so I'm going to get things in order. So I retire earlier than I expected, not like I've done any work this past year."* She'd explained she would not seek treatment again. I'd told her I understood. At her age, I couldn't force her to go through it again, not after she'd worked hard her whole life, and was supposed to be getting away from hard work.

Voices called my name, the recollections and conversations weaken from my memory, and I realized the gathering was concluding. I also realized more hard work was now upon us. Unfortunately, the tasks associated with the loss of my mother were not yet over. Even before the wake and funeral, I had begun to go through the paperwork with my brother James. He and I, the eldest and youngest, were the only ones who'd remained close through the years. Along with him, my friends were my glue, and I would need my friends even more for this.

Chapter 3

It was now the end of my second week home. Will had to return to Miami for work, but I was staying to finish all the estate stuff. I was also heading back to stay with Olivia to get some more quality friend-time.

When I'd come home in the past to visit without Will, I often stayed with Olivia. I adored being with her and her family surrounded by all that love. Her husband Mike is one of Will's old friends from high school. In fact, it was the same Christmas when Will and I began dating long-distance—I'd been lucky enough to meet Olivia. That Christmas we had visited her and Mike, and she and I had hit it off right away. When Will had returned to Miami after the New Year, Olivia and I stayed in touch and had become close friends on our own. Eventually I moved to Miami to be with Will, but my friendship with Olivia continued and became stronger over the years, bridging the distance.

Olivia, fortunately for me, had also been my bridesmaid at my wedding. Being that the wedding was in Ottawa and me in Miami, she'd helped me with all the wedding preparations. She'd have done it all anyway, even if the wedding had been a world away. She's helped me many times over the years—and now she'd be helping me again with the passing of my mother. I'm not sure what I'd do without my Olivia. Little Liv, with her short blond pixie-style haircut and a little pixie voice to match. She may be little but she's a high energy, multitasking Super-Mom. Her daughters laugh when I imitate her rushing around the kitchen in turbo-speed doing everything all at once. We coined the name *Octopus Woman*, saying she's the mom with the eight arms. And like most mothers, she puts everything and everyone before herself.

Today, after going to see her daughters perform in a horse show, we were headed out to see *her* mom just the two of us. We'd hit Kingston as the car clock showed 12 noon. Like most of my friends, Olivia wasn't originally from Ottawa, she'd grown up in Kingston where her mother still lived. Unfortunately, one of the things she and I had in common was that both our mothers had been sick with cancer. Mine was gone now, and hers was barely holding on.

We spent the afternoon chatting and telling stories with her mom Pam, *shoot'n the shit,* as we call it. Pam was weak but led most of the conversations. The visit was short, but it was warm and joyful though I'm sure the *reason* for my being home had forced a scary reality on both of them. I hated that I represented their potential future.

On the drive home to keep Olivia's spirits up I recalled the laughter of the afternoon's dialog and stories. The rest of the day and evening was a quiet one at home with her family. I chose to go off early to bed to get whatever sleep I could manage under the circumstances. I reminded myself not to overdo things and to *not* surround myself with too many of the morbid chores related to my mother's death. I'd make sure to spread those things out between visiting with my friends, and spending time alone, but I knew tomorrow would be back to scary reality for me. I also knew I would have to do this next part alone, especially to keep Olivia from seeing more of her possible impending future. Tomorrow was go *through Mom's stuff* day.

* * *

Today's goal was sort and pack, oh and also not crying.

I wrapped up Mom's good china and stemware, packing and storing it away with all her valuable things I planned to ship later to my home in Miami. But until my husband and I sold our condominium and purchased a house, those items would have to wait here at my mother's house in the meantime.

Systematically I went through my mother's clothing, sorting out the items suitable for the shelter and those items that would go to other charities. There were suits and casual clothes, shoes and purses, coats for all seasons with matching scarves and mitts for all. The sorted clothing was put into bags to take to the local women's shelter. Though my mother was also not a fan of shopping, she oh-my-gosh had a ton of clothes. I tried not to think about what it would have been like to do this at my aunt's home, with all her clothing and trinkets, but each time I opened a dresser drawer, my mind jumped from pieces of clothing to memories of both of them. My mom's sister, Kay, who was older than my mother by 9 years, was a real shopper. Even in her 80s, she'd been a sharp dresser.

Sadly, a month prior, when I'd been home for Mom's 75th birthday, my aunt had landed in the hospital with a mix of strange symptoms; bruising on the arms and a tooth infection. Her eyesight had been failing her for years, but she was still quick as a whip, but we figured the bruises must have been from her bumping into things. And rare for a woman her age, she still had most of her teeth, and with the care she took with them, the infection seemed unusual as well.

During that particular visit home, James and I had taken my mom to see her in the hospital. We'd had Mom in a wheelchair to navigate the hospital. Though frail, my mother had gotten up from the wheelchair and shuffled over to where my aunt had lay sleeping. There'd been pain clear in her movements as she'd bent to caress my aunt's hair. When my aunt had awoken and lifted her head, my mother had bent down as if to whisper something in her ear. My brother and I had stood in the doorway awhile, giving them a moment and allowing my aunt to gain clarity as to who was there to see her. We'd stayed only a short time, but I'd told her we would come back on Mom's birthday and that I'd smuggle in cake for her. As promised, later in the same week, I'd returned with my mother *and* my husband in tow, with a big piece of cake for her. She'd squealed with joy at the offering, but it had been more about seeing us than the cake. She'd told us how she *didn't feel sick,* and had said how amazed the doctors were that she'd not needed to come to the hospital sooner, considering her diagnosis of a rare form of leukemia. When the doctors had asked her how often she'd been to the hospital in the last little while, they'd been astonished at the length of time. She hadn't been in a hospital since the birth of her last son, over forty-five years now. The doctors also couldn't believe how rapidly her condition had progressed despite her not having any other issues.

She'd told me, *"I don't feel sick."*

"Do you want to feel sick?" I'd responded.

She'd laughed. *"No. The doctors say I don't even look as sick as I am,"* she'd said, giving me a little smirk.

"Do you want to look sick?" I'd tossed back. She'd laughed again and squeezed my hands. I'd climbed into the bed with her then, and my husband took our photo as we cuddled. The doctors had given her six months to live, though to see her, you would never have known she was terminally ill. Two weeks later while sitting at my desk at work in Miami, I'd gotten a call from my brother, telling me Aunt Kay had passed away. I'd had the photo my husband had taken that day pinned to the wall behind my computer. I'd gazed at it through tears, realizing that was the last time I would see her. I'd also realized I would be taking my third trip home in three months *and* it also meant having to put a stop on my immigration process, allowing me to leave the country once again. Work—HR in particular, had made me feel as though I had inconvenienced them with postponing it. So much for the *human* in Human Resources. Aunt Kay's service had been beautiful, and my Uncle had given the eulogy. He'd told the story of my aunt's life and I had learned much more about her as a result. We'd all learned a little more about her that day. Some stories made us cry, some made us proud, but as he'd hoped, most made us laugh. My Uncle is a fantastic speaker, and we were in awe of how well he kept it together through the whole day. We had all wished we had recorded his speech, one written so well and so well delivered.

I moved to another drawer and pulled it open. The recent memories of my aunt's funeral lost its colour as I stared at my Mom's wedding album. Under it I found her wedding dress shoved into an old department store shopping bag. I put the wedding dress aside to pack in a *ship to Miami box*, and then plunked down on the floor to flip through the album. I loved seeing the special photos. Loved seeing the younger versions of my parents and grandparents. I adored the ones of Mom and Aunt Kay together, especially the one of Aunt Kay helping Mom to get ready.

It had been after the sudden passing of my aunt when my mom had taken a turn for the worse. She had been the last of five siblings, her three brothers had passed away quite a few years before and it had been just the two of them for the longest time. My aunt had still had her husband, but my mom had remained single since the divorce when I was a kid. Their closely timed deaths had made me think of how with most elderly couples, when one died, the other often followed close behind. Prior to my aunt's death, the doctors had said Mom might have a year, but after Aunt Kay died, I think she gave up. Being without her sister was too much, and I knew it. I'd been back in Miami again when I'd gotten my regular call from Mom. She'd sounded tired, but I could tell she wasn't herself. As we signed off, I'd told her, *"I'll talk to you later in the week."* She'd given her usual, *"Okay dear,"* which always sounded more like '*Deah*', the way she said it. The following week she'd required sedation to deal with the pain and before I could be on a plane back home to see her, she'd passed away. We wouldn't *talk later in the week.*

I looked back at the wedding album to shake off the memory of our last call. I needed to if I was to get through this and complete the task. So, to the closet I went, starting from front to back, I unhooked clothes from hangers and packed them into the shelter bags. But as I reached the back of my mother's closet, the weight of the task finally hit me.

There, wrapped in a dry-cleaning bag, was the dress my mother had worn to my wedding two years prior. Below it were the shoes and purse she had dyed to match. She had been proud of that *find* and had loved the bold colour choice of the deep raspberry. It was a sleeveless, fitted, knee length dress made of lightweight twill with a matching jacket of the same length, and she'd looked sharp in it.

Funny thing about a wedding—something you don't realize until you're the bride, is that you don't get to see your friends and families arrive. You don't get to see the groomsman and your future husband go down the aisle, nor do you get to see your bridesmaids go down the aisle. It wasn't until I viewed the video from the wedding that I got a glimpse of how happy Mom had been going down the aisle in that dress she was so proud of finding. She'd smiled so big that day you'd swear she'd had a hanger stuck in her mouth. A three-piece Celtic band had played at the wedding, friends of Mom's. They had played for the guests prior, for the wedding party and for my arrival. In the video, as Mom went down, you could see her glance over to them and *wink*. These are the things you miss when hidden out of view.

And now, the last thing I wanted to do was package up that dress. But thinking about what Mom would want, I mustered all my strength, telling myself that someone else would get the same joy she had gotten from it, from something that was *just a dress*.

Chapter 4

What's today? It was *time with Mac day*, and a day to just hang out.

Mackenzie, *Mac* for short—one of my best friends, was the one who had suggested the women's shelter for donating Mom's things. She'd also volunteered to help me take the many bags and boxes over to the shelter in her family van. Mom would have liked that her clothes were going towards helping other women.

When I arrived at Mac's and I headed up the walk to her house, I grinned and took a quick peek over my shoulder at the van. My Mac was now a mom with a minivan.

"Stop staring at my *precious*!" Mac called out from the top of the steps.

"I would never have pictured it when we were teens—you with a minivan," I said, climbing the steps to the front door.

As long as I have known Mac, she has always been a fashion plate, latest hairstyle, clothing, and all the latest trends. And like always, she welcomed me with a *smiling* mouth full of bright naturally white teeth. Those big brown almond-shaped eyes of hers full of love and mischief sparkled back at me. She swept her long dark-chocolate coloured hair over her shoulder to let it run down her back. Me, her complete opposite, having dirty-blond hair—*dishwater* blond, my mom called it. Grey-blue eyes to her dark ones, and my teeth—well, from grades 8–11 I'd had a mouth full of braces. But long since freed from that torture, I greeted her back with an equally mischievous smile.

"Hey, miss jeans'n t-shirt, didn't I see you in a dress the other day?" Mac said, crossing her arms in front of her.

"Yeeees," I said, cringing for effect. In the past, when Mac donned the latest in high fashion, I was in my jeans, t-shirts, and sneakers. She'd tried many times to fancy-me-up, but it never felt like *me*. Though, she had helped me find that perfect dress for the funeral.

Growing up, the two of us had lived in different areas of town, after junior high, we had ended up at two different high schools. After grade 12, I'd left town for college. Sometimes I'd come home on weekends, and Mac visited me once, but our lives changed, and we'd drifted apart. Happily, years later we reconnected on *Facebook*, and we were tight again, tighter than *Botoxed* skin—her words not mine.

On this occasion and much like with Olivia, Mac and I had scheduled to visit with her Mom, Monica. So we hopped in her van and were off.

Like always, there was food. Monica liked to feed me and with my rubber arm twisted, I was always happy to oblige her. As I'd suspected, the visit went on eventually ending up as a cry-fest, though the hugs we exchanged were welcomed. And like usual with my visits with friends in Ottawa, this one with Mac and her mom, passed too quick.

Back at Olivia's, I hid up in my temporary bedroom to call Alison. I'd wanted to tell her how her words about the funeral and wake had been *bang-on*.

On the first ring, she picked up. "Spook, how ya do'n?" Her words were soft as if waiting for an onslaught of emotions from me.

"I'm good," I assured her. I was for the most part. "You must have learned a lot about grief at your jobs," I added. She was always involved in work that concerned helping other people—usually those less fortunate. I heard her breathe what I assumed was a sigh of relief over the fact I seemed to be holding my own.

"Guess you could say I learned a lot on the job, but I learned much more going through it. A witness only sees so much, but the injured party gets it fully." There she was again with the perfect words.

I grinned. "You've got it all covered—life experience and work," I said. That work list was a long one; group homes, Children's Help Line,

Children's Wish Foundation, and in her current job as a property manager at a seniors' housing complex.

"It's just life," she said, laughing out the words and deflecting the attention. Modest was her middle name. We continued chatting about different things; my time so far in Ottawa, what she'd been up to, and how her family was doing, normal Spook-to-Spook conversation.

"Well, I just wanted to tell you that you're amazing, that's all," I said.

"Thanks, Spook."

I could picture the blush on her face. "No, thank you," I said, "have a great evening—love you."

"Love you too, Lynn," she said, ending the call.

After my dose of Spooky, I sat thinking about how we'd lost each other in the year after she'd move to Calgary, and as with Mac, it had been several years later, about a year before my mom got sick that we'd found each other again, thanks to good old *Facebook*.

Chapter 5

Heading into another week in Ottawa, I set plans for another visit, this one with Vicki, a former coworker turned close friend.

Vicki works as a technical writer and is a master of the English language, not to mention after four years of living in the Dominican Republic and with no formal training, speaks Spanish fluently. It makes me laugh sometimes because one of her biggest pet peeves is my poor spelling, and she experiences it a lot with our emails. We communicate via email habitually. We keep each other motivated with talk of life, love, food, and exercise. Considering I hate my current job and live too far away from everyone, most days I wouldn't survive without her emails. She is also exceptionally good at knowing what I needed on my visits. *Food*. And today's adventure would involve a long drive across to Wakefield, on the Quebec side to visit with a friend of hers who had a bakery business out of her home.

As Vicki drove, I stared out the window letting my mind wander. It ran through the blur of these past weeks, the memory of all the love from the wake surrounded by my friends and family, and the recent visit with my other girlfriends.

"I saw your friend Duane and his parents at the wake," She shot out, her words pulling me from my musing.

I straitened in my seat. "Ya, I hadn't seen him in a long time. I hadn't expected to see him or his parents." He was an old friend from my high school days.

"It was his mom I was surprised to see though," Vicki said, taking a quick glance my way.

"You're not the only one." I rubbed my eyes and took a better look at where we were. Not that I knew where we were, I hadn't been paying attention to the road signs or the twists and turns.

"I saw you go over to her when she was looking at the photo boards set up for the visitors." She took another quick glance at me, most likely checking to see if I was okay. "When she turned around and saw you behind her, you reached for her," Vicki added.

"Couldn't help it." I twisted in my seat to face her as she drove. "I had to put my hands on that sweet little face of hers."

"And she reached up and did the same thing to you, I recall." Vicki turned her head again and gave me a quick smile.

"We locked eyes and both of us lost it—cried big time." It had been like we'd locked on to each other's souls. I cleared my throat and pulled back any wavering tears. "Duane said when he told her that my mom had passed away, she'd said, *'I have to go to her'.*"

"Well, you had a major Lynnie premonition about his mom, right?" Vicki recalled. Then she honked the horn, gaining on someone attempting to drive and read a map at the same time. "Get a GPS, loser," she called out as we sped past. It made me laugh right when I needed it. "Didn't you have one of your *feelings*?" she said, emphasizing the word.

"Two," I said, "I had two spidy-sense moments about her."

"You know I dig this stuff—even if I don't believe it, but tell me again." She gripped the steering wheel as though she was racing.

We were alone on the road now and I laughed again and held my grin.

"What?" she asked, when she noticed me smiling in her direction.

"Nothing, nothing," I said, still grinning, moving on to recap the story. "It was in the fall, a few years before I moved to Miami. I'd had this *urge* to call and talk to Duane—nothing foreboding, just a *feeling* I should call. I'd asked how things were going with his work and friends. He'd told me everything was cool, nothing new to report. Then he'd made a comment about his mother that had gotten my internal alarms going. Something like, *'She's good, been teasing her lately about her being forgetful, but other than that it's all good'.* And that's when the words came. *'Get your dad to take her to see a doctor. She needs to get checked out,'* I'd told him." The memory of it made me fidget in my seat now.

"Didn't his mom wait tables at a diner near their home? Shouldn't a woman her age be retired and playing with grandchildren? Gawd, she's such a tiny little thing too."

"Yup." I felt the same way. Other than being a smoker, she'd always appeared to be in good health. I'd had no reason to think she might be ill, but still the words had come out. "Duane has witnessed my strange insight before, and he knew I wouldn't have said things like this lightly. When he'd said nothing back, I'd pushed it home, told him, *'there's something not right—get your dad to take her to the doctor as soon as possible'.*" I sucked in a breath remembering the urgency. "He'd promised me he would talk with his dad and get her in to see the doctor. And he did as promised. What they'd found was deadly, a brain tumor—cancer." I swallowed, tears were sneaking in again. "She'd gone in for surgery to remove the tumor, but when they'd opened her up, her brain had swelled. They'd waited until the swelling went down, but they'd had to close her up without removing the tumor. Only other options were chemotherapy and radiation treatments."

Vicky shook her head. "The poor little thing. Cancer is a nasty bastard."

I took in a deep breath and let it out slow and continued the story. "When Autumn led to Christmas, I'd gone over to see her, but she was very weak, and she'd not been herself. We'd sat on the couch together and she'd clung to me not wanting to let go. She had always been a big hugger and never let me leave the house without a series of hugs that led to the front door, but this time she wasn't able to get up. I'd been at the door to leave when Duane had asked me, *'Is she gonna make it?'.*"

"He knows you can't see that stuff, right—not exactly?" Vicki asked.

I nodded. "He knows, but he also knows sometimes my feeling or my *not* feeling, means something too. Told him I didn't see her dying, couldn't picture it—couldn't find the image if I'd tried. But it was all I gave him." I hated that part of the sensing or whatever it was I had.

This weird knowing stuff, happened to me here and there, and people seemed to get a kick out of it. I tried not to think about it as anything other than strange feelings. When people took it too seriously, it made for a heavy weight to carry for something I questioned myself, and I loathed it.

"What were you supposed to tell him? It's not like you have actual superpowers—no offense."

"None taken," I said. Vicki was a skeptic, but she still loved a good story, so I finished it. "A few weeks into January, Duane called me again—told me, '*Dad said she's not doing well, she's sleeping all the time. Based on what the doctors told him, Dad thinks it won't be long now.*' I hadn't been sure the reason for his call, maybe to let me know the situation— in case I wanted to see her again before it was too late, but again, the words came, and I'd said, '*No, Duane. Tell your dad to call the doctor. Something's not right here—she's not going to die—it's something else.*' He'd said his dad was convinced she would die, so I'd repeated myself, '*No! It's something else, call your dad now.*' After we'd hung up, he'd done what I told him. Again."

"Clearly there's a happy ending—because she is still alive." Vicki's eyes were wide as she glanced over at me.

I smiled at the skeptic. "Yes, his father had called the doctor to come to the house. And wouldn't you know it—it had been the tremor medication she'd been taking. It would have killed her if she'd remained on the too high dosage. Once they'd fixed it, she was fine and back to her normal upbeat little self."

"At the wake, you and she were wrapped around each other crying," Vicky reminded.

I nodded again. "It was the first time I had cried the whole day actually—not because of the day, but because it had been over ten years that she'd been in remission, and I hadn't seen her since that Christmas. Duane nicknamed me the *Oracle* after that. Now, whenever he asks for my advice, he jokes and says, *The Oracle knows!*" I laughed thinking about it. "I throw the saying out there sometimes for fun. It's not as if I know everything—for sure I don't."

"But somehow—someway, you sometimes do, and when someone needs it," Vicki the skeptic threw in, laughing along with me.

"Perfect—we're here," she said, switching the conversation as we pulled in the drive.

Perfect indeed, the woman's kitchen was stacked with homemade cookies, cakes, pies, and cheesecakes. Good thing they were all orders she was filling and not *for sample* items because I'd have put her out of business. The place smelled amazing, and with all those luscious desserts baking and cooling, they and the visit were excellent distractions. Once again Vicki knew what I needed.

I'm blessed to have these women of such strong character and bravery in my life, ones who have taken on challenges and struggles that might have broken lesser women. I have lost a few of these women over the past year, but I have also regained friendships assumed lost. Each of them I have met in different places and phases of my life. Unlike most clusters of friends, they are not part of a group of girls who've known each other since childhood. One of the special things about my closest girlfriends is their ability to *come together*. They know *of* each other through me and are familiar with each other because of the coming together. It would be something I wouldn't fully understood until much later, that in the coming months this ability of theirs to come together, would prove to serve a greater purpose.

Chapter 6

By week's end I had all of Mom's valuables packed and the things I wanted to keep for myself, tucked away into the closet of a bedroom.

Mom had used the bedroom as an office when she was still working, but for the past year she'd used it only to play bridge on the computer. She could play for hours. She was quite the brilliant card player but lacked the patience for teaching the game and I often gave up trying to keep up with her. At the funeral, there'd been members of her bridge club from years ago. They had joked that the gatherings had turned into more of an excuse to get together to talk about the latest gossip, but my mother had lost interest when the gatherings changed from cards to chatting. She'd wanted to play cards. She should have taken up poker, she wasn't a gambler, but she had a good mind for cards and strategy. She'd been an avid reader too, often reading three books at a time, not literally, but she would have three on the go, from which she would jump back and forth. She often reread the same books multiple times if she liked them. She particularly loved mystery novels.

Me, I never read, well, not until recently. Before, I never got the point when there were so many good shows on the TV and movies in the theater. She and I had spent lots of time watching mysteries on the local channels, sometimes renting or attending movies to see the latest mystery thriller. After a good one she would often say, "*I should write a book, bet I could spin a fine tale.*" And, since she would often say she should write a book, I had gotten her a journal to do just that. "*Write all the funny stories from your teens and your years as a nurse,"* I'd told her, *"all the stories I loved to hear."* I told her to write about when she had adopted me, put any memories *she* loved, and any quotes or even recipes she felt were important to share. I bugged her often—asking her if she'd started her book yet. But she'd always say, *"I'll get to it."* With that memory, I moved to pack the last item, the journal, into the last box for my future shipping.

I stopped to examine the journal. In opening it, I noticed she'd shoved various papers in between the front cover and the first page. Among the contents were her last business card photos, and an email-print-out titled *Lynn Westlake and Will Lockridge,* listing all the dishes she'd purchased from my bridal registry. She'd added a handwritten list of dates and notes recalling all the significant moments in her life. Along with that was a tiny piece of paper I swear looked a hundred years old. On it was written a registry number, a date, May 3rd, and the words 34 weeks, along with 5 pounds 5 ounces. It was my birth information written long ago on a piece of notepaper. It was thin and delicate with age and I had no doubt it was the most precious item she'd put in there. It made me think of her last version of my adoption story, *and* it made me laugh. "Thanks, Mom," I whispered.

It also reminded me I still hadn't heard a thing from the Adoption Disclosure people. I'd filled out the forms to search for information on my birth parents ages ago. Mom had remembered little or perhaps chosen not to share much. I knew next to nothing about my birthmother, only that she'd been young, about 18 when she'd had me. I had no info about the birthfather or family, nor any medical or ancestral information about either. The woman who'd helped with the forms told me that unless a birth relative was searching for you and a match was made, that you might never hear anything, *ever.*

Refocusing back on items from the journal, I found a letter dated November 19th, the same year as my birth, written by Mom to *her* mother. I opened it. It contained writings about how Mom's children were all doing, how I was finally gaining some weight, and it had touched on each one of us and our little lives. I found it fascinating to read about life with my new family during a time which I had no memory of. Then I read the oddest thing.

She had written about a presence, a protective essence in my room, wrote that she sensed it whenever she would come to get me out of my crib. She'd written, 'I felt it again Mom, in Lynn's room. It's a feeling as if someone is there. It's silly, but it's a good feeling, like she's protected.' The words shocked me. My mom never let on she believed in that stuff. God yes—spirits no, but perhaps her younger self had. It touched me to read those words written from daughter to mother, but I had to wonder why she had selected this one in particular. It also made me want to read the rest of the letters I'd found. Earlier I had uncovered boxes of old letters to and from my mother and my grandmother spanning many years. My grandmother was a stranger to me, but I'm sure those other letters could give me insight into my grandmother and the younger version of my mother. But for whatever reason, Mom had chosen to put this one in the journal. Why? Another mystery perhaps.

I set aside all the contents and reread the words she had written on the first page of the journal,

> June 21
> I'm going to start this epistle about my life and also notes on the family.
> At present, I'll start with this past year then switch to the past ~~past~~.

She had already crossed out her first mistake… but it was all she'd written. She died less than three months later, never writing another word.

I gathered the mix of papers, putting all the items together again and placing them back in the journal next to the two sentences she'd written. I set it in the last box, sealed it, and put it in the back of the closet. "See you when we get a new house," I said.

Chapter 7

Rounding out the end of the fourth week I had finished what was needed and was off again to the airport to catch my flight back to Miami.

"We're here," James said, pulling me from my fog as we stopped at the passenger drop-off area. He got out and grabbed my suitcase from the backseat.

"Mom would be proud of us—we did it," I said, as we did the awkward brother-sister hug, meaning we'd survived getting all her affairs in order before I had to leave again. Part of me didn't want to go back to Miami and leave my family and friends, but the other part of me needed to feel normalcy again—back to my other world, my husband, and my stupid job.

A wave goodbye and off I went, dragging my suitcase into the airport.

The Ottawa airport is a small airport, but it's an efficient one. Ottawa is the capital of Canada, but you wouldn't know it by its tiny airport and limited flights. And as I've done a million times before, I went through the usual airport dance. I'd given myself plenty of time to finish the routine and was now at the gate with time to spare. I made myself comfortable near the call area for my flight and gazed out the big window recalling another type of dance I'd had.

My long—very long, hit and miss style cha-cha with Will that I'd been doing since I was a teenager. We'd met in high school, dated for only a few months but to a 14-year-old girl it was a lifetime. Will was a senior and one of the cutest guys in school. And I was, well—*me*, in grade nine—new to the school, and completely out of my element. It was November of my freshman year, while I'd been sitting with a friend in the bleachers watching a lunchtime event, square dancing, floor hockey, or something equally dull, when Will and another guy sat down in the stands a row behind us. My girlfriend and I had been reading the horoscopes I'd cut from the daily newspaper, when I'd caught a voice say, *"Hey whatcha got there?"*

It was *him*—the cute blond-haired guy with the big blue eyes. Was he talking to me? No way—but he was. Grabbing a little confidence, I'd turned and told him, *"It's the horoscopes from the newspaper."* Continuing my bravery, I'd asked, *"When were you born?"*

"February 3rd," he'd replied.

"That makes you Aquarius," I'd told him. Then with a smile I'd recited his day's predictions. Finished, I'd turned back to my friend, whose mouth had been gaping open the whole time. Thankfully the end-of-lunch bell rang, because I'd been all out of courage and we had to head off to class. He must have had a spare because he didn't leave when we did. I'd managed a, *"See ya!"* like it was no big deal, then turned to maneuver down the bleacher stairs, thinking *Oh, that didn't just happen—did it*? But it had. Next day I'd sat on a bench in the main hall by myself reading the latest horoscopes, waiting for one of my friends to show. As I'd read, a shadow spread across the newsprint, and I'd looked up. There he was, standing there grinning at me. Then he'd sat down next to me. *"So, what does my future say today?"* he'd asked. From that moment on we'd spent our lunchtime together. I would bring in the horoscopes and we'd read them and chat for the lunch period. We did other things too, like go to school hockey games or hang out at his house. He'd told me that his mom had talked to him about the age difference, and that she'd said, *"If you really care about each other you can make it work despite the age difference"*. I loved her for saying that.

That same year Will invited me out for New Year's Eve. Our first stop was his friend's place. It was a toga party with everyone dressed in bed sheets and walking around barefoot with drinks in their hands.

The song *Rock the Casbah,* by The Clash had been booming through the house. To this day, if I hear that song, it's still the first image that comes to my mind. After the exchange of New Year's cheer, he and I were on our way again to the main party. I'm not sure whose house it was, but there'd been a band set up to play for the night. It was here I had my first sip of Champagne, and at the stroke of midnight, as everyone cheered Happy New Year, I had my first New Year's kiss. It was amazing, well, 14-year-old girl amazing. However, when January came, and we were back at school, things between Will and I changed, well he changed and pulled away. His 19th birthday was approaching and soon before it did, we'd broken up. It was still a joke between us even now it's what had ended our relationship. He'd then been old enough to go out to bars, I wasn't. He'd graduated the following June, but I had another three years.

"Final call for passengers flying to Miami!" a voice sounded from above, shifting me out of my memory. Time to go.

I grabbed my carry-on and then passed through the gate, handing off my boarding pass to finish the airport dance. Once seated in my designated spot, I peered out another much tinier window, and let my eyes glaze over again.

"Something to drink?" the flight attendant asked, the words fazing me back.

"No, thank you." I smiled. She turned her head away to ask the next person the same question in robotic form.

I rolled up my sweatshirt and leaned it against the frame of the window. I was alone in my row with no one to squish in next to me, and as my head met the sweatshirt, I was out.

The jarring motion of the landing threw me back to the land of wakie-wakie and into this time and space, back into the land of the sun and sand, back to Will.

As usual, he was waiting for me at the luggage carousel with arms open and a big smile. He rescued my luggage from the conveyer belt and the two of us went out into the heavy Miami humidity and across to the parking area.

As we drove through the exit gates, I watched as a little old man clutching a red gift bag rushed along the walkway. The bag had a stylized image of a Christmas tree, with a shiny gold angel at the top of the tree.

I love Christmas. It's not about the gifts—it's the *feel* of it. Something about it, something perhaps magical I can't quite put my finger on, but it didn't matter. I always took it all in, the colours, the sounds, the smells, and the food, can't forget the food. Realization came, and I let out a, "*Huff.*" This coming Christmas would be different, oh so different without the matriarchs of the family.

With the rush of thoughts and emotions, I pushed back tears and tried to refocus on the red gift bag, but the old man had gone out of view. The thoughts of the coming season pulled me back to another Christmas, the same Christmas I'd spoken those words regarding Duane's mother. It had been in the middle of that scare I had gotten another feeling—a small one—but it was definitely one of *those* feelings.

Sometimes like a push or pull, do or don't do, say or don't say something, that I often got, this time it was a push. I'd been filling out Christmas cards, when I'd gotten the push or persuasion you could say, to address a card to Will's parents. I'd addressed one for him as well, hoping his mother would get it to him. I'd had no clue where the need to do this had come from, but my intentions had been simply to show him I was well and that I was sending good wishes for Christmas. It had been over five years since we'd last spoken, but I'd assumed his mom would get the card to him as she'd done so many times in the past. To my surprise, two weeks later I'd received a postcard in the mail. It had a picture of a scuba diver and shark on the front, and on the card side was written,

> Hey there,
> Just rec'd your xmas card.
> Started vacation today, Cocoa Beach/Orlando next 3-days,
> Then up to Ottawa Dec. 22 – Jan. 1 at home. Call me.
> Take care, Will

We'd gotten together for a few hours at my house over Christmas. He'd told me it had been two years since he'd been home. He'd said how bizarre it was to get my card since he'd scheduled to come home for Christmas. He'd also asked me *why* I'd sent it to his parents. I'd said,

"Something told me to send it," that I figured his mom would get it to him the way she always had. I'd told him I hadn't expected to hear from him, only wanted to wish him happy holidays. That's when he'd told me something that'd crushed me. He said his mom had passed away two years ago as of that past August. I'd cried when he'd said it—I'd cried for his loss and because I hadn't been able to say goodbye to her. I hadn't known she'd been sick, and I hadn't been there for him. He'd told me she had started to feel unwell a few years prior and when the diagnoses came, the illness sped quickly, taking her to the final stages and to her passing.

She'd been our helper. After high school, she was the one who'd readily facilitated Will and me keeping in touch. When he'd later moved South to Florida, staying in touch had become much harder, but with her help, we'd managed. What hit home most, was it had been around the same time Will and my contact had dissipated when her illness first started.

The news about his mother had been heartbreaking for me, though the rest of our visit had been as if no time had passed, which was great for both of us. Over the next year and a half, we'd chatted, stayed in touch by phone and email. That fall, he'd asked me to come visit him in Miami. Even though we'd both been single at the time, I'd let any romantic feelings fade long ago. Besides, I was happy we were friends again—not to mention I could visit him where *he* lived this time. But surprisingly to both of us, things changed three days into that Miami trip. And though we'd gotten to know each other as friends again—not the awkward teens of the past, but as adults, something more between us had sparked. I'd known spending that much time with him was a big deal, considering things in his world always changed so fast. We'd both been happy with how the week had begun and how it had ended. No regrets. When I'd returned home, I'd written him a long email telling him I was proud of the person he'd become and that his mom would be proud of the man he had become. In ending the email, I'd put how happy I was we'd had the time together, that there were no expectations and no worries, and I'd thanked him for being such a gracious host during my stay.

The emails and phone dialog continued over the next months, but we hadn't talked about what had transpired on the visit. He'd told me he wouldn't be home for Christmas that year, but I'd been okay with the idea I might not see him again for a long time. I had gotten used to our infrequent visits, even if the last one had been different. Then, on the day after Christmas, he'd called to tell me he'd be coming up on the 28th and he'd said, *"It would be really great to see your face when I get off the plane in Ottawa."* Being the nice friend, I'd picked him up and a pizza along the way, and we'd headed back to my place to hang out. We'd been sitting on the couch eating pizza and watching TV when I'd turned to him and asked that forever-pending question. *"Do you ever think about us as a couple?"* To which he'd replied, *"All the time."* And by the end of that visit, we'd decided to try a long-distance relationship, see where it would take us. A year and three months later I moved to Miami. Six months after that we were engaged, I had gotten my first work visa at Christmas, and had started my first US job the January that followed. In July we'd gotten married back in our hometown surrounded by our friends and families.

What was it about Christmas? Other than I loved the season, I wasn't sure, but amazing things seemed to happen then, and the push to send that Christmas card had changed my life. It was the first time one of my *feelings* had been for me and not for someone else. Some call it intuition, but this had been *strong* intuition—or maybe it had been just dumb luck.

"Lyyynn," Will said, stirring me. "Where are you, daydreamer?" He squeezed my knee, making me jump and laugh.

"I'm here. Reminiscing is all." I smiled, beaming love back at him.

When we pulled up to the condominium, Will dragged my luggage out and wheeled it inside for me. Knowing I was exhausted and a little off my game, he let me be and I wandered into the apartment and straight to the bedroom.

I slumped down on the floor and pulled two boxes out from under the bed. One was full of photos, cards, and memories, the other contained all my important documents. I took an envelope from my purse, opened it, and unfolded the papers. In a slot all its own I slid in copies of my mother's official death certificate along with the memorial card from the wake. I flipped to the front of the files, under *A,* and found my photocopied adoption forms.

It had been three years since I had filled out the original forms and mailed them off to the government agency black hole, waiting for a match. A year before I'd moved to Miami, a letter had arrived that was both informative and sad. The letter was from the Adoption Disclosure Agency and it contained the names of my birthmother and her parents. It stated where and when she'd been born. Mentioned she'd married ten years after my birth—not to my birthfather, but later divorced. Finally, the information I had been waiting for—but not exactly. It also had information detailing how she had passed away due to breast cancer, ten years in fact before this letter had even gotten to me. The reason it had been sent, was not that they'd made a match, but that the information was legally available due to her death. At least I had a bit of information and some medical history to work with, but it seemed no one had been looking for me.

The dates had showed she'd died in her early 40s, and I'd been having myself checked every year since, as I had no record of when she'd first been diagnosed. Soon after receiving that letter, I'd contacted the agency again regarding information about the birthfather, but they'd said all first searches needed to be finished before any second searches could be started. However, I was also told a bill would be passed soon which would open all closed adoption files to both the adoptees and their birth families. I'd decided I'd wait until I could do the inquiries myself. I had put the inquiry aside, but now after Mom's death, I knew it was time. Time to go online to the provincial website and fill out the new open-file forms.

Still sitting on the floor, I took out my laptop from my tote and I started it up. I went to the disclosure website and filled out the forms. I send a copy to myself at work for printing tomorrow on my first day back.

Yup, a month away dealing with death and tomorrow I'd be back at work. Oh joy.

Chapter 8

Monday mornings were tough enough as it were, tougher after the month I'd had and even tougher since I hated my job and would have rather been anywhere but here.

With the layoffs this past summer, the company had gone from 2300 employees down to 600. I tried to think of it as though they needed me and didn't want me to leave. Either way, the place was bad. Everyone was unhappy, there was too much work and not enough manpower to get things done. Everyone remaining felt overworked and trapped because the economy was so bad, and they figured they had no other choice but to suck it up and do the extra work. Bad, bad, bad and more bad.

Will had started my green card paperwork process, which meant once I got it, I could work anywhere I wanted or choose not to work if that's what I wanted. It would be great to walk out of this place for good. Twice now Human Resources has screwed up my immigration visas, making the whole process more painful with the stop and restart of having to go home for two separate funerals. But HR didn't care, the idiots still got the dates wrong, though I managed to get back in the US on a wing and a prayer.

Leaning my elbows on the desk, face in my palms, I stared through a mindless fog at the computer screen. Pushing through the fog, I printed the new adoption information forms, and then forced myself to make a call to the representative at the government agency.

The woman on the phone explained what type of paperwork to expect, but not to expect much in the file, since as a 3-month-old, I had not been in the system long. She informed me however that in the meantime I could request a copy of my original birth record and adoption record. Those would have my registered name at birth and possibly the name of my birthfather. She added that I would receive those records fairly fast, but anything else in the adoption file could take up to a year, that's if anything else existed. Whatever information I could get I'd be grateful for, so I sent off the request forms. And again, I would wait.

* * *

Over the next days that passed, I tried to deal with my losses, but continued in a haze—still moving forward with my life, all the while trying to help my friend Olivia deal with her situation. Before I had left to come back, I had told her, "*Just go, be with your mom, for no other reason than to be with her.*" I hadn't been able to do it with my mother, so I'd pushed her to go. As more days spilled over to a week, and the week spilled over into another, in the middle of the second week, things came to a screeching halt. Though Olivia had made it there in time to be with her mom, Pam passed away only ten days after I'd gotten back to Miami. And as par for the course, immigration screwed me again. With my green card in mid-process, I was stuck in the country and unable to be with Olivia and her family. I counted myself lucky of the fact Pam and I finally met on my last visit home, that we'd talked, and we'd hugged. But dealing with still more loss, stuck in the US and without my friends and family around, my haze continued as Olivia's *started*.

This past year has been a doozy. Alison's mom passed away in March, my aunt in August, followed by my mother in September, and now in October we lose Olivia's mother. That malicious monster, Cancer has taken them all.

Days continued to spill into weeks, and those weeks into months; November, December into Christmas. January slid in with a hint of haze still lingering and I'd all but forgotten about the adoption forms. I'd figured it would take forever to get any information back, but when the last week of January arrived, I received an interesting surprise.

Checking the mailbox after work as I regularly do, I found two manila envelopes shoved inside addressed to me. I tore both open before leaving the mailbox area, attempting to read as I walked heading to the stairs. I passed through the front lobby, trying to comprehend what it was I was reading, and stopped short in front of the stairwell.

There in my little hands were the copies of my original adoption record and birth registration. Reading from the top, I recognized my birthmother's last name, *McMillan*, from the original letter I'd received years ago. With a Scottish name like that, I'd expected a modest first name to go with it. *Wrong*. Instead, there it was... my official first name... *Yasmin*.

Clutching the letters, I raced up the three flights of stairs to the apartment. Through the door the first thing I did was power on my laptop and then Google the name on the internet. My birthmother had been a teen in the late 60s, in Canada nonetheless, and how she'd come up with a name like that I hadn't the foggiest. Confused by her choice, the confusion only got worse when I found that this spelling was particularly uncommon, the more common use being *Jasmine*, though Yasmin it stated, was an original version. Researching further I found the origin was from Old Persia and over the centuries, it had mutated into different forms.

"Yasmin, Old Persia—really?" I questioned aloud. The name conjured images of a dark, exotic woman, gypsy or Middle Eastern-looking women from those Arabian Nights movies, but certainly not me. But I was Yasmin—well at least the day I was born, I was. Desperate to share my confusion, I send off an email to my girlfriends telling them about the name. In a rush, their email responses came back all sporting similar reactions. Stuff like *Wow, how bizarre* and *You don't look like a Yasmin*.

Then to add to the confusing information, when I finally scanned the second page of the birth registry, in the spot where my birthfather's name should be—there was.... *nothing*. This left me with the original question—who was my birthfather? Who was he—who was I for that matter? I had no one I could ask. How else could I find answers? Questions burning my brain, I remembered a friend of my mother's had used a private detective agency to track down a family member. Figuring I'd know the company name if I saw it, I went back to Google.

Bingo! I found it and sent them off an email without hesitation, inquiring about finding information on my birth relatives. Then I waited, again.

* * *

And waited... and waited some more.

There was still no reply by the time Will's birthday arrived in February. I had gotten out of my depressive funk, glad to push free of the haze, and I was content to take the next few months to refocus on my life, on Will, selling our condo and finding a new home, and finding my way back into the world and my happiness.

Chapter 9

May arrived in Miami, and our condo was still up for sale.

The current market was bad for sellers and we'd had our place on the market for the past two years. During which time though, we'd saved plenty for a new place. We wanted a house—for many reasons, but the main reason was for friends and family to have a place to stay when they visited. In hopes of a sale today, we tidied the condominium for the showing, making the place appear as though no one lived there. Then we waited while the prospective buyer took a whole five minutes to view it.

Usually we escape for a short walk around the property, while our agent showed the place, but this time, Will and I were heading out to see another home for sale, one that was having an open house in our favorite neighborhood. The community we liked wasn't small, but it wasn't overpopulated like other parts of Miami. It's similar to where we live now with beautiful, lush surroundings and tons of mature palm and live oak trees, and part of the reasons we love it so much. The other reasons were because it was not one of those patchwork communities where all the houses look the same—where everyone has to have the same paint job and landscaping. Every house on these streets was different, but with similar large lots, with older homes with tons of character.

Will easily found the street and turn onto it, and then we slowed to a crawl. There, near the end of the street I saw it... *the house*. From the website's photos I had already fallen in love. Many of the houses we'd looked at had appeared perfect until you got inside and checked it out, but this place was looking good so far. Another great thing about this house was its location, two streets in from a main, easy to find, but still quiet. It was also near the end of the street, one house away from the end. Not quite a corner house, but only one neighbor besides, and on the other side was a large green space next to a park. Will pulled into the half-moon driveway and shut off the car. Since the open house was going on, the seller's agent was already on the front step waving at anyone who would venture to stop.

The front of the house stretched out on both sides from the large double front doors. Along the sides of the house, there were dark green leafed bushes covered in delicate white flowers. Their fragrance was evident as we walked up the path to the front steps. Like many houses in Miami, the outside of the house was stucco. This one was painted in a soft pale yellow, framed by the lovely green and white of the flowering bushes. The agent welcomed us in, and I stepped through the front door.

A little tingle of soft cool air tickled the fine hairs on my neck and arms. *Must be the A/C* I figured and ignored the sensation. We stood in a small entryway separating the doorway and main hall which attached the split floorplan of the living spaces. The interior of the house was bright with large windows along the back. The nearest room had a stone fireplace which I always considered funny for Florida, but now I like the idea, because we get some cold winter days, and *weeks* if we're lucky.

We walked through the living room to the large kitchen that had an island big enough to put four barstools on one side and prepare a feast on the other. The kitchen had an open concept view to part of the living room and to the dining area, with both areas opening out to the backyard.

Will moved to stand in front of the big windows to check out the large backyard and pool. I listened as the agent described the house.

"If you go right down the hall to that side of the house, it has two of the four bedrooms and a large full bathroom and leads around to the hall opening to the kitchen and garage. If you go right to the other side of the house, you find a half bath, a small bedroom suitable for an office, the master bedroom with a full bathroom." With a short pause, he added, "The master bedroom also opens out to the back yard."

My heart soared at the mention of finally getting my own private outdoor space and multiple ways to enjoy it. It got even better as we passed through the back-patio doors. The backyard had a large, covered patio area with an almost Olympic length pool, surrounded by thick dark green grass. A high, but light-stained wood fence surrounded the back yard, and in front of the fence were more of those green bushes with the white flowers.

I'd known Will would fall in love with the large pool. He already swims three mornings a week with a master's swim team, but he'd be salivating at the idea of doing laps in his own pool, and I watched him go off with the agent to get the *how to* on the pool maintenance.

I was falling in love with the rest of the place. The scent from the flowers was intoxicating as I continued to walk the perimeter near the fence and there seemed to be butterflies on every bush. Most them were on the bushes nearest me. But strangely, as I moved—they moved, and in the same direction I did as if following me. Or had it been my imagination? But each time I tested the movement, it happened again. They were actually following me around the perimeter of the yard. I called out to Will, but he'd gone around the side of the garage to where the pool system was.

I remained where I was grinning like a fool, facing the house with my back to the fence and the butterflies. A kind of energy swirled all around me, a tingling or tickly something—something I couldn't explain. A cool breeze swept over me and all the butterflies fluttered up into the swirl of the breeze, hovering around and above me. Will and the agents came from around the side of the house, both stopping in their tracks when they saw me.

Will gave me one of his big toothy grins. "This is the one!" he called out, walking across the yard to where I was standing. In a low voice only I could hear, he whispered, "Your mom's here—and it's your birthday weekend."

"And one week before Mother's Day," I replied.

Sold!

To top things off, while we'd been out finding our perfect house, our own agent had been working on papers from an offer he'd received from the showing.

* * *

Four weeks passed, and we were moving the last of our things into our new home. Will was off to gather the rest from storage while I hauled the last of my boxed personal items from my car into our new house.

I walked up the short steps to the front door when motion at my left caught my attention. I turned towards the neighbor's house. There on the porch was a tiny older woman wearing a long light blue kerchief. She was waving frantically at me and smiling. With each wave, she made little bounces like a child who needed to get to the bathroom. I smiled and waved back at her. She stopped waving for a second to cover her mouth as if giggling, but she was too far away for me to know for sure. Still holding the box with my other arm, I turned and lowered my gaze to the door handle, but when I glanced back up again, the old woman was gone. I'll see her again I thought and carried the box through the doorway and further into the master bedroom.

Earlier I'd noticed there'd been butterflies on the bushes out front. I'd wanted to get a photo of the bush and its flowers to send to my garden expert, Andre, so I scrambled through the box I'd been carrying and found the small digital camera. Checking its battery life, I walked back down the hall to the front door. Slipping into my favorite pair of flip-flops, I then pulled open one side of the big double doors.

I leapt to the walkway from the second step and circled around to the bushes. Before taking the shot, I stopped to admire the butterflies resting on the flowers. The larger ones resembled Monarchs, but along with those were smatterings of tiny pale-yellow butterflies and light blue butterflies, each about the size of a dime. They moved from flower to flower so fast they appeared more as flashes of colour. I raised the camera and readied myself to take the first photo.

"Yasmin!" a voice came as if speaking my name—not my name-name, but I sliced a quick glance to the left to find where the high raspy voice was coming.

There, a few feet from me stood the old woman from the porch. Being in Miami, I had assumed she was Hispanic, but seeing her up close her appearance was different. Middle Eastern, and what she wore was a Hijab, not a kerchief. The blue of the fabric was the same colour as her eyes. Her skin was dark and smooth with deep lines around her mouth and near the corners of her eyes. She couldn't have been more than 4 ½ feet tall. She took a step closer and grinned up at me, raising her hands to my face.

"Jadda?" came another woman's voice from around the side of their house. The woman rounded the hedge into view.

In that moment, the old woman placed the palms of her hands against the sides of my face, and I refocused on her. She stared up into my eyes. Still grinning, she said it again, "Yasmin."

The younger woman rushed over. "No-No, Jadda, it's Jasmine not Yasmin." She moved to lower the old woman's hands from my face though I stood still looking into those sparkling blue eyes. "I'm so sorry," she said, "*Jaddatee*—I mean my grandmother, *Mitra*—she gets confused sometimes." Then she spoke to the old woman in Arabic. I only recognized it because I have loads of Lebanese friends in Canada who families spoke the language. I'd been taught a few key phrases and not just the bad ones. She turned her grandmother to face the flowers. "Jasmine, not Yasmin," she said again, this time emphasizing the distinction.

The old gal turned to face me again, smiled and gave her shoulders a little shrug. The other woman said something again to her and the older woman turned and scurried off and around to the side of the house.

"I'm sorry about that," the younger woman said. She had a friendly smile and big dark doe-like eyes that crinkled a little at the corners as her smile widened. She raised her hand in an offer of a handshake. "I'm Dunya. Welcome to the neighborhood."

"Uhm, oh hi. I'm Lynn, uhm—thank you," I said. Taking her hand to shake. "*Marhaba*," I said, using my broken Arabic try at *hello*.

Her smile widened, and she let out a little laugh. "You speak Arabic?"

"*Baa'ref arabee showayya,*" I attempted again, giggling a bit. *I speak Arabic a little,* was what I hoped came through. "But just a few words and phrases," I finished, shaking my head and grinning at her. No matter how good or bad your attempt was to speak another person's language, most were pleased, and a little entertained by the effort, and it was true by Dunya's reaction to mine.

"*Salam,*" she said, using the complement response to my hello. "Nice to meet you, Lynn."

"I take it we're neighbors," I said, affirming the obvious.

"I live here with my mother—who's only here half the time, and Jadda, my grandmother whom you met." She turned towards the house and back, waving a hand towards her home. "My daughter, Aleah, lives here too, but she's up north at university." Her smile changed, the expression a hint of missing her daughter. "How do you like your new home?"

I cut a glance the other direction to look the length of my house and back again to her. "I love it—really love it, and I'm not even all moved in yet." I huffed out a laugh. "I was out here trying to take a photo of the bushes and its flowers to send to a friend back home. He'll be able to tell me what they are," I said, holding the camera up.

"Jasmine," she answered. "*Butterfly Jasmine* to be precise. The older Cuban gentleman who used to live here planted them all over the property. It's the Cuban national flower."

"But your grandmother, she said the name *Yasmin.*"

"She used to say that to Sal too," she said, giving a little laugh.

"Sal?" I questioned, my first thought going to my mother. Everyone had called her *Sal,* even my cousins called her *Aunt Sal.*

"Salvatore, actually. He and my grandmother used to sit out in the backyard or walk around the perimeter of the yard talking. Neither of them speaks any English, but they nattered on just the same."

"Sounds cute," I responded. The image was so clear, both trying to communicate, neither of them speaking the same language and her tormenting him as if they were an old married couple.

"He would tell her, *'Jasmine... Mariposa'*, meaning Butterfly Jasmine and she would torment him by saying, *'Yasmin'*—which is an earlier version of the name Jasmine."

"From Old Persia," we both said in chorus.

"Oh, you know that name," she remarked, taking in a deep breath. "She has been very sad since Sal left. His daughter had to move him to a seniors' home after he got sick earlier this spring. Jadda misses him dearly. She has smiled little since he left. Well, not until you moved in," she added.

"Gee, if I can make her smile, I'm proud to have moved next door to you," I said, giving her a generous smile.

"Thank you. I'm sorry if she bothered you," she said, in a gracious tone.

"No, not at all. She seems very sweet."

"She is dear to me. My mother on the other hand—is a handful, wait until you meet her." She seemed to cringe a little while trying to force a smile. "She loves Miami—and its casinos," she added, the statement speaking volumes.

"Mothers and daughters have a unique relationship," I said. I laughed and gave her a knowing wink. She smiled back as if a little message had transpired between the two of us.

"I should check on Jadda. It was nice to meet you, Lynn." She nodded and dashed towards the side of the house.

"Oh, same here Dunya, don't be a stranger. Drop over anytime, please," I shouted.

She stopped and gave another nod and a little wave and then hurried off around the side of the house. I turned and looked down at the camera and back at the flowers but didn't take the shot. Butterfly... *Jasmine.*

Will arrived a few minutes later with the remaining storage items in tow, and then he proceeded to dump the lot in the middle of the living room before coming into the kitchen where I was trying to put away dishes from one of the many kitchen boxes.

"How are you making out?" he asked, tickling my rib cage.

Slapping his hand away, I said, "Oh you know me, I trudge along." Then I placed the last of the dinner plates on the shelf. "What are you making me for dinner?"

"Me? Don't you have something ready to go," he tossed out in response.

"Oh, I see. My magic wand and I will just whip-up something special." I opened the fridge to display its emptiness.

Thirty-five minutes later there was hot pizza warming that plate I had previously put on the shelf. "Ah pizza, the food of gods," I exclaimed as I chomped the crust. "Tomorrow we have to book our flights home for Canada Day," I said, as I grabbed another slice.

"Going to be a quick one. Not much of a vacation with all the rushing around and visiting," he said, exhaustion already showing on his face.

"We weren't home for Christmas. I need to go home and see everybody. And I want to meet with the PI," I reminded him. A week before we'd moved, I'd received a response from the agency stating they had assigned someone to address my inquiry. "Oh my God," I said before Will could respond. "I need to tell you about the weirdest part of my day."

My husband sat content at the kitchen island as I unraveled the story about the old guy, *Sal*, who used to live here and about the neighbors and the butterflies. It was all such an amazing coincidence with my birth name, and not one—but two associations to my mother, both butterflies and the name Sal.

Because of all the weird stuff I've experienced over my lifetime, I often joke that there must be cosmic forces around me and why I'm always curious about these types of coincidences. Will finds my stories about these kinds of things entertaining but doesn't take it as serious. And as usual, he gave little in response to my story, returning instead to the topic of our trip home and how it was necessary. We both had boxes of stuff back home we needed to ship here. There was a closet full of boxes at Mom's house and Will had a bunch still waiting at his dad's place to ship.

As Will talked plans, I leaned against the kitchen counter and zoned out on my own thoughts about what it would be like to walk back into Mom's house again. I tried to recall all the things I had packed away, and consider what it would be like to unpack those items here, see those special things of Mom's again, and in my new home—their new home. A twinge of pain pinched in my gut and I sucked back an almost cry pushing to get out. Mom would have loved this house and all the butterflies. I hadn't been home since the funeral last September and sadly it would be a quick visit again, only a week.

I glanced towards the front door in recall of my brief encounter with our new neighbors. It was all weird and I swear the old woman had called me *Yasmin*—she'd never even looked at the flowers. She'd looked right at me—*just me*. But I *had* moved into the home of her only friend, a man whose love was those flowers. It was still bizarre… but I let it go.

* * *

The next two weeks flew by, and before I knew it, it was *fly to Ottawa* time again. I was more than thrilled to get away from work and head back up north to see our family and friends.

An email had arrived during that time from the private detective agency, this time informing me that a man named *Anthony Merenda*, now had my case. I'd composed a follow-up email to this investigator, letting him know I'd be in Ottawa this week, along with the contact information during our stay and that I wanted to meet with him if possible.

Tomorrow, we head to Ottawa.

Chapter 10

Canada Day is a lot like July 4th in the United States, lots of eating, drinking, partying, fireworks and all the national pride you can handle. But I'm proud to be Canadian, *eh.*

We walked the downtown streets of Ottawa among all the crazy Canada Day partiers clad in their red and white clothing. Many had red maple leaves painted on their faces and other body parts. Along with celebrating, the one thing I'd wanted to do once we were downtown for the festivities, was to go see the Canadian Tribute to Human Rights monumental. And since it is within walking distance of all the activities on Parliament Hill, Will and I set off to see the monument.

When the monument came into view, I happily approached it and stood looking up at the 30-foot-tall red granite façade. A fellow Canadian, a Montreal artist and architect had designed it. It had been unveiled by the fourteenth Dalai Lama of Tibet back in September 1990.

"The writing on it is the first sentence of Article One of the United Nations Universal Declaration of Human Rights," Will said.

All human beings are born free and equal in dignity and rights, I read in my head. Then I walked through the monument opening to behind the front wall. There in both English and French on granite plaques carried by stylized human-like figures, where the words *Equality, Dignity,* and *Rights.* On granite plaques on the interior known as *The House of Canada,* were other writings. These plaques carried the same words, but they were in 47 of 70 Canadian aboriginal Peoples' languages. It wasn't a fancy monument, primitive actually, but the feeling you get standing there, is something almost indescribable, but being there gave me this overwhelming sense of pride.

While I was checking out the plaques, Will said, "Many people are honored here." He glanced over to see if I was listening and continued. "In 1998, a plaque honoring John Peters Humphrey—he's the Canadian who was the first director of the United Nations Human Rights Division. He wrote the preliminary draft of the UN Declaration." Will pointed a finger at another sign. "Nelson Mandela was here in September 1998, to unveil this plaque here, commemorating the 50th anniversary of the declaration." He paused. "President Mandela had said, '*Inspire all who see it to join hands in a partnership for world peace, prosperity, and equality.*" When I did nothing but stare at him, he said, "What?"

I smiled like a proud parent watching their kid in a school play. Amazing, my husband can't remember where he put his car keys, but he could remember all of this. "Nothing—yer just cute is all." I grinned again. "Take my picture would ya," I asked, standing near the entrance where the sun shone through. I could always count on Will for the occasional history lesson, and I could also count on him to take the pictures.

* * *

Canada Day over, our time folded over to the next day. Friday, which was also, *get boxes ready for shipping pickup* day. And while Will stayed at his dad's place getting his things together, I went to my mother's — rather my brother's place now, to gather my boxes from the bedroom closet where I'd left them.

Up the way from Mom's house on a mile-long section of Meadowlands Drive, is what Vicki calls, '*Minto-land*'. There's a variety of homes and rental properties dotted throughout this stretch of the street. There are row houses, townhouses, long walkup buildings, tall multi-unit apartment buildings and the yellow brick, boxy, three-story walk-ups like the one she lives in. With her living up the street, she'd graciously offered to come over and help me move boxes.

When I come home, I don't always get enough time with my friends and it was harder with quick visits, so I was thrilled and thankful to spend time with her doing anything, even this. And like usual when visiting my mom in the past, she'd ridden her bike over. She arrived with her dark blond hair—sometimes short, sometimes long—but as she says, *'always too thin'*, back in a low ponytail so her cycling helmet fit properly. Her beautiful, dark brown eyes hid behind snazzy red sporty sunglasses. She wore a snug cherry-red touring shirt made for long rides with those little pouches in the back for supplies. Red was her favorite colour and if a piece of clothing came in red—she owned it. I was surprised her bike wasn't red, but I'm sure she'd already checked into that.

We chatted as we moved boxes from the house into my rental car. She told me about her new business venture of proofing and editing other people's manuscripts and magazine articles.

"The researching involved in the projects—the searching, solving, and verifying for them are the best parts," Vicki said. She's always had a skill for that kind of stuff. "Who are you shipping all this with?" she asked with a grunt, lifting the last box into the car.

"Not sure—Will arranged it. Supposed to be shipped to some local Miami mover and then to our new place. It has to go through a horrendous customs process. Kind of like me," I said, mocking a pain-stricken face. "The movers in Miami will handle that part for us, like a liaison I figure." I grinned. I was thankful someone else was handling the cross-border stuff. "I'm eager to go through all the boxes again. Can't remember what's all in there, other than the obvious." Mom's artificial Christmas tree made no secret of itself with a dark green limb tip poking out, along with tinsel stuck to the packing tape. "I packed some books and clothes and knick-knacks of Mom's, but I can't remember the rest." I rubbed the back of my hand against my forehead.

"Going to be hard to go through it," Vicki remarked, a hint of sadness in her voice.

"It's hard being here—her not being here anymore… it's like she disappeared." I let out an exhausted breath. "Like a bad dream," I added in a whisper. Eager to change the topic, I turned to admire how fit Vicki looked. Most people don't look great in their tight cycling gear, but Vicki *rocked* cycling shorts. She has the market on fit legs from the marathon of cycling she does on weekends, plus the to-and-from work every day. She may be a decade older than me, but you would never know it. She has the youth gene, and with it the energy of a woman *two* decades younger.

"Vick, thanks for your help with all this." I'd hoped to spend more time with her, but I had too much to do and too many other people I needed to see. Short visits suck, and I suffer girlfriend withdrawal because of it.

"No problem," she said.

"It was the distraction I needed more than the help," I said, the words catching in my throat. I gave a little cough to hide the emotions.

"Well, that was my good deed and workout for the day," she said, laughing and then she mounted her bike. "I'm off. Heading over to a friend's place for a barbeque." She grinned and buckled up her helmet.

"Mmmm I'd love me some barbeque," I shot out. A barbeque and a lawnmower were the first two purchases Will had made for the house. "Oh, hey—speaking of great food, we're having dinner over at the neighbor's place tonight." I licked my lips and rubbed my hands together at the thought.

"Enjoy!" Vicki called out, having heard me speak about past meals with them. She pushed off with one powerful thrust of her pedal and was up the hill in a flash. I watched her climb the hill with no effort.

I *gasped* and counted myself lucky I didn't have to keep up with her on that bike. Then I returned inside to say bye to my brother and to let him know I'd be back tomorrow to help organize the remaining stuff he wanted to keep. One quick hug with him and I was off.

Back at my father-in-law's place, I found him and Will sitting on the basement floor going through boxes of old swimming awards and medals. Thankfully, it was the last box they had to go through as all the rest were stacked and waiting by the front door.

"What time are we heading next door to see Andre and Louise?" I asked, rubbing my stomach in anticipation. Visiting with them was one of our favorite things to do when we came home, mostly because we adored them, but also because Andre was an amazing cook.

"We'll finish up here and head over," came the comment from Will's father David, followed up with a smile. He enjoyed the visits as much as we did.

Fifteen minutes later our three grinning faces rounded the corner to the neighbor's backyard. We were greeted by the amazing aroma of something spectacular cooking on the barbeque and Andre waving his tongs in welcome. His welcome was followed by Louise bursting through the back door with serving dishes full of more tasty treats in both hands.

As we all found our places around the patio table, Andre moved the platter of food from the barbeque to where we sat. "Wine anyone?" he asked, lifting a bottle of white in one hand and a bottle of red in the other.

Will and I raised our wine glasses in unison. "Yes—please!" we said in response, followed by laughter as our love for all things Andre and Louise gushed out.

Dinner was fabulous like usual and so was the dialog and entertaining stories the happy couple shared. As evening moved on, David headed home early, while the four of us continued to drink more wine and tell more stories. Andre and Will moved off to poke at the still burning coals of the barbeque and continued to talk travel and tourism, while Louise came over to my side of the table to sit next to me and chat.

She took a sip of her wine, and then said, "Joan told me you two met in high school, that she helped you both stay in touch after." She took another sip. "Until the wedding I never knew who she was talking about. Your speech brought things full circle—it was you she spoke of."

I only nodded, I had a full sip of wine in my mouth.

"William brought home different girlfriends through the years, but I never met this Lynn person she would mention." She smiled lovingly in relaying the sentiment.

"I always thought I was being a nuisance," I said. "You know, trying to track down Will or get messages off to him." I gave her a little laugh with my response.

"There was a time when she lost track of you. William hadn't heard from you either she told me. She seemed panicked over it. But her illness had begun around the same time though."

"Panic?" I questioned, confusion seeping in.

"Well, maybe not panic—but she was anxious. She'd worried the two of you wouldn't find each other again. She hadn't known how to get you guys back in touch. Seemed to think it was her job to do so." Louise paused. "As she got sicker her anxiety about it seemed to get worse. She couldn't find you—couldn't even get Will to contact you. She said something about *not allowed,* meaning not allowed to direct either of you—only keep communications going somehow." She shook her head. "Perhaps she was afraid William wouldn't find someone. You know—to settle down with. Guess she thought you were the one. She was right, you were." She smiled, giving my knee a little tap.

"I hate I wasn't there, I didn't get to see her before she was... gone." I shuddered a little, keeping my voice low, so the boys didn't overhear what I was saying.

"William didn't come home for two years after she died." She took a glance over her shoulder at the boys.

I nodded again when she turned back. "He and I hadn't seen or talked to each other in over five years. I hadn't known she'd died—let alone she'd been sick. I'd even sent her a Christmas card and one to pass on to Will the way she used to. He'd told me his dad had passed it on to him. He'd sent me a postcard that same year saying he was coming home for Christmas. It said to call him—the rest is history." I peeked over again to make sure the boys were still otherwise engaged, but they were unaware more than anything due to the wine consumption.

"Well, I visited with Joan when she was in the hospital in the days before she died. She kept trying to tell me how William and Lynn— you, needed to reunite. It felt like a desperation of sorts." The pain of the memory spread across her face from a frown to a grimace.

"Why was she so adamant about this?" I asked.

She shook her head. "There was something else too." She paused, quickly checking on the guys. Leaning in closer she whispered, "I was there in the hospital when William came home to see her. He had his most recent girlfriend with him. Joan kept saying, *'That's not Lynn. That's not Lynn'*. I tried to sooth her—tell her he would be okay, not to worry, but she wouldn't listen." Louise sat up straight, pressing her lips together as if pondering her next words. When I said nothing, she leaned in again. "You know, I told no one about this, ever—not even Andre." She paused again. "Joan told me never to tell anyone." She put the palms of her hands against her cheeks and drew in a long breath. "She told me something strange—something that was, well, I think it must have been delirium from the pain medication she was on."

"What did she say? Please tell me," I pushed, but still whispering. Stunned already at what she'd shared, I still needed to know more. Loud laughter came from the boys over some story Will was spewing and we both turned a quick glance their way and then back again as if hiding like mischievous children. "Go on please," I said. The hairs on the back of my neck tingled. I was having one of *those* feelings, but this time... no words came—not this time, and they usually did. Instead, I kept quiet as my brain hummed. Something about this sensation was different. Seldom do I question my feelings, they're just, well—no big deal. But this one—this sensation, hinted of importance.

Louise took another long deep breath in. Letting it out, she said, "During one of those moments—when it seemed her pain had subsided, Joan had looked over at me, leaned to the edge of the bed and curled her finger motioning me to come closer." Louise took another deep breath. "She could hardly speak with the failure of her lungs. It was painful even for her to breathe. I told her she didn't need to talk, that instead I would give her updates on my family—but she begged, *'No, listen please'* she'd pleaded. I gave in and moved my chair closer and leaned my face nearer to hers to keep her from straining any further. Then she'd said, *'A few years ago, a man approached me in the park. This man was like no other I had ever seen. He had an aura about him and he smelled like the sea and sunshine—beautiful like a day at the beach. He sat down beside me on the bench. I wasn't scared, it was peaceful in his presence. He told me a story about four mothers and four daughters and how they kept the balance'*." She paused and gently rubbed her eyes as though the pain of the memory weighed on her.

For me, the words brought images of Mom leaning in to talk to my aunt in the hospital bed. The memory made my chest ache, and I was dizzy. Louise took my hands as if trying to hold me in place, but I hadn't moved. I was fixated, and my body was humming still.

"You have to realize," she whispered, "I thought she was completely out of it. She insisted she needed to tell me—so I continued to listen. She'd said, '*The balance was off, but he had made it right, and now he needed my help. He told me it was my task to make sure Will stayed connected with Lynn*'. Joan had told me this encounter had happened around the time her illness had started." Louise paused again and gave her head a little shake. "I asked her who the man was, but all she told me was his name. *Gabriel*. I was sure it had to be the meds making her delusional, but still she'd said she had one last thing to tell me. This was the part of her story I hated the most," Louise said. She winced even before she said the words. "Joan said she'd assumed she had let Gabriel down, because you and Will had lost track of each other and she didn't know how to reconnect the two of you… because she never saw the man again."

"What?" I gasped out. Who the hell was this guy messing with her? Was he real? Was it a weird drug influenced dream she'd had? It sounded like a story from a fairytale, but I'd been glued to Louise's every word, and needed more.

"I told Joan again not to worry, but she had said, '*I'm sick because I failed and may die because I'm telling you about it. He had said sharing the secret will bring on illness or even death, but I have to pass it on. I must make the sacrifice. Tell no one what I've told you,*' she'd said, '*it could make you sick.*'" Louise sucked in a breath as if she were trying to swallow the horrid memories. "I didn't understand what this was all about. All I could do was hold her hand while she painfully spoke. I'd told her I wouldn't tell anyone, but that she should rest. I'd told her Will and David would come to see her soon—that she needed her strength." Louise paused. "Then the oddest things happened. The strain I had seen in her face lessened—like a burden had lifted from her. We never spoke about it again… she died a few days later." Louise crossed her arms over her chest like a self-hug and took in another deep breath.

I tried to absorb her words—the story. Louise tried to reassure me it was the medication fog and a story full of nonsense, but it was clear in her shaky words, I wasn't the only one she was trying to convince.

"Don't worry, I won't mention this to Will. He has his own painful memory of her in the hospital," I said, placing my arms across my chest hoping it would help the ache, but my body continued to hum with pain. Another roar of laughter came from behind us, making us both jump and turn in our seats.

The boys glanced up to see we were staring at them. "What?" They said in harmony, questioning the painful looks on our faces.

"Nothing—nothing," I responded quick for both of us, reaching for my wine glass, and faking a smile.

Louise in a fluster, stood and gathered empty serving dishes. And the wonderful man he was, Andre sprang over straight away to help her.

"I'm getting tired—you?" I questioned Will when he let out a long-drawn-out yawn.

"Uhm ya a bit tired, a bit tipsy too." He laughed as he tipped his glass, finishing the rest of his wine. "I'll let our hosts know we are taking the long 30-second walk back across the lawn to home—and to where our beds were calling us," he said, gathering our dinner plates to take inside.

Laughter came from the open screen door as both Andre and Louise brushed through followed by Will. Andre and Louise were not big drinkers—they were just big *pourers*, and we often ended up tipsy. We always laughed a lot on our visit, so much so my facial muscles always hurt the next day, not to mention my sides from splitting a gut. We exchanged final hugs, and I pushed away any thoughts of the bizarre story as we went on our *tipsy* way.

Chapter 11

In anticipation of a hangover, I opened one eye, but was pleasantly surprised to find I was only mildly dehydrated, nothing a big glass of water and an aspirin couldn't fix.

My plan was to go by Mom's house first to tidy up the rest of the boxes, then swing over to Mac's to hang out over at Mac's place while she did her typical mom and homemaker stuff. I figured since both places were in the same end of town, I could squeeze in the visit with her. But when I arrived at Mom's house, I had found a note on the entry table left by my brother James stating he'd already done up the boxes for me. His note explained that he'd been awake and at it since 5 a.m. packing and tiring himself out in the process. Now he was down for the count, off taking a nap. Big brothers are great, and his help meant that I was also free to continue over to Mac's.

On the drive to Mac's, I mulled over other times when James had taken over, back when we were kids. Well, I was a kid—him being 10 years older. When my parents divorced, he was already grown and out of the house. Though he often humored me with pretending to be a kid and still does it now even though we're both grown up. We both liked scary movies and stuff like ghosts and monsters. On one occasion, for my 16th birthday, he had taken me to see a friend's wife who claimed to be a fortuneteller. I was already uncomfortable with the idea when I got there, but to add to it, the woman had started the reading off with, *"You're afraid of water."* Not as a question but more like a fact. Strange thing was, I *had* become increasingly afraid of water over the years, but I'd told no one.

Rejecting the comment, trying to hide the truth, I'd said, *"No—not that I'm aware of."*

Then she'd asked, *"Do you remember an accident where you almost drowned?"*

Truth this time, I didn't recall this *almost drowning event,* and had said, *"No."*

She'd gone on to give me a story about me on a lake. The story wasn't anything major, but I swear I'd seen the whole thing in my head—every detail as she'd described like it was a real memory. *There was a big lake, a canoe with me in it. There was someone else in it too, but I couldn't see who it was—couldn't feel who it was. The sun was setting, and the canoe became very tippy. Then I was in the water, under the canoe. When I came up out of the water, it was dark, nighttime—suddenly I was back in the boat.* When the images had vanished, I'd focused back on the woman. I hadn't known what had just happened, and the woman just sat there staring back at me saying nothing further about it. She had that look on her face where people say, *'you looked like you've just seen a ghost'.* Who knew what she'd seen. Hell, I couldn't explain what I had seen, but it— whatever it was, had rattled this fortune teller. Before I'd left, she'd handed me a light pink-coloured stone, and her hands had shaken as she'd given it to me. She'd told me it was rose quartz, and it was good to *keep on your person*—good for my wellbeing, apparently. She'd had a huge bowl of crystals and rocks sitting on the table as well, and she'd told me to pick another stone. I'd gone for an irregular-shaped, silvery-black stone with a smoother slick surface that had reminded me of how the water had appeared in the memory—vision, or whatever it was. When I'd closed my hand around it, it had felt good against my palm. She'd said it was *Hematite* and called it my *career stone.* What a joke I'd thought, thanks for the guidance—I'm 16, what do I need a career stone for?

Several years later, I'd read-up on precious and semiprecious stones and found out some ordinary stones were often used in magic. The properties of stones or gems could be activated through prayer, charming, or ritual, and that quartz, *rose quartz* in particular, was used for healing and other things like psychism, power, success, speaking with the dead, and spiritual attainment. I'd had to look up the term *psychism* and found it referred to *the doctrine proposing the existence of psychic phenomena*. Coolest thing I found about the black stone was that it isn't just about career success, it's also for healing and for grounding and foresight.

I pulled into Mac's driveway, letting go of the birthday memory. Getting out of the car I spotted Cooper, Mac's boxer, lounging on the front lawn. He got up from his usual spot, made one loud bark and turned to go up the front steps as if saying, '*follow me*', so I did. I loved the old guy, he's more like a family member. He was great at guarding the house and watching over the kids *and* he's Mac's best buddy. Funny, he looks scary on the outside, but he's a marshmallow on the inside.

When I hit the top of the stairs, I yanked open the screen door to see Mac standing in the kitchen as usual. She was wearing a long dark brown peasant skirt and matching brown tank top. Her hair was up in a top knot, she wore no makeup, and she was barefoot. She's become very bohemian in her style over the years, going from a metropolitan high-style type, to a natural earth Mother. Everything was organic in her kitchen, and she even had a composter out back. She was a little curvier than she'd been in high school, but the curves came from birthing two sons—now 7 and 4. It looked good on her though and added to the sexy gypsy-thing she had going on.

"What are you cooking now?" I bellowed, finishing with a laugh.

"Westlake, you're a walking stomach. How do you stay so thin — hollow leg?" She threw back at me, followed up with a big welcoming grin. Her smiley face with all those perfect white teeth reminded me of a pack of *Chiclets*. I'd been tortured with braces, my teeth were good, but they'd never look as dazzling as hers.

On the counter was a large container of her homemade hummus and I grabbed a carrot, dipped it, and shoved it into my mouth before she could say a thing. I laughed again, nearly choking on the carrot.

"Serves you right, ya little glutton," she said, laughing with me.

My stomach growled when I spied the two huge racks of muffins cooling beside the stove. I reached for one but stopped when I bumped the huge textbook sitting next to them. It was tan with a dark green title across the top, *Natural Healing, Homeopathy & Naturopathy*. "What's this?" I said, giving the book a little shove her way.

"It's a book." She coupled her sarcasm with another big toothy grin.

"Smart-ass."

"I'm taking a course. Figured you'd think it was cool, no?" She spun the book around showing me the contents list and then continued with mixing whatever was in the bowl in front of her.

"What about the jewelry stylist-sales job?" I asked, continuing to admire the book, and peeking over at the contents in the bowl.

"Oh, I'm doing that too. Have to keep a bit of the old Mac alive too, ya know?" More stirring.

"Mother, housewife, homeopath, and fashion plate—sure no problem," I said, poking fun. But I was confident she could do it all and more. I took a longer look at her. She wore long dangly wooden earrings, and a matching pendant suspended on a braided cotton lanyard that hung just above her navel.

"You like?" she asked, seeing me gawk at it. She modeled the piece, lifting the necklace by the wooden pendant. "It's from S&D," she advertised. The company did high-end costume jewelry, catering to celebs and now to the public. Most of the stuff was much too fashion-forward for me, but I loved the pendant she was wearing. "It's the new line," she said. "Has a *Native Indian* influence—and I quite like it. It's a change from their typical flashier lines."

"I like the pendant," I said, taking the wooden piece in my hand. "Is it a deer?"

"Elk," she corrected. "The elk is supposed to be a symbol of psychic self-defense and protection. A rune of an elk—like this one is worn to defend against malevolent spirits and makes one brave while facing fears of the unknown."

"Really?" I raised my eyebrows in surprise and tried not to giggle.

She took the piece from my hand and rubbed the wooded animal between her own fingers. "That's what they say." She stuck out her tongue at me.

"Can always use a little warding off of malevolent spirits." I chuckled. "How can I get me one?"

"I think I know *someone* who can get you one." She beamed.

As Mac continued to mix and bake, and then mix something else, I relayed the latest about Will's globetrotting work trips and the stuff he'd brought back for me. I shared how I especially liked the things with a protective element to them. I had charms, small statues, and different pieces of jewelry you're supposed to wear for protection. "My favorite piece is a long oval-shaped rose quartz pendant, wrapped in silver wire on a black lanyard—like the one you're wearing," I told her. "Wearing rose quartz is supposed to be good for your wellbeing. It works—kind of makes me feel good, peaceful, relaxed—safe sorta," I added, just as voices boomed from the back room.

"Boys! Keep it down, I'm visiting with Lynn and can't hear myself over your screeeaming!" Mac belted out. She smiled again, handing me a warm muffin. "What else is on your plate for this visit?" she asked, now in a contrasting softer tone. She leaned a hip against the counter and split apart a muffin for herself.

"We're going over to Olivia and Mike's for dinner tomorrow. The day after, I'm meeting a private investigator," I said, keeping it all nonchalant, and shoving a piece of muffin into my mouth.

"What?" Her eyes widened.

"Dinner at Olivia and Mike's," I responded, keeping back what she was truly after.

"Uhm no, Lynnie—why are you meeting with a PI?" she fumbled out, giving my arm a pinch. "As if you don't know what I meant by *what*."

Making her wait, I chewed slow and rubbed my arm, and grinned. "Remember how I put in a search for my birthmother—but only got *some* of the paperwork?" I paused, swallowing another bite while she digested the statement. "Well, I wanted to see if I could find more information. Best-case scenario would be info on my birthfather, since he wasn't named."

"Ya, but where did you get the idea to hire a PI? Seems a bit extreme, no?" Mac nibbled the edge of a muffin.

"I'd like to know more about my birth-family. I'd like to know if my birthmother had any siblings or any other children. It's my unknown life and I'm curious. But I have no expectations," I said. I gave her the short version on how I'd gotten the name of the agency and that they were reputable. I explained we had already corresponded, that they had copies of all the paperwork, and would assess if there were sufficient leads to find more information. "Need more, something—anything." I sighed. Mac waited, she seemed to know I had more coming, and I did. "It's hard knowing I came from another family line. I don't have that genetic thing with my family that you and all my friends do. Maybe I could see what my birthmother looked like—if there's any resemblance," I mused, shoving the last piece of muffin in my mouth, halting my rant.

"What if you uncover something not so pleasant?" Mac's eyebrows crinkled, and her lips tightened together.

"What if I do? I am who I am, Mac. I'm not going to change because I find more information. It's scary not having any family medical history—I'm in the dark." I stopped and took another muffin from the rack and nibbled the muffin's coarser top edges. "Best part of the muffin," I said, giggling a little, trying to redirect her worry to things less serious.

"Wow, I don't know what to say." Mac shook her head as if still trying to grasp the idea. "I guess I'd be curious too. Hard to imagine being in your shoes," she said with a grin and glancing down at my feet.

"It's still weird for me too." I said, doing a little toe-step, showing off my not-so-fancy flip-flops. "Who knows, the PI may find nothing." I forced a smile.

"Hey—speaking of weird. Yesterday I was watching a show on fortune tellers—do you remember when we went to see that psychic? You, me, and Deb?" she asked, switching the subject herself.

"Gawd, what were we—like 20-nothing at the time? Felt like we'd been there all day too." The woman's method of reading took the whole afternoon, but she'd told us some amazing things. That had been my second experience with a fortuneteller.

"She made us choose those angel cards from the little box, remember?" Mac said, before pouring a creamy mixture from one bowl into another containing a bunch of dry stuff. She mixed again.

"And the stuff she told each of us was bang-on," I recalled.

"Ya, she was very specific. None of the readings could've been swapped out for the other."

When I tried to put my finger in the bowl, she gave it a tap with the spatula.

"She said you were afraid of fire?" I said, rubbing my fake injury.

"Auh, don't remind me—majorly afraid of fire. Creeped me out when she'd said I'd burned to death in a past life. Nice, right—Not." She shook her hands and cringed as if she'd touched something icky, and then she continued stirring. "I seem to recall she said you were afraid of water and drowned in a past life—Hello."

"She's the second psychic-reader to tell me that," I said. The water—the fear thing, the drowning—well almost drowning. Mac knew the story about the other lady, I'd told her when we were teens, but I wasn't sure if she had remembered it.

"She'd also said your *third-eye* was open—that you had a sense for things like she did," Mac said. "You know you kinda have that sorta thing going on, Lynn. You've always been tuned in to the unseen world." She followed with a "uuuoooowwwwhh," making a weak attempt to be scary.

"Whatever," I laughed out. "I wouldn't take it so serious." I'd laughed, but I knew there were many things I'd *sensed* and seen over the years, and I knew no one who could relate. I'd never forgotten how it had felt being at that fortuneteller's place with my friends. The way this woman's words had affected me. I'd tried to play it off as a cool adventure like the others had, but part of me had known her words had meant something. They'd felt like something... *true*. I'd even search the term *third-eye* and found that in some Eastern and Western spiritual traditions, it's often connected with visions, clairvoyance, and something to do with the ability to detect chakras and auras. Other stuff I found mentioned precognition, and out-of-body experiences, and how people who've developed the ability to use their third-eye are sometimes known as *Seers*.

"Who've you seen on this visit so far?" Mac asked, shifting the focus.

As she moved the rest of the muffins from the rack into big plastic storage bins, I told her about my visit with Vicki and the chore of moving boxes. Then about how Will and I had gone for dinner at the neighbors, but I abandoned telling her about my conversation with Louise. She'd already been miffed over my using a PI, so I wasn't sure she'd be able to handle that part. I needed to tell someone—just didn't know who could handle it. The encounter with Dunya's grandmother had twisted me up, but I had tried not to read too much into it. I'd told Vicki about the incident in one of my emails to her, but she'd just confirmed it was *Butterfly Jasmine* and considered it a funny coincidence. She'd pointed out had I *not* known my birthname, I wouldn't have thought anything of it. Vicki was a fact person. Mac was more open for mystical possibilities. I'd tell her sooner or later about it, but I'd let her adjust to the PI thing first.

I eyed the vast array of spices Mac had near the stove. Then I picked up each bottle one at a time, opening the lids, and sniffing. Most didn't have a label on them, and I couldn't tell what they were—not that I could tell by sniffing either, I was just curious. "What's with all the spice tins, Mac," I asked, determined to smell each one.

"Ya, been expanding my spices and herbs. I was missing a lot they recommend in the training course. My hubby keeps calling me the *Kitchen Witch*." She laughed amused at the idea. "I have to make time to put labels on the rest. I don't want to mix up a batch of something nasty, or cause someone to break out in a rash or grow a third arm or something," she joked.

Rubbing my stomach, I said, "Maybe I should've asked what was in these muffins, before gorging on them. Tell me they get rid of wrinkles or something equally useful." I widened my eyes for confirmation.

"Sorry, just plain old carrot and bran, oh, and a little eye-of-newt," she finished, winking at me.

I smiled back at her and gobbled up the last bit of my second—or was it third muffin?

"Still hungry there, Lynnie?" she asked, giving me a big eye-roll.

"Naah I'm good—doing dinner at Olivia's tonight, she'll make sure I'm all filled up. Just showing my appreciation for your cooking." She grinned and shook her head at my never-ending appetite. "What do you have going this evening?" I prodded.

"Monica's coming over to show me a few pointers with the old spice spectrum. She thinks I'll cause someone bodily harm with my *experimental* cooking." Her tone may have been lighthearted, but I knew better. Monica—Mac's mom, she's the *real* cook/baker in the family, so there was a hint of truth to what Mac was saying. I'm sure her mom *was* worried about her use of spices.

A little giggle escaped me at the thought of Mac and her *reckless* spices.

"What? Don't laugh. You know how she is. '*Those are not just spices, Mackenzie*'," she said, doing a stellar imitation of her mother, making me laugh harder.

"Well, you better get labels on those tins before she comes over—or you're in deep shit." I said, giving her my best pretend bulgy-eyed distressed face.

"Ooohh you're right—crap!" she squealed. Panicked, she grabbed the label maker from the top of the fridge.

We spent the rest of our visit chatting about her family and their goings-on, and labeling tins to prepare for *Professor Monica*. It was always an easy relaxed time at Mac's, no pretention or restraint of topic. Sometimes our conversations got emotional, from gut-wrenching laughter to mascara-running crying, but we cherished both.

Finished with the labeling and the visit, I yelled my goodbyes to the kids in the back room. Then Mac and her buddy Cooper escorted me to the front door. We hugged as always, and I told her I'd check in later on the PI stuff once I had something to report, or even if I didn't.

"Blessed be," she tossed out in jest, placing her palms together over her heart in a mocking *Wiccan* salutation.

"Merry part," I responded, bowing my head and copying the hand gesture. I blew her a kiss and turned towards the car.

She waved from the front step as I pulled away, and like my mother often did, I honked the horn twice in a final salutation.

Chapter 12

From the driveway at my father-in-law's place, I spotted Will and his dad walking from the far end of the street, most likely from another walk around the neighborhood.

"Hello boys!" I bellowed from the front stoop.

William waved crossing both arms over his head as if he were flagging me down. He jogged his way up the drive and then wrapped his arms around me, then he planted a kiss, making a squeaking noise against my cheek.

"Auh gross, you're all sweaty," I said, trying to push him away.

"Going to hop in the shower and get ready. Then we'll head over to Olivia and Mike's," he said, freeing his grip on me.

"I'm gonna have to change my shirt now—ya big goon." I stretched my shirt out to examine the sweaty-boy marks. "Sheesh," I said. His dad laughed and turned me towards the doorway, directing me inside.

While Will showered, I scrambled through my suitcase to find another shirt to wear. I grabbed a thin long-sleeved white thermal t-shirt and changed out of the sweat-marked one. Hurriedly, I redid my ponytail, tidying the strays that had come loose.

We took our usual route to their house, a route we had taken a million times before, completing the left–right-left-right turns from the main road into the community. We turned onto their street, and then a few houses down we pulled up to house number 222.

Likely hearing us pull up, Olivia came out the front door to greet us. She was followed by her daughters and their new black lab mix puppy, *Bella*, who trailed behind them. "Hello, my dear," Olivia squeaked as she wrapped an arm around my back. "How about a glass of wine?" she said, more a statement than a question.

"What took you so long to offer," I shot back, and wrapped my arm around her shoulders. She giggled.

"Girls grab the dog and get her back inside, please!" she said, beckoning to her two lovely imp-like daughters. Olivia's girls are amazing creatures, both athletic and tenderhearted, with big, beautiful eyes like their mother. All of them had this elfish look about them, with petite little bodies fixed with the high sprite-like voices. They could definitely pass as relations to the *wee fairy-folk*.

"Get the magic juice flowing," I said, squeezing her again.

We scampered up the steps followed by Will, the doggie and the two fairy elves.

The visit progressed with its usual mix of social wine and food served out on the patio, along with the occasional, "*Mom!*" coming from inside the house.

The first bellow had come from Rachel, Olivia's youngest, saying she'd pinched her finger in a drawer. Remedy one, a small bag of peas from the freezer to put on the finger to ease the throb and potential swelling. The following hour later, it was the older of the elves, Katherine—or Kate, named after her great-great-gran. Kate, it seems had cut her finger trying to slice '*super-duper*' thin pieces of cheese and had nipped off the side tip of her index finger. She'd been more upset it had ruined her nail polish. Mom to the rescue with disinfectant and a bandage that was the exact size, shape, and comfort for the injury. But what really topped it off, was after Mike had ranted about how his daughters *needing to be more careful*, doesn't he go and burn his forearm on the barbeque lid. Once again Nurse Olivia to the rescue with the burn compress, ointment, and perfect dressing for the injury.

"Okay people, Mom has had enough doctoring for one night. I want to relax and enjoy my wine and visit with my friends, pleeeease!" she roared, collapsing on the lounge chair next to me, wineglass still in hand. She rolled her eyes and took a big sip of her wine.

I laughed. "How's work handling things while you're off on vacation?" I asked. They had a meltdown every time she was away from the office. She's the one who keeps everything organized including the doctors. When she's not there everything goes to hell.

"Dr. Rick has been calling me every day since I've been off, and it's only been two freak'n days. I swear the man would lose his big nose if it weren't attached. I like being needed—but come on," she huffed out, then took a sip. I laughed again, and she followed with, "How did box moving day go—did Will and his dad get everything done at their end?" She took another sip of wine.

"Well enough," I said nodding, trying not to allude to the slow pace the boys had taken to go through their stuff. But she knew.

"Hell, I still have boxes of Mom's in the office I've yet to go through," she remarked. "There's stuff in those boxes from Mom *and* my Nan. I wouldn't doubt if there's stuff from my mother's mom in there and so on," she dragged out, laughing at her own words.

"Long line of women," I said, baffled yet entertained.

"You don't know the half of it. Get this—my great-grandmother Katherine, whose mother abandoned her as a child, had two half-sisters from her father's second marriage. He was a surgeon by the way. Katherine had one daughter Phillipa—my grandmother. Phillipa had a daughter—my mom, Pamela. Mom had two daughters—my sister and me. My sister has two daughters and well—I have two," she explained. She paused and made a face as if questioning the order she'd just recited and took another sip of wine.

We continued to talk about all the women and their lives though I had a little trouble keeping up with all her rapid recollections. Other than lots of women in the family, there was another common thread, all the women seemed to be involved in the medical field. Liv's grandmother had worked for a doctor, her mom had been a nurse, and Olivia works for a group of doctors. No wonder Liv was good at fixing boo-boos.

As Olivia finished detailing the long list of women in her family, I glanced over to see the men fiddling with Will's camera. Mike's laptop was up, and he was trying to connect the two. To halt Olivia's storytelling, I pointed over at the boys, and together we rose from our lounges to go see what all the fuss was. I circled around and found that Mike had a photo of *me* on the screen. It was one Will had taken on Canada Day at the entrance of the Human Rights monument.

"We weren't sure what we were seeing. Hard to see on the camera screen, so I connected it to the laptop to get a better look," Mike explained.

"What's the big deal about the photo?" I asked, leaning in closer.

"Well, it… kind of looks like you have wings." Mike pointed to the area on the picture above my shoulders.

"Wings? Are you drunk?" Olivia slurred, leaning in. "Oh, wait that's me," she said with a laugh and a snort.

Will laughed and moved over so I could see better. Mike enlarged the photo such that I was the only thing in the frame.

There I was, standing dead center in the opening. Behind me, filling the opening to the stone archway, were what resembled an expansive set of wings. The tops were about a foot above my head, with the bottom tips poking out near the back of my knees. They weren't solid, more translucent like thin tissue paper, with slight division of what resembled feathers lined up and stacked like you'd see on a bird's wing. "It's got to be a play of the light shining through," I said, bewildered.

"Well, it's not like you have wings—but it looks like you do," Mike said. He turned and gave me a smart-ass grin.

"Maybe it's a reflection of sun off the stone or something—but isn't it cool?" Will boasted, like he'd captured it that way on purpose.

I stared at the photo, reaching for the mouse. Enlarging it again I scrolled up and down looking at, *my wings*. I reached back and rubbed my shoulder, wondering what having wings this size would be like, feel like. The fine hairs on my neck tingled, stopping me from entertaining the idea further. "That's a keeper," I said, and the heightened sensation on my skin dissipated. I turned to head back to the lounge chairs and Olivia followed while the boys continued with going through the rest of the photos. "Let me know if you find any other mysterious photos," I said, dismissing the findings, turning my attentions back to Olivia. "Liv, do you still have that blue jay that comes around the backyard squawking for peanuts?"

"Oh ya, we have two now. I used to say the first was Nan keeping an eye on us—now the second one I think is Mum," she shared. "Why?" She sipped.

"Was thinking about the last time I was here, when you told me the story," I said, then segued into my story about the butterflies indicating we'd found the right house.

Olivia loved the idea about Mom being there, but I wasn't ready to tell her the other story, the one about the Butterfly Jasmine and my new neighbors. Instead, I just told her I'd met the neighbors, and that they were very nice. I did however fill her in about going to meet the PI. She thought it was cool, as I assumed she would, and she was just as curious about things as I was. Olivia is the most emotional of my girlfriends—it isn't a bad thing, it just means I'll have to ease her from the minor stuff, and later—gently, go onto the big stuff, like Louise's story. All were better explained when she was sober too.

The night ended like always, Mike had made another spectacular meal, and we all drank without care, and because we were full of magical food and wine, we stayed the night, crashing in their guest room.

✷✷✷

The next morning back at my father-in-law's, I cleaned up and readied myself to meet with the private investigator.

The weather was cool for July, much better than the humidity of Miami and I was comfortable in my cargo pants and short-sleeved t-shirt, and I even kept the car windows down as I drove. I'd arranged to meet the guy alone at the local coffee shop and told him what kind of car I'd be driving, so he knew when I arrived.

I pulled into the parking area and got out of the car. In the second row of cars, there was a large man leaning against a black Escalade. He wore a white golf shirt and dark jeans and he seemed to be checking his phone. I locked the car making the alarm beep, and he glanced up. He gave a friendly grin and started over towards me. Tucking a folder under his arm, he adapted a little jog as he hustled himself over the grassy divider between the rows.

A stride before reaching me, he extended a big hand, and in a deep voice, said, "Hi, I'm Anthony Merenda. You must be Lynn." He stood just over 6 feet tall, carrying no less than 250 pounds of what suggested thick muscle, but his smile was genuine and calming.

Losing the proper response, I said, "That sounds like an Italian name." I winced and shook his hand. The palm of his hand was warm and smooth, but it still had a roughness of calluses, and typical if he were someone who lifted heavy weights in the gym.

Without missing a beat, he said, "You bet. My mother named me after *Saint Anthony*, the Patron of Lost Things and Missing Persons. Guess it suits, considering the business I'm in, eh?" He grinned again.

His dark midnight-coloured hair was cut short, not military style, but still tight to his scalp. He had large dark green eyes, like the colour of old wine bottles. He had typical Italian good looks you might see in an old gangster movie. On the left side of his upper lip was a small but deep scar that looked as though it had been there forever. Still at a loss for words, I grinned back at him and let go of his hand.

Together we turned and walked across the parking lot.

He reached out in front of me when we closed in on the front door of the coffee shop and pulled open the door creating a big swoosh of air. I turned to say something, and he nodded at me, motioning me to go inside. The thought lost, I turned back and went inside.

"Coffee?" he asked.

"No thanks," I said.

Anthony moseyed up to the counter and ordered himself a coffee while I walked over to the farthest booth to find some privacy.

Sitting, I watched as he thanked the girl behind the counter, spun around and sauntered over to where I was waiting. It was cool in the coffee shop, but my hands were sweating. Nerves I figured, and I tried to dry them on the sides of my pants.

"Can I get you anything—my treat?" he asked again.

"No. No thanks, I'm good," I said, and clasped my hands together in my lap. With the way I was feeling, the last thing I needed was a coffee or a sugary donut.

"Well, let's get to it," he said. "I'm afraid I have little to tell you at this point." He paused and took a deep sip of the hot coffee.

"Oh," was all I got out, disappointment spreading over me.

"Wasn't able to find any family members—yet. But I found out what high school your birthmother attended. I'll try to track down a classmate or possible friends from the time."

"I figured she went to school in the east end of town," I said, "Well, based on the address they had for her when I was born." She would have been pregnant her whole senior year if she attended at all. In those days, they didn't allow a pregnant girl to stay in school.

He flipped through the folder. "As for her cancer diagnosis, it looks like it was about a year before her death, but it's all I found so far." He flipped more papers. "Couldn't find anything on the ex-husband, not even anyone who may have known him."

I wiped my hands on my jeans again. "I'm not too concerned about her ex, but more whether she had any other children." It was one of my many curiosities, my birthfather being the main, but other family members would be a great start as they may know more about him or have photos of her.

"No mention of any other children," he confirmed. "Also, both of her parents are deceased. I'm sorry I don't have more for you, but I will keep at it. I'm trying to track down her earlier jobs. Between her school friends and work friends, I may be able to piece together more for you." His voice softened as if trying to reassure me. I'm sure he saw the disappointment on my face. "Strangest thing though—it wasn't what I found, but more what I couldn't find." He trailed off looking a little mystified, then cleared his throat. Then he added, "I couldn't find one thing on your birthfather. There is no mention of him or any medical records on any of the birth or adoption files. Back in the day, medical information was required for the records—even if the father wasn't named, it was mandatory for the adoption process."

"Could have been left out to avoid public embarrassment, or impact on the boy's future," I stated. Or she could have kept his name a secret to avoid her own embarrassment.

He must have sensed the wheels turning in my head because he said, "Have no fear, Anthony's here." He laughed, trying to shake me from my hopelessness. "I've just dug into this, Lynn. Something is bound to turn up. Good or bad, you'll have your answers—I'm sure. Even I'm intrigued. It's like a real mystery, and an investigator loves solving mysteries. Don't give up on me." He reached over and patted my shoulder.

The meeting was short, and we left the same way we'd come in. We said our goodbyes, and he marched off to his car in pursuit of answers.

I sat in my car still in the parking lot recapping the conversation along with the events of the week *and* tried not to cry. I had gotten nothing—nothing but more questions. I tried to convince myself I'd filled up enough joy from visits from my friends, but... I still had too many holes. And tomorrow at 7:00 am, we'd be in line at the airport, doing the dance again.

Chapter 13

The trip home had been long, making the day short. After unpacking and doing laundry from the trip, all we had time for had been a quick uneventful dinner and then it was off to bed.

Later to bed, early to rise, the sun hadn't even risen yet as I lay in bed awake sulking. My trips always went too fast, and I never got enough time with my girlfriends. One visit each it seemed if I was lucky. It's hard not to be around for their daily lives. Oh, sure I get emails and phone calls, but it was still hard missing out on the real parts of their lives, only getting tidbits or recaps of events after they've happened, never being there in the moment. So many moments missed, not to mention the missed years with both Mac and Alison.

As I continued to pout, I pondered Louise's story. I turned on my side to face Will as he slept peacefully next to me. Even with little light, I could see his eyes dart back and forth under his lids. His breath was soft and steady. He always slept light and rarely ever made a sound. Unlike me, if I fell asleep on my back, I was a thunderstorm of noise as the mouth-breather. I reached over and placed my palm on the side of his face. He grinned a little, eyes still closed, saying my name in a low whisper. I quietly pulled my hand back, tucking it against my chest. Telling Will of Louise's story was not an option—it wasn't the right time. Would there ever be a right time to tell him what transpired between his mother and her friend? I closed my eyes and searched for sleep again.

Two hours later, I was up. Will was already out of bed and had the coffee brewing. I left the bedroom on the sound of him clanging around in the kitchen and caught the smell of eggs and back-bacon cooking. I headed straight for the kitchen, sniffing the air as I crossed the living room. One thing I loved about the layout of the house was that you could see the kitchen from the living room and vice versa, and as I approached, there was Will, plating breakfast and grinning like a champion.

"My hero," I gushed and smacked him on the butt as I rounded the big island. "Smells great," I said crawling up onto one of the barstools that flanked the island. Then I dug into the big helping of my Sunday breakfast, eggs, toast, and *Canadian* bacon. Made me laugh to call it that. It was written that way on the packages you find in the grocery store here in the US. To us Canadians, it was pea meal bacon or back-bacon, but either way it was lean and delicious.

"What's on your plate today," Will asked, following with, "and don't say bacon and eggs." He chuckled.

"Let's see," I pondered, savoring my last piece of bacon.

Will shook his head. "I'm going to catch up on work after breakfast. Need to get back on track and prepare for my next work trip. End of the month—don't forget," he said.

In boring contrast, I said, "Laundry, groceries, and making the food for the week. I live a glamorous life here in Miami." I smirked and gave him a long-winded sigh.

"You've got it rough." He mockingly rubbed my shoulders. "Did you want to download the photos from the trip, before you get on with the glamorous stuff?" he said, deflecting my *poor me* response.

"Ya, I'm gonna send Alison that weird, winged photo you took." I was curious what she would say about it. "She'll love seeing the photos from home too. She doesn't get back to Ottawa as much as she'd like."

With my stomach happy, I tidied up after Will's breakfast preparation mess. Then I went to check my emails. Will's father didn't have internet and checking emails on our trip home had been next to impossible. As my laptop whirled to life on the coffee table, I glanced around the living room at the few still unopened boxes from our move.

The one next to the sofa was marked *Living R* in thick black marker, and I shifted off the couch to open it.

Inside were all the small sculptures and woodcarvings from Will's travels, along with three framed photos. There was one from our engagement, and one of Will and his mom. The last one was of my mom and me from my wedding day. All the girly wedding preparation had been worth it to see that smile on her face. The lights flashed on my laptop grabbing my attention. I sighed and placed the framed photos back in the box and sat back down to log in.

Waiting again, I glanced around the room at the other boxes and over to the open spaces in the large wall unit that currently only held our TV. I didn't mind the unpacking part of a move—it was the *pack-up* part that was torture. Before our trip home I hadn't finished this room, but I was determined to get the last of our items out before the shipment from Ottawa arrived. It was supposed to be here by the end of July before Will had to leave on his work trip to Jamaica. He told me he'd work from home on the day to be here when it arrived. I'd told him I would take care of my stuff I'd packed, if he'd take care of his. He had said, *"Deal,"* but I had a sneaky suspicion I'd be taking care of all the boxes.

Focusing back on my laptop, I double-clicked on the email icon. The application sprang into action and downloaded my latest emails. Like little messengers lining up, six emails dropped into my inbox.

The first was from my buddy Luc, asking if I was home yet and telling me he was bored to death at work without me.

Next was Derek's, telling me about a crazy book he was reading, where the main character investigates paranormal activities, stating it might be one I'd like. It had been soon after Mom died when I'd met Derek. He was a consultant from South Carolina, sent to work on a project with my current employer, and I was assisting on the project during that time. With the timing as it was, I had just found out Olivia's mother had died, and I hadn't been focused on the project. Despite that, he and I had connected as if we were old friends, like we were the only people in the room, and the others seemed to be oblivious. By the end of the three-week project, we'd exchanged contact info and cheerful goodbyes. Since, we've become close friends and as a bonus, he sometimes functions as my *go-to-geek* because of his superior problem solving on the computer front. We like many of the same TV shows and he also loves fantasy and sci-fi movies and books. I even got him to read a couple of *my* favorite books, not that I've read a ton.

The third email was from Vicki asking how my flight was, followed by the outline of her activities of yesterday and today.

Vicki's was followed by Mac's email saying how great it was to see me, and that she may need help with the *'how to study for an exam thing again'* and that the whole school thing was *'wigging'* her out.

Second to last was Olivia, saying she wished we could have stayed longer and that the girls miss us already. She'd listed the chores she would tackle around home, and how she needed to get new rubber boots for the girls since they spend most of their time at the stables these days.

Last, was Alison, who also asked about my trip home. She'd written that the one visit she and I had since our 12-year gap, wasn't enough and that she and Ken were looking forward to coming to visit us at the new home. She'd ended the email with how Canada Day was always the best spent in the *Nation's Capital,* and if you weren't from Ottawa, you couldn't understand.

Turning from my computer, I reached into my computer tote and pulled out my favorite photo of her and I. The one with our faces squished together as we hugged in front of her apartment in Calgary. I sported my usual boring ponytail while her long wavy brown hair full of golden highlights streamed over her shoulders. Those amazing blue eyes of hers, the colour filling most of the eye area with only a shimmer of white at the edges, sparkled out at me. It killed me that she never ever had to wear mascara—her lashes were thick and dark, and looked as if they were meticulously curled, but were natural. She has little apple cheeks that pop every time she smiled. That gracious love-filled smile, pretty much shone all the time. She sometimes wore lipstick, but it was more like a darker shade of her already perfect lip colour. I told her she should have been a model, and that I wished I could find a lipstick in the exact shade of her lips. After searching for years, I realized the colour didn't exist, and if it had, it would have been called 'Angel Blush' or something similarly adorable. We were both the same height, but she has a shapely figure, that some would say had a *little extra*, but for the man who appreciated a woman with a little extra, they were always a goner.

She and I had worked at the same technology company in Ottawa, reconnecting after high school, and that's when the whole *Spooky* nickname had started. And it was there she met her now husband Ken. She and I worked the IT helpdesk, and Ken was one of the many on-site support guys, but he lived out West in Calgary which made him thousands of miles away from Ottawa. As part of our job, we talked to these support guys regularly, but the conversation between Alison and Ken eventually moved to off hours and grew into a nice friendship. In time they fell in love via email and conversations over the phone. After Ken's first visit to see Alison in Ottawa, he... was... a goner. She in time moved to Calgary to be with him and they later married. I'd met him a few times, but here in Miami, was the first time either of them had met Will, although Alison had remembered him from high school.

Time flies, it had been over two years—almost three, since she and Ken had been here checking the housing market in South Florida. They'd been hoping to buy an investment property near us and had made an extra stop to visit. I was sure the boys had thought we were nuts with the way she and I talked and giggled nonstop. We had been so excited to meet up that when we saw each other in the lobby of my condo, we'd run to embrace, calling out, *"Spoookeeey."* We slammed together in a powerful bear hug, like we were holding on for dear life, like our hearts might stop if we let go.

I smiled at the photo. It made me happy, but I needed more. It was difficult not being able to see her like I could with my other friends in Ottawa. But we did our best to keep in touch and up-to-date with our lives by phone and emails. Of late, she and Ken had been going through fertility treatments with no success thus far and it's been tough not being able to be there, actually *be there* with her for this hard stuff. Alison had been the only one I hadn't touched base with this past week, so I wrote her back first.

As I started the email, Will sauntered in and handed me the memory card from his camera. "Here ya go. Let me know if there's any good ones we can print off for Dad," he said, heading towards the extra bedroom we'd set up as the office. "Call me if you need me," he called as he disappeared down the hallway.

I paused on the email writing and popped the memory card into my laptop and brought up the list of photos. I scanned the list, stopping to enlarge one or two, but moved on to revisit that crazy one of me with wings.

It wasn't a bad shot, and I looked pretty in the photo. The sun cascading down made my skin look soft and luminous, contrasting with the columns of the monument's hard red granite. I further enlarged the photo to examine what I assumed was a play of sunlight against the reflective surface of the granite... but found it wasn't. There didn't seem to be anything able to cast that reflection, nor those tissue-paper-like shapes above my shoulders and from behind my knees. Could be it was a smear of some sort, I pondered, increasing the clarity of the photo. The photo option didn't help—only made the image appear as if I *did* have wings.

How could a digital camera create that image I wondered? The old-style cameras sometimes created ghostly images on film due to things like humidity, aged, or damaged film. Even the occasional camera strap created a weird appearance, but digital cameras didn't suffer the same problem *and* the rest of the photos had been clear.

Whatever.

I attached the photo and wrote a long description with it. I also told Alison about my neighbors, knowing she would get a kick out of that coincidence *and* this weird photo. I wrote a summary of the story Louise had told me, though I still wanted to talk to her about it, more about how it had made me feel. She's good for talking through emotions *and* about strange stuff. She was a believer of all things seen and unseen and I could talk to her without feeling foolish. I hit *Send*, wondering how soon I'd hear back from her.

In the meantime, I sent the photo off to Derek. He also loved the weird and unusual, but he'd be able to explain what had happened to the image. Then I sent responses back to each of the girls, saying how much I enjoyed seeing them, and agreeing it was too quick. I stated I was continuing to put away stuff from boxes and preparing for the new shipment coming in two weeks. After, I sent an email response to Luc, telling him I had a cool photo to show him, knowing full well when I showed him, he'd freak. He's had a few of his own *weird* experiences and with him being a religious man, the whole wing thing would for sure stir up conversation about God and angels.

I hit send on this last email, and my cell phone rang. It was Derek.

"Hey," I said, answering the call.

"Shortcut Jones," he announced. I liked when he used the nickname I'd coined for him.

"I take it you saw the photo?"

"Yes, oh winged-one." He chuckled and cleared his throat. "Looks cool—how did Will do that?"

"He did nothing. Just took the photo where and when I asked," I explained. "He didn't try to make the photo look that way. He'd told me it hadn't look that way through the camera's viewer either."

"Is there some statue in the back, behind you or something," Derek asked, as if already conjuring an answer to the mystery.

"It's a long walkway behind me, no statues—nothing," I assured him. "It's just a cool photo—don't you think?" I tried not to sound as if I thought there was much more to it.

"Hmmm, I'm looking at this internet site, the guy in the book I'm reading refers to it. He writes how people upload weird ghost photos here all the time. Some of them believe these are real spirits or *heavenly bodies* they're seeing in their photos," he scoffed. "But I see nothing like yours. There's lots of photos of people with things shaped like angels in them, but no people with wings."

"Do you believe these are photos of spirits that people are uploading?" I was a tad hopeful but considering how he usually finds a plausible scientific explanation for these kinds of things, I held my breath.

"Not saying I believe, but some of these photos—like yours, are hard to explain is all," he said clarifying. "You don't believe there's an angel standing behind you, do you?" he questioned, as though he'd caught me.

"Uhm, I just think it's bizarre." My words trailed off because I hadn't considered someone or something standing behind me. I'd been thinking it was just me with wings. "Well, when you put it that way—

I love the idea there might be an angel watching over me… or maybe it's a sign I'm earning my wings," I said. I tried not to sound put-off and laughed a little to make it light.

"Lynn, you know I don't believe in angels, not in a religious sense." He paused. "But I think there is a high probability there may be other entities that can appear in photos as energy. I'm not so arrogant to think *we* are the superior beings of the world, or worlds. I'm sure some experiences with ghosts and angels can be explained, but for those that can't be explained away, maybe—just maybe, we are not alone."

What was that supposed to mean—aliens? Why couldn't he give me a simple explanation and clear my mind and my overactive imagination?

"Sure is a cool pic though," he said, full of boyish enthusiasm.

"I go back and forth myself on that one," I said, sounding sheepish.

"Just sent you the website to check for yourself," he said. Then he changed the subject to that of my trip home.

We chatted about the visit *and* the shortness of it. He mentioned how he would love to visit my hometown sometime, but first wanted to come see me in Miami again now that we had the house. I told him about the nice neighbors, the flowers, and the butterflies. I mentioned that Will would be going away again, and that I was almost done unpacking, but a final shipment was still to come from Ottawa. Before signing off, he reminded me to check out the link he'd sent.

I clicked the link now sitting in my inbox and brought up the homepage to a website listing photos of ghosts, spirits, angels, demons and more. Some photos were realistic but others not so much. Derek was right, there were no other photos like mine. Even the ones grouped as angel photos looked more like those from the ghost and spirit lists. Part of me wanted to believe it was supernatural but another part of me, the *scaredy-cat* part wanted to find an explanation to what happened to the photo, but I couldn't seem to find any. Why did it look like that? Between thinking about the Yasmin thing, the angel-wing thing, and the story from Louise, I was beginning to freak myself out.

"*Bing,*" sounded from my computer, as a new email from Alison popped into my inbox.

Her email started with, '*Totally cool Spook! You should print that one off*', following with how her mom loved that place, and how the monument was one of the last places her mom visited before her parents moved out to Calgary. Her email continued on in response to the neighbors and the weird mention of my birth name. Alison, having dabbled in screenplay writing, she noted it sounded like a scene from a movie, adding, '*If you ever saw it in a movie you'd hope the writer and director made it believable*'. I laughed because the whole encounter with the neighbor had been like a scene out of a movie, but it had really happened. I know I heard what I heard, I just didn't know what it meant, and it hadn't been '*an error in pronunciation*' as Dunya had said. Alison had also commented about the photo, stating that her dad recalled her mom saying, '*There was something about the place*', that monument, '*something powerful*', and she'd had to see it one more time before moving. I'd sensed something there too, but I'd brushed it off as nostalgia. I wrote her back and told her about the meeting I had with *Anthony of lost things and people*.

Within minutes, my phone was ringing.

I pressed answer on the cell phone, but before I could say a thing, I heard, "Spook, you didn't tell me you were going to go see a PI!" Her enthusiasm burst through the phone. "I love a good plot twist," she finished.

It was my turn. "Remember when I got the copies of my birth registration—the ones missing my birthfather's name?"

"Ya," was all she gave me.

"Well, it got my overactive imagination in need of answers. And don't worry, I didn't pick this guy out of a hat. Mom's friend used this agency before—figured I could trust them. Not that the guy found much."

"Maybe you should call him. See if he's found anything juicy. Can't hurt," she tossed back with more enthusiasm.

"He's supposed to call me, but ya, I'll shoot him an email." I'd pondered the idea earlier, just hadn't wanted to hear *no* from him.

"Okay cool—Let me know what you find out—I'm dying here," she ended, faking as if in agony.

"Sure thing. Later, Spook." I laughed as I closed off the call.

I opened a new email then and wrote one sentence to Anthony,

> *Hey, finder of lost things and people, any updates for the Canadian transplant?*

I finished the email with just *Lynn* and hit send.

Chapter 14

The next two weeks back at work blurred together, and it was now the day our shipment from Ottawa was to arrive, *and* the day before Will was leaving to go to Jamaica.

He travelled a lot for his job working for an international cruise line here in Miami. He manages the shore excursions for some of the foreign locations cruise ships travel to. Along with two Caribbean ports, Jamaica and Grand Cayman, he also manages exotic locations that include New Zealand, Australia, Egypt, India, Dubai and most of Asia. But I preferred his local trips like this one coming up to Jamaica. And like he'd agreed, while I was at work, he was working from home and waiting for the delivery. He'd called while I'd been in a meeting, and he had left me a message stating the boxes had arrived, and that mine were waiting for me in the garage. I could hear the gloating in his message, but a deal was a deal. I would take care of my own boxes if he would take care of his—end of story.

When I pulled into the driveway, I pictured his boxes still piled unopened and next to mine in the garage. But when I walked through the front door and wandered the house, I saw he had moved his boxes to the office. My blue bins were in the garage, but I guess he'd had the movers take his to the office for him. Now I knew why he had sounded so proud of himself. But he still had the task of going through them and putting away all his stuff. We'd agreed no boxes left unpacked. I'd have my bins unpacked and put away by the time he got back next Friday, but I wasn't going to unpack his. A deal was a deal, and I allowed myself to stand there a moment in the garage and stare at the stack of plastic bins containing my stuff.

"Need some help?" Will asked as he came through the garage door from the kitchen, smugness spreading across his face.

"No, thank you. I'll get to it after dinner. I'm going to move them into the house to sort later," I said, giving him a face that said, *You'll pay for this Mr.* and put my hands on my hips for emphasis.

Will ordered pizza for dinner, feeling guilty I'm sure for not having the movers take my stuff into the house. Further to win me over, he poured some wine. My weakness, *pizza*—he played dirty, but I loved him, and pizza.

With a full stomach and a few glasses of wine in me, I moved each and every bin into the house—by myself. I stacked them against the front wall and framed the window in the living room, two high and three deep. It would be emotional, but I was still looking forward to going through the bins. It would be a finality of events seeing my favorite things of Mom's placed in *my* home. I had my work cut out for me, with the unpacking of stuff and the memories, but the emotional mending could wait until tomorrow. Over dinner, I'd told Will I wouldn't get to unpacking until after work tomorrow night. I also told him I'd try to con Luc into coming over to keep me company too. Will liked Luc, and he also liked me not being alone in the house. And with Luc being highly food motivated, if I promised to make him something yummy, I'd be able to convince him to come over. He might even bring his dog Raven with him too. Luc knew I couldn't wait to get my own dog or doggies now that we had the house and all the space.

* * *

Friday morning, and Will was finishing up packing his suitcase for his trip. Then with a kiss and bear hug, he was off in the shuttle to the airport. A short half hour later I grabbed my keys and tote, and I was out the door to work.

My day at work was the same as always, filled with boring unexciting tasks and projects that lead nowhere, at least not anywhere that mattered. Coworkers dropped by occasionally to chat and take a load off as the time eventually moved things closer to lunchtime. Of course this time of day always seemed to come slower on Fridays.

At my current IT job—which I hate, I have a few close friends, a few of whom have been witness to my *heightened senses*. Luc for one, who I like to call my best *girlfriend*—which he hates, meaning he's my best bud, though I like to torture him with the label. He's a bit of a loner, but at work we try to keep each other from losing our minds. We fill our workdays with lots of laughing and talks about things other than our jobs. He's Catholic, and I like talking to him about religion only because he's open-minded, but he's also curious about other religions and it's a bonus to bounce religious topics and ideas off him. He's a true believer in all this intuition and third-eye stuff too. To look at him, with his shaved head, biker-style goatee, tattoos, and edgy rock-star quality about him, you would never think he was much of a spiritual person. But he goes to church every Sunday, and he *always* wears one of those religious necklace-pendant things he told me was a *scapular*. The type he wears is a *'devotional scapular'*, a much smaller version evolving from the *'monastic'* scapular used by people such as monks and nuns. Luc told me they're either composed of two small pieces of cloth, laminated paper, or wood like his. They're about the size of a penny but square, and they have religious images on both sides of each piece. He explained how some people wore part of it hung on the front of the chest, with the other piece down their back. He wears both in the front and always hidden by his shirt, and it's supposed to be for a protective purpose and to show a person's faithfulness as a Catholic.

Luc, the electric guitar playing man of faith, also reads paranormal/fantasy fiction novels. We both prefer plausible fantasy to realm-type fantasy stories and sometimes we read the same book at the same time, so we can talk about the story. And it was regarding a mutual friend of ours, Joanna, where he'd first experienced my weird *premonition* stuff.

It was back in October of last year when I'd first gotten to know her. Her office had been near mine making it easy to chat, and with the big topic of the month being *Breast Cancer Awareness,* some of the girls in the office were talking about mammograms.

I'd told them my birthmother had died in her early 40s from the disease and I had been going every year for mine since I found out. Joanna had shared she'd had breast cancer 20 years prior, and I'd asked her if she still did her mammograms. She'd sheepishly told me it had been *many* years, but she had planned to get a bunch of follow-up tests done and one was the mammogram. That's when the words came..., *"You need to get to the doctor and you need to schedule that mammogram now,"* I'd told her. In the weeks that'd followed and when she'd still had done nothing, I'd forced the issue on her again. I'd told her she could go to the screening center up the street and that they were quick. In late November, she'd told me she would be getting the prescription soon. *Soon?* My senses had tingled again, and my rant with badgering her had begun again too. I'd kept at her; couldn't deny the *feelings* and the sense of panic I'd had while waiting for her to address the issue. I had told her to have the doctor fax the prescription to the imaging center and book the appointment *now.* Finally, in December, Joanna had gone to the imaging center. But, unlike the normal, *'We compress because we care'* send you on your way routine for a mammogram, Joanna had been at the appointment much longer than expected. They'd needed to do a second set of images, because they'd found *three* separate masses, and all had had to be biopsied. When the tests came back, not only were they malignant, they were three different forms of the disease. Luckily—if you can say luckily under these circumstances, the tumors were encapsulated, and the cancer had not yet reached her lymph nodes. Through January and February, Joanna saw several specialists that ended with her having surgery. Incredibly a day later they released her from the hospital to go home.

Now Miss Joanna, she's a tiny slip of a woman, but with a heart the size of Canada, and we've developed a close friendship since that first breast cancer talk and scare. Joanna thinks she and I share the same guardian angel, or that at least mine talks to hers regularly, and I had to agree with her on that one. Joanna fought that bastard cancer a second time *and* at this stage of her life. She turns 72 years young this August, and thankfully is now cancer free.

Over the years, I have sensed various weird events like this. Some have had a negative or evil element, sometimes associated to a person's presence, or *bad vibes* others might call it. On those rare occasions when I get a bad feeling or image, I try to push it away. Most times I get good or helpful feelings or premonitions. But sometimes—even when the information comes across as bad news, it often ends up as helpful. To me it's a bunch of bizarre coincidences and a quirky thing that seems to happen to me—through me—whatever. But the feeling I was having right now… was that I was *starving*.

Typically, on Friday, Luc and I get out for lunch and sometimes our pal Darius comes with us, and today was one of those days. We were quite the threesome. Me, well—I was me, Luc was his typical edgy-looking self, and Darius, he was the *gentle giant.* Other than our love of movies and good food, he and I were a comical contrast. He has strawberry-blond brush-cut hair and a pale northern complexion. He stood upward of 6 feet 3 inches, and weighed over 300 pounds, most of which was muscle. Even with his great size, he was as calm and quiet as a mouse—shy you'd say, but we pulled him out of that quiet nonsense frequently, and he was always happy to join us for lunch.

Out on the street in front of our building, our motley crew stood waiting for the trolley. Our ride was an old-fashioned trolley system that took passengers along a fixed route. It's never on time, but it was free, and we were grateful it took us to where the best restaurants were—namely our favorite Thai restaurant. The running joke was that they must put *crack* in the food because we were all addicted to the *Chicken Panang* they serve. Luc had said he wished they had *breakfast panang* because he loved it so much. The place had great food, the service was fast and cordial, and we were always in and out of there in less than an hour which included travel time, and it worked perfectly with our restricted lunch time.

As usual on our return from lunch, we unloaded from the trolley and walked the short 10 yards to where we always crossed the busy road. And as always, we played the '*I saved your life*' game, where you block the other person from stepping off the curb into oncoming traffic, though none of us would ever take the dangerous step. Darius with his gigantic body, often blocked my view of the oncoming cars, but still I would put my arm out to stop him from crossing, telling him, '*I saved your life*'. It was a joke for obvious reasons because it wasn't as if I could stop him if he chose to take that step.

Today was no exception, and I played the old '*stop*' game with Darius. It was Luc who made a break for it and darted across to the median separating the two directions of traffic. I followed quick on his heels and left Darius to meander across after us. He never ran, *ever*. I'm confident that if a car ever made contact with him, the car would suffer more than he would.

From the median, the two of us watched as Darius sauntered across the road to where we stood waiting for yet another opening in traffic to cross to the far side. An oncoming car slowed, and the driver waved for us to cross, giving us the opening we'd been waiting for. The driver was clearly not from Miami, they'd sooner mow you down than stop. At that, Luc took the opening and ran. I turned to see Darius step onto the median behind me, making it across the first divide finally. When I turned back, I watched as the stopped car resumed its way and sure enough, the license plate on the car read *North Carolina*. Now it was my turn, and I stepped out on to the road. An awful ear-piercing screech of breaks sounded to my right, and I turned towards the squeal.

Something wrapped around me and lifted me into the air. Before I could grasp what was happening, I was on the other side of the road next to Luc *above* where he stood — looking down at him. I was high off the ground… in Darius's massive arms. I turned my head to stare at my giant friend.

His face was red and running with sweat, pouring onto his shirt. He panted as if he'd run the fifty-meter dash. He'd grabbed me and *run* across the street. And that screech hadn't been from a car, it had been from a huge delivery truck, which thanks to Darius, just missed plowing me down and, well, *killing* me.

Luc gawked up at us, eyes bulging, mouth gaping open. "Darius man, you okay?" he said. "What the hell?"

"You can put me down now, Darius," I said. I spoke soft and smiled to let him know I was okay, but he remained motionless, blank, staring down at the ground. "Darius." I spoke a little louder this time and patted his arm.

His head shot up and he turned his sweaty face to look at me. "You okay Lynn... did I hurt you?" he asked in a strained whisper.

"Are *you* okay, Darius?" I asked back. "You can put me down now." I gently patted his arm again.

"What the hell happened? Where the hell did that f'n truck come from?" Luc asked, unnerved and pointing at the dark patches on the road. "Look at the skid marks. How did you get to her so fast—get across so fast, without getting killed?"

"Uh I, I don't know. I don't know I—I just, ran… and grabbed her. I barely remember doing it. It was… *instinct*. My brain screamed, *protect*, so I ran," Darius mumbled out, trying to wipe the sweat from his face.

Luc attempted to spin Darius's big body around, as if checking for any injuries. But there weren't any—not a scratch, not on either of us.

"C'mon boys, let's go," I directed, pulling the two stunned men along the walkway towards the building's entrance. Neither of them said another word as we walked. We continued into the building and rode the elevator to the fourth floor in silence. When we reached the entrance to Darius's secured area of the office, I placed my hand on his massive arm stopping him mid-stride. "Thanks, Darius. You saved my life."

His shy eyes looked down at me. "Sure-sure, no problem."

He still seemed confused as he turned away from me. He swiped his security card, opened the door, and passed through without looking back.

Luc and I continued down the hall to our entrance, but both stopped short of the door. "What the hell happened," I asked him, half smiling half grimacing.

Luc fumbled under his shirt for his scapulars. Pulling the two small pieces of wood free, he held them together in his fingers and kissed them. "Hell—if I know," he said. "One minute you're standing on the median—next, Darius has you clutched in his big arms beside me." He rubbed the top of his shaved head. "The truck came out of nowhere, Lynn… and those skid marks, they stopped *past* where you'd been standing on the median."

I shook my head and huffed out a breath. "Go check on Darius, would ya?" I said, pleading a little.

"Ya-Ya, sure thing." Luc seemed upset, and a bit shaken, but we continued through the door and back to our desks.

It was all confusing, but to add to the confusion, I *wasn't* shaken like I should have been. My heart should have been racing—pumping hard over what had happened, but it wasn't. My brain on the other hand, was in hyper speed.

I sat at my desk going over the event... and then other incidences that had occurred with coworkers. Nothing quite like this, but the others were equally strange. One occurrence happened right after I first began working here. I'd been assigned to work on a project with another team member. All I'd known about the woman at the time was that she was married, had a son about six years old, and was then pregnant with her second child, but that was it. We'd been sitting in the lunchroom reviewing documents, when once again—even with people banging and clanging all around us, the words came. "*How is your son making out at school?*" I'd said. I hadn't known a thing about the kid, couldn't even remember his name, but as I'd spoken the words, her mouth had gaped.

"What? I have been sitting here trying to focus on this stupid project when all I can think about is my son. He's been having problems at school. Kids are teasing him because he wears glasses. How did you know?" she'd questioned.

"*I didn't, not really,*" I'd said, and had tried not to look surprised myself. I'd known my words had been odd, but I'd sat there thinking instead how weird it was kids still did that, made fun of kids with glasses. I hadn't been trying to pick up on any concerns of hers—it had been a compulsion to say the words. I'd told her it wasn't anything I knew, more what I'd *felt*. I'd suggested she should get her husband to talk to her son about it.

"*He's not his real father, but they are buddies,*" she'd explained, adding that she'd been wondering the same thing right then. Later in the week, she'd told me her husband had talked to him about the problems at school and had helped him resolve the issue. She'd said he'd even become the kid that all the other kids looked to for help with their schoolwork. She's received a few other bizarre tidbits from me since, and she always laughs and says, *"You're freaking me out, but I like it."*

Situations like these are sometimes hard for people to take, but I'm used to it now and the varying reactions. It's uncanny when a person whom I barely know or just met, opens up and tells me things they would never tell me—or anyone else for that matter. I figure it has something to do with people needing to unburden themselves by telling *me* their stuff, their secrets. It happens to me a lot.

Another incident happened in a one-on-one meeting with a coworker, the first time we had ever crossed paths. Right in the middle of our meeting, during work dialog, I'd stopped… and the words came out. *"Are you okay?"* I'd said, though there'd been no sign she wasn't. She'd looked up from her documents, opened her mouth, and let the floodgates for all her troubles open as well. She'd talked about her life and all that had been going on. At the end of the flood she'd apologized for saying too much. When I'd asked if she felt better, she'd said a firm, *"Yes."*. I'd told her not to worry and that I'd never say a thing about what she'd told me. She'd nicknamed me *'Vegas'* that day. Like the saying, *What happens in Vegas, stays in Vegas,* but for her it was, *'What you say to Vegas, stays with Vegas'*.

There have been other events too, but this thing with Darius, it was different. I replayed the images over again in my head, and I couldn't shake the odd notion, it was somehow more—something… *special.* I remember taking a step off the curb when I sensed *it*, not with Darius— but a split second before, sensed something *new.* But before I could process it, Darius had me on the other side of the street. It'd been the first time one of my *feelings* had blended with a person's *actions.* And under normal circumstances, my heart should have been pounding through my ribcage, but instead I was calm, strangely calm. Luc had been the one who'd been losing it, Darius a little too it seemed. But me, I'd felt *safe.* Lucky for all of us, we were alive. And lucky for me again, the last few hours of my shitty workday had flown by.

I shut down my computer, grabbed my tote, and headed to Luc's desk. Due to all the commotion, I'd forgot to ask him about the favor. When he looked up from his work, I flashed him a smile, and said,

"Wanna come over—keep me company while I go through the shipment bins?"

"Sure," he said, "What's for dinner?" He wiped his mouth with the back of his hand as he said the word *dinner*.

Eye-roll. "Head home first and get Raven. I'll have something ready when you get there. You don't mind staying over—right, crashing in the guestroom? I'd appreciate it, you know—the not staying in the house for this first-time alone thing," I said, giving him a wide innocent smile, hoping he wouldn't tease me until we were out of the office.

"No prob."

"Cool," I said, turning to leave, but then he grabbed my arm.

"That was something, Lynn—really, *something*." He let go of my arm.

Clearly the event from lunch was still weighing heavy on his grey-matter. I said nothing in response, only nodded and continued to turn and go. When I glanced back quick, he was still watching me, smiling now though puzzlement still lingered in his expression.

Chapter 15

At home I pushed any thought of the day's event out of my head and went into weekend mode.

After changing into an old pair of jeans and one of Will's old t-shirts, I plopped myself down on the couch and once again woke up my trusty laptop. I was eager to see if I'd received any response from the PI. And there it was, the response I had hoped to see. It read,

Hello Lynn,

Good to hear from you, and yes, I have more information. I've located the high school your birthmother attended. I've obtained yearbooks from the previous years and found quite a few photos of her and another girl together. I've located the friend and luckily enough the woman still lives in Ottawa. I was able to track her down, and she was responsive to taking my call.

On the call, she told me she and your birthmother had been best friends. She knew of the pregnancy and said your birthmom started to show around Christmas time, but it was still kept a secret. As close as the two were, she'd not told her who the father was. She hadn't had a boyfriend at the time and had tried to brush it off as a one-night stand, some boy who apparently had gone away to college. She'd told her the boy didn't know about the pregnancy and she'd wanted to keep it that way.

The woman also mentioned a peculiar event regarding your birthmom, something about telling her she'd gone to a fortuneteller of all things. Said the fortuneteller had told her to take this pregnancy

full term, but it would be best she gave up the baby. The friend said she didn't believe the story about the one-night stand nor the fortuneteller, but I hadn't questioned her on either. They lost track after high school when the woman went out East to university. The last thing she mentioned, was how it seemed your birthmother had been looking for a specific type of family for the adoption, which she considered strange. She had been very specific, as though she'd known the people or something close to it, and that there had to be only boys in the family, no other daughters.

She asked to meet me later today, said she had more information but wasn't in an appropriate place to talk.

Try me later today, I'll let you know what else I find out.

Anthony

That wasn't much to go on, and what's with all the secrecy, and a fortuneteller, really? I'll be calling to see what else he gets, for sure. And now was as good a time as any.

I grabbed my phone from my tote. I dialed the number saved as *PI – Anthony.*

It rang once and picked up. "Hello, Anthony Merenda here." His voice sounded like an answering service though a joyful one.

"Hey there, it's Lynn—Lynn Westlake—in Miami," I responded, trying to sound as jovial.

"Oh, Lynn, hey—ya—you got my email I take it?" He sounded surprised even though he'd said to call. "Sorry, ya uhm, there hadn't been much to go on with the best friend—or so I thought."

"Or so you thought?" I shot back.

"Well ya, the email I mean—not much there," he confirmed. "But the meeting with her, was good—but strange." He paused, and I heard him take in a long breath.

"Go on," I urged. Was this guy trying to kill me or what? Not like I haven't been waiting years to hear something, well something I didn't *already* know. I mean throw me a bone, man.

I was about to burst from waiting when he blew out the breath, and said, "Well, she had nothing else to say about who the father might be, but she did have a few things to say about your birthmother." Disappointment escaped me in a sigh, but when I didn't respond, he continued. "She said your birthmother had this way about her—always knew stuff. Like a psychic gift, she said. Strange I know. She was always interested in things like Wiccan practices, spiritual stuff, Earth and stars, natural healing stuff. Said after she'd gotten pregnant, she had talked a lot about angels—not in a religious sense, but more about the paranormal connection they have with humans. She kept coming back to how incredible your birthmother's insight was."

"Whoa—really?" I don't know anyone like that—*right*.

"I can't vouch for the facts, but that's what she told me." He stopped to clear his throat. "She explained that they hadn't seen each other or even talked in years, but that they'd met up a short time before the cancer diagnosis. The friend works at the hospital where your birthmother had her cancer treatments." He paused, clearing his throat again. "She mentioned on another occasion that they'd met up, gone for a walk… in the park, near the house where your birthmother lived when you were born. Said it was the first time they had talked about the baby since the day she'd given you up." He stopped. I guessed this wasn't the type of news he was used to delivering and perhaps he was waiting for me to comment, but when I remained silent, he pushed on. "This is where the story gets a bit off." He made another throat clearing sound. "I don't know what to make of this, but the woman said your birthmom told her the baby—you, were still on your correct path… and she'd said something about the balance being kept. The friend hadn't understood the statement, figured it must have been the meds causing the odd talk—the cancer drugs I mean. She'd had explained prior that your birth mom always seemed to know stuff, but she'd considered that possibly your birthmother had been keeping an eye on you or something." There was another pause. "You still with me Lynn?" My brain was reacting, but my mouth wasn't, I couldn't find my words. "Lynn?"

"Ya-Ya, sorry, listening," I managed, "Keep going." I was almost scared to hear the rest, yet I was dying for more.

"Okay," Anthony said, followed by the sound of shuffling paper. "She said your birthmother *never* mentioned the baby to anyone, but that she always spent the day of your birth alone—in that park, the one they'd taken their walk. When they'd met that time, she asked her again about the father, but all she'd gotten from her was, '*I've written it all down and the information is safe'*. The friend said she didn't want to push her because she'd looked unwell. The last thing she'd told her was how she'd gone to see the adoptive mother—your mom, on your 27th birthday, but she wouldn't tell her anything about the visit."

He took a rather long breath in as if there were more to say, but I couldn't hold back. "Went to see my mom?" I questioned, mystified by the idea. Then the realization hit me, my mom had had this information and had chosen not to tell me.

"It was soon after that visit with your mom that the cancer took your birthmother," he finished.

"That's... some story. My mother never mentioned anything about this. I don't think she'd have kept that from me. Don't suppose I could get the woman's name and number?" I asked, curious, my mind still racing.

"Sorry, it's confidential. It's part of why she was even willing to meet me. Happens a lot in this business. People will talk but don't want to be involved in it, ya know. And she doesn't know it's *you* who is looking for information, just an interested party," he said.

"Oh. I understand," I assured him—*not*.

"Hey, I'm not done with this, Lynn. I will keep looking for more information. I have a few other leads. Got a new contact—goes by the name'a Gabriel. Says he might have a connection for me. I'll let you know what I find out either way."

"Okay… keep me posted. You know where I am." I ended the call.

Stunned into silence next to my laptop, I replayed the tale he'd told me. A contact named *Gabriel?* Just another uncanny coincidence, right? Joan had used the same name in her story to Louise. I wasn't sure what to think of all these coincidences or these stories. All I knew was that I was missing more parts from my life than I'd realized. Seemed I was missing whole chapters. What else had my mother kept from me?

I glanced at the oversized clock on the wall next to the kitchen opening. It was near 5:00 pm. I needed to find something I could make for Luc's *bribery* dinner. Being alone in the house was not on my favorites list. We had the security system, but it was too soon to feel completely comfortable. I figured that in the meantime before Luc and Raven were to arrive, I'd give a call to Alison. She could help fill the time and the gaps in my brain too, plus I could bring her up to speed on all this.

I hit dial for her on my contacts list and moseyed into the kitchen as it rang.

"Hello?" Alison answered on the second ring. She knew it was me, but still used her professional work voice.

"Spooky," I responded in anticipation of her usual response. I had an overwhelming need to giggle.

"Spook, whatcha doing?" she said, whispering her reply.

"Do I... have a story... to tell you," I tossed out. Then I swiftly dished out the story the PI had given me.

"Your birthmom sounds a little like another *spooky* person I know—not say'n any names." She giggled. "Not much to go on for your birthfather, but the PI mentioned he'd keep digging, eh?" Before I could respond, there was a loud "*KNOCK-KNOCK*" on the front door. "Maybe that's him now," Alison joked.

"He's in Ottawa, silly—hold on a sec. Sheesh, I didn't even hear a car pull up." I headed for the front door. "Stay on the phone until I see who it is, okay?"

"Yup."

I clutched the cell phone to my chest and peeked through the peephole. There was a young man on the front step, around 18 years old, clean-shaven, dressed in a red polo shirt with a company logo on the upper left-hand corner, but I couldn't make out the words.

"Who is it?" I called out.

"Hello, Mrs. Lockridge?" the voice said, "It's Juan, from Angel Movers. My pop sent me to give you the paperwork from the move."

"Did he just say *Angel Movers*?" Alison's muffled voice asked through the cell phone.

"Ya, hold on, Spook. Must be the company who handled this side of our Ottawa shipment," I whispered into the phone, then opened the front door part way.

There stood *Juan*, grinning.

"Oh hi—sorry about that. Wasn't here when the delivery was made," I explained, opening the door wider. Trying not to stare, I eyed the logo on his shirt. It said Angel Movers all right. I spied a little red car in the driveway too with the same logo on the door.

"Cute, Angel Movers, where's your wings." I flinched at my brainless comment.

"Angel is my pop. It's his company," he clarified. Without missing a beat and as if the poor kid hadn't heard the comment a million times before, he extended a hand and said, "Here's your copy of the shipping invoice and the customs forms. Is there anything else you need? Was the move okay?" He smiled and handed me the white envelope that sported the same company logo as his shirt and car.

"Thanks, Juan. That's great—the move was great." I smiled back still embarrassed for my comment, and especially with him being so polite about it.

"Okay great. Enjoy your new home." He followed up with a wave and a quick turn towards the car.

I shut the door, twisted the lock in place, then leaned back against the door staring at the envelope.

"Helloooo, Spook, you there?" Alison's muffled voice came again.

"Crap!" Had almost forgotten she was on the phone. "Sorry, Spook—thrown off by my little visitor. Will never mentioned the name of the moving company, only told me, *'they were great'.*"

"Let me see now—recap girlfriend. What's with all the bizarre shit going on? The whole name thing with the butterflies and the old lady next door—that was strange. But this weird story Louise told you, and what's with the name *Gabriel?* It reeks of the bizarre. Let's not forget that photo of you with wings, my dear. And now, Angel Movers shows up at your door, c'maaaan," she said, letting out a huge gasp followed by another giggle. "Aren't you totally freaked out—you know I'm loving this, right?"

"You're freaking me out," I said back, giggling at it all. "I keep trying not to read too much into this. You know crap like this sometimes happens around me."

"Ya, but not all at once like this," she said, followed by a loud, "*Puhh,*" and ending her rant. "Hey Lynn, can we talk more about this later? I need to head out—doing dinner with the in-laws tonight, gotta boogie."

"Sure-sure," I shot back, my brain still spasming over the stuff she'd rattled off.

"I'll call ya tomorrow. We'll go over it all again. It's kind of fun don't ya think?" She chased her response with a, *"moouaah,"* sending a kiss through the phone. "Later Spook, love ya."

"Love you too." I closed the phone and stood there stunned into silence *again*. She was right, the stuff was unusual, and it was fun in a way. Who was I kidding, this stuff was *seriously* weird. With one deep breath in and out I headed back to the kitchen in pursuit of making a fabulous dinner.

When the prep was done, and the pasta and spicy sauce simmered on the stove, I moved my attention to the living room and the bins still stacked in front of the window. "Ennie-meenie-minie-moe," I said aloud, and picked the farthest bin to the left. I moved it to the middle of the room and pealed back the lid. It made a snapping noise, flipped from my hands, then fell to the ground. Inside, the bin revealed a top layer of bubble pack I'd used to keep things protected and from shifting. No longer needed, I tossed it aside. The next thing I saw was Mom's journal.

The tan leather-bound book had the word *journal* stamped into the leather. I lifted the book and sniffed. Mom had resorted to chain-smoking near the end of her days, and the journal still smelled of smoke. I flipped it open and pulled out the loose papers to set them aside. The inside cover of the journal had a light-yellow paper that sealed off the edges of the leather ends. The starter page had a space midway with the label *This journal belongs to…* where you can fill in the name of the owner. Mom hadn't filled this in, and I'd chosen not to fill it in for her. A turning of the page revealed the entry she'd made, and I reread the two lines.

I wasn't sure why I'd kept the thing. It made me sad she hadn't filled it with anything. I fanned the pages thinking I could put a dryer sheet or *three* in-between the pages to rid it of the smoky smell. A flash of something in the pages caught my eye, and I stopped. Thumbing back through again, slower this time, I found it about an inch thickness in… more of Mom's handwriting… pages of it.

Chapter 16

The first page was dated May 3rd—my birthday.

Locked in place I stared at the page struggling to grasp what I was looking at. How had I missed this? But I knew I'd only looked at the first few pages before packing it away. She hadn't written on the next page, and I'd assumed the sentences on the first had been all she wrote. I'd been more concerned about the items she'd stuffed in the journal and never checked the rest.

I stepped backward a few feet from the open bin maneuvering myself to the closest couch, my eyes still glued to the first page. The noted date was May though the very first page had been dated June. I thumbed further to see she'd filled a dozen or more pages. Making myself comfortable I sat cross legged on the cozy couch, and then I read,

> *May 3rd.*
> *It's Lynn's birthday, and one week before Mother's Day. Lynn and William arrive this week for another visit home.*
> *The doctor says I'm cancer free. He told me the tumor could have been growing for a few years before they found it. I hadn't been feeling well for some time and losing all that weight before Lynn's wedding had made me worry. I hadn't told Lynn, she would have pestered me into seeing a doctor. Had I gone in back then, the findings would have ruined their wedding plans. I may be cancer free now, but Lynn was right, I should have gone in sooner to see the doctor. I can be such a fool sometimes.*

"I knew it," I blurted. She hadn't been well, the little devil. Why she'd always believed she had to keep that stuff from me, I never understood. I read on and I tried to imagine my mother's voice and how she would have sounded if she were speaking the words.

It was after Lynn and William's engagement, when I told Kay about the visit from Lynn's birthmother.

There it was—in my mother's handwriting, *birthmother*? It meant the friend's story was true, but it also meant that mom had kept *this* from me too.

The woman had told me not to tell anyone. Something about how exposing the secret could cause illness or affect my life expectancy. I'd thought it was a crock. She'd even said, 'the person you tell now shares in the burden of keeping the secret'. She said the closer the person was to the source of the secret, the deadlier the results would be, and writing any of it down would be the same as telling someone. She'd said exposing the secret would cause illness, exposing the secret more than once or placing it out in the open would cause illness resulting in a slow death. Telling the source directly would cause illness and death soon after.

What? I could almost excuse she'd kept her health issues from me, but how could she keep a visit from my birthmother from me? And what the hell was this crap about more secrets?

I reread the passage again, swallowing hard after the words *illness and death*, stopping to take in a breath before reading the next line. It made me think of how quickly she'd deteriorated after the wedding. It had been a year since I'd seen her, and when I did, she'd become noticeably thin and frail. She'd seemed to have aged ten years in only the one. She'd even walked as if in pain. It was shortly after that visit, James had had to rush her to the hospital. She'd been suffering from a severe pain in her side. It wasn't long after they diagnosed her with cancer. "SNAP-SNAP," followed by bubbling sounds coming from the kitchen shifted me out of my memories.

Up fast bringing the journal with me, I found the pot with the pasta had boiled over. I set the journal on the island counter to tend to the little overflow of water. Turning down the heat, I then repositioned the pot to cook the pasta an additional few minutes. I reduced the temperature for the sauce as well, stirring it gently to make sure it wasn't damaged. The clock over the stove read 7:30 pm. There was still lots of time before Luc would arrive, so I pulled out one of the island's barstools and sat down to resume reading.

What else had my mother been keeping from me? My eyebrows pinched together, and I read on,

> She was convincing, but I didn't know what to think, a coincidence maybe? I'm not the type to believe this kind of mumbo-jumbo, but she'd seemed like a normal, educated, and sane woman. It had been a shock when she'd arrived at my door. I'd had no idea she even knew where I lived, but she had known our names from the adoption. I hadn't recognized her, it had been 27 years since we'd first met, and she'd only been 19 at the time. Was it a coincidence too that she arrived at my door a week after Lynn's 27th birthday?
>
> She hadn't looked well and had told me she had little time. I didn't realize what she meant by 'time' until that letter. Lynn had come to me 10 years later telling me of the Adoption Disclosure papers, and the letter she'd been sent about her birthmother. It showed a record of who the birthmother was and that she'd died ten years earlier, of breast cancer. The date showed she'd died soon after being at my home, when she'd told me the story, told me the secret.
>
> I knew I had to tell someone about this meeting and Lynn's letter. I told Kay. Who else could I tell? Was it another coincidence that soon after telling Kay I'd felt my health wasn't right? I'd chalked it up to getting old and slowing down, but then the weight loss started. Months before the wedding I'd had to have my mother-of-the-bride dress taken in, twice. I'd been wondering if telling Kay about the visit and this so-called secret had caused me to get sick.
>
> Did I believe this woman? Could all this be true or was I losing my mind? I'd been suffering excruciating pain and James had to rush me to the emergency room. The diagnosis had been cancer. I'd gotten through 74 years with no major illness and now I had cancer.
>
> This woman arrives at my door, tells me that by sharing the secret she'd sealed her own fate. But if she already had breast cancer, how could she say telling me would affect her health. How could words cause your death? Maybe she was crazy, maybe it was just the ramblings of a sick desperate woman to pass word to her adopted child. Too many coincidences.

I am cancer free now, so does that mean telling Kay did nothing since it didn't kill me? Maybe it made me horribly sick or maybe it's just a bunch of malarkey. Would I get sick again from writing this down or would I be fine? Now who's crazy? Have the radiation treatments done something to my brain?

This was not how I expected to fill this journal. I'll tell Lynn all about it when I'm back to my old self again. Though, finding out that her birthmother came to see me, and I didn't tell her, she'll be angry. Especially since the woman is deceased now. But she would get a kick out of the story I'm sure, and that would keep her anger short lived. I hope.

I can't wait for them to get here, just wish they lived closer.

"Mom is this for real?" The pages were reading like a mystery or fantasy novel. Had she started to write a book, a fiction one instead of a memoir? I was determined to read more of this—this crap, but the room had gotten dark. More time had passed than I'd realized, and like an idiot, I'd been trying to read by a small crescent of sunlight cracking through the far side of the patio door.

I reached over and tore a corner off an envelope from the stack of mail on the counter. Marking my place, I wedged the piece in the crease of the journal page. Off the barstool, I headed to the far wall near the living room to flick the light switch. The kitchen lit up scaring away the pending darkness. But then the light flickered.

I scrambled to the living room and over to the coffee table and powered off my laptop to avoid any power surges. I grabbed my cell phone and turned to the lamp on the side table next to the couch. I turned the small stiff knob on the lamp in hopes for more light, and perhaps a hint of clarity to what I'd just read. But the lamp made a crackle sound, flickered, and then concurrently both the kitchen light and the table lamp went out.

There I stood, in the dark and in confusion. "Great!" I shot out to nobody then headed back into the kitchen. I misjudged the distance in an attempt to round the island and meet up with the stove, the handle of the saucepan jabbing me in the stomach. Rubbing the sore spot with one hand, I ran my other hand along the edge of the stove to find the knobs. Not that I needed to turn off the stove, there was no power, but when the power came back on—so would the stove. Finding the knobs, I turned both burners to off.

"Now where are those damn flashlights?" My brain was spinning over the urgency for light and the urgency for reading further. "Hall closet," I remembered. Then I patted the side of the stove, then the wall to find my way to the front hall. I turned to go down the hall but then paused to take a quick glance towards the living room window. Through it, I could see the streetlights and lights of the house across the way were still on. "Oh, I see, only my house—great." Okay Westlake, deep breath, don't fall apart. "No biggy—alone in the house—no biggy," I mantra'd aloud.

I faced back down the hall again, but to no avail, though foolishly trying, my eyes wouldn't adjust to the darkness. With no windows down the hallway, all I could see was dark on dark. Shuffling, I patted my way towards the hall closet and hopefully to the flashlights.

Doorknob. "Bingo!" I yelled. But in the closet, all I could find were towels and sheets. At the bottom of the closet should have been the toolbox. *Right*—Will had moved it into the garage now that we had one to keep our stuff. "Crap!" I yelled to the darkness. I turned and shut the door, then felt my way back down the hall. I stopped every few feet to listen.

Listen for what—my heart beating in my throat? "Get it together, Lynn—Luc will be here any minute."

At the kitchen doorway again, I glanced back towards the living room window to see that the streetlights were still on. I needed a plan B. "Candles," I said aloud. They were in the bottom drawer in the kitchen. I shuffled my feet across the floor, hands stretched out in front of me, making my way to where I hoped the drawers were. *Relief*, I gripped the handle of the top drawer and knelt to locate the bottom one. I pulled the bottom drawer out and reached in.

The tiny hairs on my arms tingled. I knew what should be in the drawer, but in the dark and with my overactive imagination, I shivered a little as I rummaged around for the candles. "Voila!" A reprieve. I grabbed hold of the four small candles I had hoped would be there. Feeling around again, I found the handy-dandy-mini-BBQ-lighter. I lit one and found a dish on the counter to set it in. Then I lit a second and placed it with the first. I set the other two aside just in case I needed them later.

The two small candles threw off enough light that I could continue to read, not well mind you, but I couldn't stop now. I needed to know what else she'd written—what else she'd kept from me, and what the hell this *secret* was? Resuming my seat at the island, I grabbed the journal and flipped to where I had placed the makeshift bookmark, and read the next entry,

> *July 27th.*
>
> *It's one week before my 75th birthday and the cancer is back. I told everyone I'm not going to do any more treatment. It was all too much last time. Too hard on me, too hard on James and too hard on Lynn being far away. No way I'm letting her come back here for that.*
>
> *Lynn and William are coming home for a week for my birthday, to see family and friends and that is all it should be.*
>
> *Thought I was in the clear. No, I didn't. I knew something was wrong. I had already felt off, damn it. I swear it was a week after I wrote the stuff about Lynn's birthmother too. I knew something wasn't right. Could it have been me writing it down? Or does having cancer make you delusional or irrational? Was this real or was I losing my mind? If Lynn sees this, will it kill me? Maybe she needs to know, maybe she needs to have all the facts. Or maybe I've already lost my mind. The doctors say I have a year or so.*
>
> *Kay told me she hasn't been feeling well. This can't be why, could it? Could she have told someone? Why would she? If she'd thought it was a joke, she might tell someone for a laugh. Not as though making light of it was damaging. Or was it?*

"BARK, BARK, BARK!" cut the silence, scaring the crap out of me and I knocked over the candles—all of them. And of course, the two lit ones went out before hitting the floor. As the barking echoed from beyond the front door, I was in dark, *again*.

"Aaahhheeehhhaaa!" I let out in response.

My frustration was followed with an even louder banging on the door and a, "Lynn! You in there? You okay?" Luc's voice was chased by more hard knocking.

Taking a deep shuddered breath, I turned. Hands stretched out in front of me, I headed towards the kitchen opening and aimed towards the front door. No electricity after all and the security alarm tech guy hadn't installed the battery pack on the initial visit. It wasn't as if the alarm would go off, so I didn't hesitate to unlock and swing open the door.

There stood Luc with his knapsack, and his dog.

Raven made a soft, "*Woof*," and stepped through the doorway ahead of Luc.

"Well come on in, Raven. Welcome," I blurted, sounding as if I had been holding my breath, and well, I had. "Hey Luc, come on into my den of darkness, muah-hahaaa," I said, using my best *Bela Lugosi* imitation and channeling a little *Abbott and Costello meets Frankenstein*.

"What's with the lights, Lynn?" he asked, stepping across the threshold and turning towards the living room.

"Mood lighting?" I said, questioning. "Lights flickered and went out a few minutes ago. Tried to find the damn flashlight, but could only find candles, aaaand they're somewhere... on the floor... in the kitchen." I smiled in the darkness. "Raven's barking scared the crap out of me, and I knocked them off the counter," I said, letting out a "*Groan*." I locked the front door behind us, and then I followed the two of them as they made their way towards the living room.

"Smells good in here, what's for dinner?" he asked through the darkness. His knapsack made a crunch and thud as it landed on the couch.

"Oh ya, I almost forgot," I said, turning outstretched hands out towards to the kitchen, leaving Luc and Raven to fend for themselves in the darkness.

"Forgot? What could have possibly kept you from slaving over *my* dinner?" he joked. Even though it was dark, knowing him, he had his arms in the air in mock protest. "Lights went out, but the food's still hot, yes?" he continued, as he made his own way to the kitchen.

"Ya-ya, no worries—your dinner is safe. But yer not gonna believe what I found in the boxes from Ottawa," I announced. I felt my way to the island, then knelt to the kitchen floor.

"Priorities, food first—boxes later," he said, his voice coming from the vicinity of the stove.

I shook my head and reached around on the floor trying to find the scattered candles. "Damn it—the wax dripped everywhere," I said, trailing with a frustrated *sigh*. "Grab Raven would ya—I don't want him to walk in the wax." But before Luc could grab a hold of him, a big warm wet tongue licked across my face, poking me right in the eye. "Oucheeeewwww!"

"What now?" Luc tossed out from the darkness, still trying to find Raven.

"Raven… tongue… wet face… eye…." I laughed letting go of my frustration. "Love you too, doggie," I told my face washer, patting him on his side. Thankfully, the candles had not travelled far from one another and I managed to find them all. Then I stood up.

"*CRACK*" went my skull to granite as it met the overhang of the island. I followed it with an "Ouch!" and my words were trailed by another sloppy lick from Raven, aaaaand I dropped the stupid candles again.

"Holy shit—you okay?" Luc asked, laughing out the words.

Wounded and wet, I sat on the floor. "Laugh it up smart-ass. How about you come over and find the damn candles this time—damn it!" I hollered from my place on the floor.

"I'll try," he said, stifling a laugh.

I pressed my palms to the top of my head, praying I hadn't split it open. Luc found his way around the island and when I detected him closing in on me, I put my hand out to avoid being stepped on. "Watch it, man," I said. Then as if to magically absorb the pain, I placed my hand back on my head. Wishful thinking but it was all I had.

Sitting in the dark, on the floor, dog gob on my face, eye watering, I let out another long pathetic *sigh*. Raven panted near my head as Luc grunted and crawled around trying to find the candles.

"Got them!" Luc shouted in triumph.

"My champion. Hey, light the damn things would ya?" I reached for the ledge of the island and pulled myself off the floor. I patted the island for the trusty lighter. Finding it I clicked it on and passed it to Luc. And as he lit the candles, the journal revealed itself through the dim light. "Check it out," I said, turning it towards Luc.

"That your mom's journal?" Confused, he asked, "Why wouldn't I believe it? You already told me about it."

"Well, it's not the journal—it's what I found in it." I gave him a little eyebrow raise for emphasis. "I thought she'd only written on the first page, but she wrote more—way more." I lifted the journal and displayed the first page, then I flipped to the start of the other entries. "There's some strange stuff in here. I mean it's her writing, but it's the content I'm struggling with. It's like a mystery—sort of. Stuff I wouldn't expect from my mother," I said, glancing at him then back to the pages.

"What? Did she write about hidden jewels or money she left you?" he asked with a chuckle.

"Nope," I said, and placed the journal back on the counter letting out another, *sigh*.

Now that the kitchen was lit again, I refocused on dinner, getting the pasta bowls and the cutlery. I maneuvered around the kitchen, my every move paired by Raven who sensed it was dinner time, *his* in particular.

Luc noticed, and said, "Here, I'll feed Raven his kibble. It'll keep him occupied while we eat." He turned and headed towards the living room. "Come on Raven, here ya go," he said, retrieving a large plastic container from his knapsack. He placed the bowl just inside the kitchen, and the container on the floor near the side of the couch. Raven munched away contentedly as Luc shuffled back eagerly to sit down for his dinner.

I'd already put Luc's bowl on one side of the island and mine on the other in front of me next to the waiting journal. "Do you want to hear about this or not?" I asked, patting the closed journal.

Luc having superb manners only nodded, his mouth was already full of pasta.

As we ate by the low light, I summed up what I'd read thus far. He said nothing, only continued to eat. I opened the journal to where I had left off, and then read aloud,

> *July 29th*
> *Kay is in the hospital....*

I halted, flipping back a page. The handwriting had changed—not much, a slight change from writing to printing, but was still in my mom's handwriting. Odd.

I started over,

> July 29th
>
> Kay is in the hospital, they don't know what's wrong with her.
>
> I told Kay this stuff about the secret is real, and we are sick because of it. I reminded her of what Lynn's birthmother had said; how telling the secret was to be for 'unselfish reasons only'. Reasons like making sure the source was safe, or so the secret wouldn't be lost. The woman had said to make sure Lynn had the information, but only if the secret was at risk. Kay told me not to believe in such drivel and that we are sick because we just are. She said that she told Mick, but of course, he didn't believe it. She also mentioned the story to her neighbor-friend. The woman thought it was a wild tale and told Kay that's where all these crazy movies come from the young people love so much.
>
> Kay had told two people and now she was sick too. How can I ignore it now? Could it be a fluke? Kay said, if I didn't get a chance to tell Lynn myself, even though she didn't believe it, she'd make sure Lynn knew the story.

Stopping, I glanced up to see Luc's eyes wide and staring as he spooned more pasta into his gaping mouth. I gave him a chance to say something, anything, but he only continued to chew and stare at me.

I shoved in a few mouthfuls of my dinner myself before the pasta got cold, and then I read on,

> July 31st
>
> Kay just called. The doctors diagnosed her with Leukemia, a rare form called Chronic Myelogenous Leukemia, CML...

I sounded out the 'M' word, but it didn't matter, it meant *malevolent*. Without looking up, I continued, I knew what was coming.

> ...and they're only giving her six months.
>
> How did this happen? Kay is never sick. She even told the doctors it's been years since she'd been in the hospital and that was to give birth to the last of her four sons who was a grown man now. They

couldn't get over how advanced the cancer had become, considering how good she looked and felt. Oh hell, I had ignored my own symptoms far too long. I'll be going up to see her at the hospital tomorrow to get more information. Coincidence my fanny.

August 1st
James and Lynn took me up to see Kay at the hospital. They stood at the doorway while I went up to her as she slept in her hospital bed. I touched her softly, and she woke. I whispered in her ear that it was me, Sally. I told her again the secret was real. Told her, we're both sick, both dying. But she kept saying, 'No Sally, it can't be true'. I made her promise she would tell Lynn what happened, tell her everything. She promised that if I died first, she would make sure Lynn knew it all. She swore she would remember everything I told her and pass it to Lynn. She promised me.

I cut short my reading and glanced up at Luc again. "I remember that day. I remember her doing that. My brother and I stood in the doorway and she bent down to Aunt Kay in her bed. She said something to her, but we couldn't hear from that distance." The image of them was clear in my mind, the painful way my mom had moved from the wheelchair to the bed, her leaning down and stroking my aunt's hair, and whispering.

"You okay?" Luc asked. He got up from his seat and headed to the sink to rinse his dish.

"Ya... this is all so.... bizarre, don't you think?" I tried to hide my pain, my loss.

"Bizarre? From you? I wouldn't expect any different," he said, "but I am confused about this secret thing." He made a silly face as if trying to keep the mood light. Was probably all he could do with all the heavy stuff weighing in the air.

I smiled, pretending his silly expression was working. "There are a few more pages," I said, "Let me keep going." I was confused too, but I had questions I wasn't ready to share at the moment. Luc said nothing more, only sat again and gave me a chin raise to go on.

August 3rd
It's my 75th birthday, I made it! Lynn made lasagna and chocolate cake for my birthday.

I kept thinking I should tell her, but it never seems to be the right time. How do you tell a person something like this? If she finds this journal, she'll surely have lots of questions. I'll do my best to show her the journal and she can ask me all the questions she wants then.

Kay will tell her if I can't.

William and Lynn brought cake in for Kay at the hospital today. Lynn had promised her she would. Kay was thrilled to see them. William took a photo of Lynn and Kay cuddling up in her hospital bed. Lynn told her to listen to the doctors and to behave. Kay won't, no bloody way if I know my sister. Lynn said she'd be back at Christmas time. That's Lynn for you—always pushing for optimism, not letting the thought that Kay might not be here at Christmas even enter the conversation.

I told Kay I was writing everything down, but of course she told me not to worry, that she'd make sure Lynn knew the story. It's best Lynn isn't here to watch my decline. I can keep her from knowing how bad things were getting. James wouldn't say anything if I told him not to.

"Both of them always kept stuff from me," I said. "Only the bad stuff. They always assumed they were protecting me, I guess. Sometimes it was family stuff, like years back when my brother was in the hospital with double pneumonia. She'd played it down like it was nothing, until I saw him for myself, hooked up to all those machines in the ICU. Sometimes it was about problems with finances, like when I was a teenager. We had to sell our house because my dad had stopped paying his alimony. And before she'd died, she'd gotten herself in debt while she was going through treatment—never mentioned she needed money," I ended, huffing out my words.

Luc still said nothing. He only watched and waited for me to read more. There'd be plenty of time for me to rant later, so I kept going,

August 5th

Lynn and William left today back to Miami. Wish they could have stayed longer, but they have all this ridiculous immigration nonsense to deal with. William is getting his US citizenship done in a few weeks.

Kay is supposed to go home from the hospital this coming weekend she tells me. It feels, much better being at home than in the hospital. Anything is better than the hospital. They are good to you

there and the advances in medicine have come a long way since my days, but being home, there is nothing better.

"It's nice she could be at home," Luc cut in, "Have the doctors and nurses come to her. Would have cost crazy-money to do that here in the U.S. though."

Those were my thoughts exactly. She'd wanted to be home, and we made sure she had what she needed for each stage, but the last stage had come too fast. Keeping those thoughts to myself, I pushed further on with the next journal entry,

> *August 9th*
> *I spoke to Lynn on the phone. In honor of William's mother who passed away 9 years ago today, they went to that big tropical garden near where they live. Apparently, she was a big flower and nature lover. They'd said it was the perfect place for celebrating her life.*
>
> *I still haven't talked to Kay since she got home. Every time I call they say she's either resting, or the doctor is with her. I'm more than perturbed with it all. I understand she's tired, I'm tired. I'm tired all the time. I tell Lynn I will keep going, eat well and try to stay on this Earth as long as I can, but I'm exhausted. If she knows I'm weak, she'll come racing back here too. As much as I want her here, I don't want her to see me like this. I didn't want her to see me go through the chemo or the surgery, and I managed to keep her away for both. She's a tough cookie, tougher than I give her credit for, but she's still my baby.*

Tears welled in my eyes and I sniffled back a potential gusher. I dabbed my nose with the paper napkin I'd used with dinner, then continued,

> *What's the date? August 13, I think. Thomas, my nephew, Kay's eldest, called.*
>
> *She died. Kay died. My sister is gone just like that. What happened? I don't know, and I don't understand why no one told me she was that bad. Didn't even get to talk to her, didn't even know she was so close, they'd said 6 months. No one told me.*
>
> *I can hear James. He's talking to Lynn at work right now. She'll be crushed.*

"Oh gosh, I remember the call too—like it was yesterday. I'd bawled my eyes out sitting at my desk," I said, pausing as my breath caught. Luc remained quiet still. He was hard to read, but not as hard as this damn journal... but still... I kept going,

> Kathleen, you beat me to it. How dare you leave me? How dare you go before me? You promised you would tell Lynn. You promised. Lynn is coming home, James told me. She'll be on a flight this Sunday. How many times has she come home in the last few months? Three, four, none for good reasons. I must tell her everything. I have to this time. I didn't like being kept from things, being kept from Kay.

I took in a long shaky breath, dabbed my nose a few times, and pressed forward,

> August 16th
> Lynn arrives today but William won't be coming. He's waiting on his citizenship interview or something, can't leave the country now. Lynn said she'll buy me some new clothes for the wake and funeral. None of my good clothes fit anymore. Can't go out in my nightgown.
> I'm tired. The doctor is coming over to give me another assessment. What more could he possibly tell me now? I know I don't have long, not the year they said I had. But I still had time. There would be time to tell Lynn.

Still staring at the page, I said, "She keeps saying she will tell me, but she never did. I could barely have a conversation with her on that last visit. She slept most of the time. If she wasn't sleeping, she was staring off deep in thought, and smoking like a chimney." I should have pushed her to talk more, but it was too late now. I needed more, needed answers. I was thinking I'd find them here—hoping—wishing, I read on,

> So tired. Wake was yesterday, or was it two days ago or was that the funeral? I don't know. Tired. The doctor came. He said I'm doing good and to eat what I want when I want. James told me I'm at the bottom of the palliative mortality pyramid, first stage, I have four more stages to go. That must be good. Just sleepy, can't focus.
> Lynn said she's heading home to Miami tomorrow morning. She's going to stay overnight and leave for the airport from here. James will drop her off.

Trying to figure out how I will tell her all of this before she goes. I still have time.

"Mom, why didn't you tell me?" I said, questioning my dead mother for the umpteenth time. Luc had been alarmingly quiet, but I didn't want to burden him with my painful rants. I gave my head a shake and kept reading,

> *Lynn woke me before she left for the airport. She lay in my bed, smiling at me. She said it was 4:00 a.m. and not to bother getting out of bed, that I could go back to sleep after she left. Was nice to see her smiling. Made me smile. Makes me smile now.*
>
> *I had my chance but didn't take it. How could I have told her then? I couldn't, just couldn't. I'd wasted too much time pondering things while she was here, ignoring her. Now she's gone.*
>
> *I never liked keeping things from her, but I've done it too many times over the years. Thought I was protecting her. Protecting her from what? She always found things out, eventually. She's always handled the tough stuff well, better than most it seemed. I didn't want to disrupt her life. The reality is she's the strong one and I'm the coward. I was protecting myself from seeing her in pain, not protecting her from the pain. I'll write all of it out, give it to her next time she's here. Still time.*

A "KNOCK-KNOCK!" sounded and Raven jumped up, startling me as he raced to the front door. He'd been lying at the foot of my stool, but I hadn't realized it. Luc and I both shot glances towards the front door.

"Oh man, who the...?" Luc said, his throat sounding dry as if finally finding his voice.

Luc didn't move, but I got off my stool and headed for the door.

Raven came over to me tight at my side. Then he growled when I was within reach of the doorknob. It was low at first, but in the dim light as I reached for the doorknob his growling became a deep guttural snarl. I touched the doorknob...

...and the lights flickered and came back on so bright it marred my vision. The stereo—I had forgotten was on—blared, spewing out *CCR's Bad Moon Rising*. Ya—not creepy at all. And of course, the security alarm went off. Raven stepped back, but only a little as I swiftly disarmed the alarm.

"Who is it?" I called out, as Luc came to stand with me at the door. I chose not to unlock the door, not yet. We waited for a response.

"Oh, hello. I'm sorry to disturb you at this hour. I'm looking for the *Abboud* family, *Mitra Abboud* in particular," said a beautiful deep voice from the other side of the door.

"They live next door," I said. What did this person want with Dunya's grandmother?

"Correct, right you are. I have tried their home, but no one is currently within. May I leave a message with you, perhaps," the voice asked, in the same gracious tone. There was a slight accent, Middle Eastern I assumed considering whom he was seeking. "Perhaps a note, with my name?" His voice chimed, sounding almost musical.

"Uhm sure—just a second." Flustered, I turned from the door.

"What are you doing?" Luc asked me as I ran to the kitchen.

"Getting something for the guy to write on—what does it look like I'm doing?" I raced back with a small pad of paper and a pen. "Hold Raven while I open the door." Luc took hold of Raven by the collar, and I unlocked and opened the door.

Under the porch light stood a very tall, well-built man with stylishly coifed black hair. The sheen and colour reminded me of shiny black feathers. He appeared to be in his late 30s, possibly early 40s, with naturally tanned coloured skin. The skin of his face, neck, and hands were the only areas visible as he wore an elegantly tailored white linen suit, with a white shirt, shoes, and tie which reflected the flawlessness of his impeccable skin. His amazing eyes were deep-set beneath dark eyebrows the same colour as his hair, and his eyes were shadowed by long thick eyelashes. Accompanying those amazing dark eyes, was a strong masculine nose. Finishing his face were full lips curved into a half-grin revealing perfect straight white teeth. To call this man handsome would have been an absolute understatement. Although the evidence of his ethnicity was subtle—his magnificence was not, and I couldn't help staring.

"My apologies for the intrusion. My name is Shamsiel." He glanced at my hands. "Is that paper for my use?" He asked, gesturing towards the pad in my hand, his movement breaking my dreamy gaze.

"Uhm what? Ya—I mean yes, sorry—here, and a pen... you can write them a note, like you asked." Stumbling through my reply, I handed him the pen and paper.

He wrote fast and handed the items back. "Thank you for your kindness." He gave me a subtle nod. "Thank you again," he added, his words softer this time. He turned and proceeded back down the stairs to the walkway, and I glanced back at Luc.

He was staring—not at him, but at *me*. Busted. For sure he'd caught me gawking at the guy. When I looked back in the direction that the man had walked, he was gone, *vanished*. I poked my head out the door and looked both ways up the street. Still nothing, no one. "That was weird," I said, shutting the door. I locked it and reengaged the alarm.

"What did he write?" Luc asked, letting go of Raven. "Ya might want to wipe the drool off your lip." He laughed and smacked me in the arm.

Ignoring the comment and still a bit dazed, I lazily rubbed my arm where he'd smacked me. "Oh man, I don't know," I said, annoyed with myself. I hadn't even looked at it when he handed back the paper and pen. I'd been too preoccupied with my *staring*. Looking now at the pad, I examined the elegant handwriting. One word, *Shamsiel*, was followed by something that resembled Arabic writing.

"Who's this neighbor?" Luc asked, following me back into the kitchen.

"Oh geez—where do I start. Been a lot of strange things going on over the past few months. Some of it you already know. Not the usual strange, but super out-of-this-world strange." Even for me. "Not sure what to make of it all. And now with Mom's journal and this stuff about some *secret*, it's all messing with my head," I muttered. I placed my hands on my head, which for obvious reasons was aching again.

"Like what happened with Darius today," he said, reminding me of the day's earlier bizarreness. "I went by his desk after you left. See how he was." He rubbed his goateed chin. "What I wanted, was for him to tell me what the hell happened. But when I asked him about it, he shook his head. All he gave me was, '*I can't explain it — one minute I'm standing there and the next I'm on the other side of the street with Lynn in my arms'.*" Luc passed a hand over his shaved head. "Said, all he remembered was the *compulsion* — he'd called it, and how his brain yelled, *protect.* That was it — just went back to just shaking his head." Luc shook his own head. "I told him not to worry — you were fine — it was all cool, but he seemed confused. He wasn't injured, was okay — seemed more worried about you than anything," he finished. He rubbed both hands over his head, swiping back and forth over the shadowy parts.

"Sounds similar to what my whatever — premonitions sometimes feel like. Like a compulsion or urge — for or against a feeling... or action. I've had nothing like that since Joanna and her breast cancer scare though," I said, cringing at the memory of how close we'd come to losing her. "And the neighbors, let me tell you about what happened there."

Maybe Luc could find clarity in it all — I couldn't. We resumed our seats at the kitchen island, and I told him the story about the old woman, the butterflies, and *Yasmin* thing.

He rubbed his head a few more times and there was a long pause before he responded. "It's coincidence — don't you think?" It sounded like he was trying to convince himself.

Instead of answering his question, I told him what the PI had told me, pointing out how the journal mentioned the same visit from my birthmother. "Sound like a bunch of coincidences?" I questioned him back.

He gave me a weak smile and looked at the journal. "What else does the journal say? Does your mom go into more detail — I mean about the secret?" he said, in a gentle but still curious tone.

"I've only read as far as what I've read to you," I reminded him. We both stared at the journal that was still open to where I had left it before the knocking on the door.

"Well then, read on." He smiled big to show his support.

I picked it up and slowly turned the page. The next contained a page full of disheveled handwriting. Mom's handwriting had gone through changes the same way her body had.

Letting out a little gasp, I refocus on the now weak and barely legible scratches, and read again,

> *Aug 30.*
>
> *talked to Lynn on the phone. didn't know what to say. had nothing to say. the sadness is crushing. Kay is gone. need strength to put the story down. worth the sacrifice. I'll leave it where Lynn will find it. the pain is bad. can't think. Lynn, I hope this finds you.*
>
> *it was in May, after your birthday, 27. your birthmother came to the door, asked to come in. I should have told you. don't be angry. we sat on the couch. she told me a strange story. said it was real. she believed it. now I believe it.*
>
> *she said when she was 18 years old she sat in the park near her house, a beautiful man came to see her. his name was Gabriel. he said she was part of something big. something that would change fate, change humanity. she said her role was to have a child, a daughter. but she could not keep the baby, had to place her with the right family, keep her on her path. a family who fit his description, no other. no other daughters, only sons. place her where the line of sons is strong, keep her hidden, keep her safe.*

I was struggling to read, both from the chaotic handwriting and the realization of how weak she'd been near the end. Without looking up, I said, "It's like what the PI told me, well—sort of. The woman told him it was like my birthmother knew who should adopt the baby— adopt me." I glanced up to see Luc sipping his water and watching me through the rim of the glass. His eyes were wide and again he said nothing. I looked back to the scratchy words and read,

> *she said on the same night, she had a dream about four women. a witch, a healer, a linguist, and a scribe. all of them held books in their arms. they stood together and behind them stood four men. Not men, angels, she'd definitely said angels. claimed that as the months passed, her belly grew. said she lied to her best friend. told her she'd had a one-night-stand. said he didn't know she was pregnant and would not tell him. told her mother, asked her for help with the adoption. she said our family was exactly what was needed. said you needed to be with us, no one else. she told me her time was short. said you were on your path, but you may lose your way again. I didn't understand, never have. but there's more.*

"Is this a joke?" I said, before reading the pending *more*. "No offense to my mother, but it sounds like my birthmother got knocked up and lost her mind. Then she shows up on Mom's doorstep 27 years later with some wacko story. Aaaand my mom thinks it's real because she got cancer?" I reread the paragraph over again in my head, but it was no clearer the second time.

"Keep going, Lynn. Maybe it gets less *wacko* in the next part," Luc said.

I stared at the journal and my eyes watered. I blinked to clear them, then read the next sentence in my head before sharing more of my mother's delusion. *'you had to be reunited with the water-bearer she said, to stay your course.'* "Oh my God," I said in response to the short bit I'd read.

"What? Dragons?" Luc asked, sounding serious.

I hoped this was a joke. Knowing the words would be clearer than an explanation, I cleared my throat and read aloud,

> you had to reunite with the water-bearer she said, to stay your course. your birthfather's identity would be found where the water-bearer resides. I don't know what that means, I'm sorry. she said the words are not always what they seem. she said something about how the balance must be kept. it was all very confusing. still is. I thought she was crazy or something, but now I know she wasn't.

"What the hell is a water-bearer?" Luc said, cutting me off.

I ignored him and continued reading this time again in my head. "Oh wait, it gets better," I huffed out, then reread the part aloud,

> she also said you would need a cipher, from the South. he won't know he's the one. he'll show himself. while everyone can see him, only you will hear him, the puzzle and problem solver. he is spiritual, but not religious. it will be a chance meeting turning into a great friendship.

The last part sounded like a riddle and made me pause. As if I needed things to be more confusing. I didn't look up, I was afraid to see Luc's face. It was like reading one of our urban fantasy books we loved so much, but I wasn't loving this. There were still no answers yet, only more questions. And knowing that I was coming to the end, I swallowed hard yet kept reading,

>*the last thing she told me, the biggest thing, was tell no one what she told me. said if I did, it would cause me illness. telling you is the sacrifice. there is no other way for you to know, no one else to tell you, to carry the secret forward. Kay promised me, said she would tell you, but she's gone. making that promise may have sealed her fate. I waited too long, had to write this all out. make sure you had it all if I wasn't strong enough or brave enough to tell you face to face.*
>
>*I'm sorry I kept this from you. I'm sorry I kept so many things from you. you've always been the strong one. I should have trusted you could handle it. you always did. forgive my writing the pain is unbearable. I'm exhausted my dear. need to rest.*
>
>*I love you, my daughter, my heart.*

Tears crested on the rims of my lower lids. My brain was spun, and my heart fractured, and I wasn't sure if I would cry or scream, or both. Painfully slow, I raised my head and stared dumbfounded at Luc. His mouth was gaping open. It must have been like that for a while because the corners were all dry.

He closed it suddenly as if realizing it, then opened it again, and said, "Your mom has quite the imagination—quite the storyteller, yes? Was your mom into this mystical stuff too?" A hint of fear flushed in his face, most likely at what I *might* answer. And he may have been on the verge of a few tears himself.

"No...," I managed while trying to clear my throat. "My mom... she never believed in any of this stuff. She was a nurse—a fact person... not someone into fantasy on any level. It's strange for me to read her words. She even says at the beginning how she thought my birthmother was nuts." I gave my head a little shake like it would stop the spin. "She starts to believe. It's unlike her." I took in a deep breath and let it out in a shudder. "I have one more story to tell you. But promise me you won't bolt for the door—leave me sitting here... because I'm about to completely lose it myself."

"Right now—at this moment... I'm not sure if I could get any more freaked out than I already am—go ahead," he said, licking his dry lips.

He stared at me with apprehension and disbelief, possibly mirroring my expression.

"I wouldn't be so sure about the *get anymore freaked out* part." I grimaced, fearing he might bolt after hearing only a few words of what I was about to tell him. I hadn't even shown him the photo yet.

"I'm too unnerved to go home and be alone now, anyway." He grinned, part joking—part not. "Shit—give it to me," he prompted, getting up and going to the fridge. "Got anything to drink? I'm going to need something a little harder than water." He opened the fridge door, leaned in and grabbed two beers, then returned to his seat.

He cracked both open and handed me one. I sat up straight, took a deep breath, and then a long sip. Then I told him the story Louise had shared with me.

Through the telling of the story, we continued to review all the bizarre events and info. I pointed out the similarities between Mom's and Louise's stories. And as I spoke my thoughts and the words out loud, a sense of clarity and lucidity of all the details flooded over my brain. Although the information still made no rational sense, it somehow felt better to talk about it. By the time I finished with the photo story, we were both burnt out. And we resigned to sleeping on the couches, still too freaked-out to go alone to our rooms to sleep.

Raven followed me as I went down the hall to the closet again to gather up what we needed. I pulled out two pillows, two big blankets, and two flat sheets, then returned to the living room. I made up one of the couches for Luc and the other for myself. Being I wasn't ready for bed, I grabbed the large pad of paper off the counter before shutting off all but the hall light. It was just in case one of us needed to find our way to the bathroom in the middle of the night and had nothing to do with either of us being freaked out of course. Right—*sure.*

When I came back to the room, Luc had his blanket tucked around his legs. He had the side table lamp turned on and was flipping through a guitar magazine he'd brought.

I sat down in the middle of my couch and placed the pad of paper on the coffee table in front of me. I drew a small circle to test the pen, and said, "I'm gonna write out all the strange things I can remember from the past few weeks." I raised my eyebrows. "Wanna help me with this?"

Luc sat up and leaned against the arm of the couch, legs outstretched.

He sat there silent, staring at me for what felt like thirty minutes when I'm sure only seconds had passed. "Well?" I asked again.

"I'm having a hard time digesting all this," he said, closing the magazine and setting it on the side table. "You're right about the coincidences, too many for my taste. You know I'm a religious person—but I'm a spiritual person too." He paused. "Part of me thinks this is a totally cool story. The other part—the religious part, thinks it's… well, that it's something way bigger." He slid his legs over the edge of the couch, putting his feet on the floor with the blanket still over his lap, and leaned in. "What if it's all true? What then? How am I—how are you—we, supposed to deal with this—whatever this is?" He raised his hands in question, palms up as if waiting for the answer to land there.

"Well… how do you think I feel? Secret—illness—death—water-bearer—cipher—really? It's not some mystery I've stumbled on here, it's a mystery about me—or at least it relates to me somehow." At least I thought it must. "I don't expect you to get involved. If you're not comfortable with this I understand. You're a good friend Luc, and I'm hoping you'll support me looking into this. There are too many questions here that I need answers to," I told him, placing my palm on my head again, attempting to sooth the still aching spot. "Some of this stuff is seriously messed up. Some things could pass for coincidence, but either way I don't know what it all means. Or if it means anything." I kept rubbing my head. I think I was hoping for a sign—a sensation of any kind, but nothing came.

"You know you can tell me anything, Lynn. I just don't know how much I can help." He gave a little shrug in complement to his own confusion.

"Just make sure I don't lose my marbles, yer all I got here. Will doesn't get me when I talk about the strange and wacky world of paranormal stuff. He understands things he can actually see. It's the unseen he struggles with, so I'm not sure how much of this I can throw at him." I rubbed the top of my head with both hands now, the strain and confusion had hit a peak.

"Okay," he said, "Let's make a list of things in the wild and wacky world of Lynnie." He took the pen and paper from the coffee table. Then he looked at me. "Number one...?" He wiggled the pen in the air.

I gave him a smile of relief and grabbed the pen and paper back. Pressing pen to paper, I wrote the first item, saying it aloud as I wrote the first curious event. "My birth registration had the name Yasmin, but no record of my birthfather." I continued the list in a chronological order of events whether fact, coincidence, or just plain weird. I filled in the parts similar from Mom and Louise's stories and ended the running list with. "Strange visitor knocking at the door and the lights coming back on when I opened the door. Raven growling at the door. A stranger looking for the neighbors, specifically *Mitra* the grandmother. Leaves a message writing only his name and something that looks like Arabic." Stopping, I put the pen down, and glanced at Luc. "Done!" I announced.

Luc stared at the list not blinking and started nodding his head. I figured I might have to tackle him should he make for the door, but he sat where he was.

"Can you think of anything else—anything I've left out?" I asked, trying to shake him from his head-bobbing.

"Nope, nope—think that's it," he said, still nodding his head. "Fact, fiction, nonsense, or coincidence—there you have it." His eyes bulged, and his head nodding stopped. He blinked a few times and his eyes relaxed.

I leaned back and stretched out on the couch, snuggling in under my big blanket. The reaction I'd gotten from my couch-mate still worried me even though his head nodding had stopped, and his eyes now rested comfortable back in their sockets. Raven came then and laid on the floor beside the couch, and a sense of something resembling *ease* washed over me. I tried to process all the things that had happened, all I'd been told, what I'd read, and all that I'd written out.

Luc stretched out and tucked his blanket around his legs again. "You know," he said, pausing for a moment. "You should put all of this in a spreadsheet." He paused again. "Do some cross references to the connections and similarities," he added, revealing the analyst in him, but I could tell he was more than just a little unnerved.

"Right now, all I want to do is sleep and hope I don't have any nightmares." I pulled the covers close around my neck. "Thanks for staying over, Luc."

"How long is Will away again?" he asked, giving a nervous chuckle, pulling up his own covers.

"Shut-up. You're as scared as I am," I huffed out, staring in his direction. He'd closed his eyes and shuddered under his blanket.

I grinned a little, knowing I was right. He was just as freaked out as I was. "Good night Luc."

"Sleep tight," he whispered, letting out a long exhalation.

Chapter 17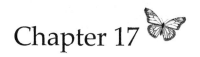

**Monument to Canadian Aid Workers – September 12th, 2001,
Rideau Falls Park, Ottawa**

With closed eyes, Michael sat on one of the two granite benches available at the site for visitors.

"Don't you think this meeting place is a bit of a cliché?" Gabriel said, appearing beside him.

Michael opened his eyes and tilted his chin up to gaze at the rectangular bronze arch with its two bronze feathers that made up the 3 1/2 meters high monument. "It's a beautiful place," Michael said. "I often come here to reflect... reflect on one's actions... or inactions as it were." His gaze followed the feather along the top of the arch. "John Greer's design is titled '*Reflection*' after all."

"And yes, we all know the three key messages the monument represents," Raphael said, his voice coming in defense as he appeared behind them.

Michael remained seated on the granite bench still staring up.

"First—it is intended to show appreciation to Canada's long-standing activities in international development and humanitarian aid. Second—it honors all Canadians who died while serving in these fields abroad, and third... it pays a personal tribute to both *Nancy Malloy* and *Tim Stone*," Raphael said, staring over to his smug friend.

"Part of the project was to create a permanent list of all Canadian aid workers who lost their lives in foreign deployments. The list currently holds 88 individuals, marking their names, their birth and deaths," Gabriel said, finishing for him.

Uriel appeared in front on the left. "Always the know-it-all," Uriel said. "What do you have to say about our current situation? We are in a state of unbalance once again, my friends." He too stared at Gabriel.

"It was you who said, '*I have already set things in motion. I have ensured that the balance will be upheld*'. Did you not?" Vretil said, uttering the mocking words as he arrived next to Uriel. Pushing his point, he added, "You call what happened yesterday balance? Thousands have died, and the people are at odds once again. And who in the hell is this *Bin Laden, anyway*? What evil watches over such a man? He shames his own people and religion by claiming that the return of *Sharia law* will set things right in the Muslim community, and that all other ideologies must be divergent. He believes all civilians—including women and children, are justifiable targets of *jihad*." Vretil looked to the faces of his brothers, searching for opposition, but found none. "Now the people who are part of the Muslim community—who have lived in North America their whole lives, are afraid and the people who are non-Muslim are afraid. This one man and his actions against the Americans have caused this ignorance towards the Muslim population as a whole. How can people not realize he and his followers do not represent the Muslim community? His beliefs are not their beliefs." he stated, his voice rising in protest, making clear his care and concern for the humans.

Michael stood and walked over to where his lone brethren stood. Grabbing Gabriel's arm as he had done 34 years earlier, he leaned in and whispered, "What do we do now, Arch of Revelation, Creativity and Faith?" His face gave no expression, but his eyes sparkled with restraint.

Gabriel patted Michael's hand. Pulling free Gabriel took a step towards the others. "You think what happened yesterday was my fault—that my action long ago and the events that followed are related? That somehow I impacted the balance?" he questioned.

"No, Gabriel. We are not accusing you of anything. We just don't see how your actions have helped," Raphael stated, his voice leveling as if to avoid further confrontation. "How exactly will five be better than the four of centuries past? We have yet to see any change."

Before Gabriel could answer, Uriel cut in. "The human population increases, and the evil seems to follow. How can one more make a difference?"

Measured, Gabriel spoke again. "You know why... you all know why. He, who watches over all, has given me this chance—given us this chance... to show Him... what He once believed about the human race... is still true."

"What's truth—that humans will destroy themselves?" Michael asked, still standing behind Gabriel.

Gabriel took a deep breath before speaking, searching for patience. "You condemn them too quickly when you know not all of them are self-destructive. As *He* does, we believe they can create their own balance. We are here to watch over and perhaps guide or inform, but never influence. For generations there has been four. Two are direct descendants from the first, but all carry the secret of mothers past. When a mother was unable to pass it to a daughter, they chose another—another to carry the secret for a new line. Many have sacrificed their lives to keep the balance." Gabriel paused and took in another deep breath before continuing. "They all risk the same consequences. It is through their sacrifices they show *their* belief in humanity. I risked my own place with Him by doing what I did. I needed to show Him I believed in their humanity, that I believed in what the four of you had done from the beginning." Stepping forward, he said, "We are Five now. We are stronger together as they now will be." He ended with a sigh.

Uriel and Vretil moved around Gabriel to stand at Michael's side, flanking him. Raphael stayed near Gabriel.

Michael's voice came in a soft reply. "How will this help the four? It's not like the existence of a fifth can ensure future daughters for their lines?"

Gabriel turned to face them all. "That's the thing Michael—it is no longer about passing strength between mothers to daughters. It's about the gathering," Gabriel said. He smirked, glancing over to Raphael, knowing more questions would come.

Raphael shot a glance to Uriel, to Vretil and then to Michael. Together, wide-eyed with confusion, they stared back at Gabriel.

"It was part of the deal," Gabriel added.

"What *deal*, Gabriel? You never told us about a deal," Michael said, pushing, his voice growing harsh.

"You couldn't possibly think it was as simple as adding another to the mix, did you? Originally, *He* allowed things to continue with the four as long as they could show and keep the balance. They can no longer do it by merely passing on to the next generation. There must be a *coming together* I was told. A collective show of strength and...." Gabriel halted.

"Aaand?" Michael shot out, cutting him off, the harshness in his voice doubling.

"And... there'll be no help from the mothers," Gabriel said, ending fast in hopes for little impact. There was a collective *gasp* as Gabriel panned the faces of his brethren. He had known the day would come when he would have to explain the repercussions of his actions, and that day was now. He'd known they'd all assumed things would continue as before, only now with five instead of four.

Raphael moved over to stand next to the other three. He turned to face Gabriel as the others had been doing. "How are they to get the information they need? What will they do with it when—and if, they find it on their own? None of them knows the burden they carry. It's currently held with their mothers. And how will they find each other?"

"We need more time—they need more time," Uriel shot out, panic clear on his beautiful face.

"We have time," Gabriel said. "Not all whom are needed are in their places yet." Addressing no one in particular, he added, "Was my Charge not at the same company as Raphael's Charge?"

Raphael was quick to respond. "Yes, but the two never met—yours no longer works there."

Turning to look at Uriel specifically, Gabriel continued, "Did she not work with your Charge as well and did they not become friends?"

"Yes, but your Charge is no longer at that IT job, she was let go a few weeks ago. I love computers," Michael admitted, "But the IT world too is a mess, layoffs everywhere."

Uriel stepped forward to stand beside Gabriel who now stared off towards the empty granite bench. "Both Vretil's Charge and mine have not been in contact with yours for over 5 years," Uriel said. "Vretil's Charge is on the other side of the country. Mine—due to unforeseen problems, is only the 5th generation in her line—and we need the strength of the generations more than ever."

"Where are your Charges now?" Gabriel queried all, his gaze still fixed on the bench.

Raphael spoke first. "Mine is still at that IT company. She has two daughters now and so does her sister. Her line continues to be strong."

"It is no longer about the line," Gabriel reminded him. Patience waning, he turned back to face them, but looked to Michael for his response.

"Mine escaped the layoffs. In fact, she and her coworkers were buzzing about the tragedy. They ended up watching the events unfold in the boss's office," Michael said. "It was the only computer receiving the online updates from the BBC website. They'd tuned in just before the other plane hit the second building. I'd watched her as she stared out the windows to the pastoral scene of the farm across the street. It seemed to take her deep into thought while all of this horror was taking place in New York." Michael paused. "She is still in contact with yours. She has no daughters, although she is raising a son alone—a son not of her flesh and blood. A selfless undertaking of love." His approval was clear in his voice and his proud expression.

"And you?" Gabriel turned to Uriel. "Arch of *Presence, Poetry and Prophecy*, where is yours?" Gabriel teased, but only for Michael's earlier mocking of titles.

"Mine is on her honeymoon as a matter of fact—at a friend's family cottage," Uriel said, with an air of merriment. "Her friends had it all decorated for them with a bottle of wine and petals on the bed and a big welcome sign." His expression changed suddenly from one of joy to sorrow. "They woke yesterday morning, had the radio on and heard that dreadful noise they play when there's an emergency. They'd had a satellite connection, turned the TV on and were glued to it for hours... they are there for a few more days," he added.

Lastly, Gabriel turned to Vretil. "What about yours, oh quiet one?"

Vretil stood firm. "Well, mine is far away in Calgary, but her mother moved out there last year to join her. At least they are in the same place now, but she has no children of her own yet," Vretil shared with reluctance. "She is ready. Her mother is strong enough, and she will make the sacrifice for her daughter if needed." He tried to hide his fear on the matter and pretended to be admiring the feathers on the arch.

Michael turned towards Gabriel. "How are they going to keep the balance, Gabriel? All but one is in contact, and by the looks of yesterday's devastation, things do not seem to be getting better—only worse. You know *He* will not look at this situation with optimism for the human race, *and* you know as well as all of us, we cannot interfere." With a grim expression he shook his head.

"How quickly you give up hope, my friend." Gabriel responded. "My Charge will unite the four and they will find the information they need. He, as you mentioned, has been watching over since I set things in motion. He has witnessed my Charges ability to perceive things hidden from the normal senses, and *He* has not abandoned our cause."

Michael looked to each of his brothers and nodded. "So, we wait a little longer. It's not like any of them have discovered their roles yet— so yes, we have time. They'll find the clues themselves and once they do, they can go to the mothers for confirmation. But until then, the mothers cannot tell them directly until they ask, correct?" Michael confirmed.

"Shamsiel has not yet revealed the descendant of *Those Who Watch*, nor has the metaphysician, the one He called *The Cipher*, been made known to us. They will need The Cipher's help," Gabriel informed them.

Gabriel regarded Michael approvingly, but then his brother's acceptance turned to rage again. "Shamsiel?" Michael shouted. "What the Hell does he have to do with this?"

Gabriel cringed.

"Cipher?" whispered Vretil.

Chapter 18

The sunlight broke through the large living room windows a little too early for my liking. We'd both needed a good sleep, especially after the events and discussions from the night before, but sleeping on the couches hadn't helped.

I looked over to where Luc slept. He had his face buried under a pillow, facing the couch with his back to the world. I stirred then, and so did Raven. When I stood, he stood. And when I went to the kitchen to start the coffee, he followed. He sat, giving me the head-tilt dogs often do, and continued to watch me.

I filled the coffee maker and hit the on-button. The kitchen filled with the aroma of fresh brewing coffee, setting a calmness to the morning. I turned back to Raven. He was still staring at me. "I'll have to get a doggie," I told him. "At least so you have someone to play with." Could swear he nodded. Strange. *Strange?* Everything was strange lately. "How about I let you out into my big new backyard and you can go… do yer thing?" He followed me to the sliding doors. When I cracked the doors, he pushed his nose through, forcing them wide, and was off at a sprint. "Had to really go, eh, buddy?"

"Who are you talking too?" Luc's sleepy voice asked from the living room.

"Uh, that would be your dog—excuse me."

"You let him out?" he asked, a slight panic in his voice.

"The yard is fully fenced—he'll be fine," I assured him. Rolling my eyes, I turned back to the glass doors. I could see Raven sitting on the back step facing the pool. "We'll worry about his *business* later," I said. "Coffee?"

The sound of papers rustling came from Luc's general direction, and when I glanced through to the living room, he was holding up the pad of paper that contained the list of *strange* I'd written the night before.

"Let's see." He turned to look at me over the back of the couch. Then he summarized, "Birthmother gave you an unusual name, Yasmin. Butterfly Jasmine surrounds your new house. Your mom loved butterflies, her name was Sally, Sal for short, and the guy who used to live here—who planted the flowers, his name was Sal. The old woman next door appeared to call you Yasmin, but her daughter says she meant to say *Jasmine*, but you said she never looked at the flowers, only at you." He looked over at me again. "That's a lot of weird coincidences and that's only part of this list."

"What do you want me to say?" I stared back at him holding the two empty coffee mugs I'd grabbed from the cupboard. "It's confusing and exciting, but it makes my head ache," I said and put the coffee mugs next to the still brewing pot of normalcy.

Luc went back to the list. "Next, you go home, have a photo taken, where you look like you have wings, and Will's Dad's neighbor tells you a story about Will's mom that involves angels. Ah, hello—what the...?"

Luc read the next set of weirdness, and I continued with my attempt at normalcy, pouring my favorite vanilla creamer into both mugs. Brewed, I poured the fresh coffee it into the mugs combining the fresh scent of vanilla and coffee to the room. Then I scooped up the mugs and went back to the couches.

I set the hot mugs on the coffee table and then dropped onto my couch. Trying to focus, I put my hands over my face. Pulling them quickly off, I said, "Okay, what about Darius and his super-speedy fast moves? Not sure how it fits with all the other stuff about mothers, daughters, and angels. And it's not that he wouldn't have tried to save me, but it's not like him to move at lightning speed." Still confused, I put my hands back over my face again.

"Yesterday and last night seriously added to the weirdness factor. The *Angel Movers*, the lights going out—and only at your house. That guy showing up at the door, the lights go back on, and Raven being all growly," he recapped, leaning over the couch to check for Raven at the back door. "Looks like he's guarding the place. Keeps getting up and looking around. Sits down for a minute, and then he's up again."

I huffed through my hands and let them drop to my lap. "I'm not sure what to make of it all. I'm used to strange, but this stuff is off the chart." I leaned over to grab the note from last night's visitor. "Guess I'll be going over to pass on the message to the neighbors." I pushed up from the couch and strolled to the front window to peek over to the side to their house. There was still no car in their driveway.

We spent the rest of the morning fiddling around the kitchen making breakfast and chatting about the events from last night and the theme that seemed to be recurring, *angels*. But by 11:00 am, the neighbors still hadn't returned home. I doubted this message would yield any insight on the other stuff, but a girl could hope, and I was curious to see the old woman again.

As the morning moved on to afternoon, Luc gathered his belongings to go. On the back step, Raven at my side, we watched Luc wander and *hunt* to complete his chore. Raven continued with looking at me again, occasionally glancing over towards his master when he heard his name mentioned.

"Man, that is one big backyard, Lynn. Hey—just heard a car pull in next door." Stopping to listen, Luc said, "We'll get out of here, so you can deliver your message, and enjoy the rest of your Saturday."

The three of us headed back into the house. Luc grabbed his stuff and leashed Raven to go out the front. Cracking the front door, I spied Dunya carrying groceries from her car to the house.

Stepping out, she spotted me and tried to wave, but the bags were too heavy. Conceding, she called out. "Lynn!" She followed it with a smile and a laugh, almost dropping the bags of groceries.

I waved, but she stared passed me to the front door. I turned to see what had caught her attention.

Luc stood on the top step with Raven tight to his side. Luc was staring back... at my neighbor. He was grinning like a fool, a fool in love that is.

I snapped back to look at Dunya who was now teetering on dropping her groceries yet still smiling. She tilted her head down. Well-well, what do we have here—a love match? Before I could comment, Luc handed me the leash, vaulted from the stairs, and promptly ran across the side lawn to aid the damsel in distress with her groceries. I had a firm grip on Raven when I saw Mitra come from around the other side of the car. I glanced up again to see Luc had grabbed two of the bags. From across the lawn, Luc and Dunya watched as the old woman came towards me at a slow run.

She was flapping her arms. "Yasmin... Shamsiel... Yasmin," she squeaked, her tiny voice and words changing swiftly to words in Arabic.

Dunya quickly set the groceries inside the doorway intent on corralling her run-away grandmother. "Jadda!" she called after her. "Oh, Lynn, I'm sorry." She gave Luc a sideways smile and together the two of them headed back my way.

Mitra stopped directly in front of me, clasping her hands to her chest. Her smiling wrinkled face beamed up at me. I smiled back at her. Beside me, Raven lowered to the ground. When the other two met up with us, I said, "That's my buddy Luc, by the way." I smacked Luc on the arm to shake him from his gawking at my lovely neighbor.

"Oh, hi, ya—I'm Luc, and this is Raven," he sputtered out, ignoring the old woman.

Raven came to his feet and gave a soft, "*Chuff*" as if saying his own *hello*.

"I'm Dunya, please to meet you." Her chin tilted, and she did her shy thing again, peering from under heavy lashes long enough they cast shadows over her cheeks.

"Pleasure's all mine," Luc said.

Raven, "*Chuffed*" a second time.

"Hello, Master Raven," she said kneeling to look him in the face. Raven raised a paw in greeting. How to win a girl—lesson one, introduce her to your dog.

Redirecting, I said, "Mitra stills seems fixated on the butterflies." The old woman continued to beam up at me.

Dunya turned back at the sound of her grandmother's name. "Oh Lynn, she has been saying it every time she sees you, and last night she started with this stuff about how '*Shamsiel is here*' and the arm-flapping. She's not normally like this." Dunya gave me a weak smile. Then her grandmother went back to flapping her arms and scurrying around us again.

"Oh wait, *Shamsiel*—Shamsiel was here. He was at my door last night. He was looking for you guys—your grandmother, actually. Here." I pulled the note from my pocket and handed it to her. With all the distraction, I had forgotten about it.

"Okay Lynn, I'm out of here—but I'll call you later," Luc said, crossing the front lawn with Raven in tow. "Sorry, I've got to head out," he added, hefting Raven into the hatch of the car, turning to smile a Dunya.

"Nice to meet you." She smiled back, then waved.

"Ya, no problem, Luc—thanks eh!" I called back to him, my words overlooked due to the flirt-fest.

"Wonderful to meet you, Dunya," he called out as he climbed into his car. He waved and then drove off, leaving me with a moony eyed woman and her arm-flapping granny. Turning back to Dunya, I noticed she'd gone from staring at Luc to staring at the note. Her face scrunched as if puzzled or possibly at the departure of her new prince charming.

"Last night, Jadda kept saying, '*Shamsiel is here*', but in Arabic of course," Dunya said. She looked up from the note, her expression strained. She opened her mouth but seemed to struggle for words.

"What is it? Is everything okay? Who is this Shamsiel?" I said, a tad too anxious, but I was dying to know.

"This name... *Shamsiel*, is not common... in fact it is rarely—if ever spoken. It comes from an old language lost long ago." She paused. "Shamsiel was the name of one of the 20 leaders of the Watchers," she whispered, then paused again.

"Watchers? Like FBI or something?" I was grasping here, but she wasn't giving me much.

"No... have you ever read the book *Paradise Lost* or more specifically, *The Book of Enoch*?" She posed the question and looked back down at the note.

"I'm not much of a reader," I confessed. "What do those books have to do with your grandmother and this Shamsiel guy?"

"The Book of Enoch... it's about angels," she whispered.

She'd just said *angels*. The reference screamed through my brain. I was searching for some recollection, but my expression must have given me away.

"Lynn?"

"Dunya are you trying to tell me your grandmother is talking about angels, and that's what all the arm-flapping is about? And not the butterflies like before?"

"The note, Lynn...." She paused again and let out a breath she'd been holding.

"Yes, it's the man's name. What?" I questioned. "The other part is written in what I assumed is Arabic—do you know what it says?"

"Yes. It says... *Watcher*, Shamsiel Watcher," she said in a whisper again, this time looking over her shoulder and back at me.

"Okay, back up here. Your grandmother talked last night about this man, and then the guy shows up at my door looking for her? He asked me to pass on this note and all it says—is his name?" Confusion mounted along with anxiety as that tender spot on my head began to ache again. "Is this guy trouble? What does he have to do with those books? What's the mystery? Sorry, you've lost me here," I admitted.

Dunya shook her head so fast she must have rattled her brain. "I don't know... I mean I don't know the man. What did he look like?"

"Well he was tall, dark and handsome—very handsome. Dressed all in white. I would say late 30s. It surprised me when he mentioned your grandmother. Figured he was a relative or something. Why do you look so worried?" I asked.

"Lynn... let me get Jadda inside and I'll come back over. Would that be okay?" Dunya wrapped an arm around a now giggling Mitra.

"Of course, sorry to press—it's none of my business, really." I was suddenly embarrassed for pushing her. I mean I hardly knew her, and well, all these things were making me a crazy person.

Mitra grinned and waved back at me as Dunya ushered her along.

"Don't worry about explaining," I told her, as she crossed the lawn. I was still secretly hoping she would come over to explain. Maybe we'd have a big laugh after, and it would just be a funny story to add to the rest.

"I'm sorry, Lynn," Dunya called as she maneuvered Mitra through her front door, "So sorry," she uttered before the door shut.

I went back into my house to wait.

After sitting on the couch for an hour, I'd given up the idea she'd be over. Perhaps she was trying to find a way to explain the anguish she'd shown when trying to clarify the note. Maybe she would come — maybe not. In the interim, I needed to satiate my curiosity about that book, *The Book of Enoch*, and took to my laptop for answers.

Online I found tons of references which made me feel like an idiot having never heard of it before. The *Wiki* page described the first part as Dunya had said, the fall of *The Watchers*, but it also mentioned how those same angels had fathered something called... *Nephilim*? The information seemed a bit out there and gave me the feeling my grey-matter might be oozing out my ear, but I kept with the research. The rest of the book depicts this Enoch person visiting heaven, through visions, dreams, and revelations. Says Nephilims can be found in both Jewish and Christian texts. The Watchers and the Nephilim were often portrayed as evil creatures or monsters. Other references described them as gentle giants and beings of free will. These Fallen Angels, or Watchers, were sent down by God. A legion of 200 angels to watch over humans. And Archangels were considered the *good* Watchers, but they were not part of The Fallen. *Whatever*. Done with the brain ooze, I leant back against the couch trying to digest all the stuff I'd read, *plus* all the stuff that had been happening.

"Rap! Rap! Rap!" sounded at the front door.

Hoping it was only Dunya, I got up and hustled over to answer. I flung open the door and there she stood, wringing her hands, chin down, eyes peering up in concern this time. "Hi," I said, giving her a welcoming smile. She looked as though she needed it. "Dunya, get in here. You look distraught—what's going on?" I asked, extending my arm. I led her to the living room and to the comfy couches.

She sat but leaned forward, hugging her knees. "You're going to think I'm nuts—you're going to think we are all nuts." She rocked back and forth on the couch, still clutching her knees.

"Can I get you something to drink? Water, tea… shot of rum?" I joked. I was ready to ply her with whatever she needed if it meant I would get answers.

"Yes, please—water, thank you," she responded, still hunched.

I returned with a cool glass of water and set it on the coffee table in front of her, then flopped lazily down on the adjacent couch. She still seemed reluctant to speak, so I said, "What if I tell you something crazy I've experienced first? Then you might not be afraid to tell me yours. I've been witness to lots of strange things in my life." I gave her a few quick eyebrow raises. "You may think I'm the crazy one." I added a sympathetic grin. "Please don't be afraid to talk to me. I have an open mind and it's more open lately than ever. Do you want me to go first?" I asked again, trying to reassure her.

She gave a nervous laugh. Relaxing, she let loose her arms from around her knees and rested herself back against the couch. "Uhm okay, you go first," she said, sounding like a teenage girl ready to play *truth or dare*.

"Okay… you remember the first day we met? You know—the day Mitra spoke the word *Yasmin*." She nodded. "Well… okay, here goes.…" I told her all about my birthmother naming me Yasmin, and how thrown off I was to see this old woman running towards me calling me by my birth name. To top off the weird for her, I added the stuff about the name of the guy who used to live in this house, *Sal,* and how my mother loved butterflies, how everyone called *her* Sal. "Do you think this makes me crazy or what?" I ended, giving her a cheeky grin.

She blinked and stared back at me, and then she blinked some more. Her mouth opened as if to speak, but she closed it again. She leaned forward and took the glass of water in both hands. Bringing it to her mouth, she took a big gulp. Lowering the glass, she said, "My turn now." And set the glass back on the table. "Yasmin is from Old Persia. My grandmother's name is also Persian. Hers means *Angel's Name*. I was told people with this name were known to be excellent at analyzing, understanding, and learning, and my grandmother has always been brilliant." Her face beamed. "She is quite old now, but she knows things—things no one from outside her generation understands. We have always been close, she and I."

I nodded, letting her continue.

"Jadda once told me people with her name were inclined to be mystics… philosophers… scholars, and sometimes teachers. Because she lives so much in her mind, she tends to be quiet and introspective. I find when I present Jadda with an issue, she sees the larger picture, and her private reflection, her analysis of people and the world events, make her seem distant and sometimes even melancholy. When the events of 9/11 occurred, she did not fear as others did. She'd told me, *'They are watching… the balance will be kept'*." Dunya took in a deep breath, letting it out as if liberating a burden.

"Balance, eh? I've heard a lot about the keeping of balance lately. Your words about your grandmother don't come as any surprise—if you can believe it. But… I haven't figured out what it all means, yet." I paused. "Do you think… Mitra was calling me by my birth name after all?"

"Yes," she replied, sitting up and reaching again for the glass. She took another long sip.

"You do?"

"She told me later—that same day, but it was confusing since—well, you don't look Persian." She gave a little laugh. "Earlier today, after we returned inside, she'd said in Arabic, *'The angel is here, Shamsiel is here, and the balance will be kept'*." The words left her in a whisper, and she glanced over her shoulder. She took another sip of water and continued, "She told me the story of Shamsiel—how he was once a Guardian of Eden. In the Book of Enoch, he is referred to as a fallen angel who teaches humans the signs of the sun. He was supposedly the 16th leader of the 20 leaders of the 200 Watchers who fell."

"Watchers—from the Book of Enoch," I confirmed. "I looked it up online before you got here."

"Oh yes, the first section is known as *The Book of the Watchers*," she confirmed. "Enoch received heavenly visions on divine judgment. It tells the story of a rebellion of angels, fallen angels as I mentioned." She stopped, checking I'm sure if I understood the story, and took another sip. "My grandmother thinks Shamsiel was here at your door."

"Whooaahhh—back up. She thinks an angel was at my door?" I gasped and gave my aching head a rub. It didn't help. "What... am I supposed to do with that?"

"See—I knew you would think we were crazy!" She put her palms up to her cheeks.

"C'mon Dunya, the guy was gorgeous, and I would even say heaven-sent, but really... an angel? And even if he waaaas an angel, what was he doing at my door? Okay wait, he was looking for Mitra — why?" I asked, assuming there was a more rational explanation.

She lowered her hands and stared at me for a moment, then said, "Jadda told me an angel is a spiritual, supernatural being found in many religions." Her words were steady as was her conviction. "The nature of angels and the tasks set for them vary in traditions. In Christianity, Judaism and in Islam they often act as messengers from, well... *God*. Sometimes they act as warriors or guards. I'm sure you've heard the term *guardian angel*—it's very popular in modern Western cultures."

Mildly amused, I said, "Dunya, I'm not a religious person—I consider myself more spiritual, open-minded, but I'm not so arrogant to think there isn't something bigger and more powerful than us. The romantic in me loves the idea of angels, but I'm not sure what this all means. Do you?" Before she could answer I said, "I don't *not* believe, I just don't know *what* to believe." I wanted to make sure that part was clear, didn't want her to think I thought she *was* crazy.

"Do you believe any of what I'm telling you?" she questioned back.

"Do you?" I threw right back at her, quicker than I'm sure she thought she'd get.

She drank the last of her water, put the glass down, smiled, and then stood saying nothing. Instead she turned and went towards the door to go. I stood and followed her. She stopped with her hand on the doorknob, then turned back to face me. "I believe... my grandmother believes... and I believe we—you and I, will be great friends... and I also believe someone, or something watches over us." Turning back, she opened the door. Pausing, she glanced back at me again. "May I come over again sometime… to talk… to *hang out*?"

Smiling, I said, "Of course. You are welcome here anytime. I have tons more bizarre stuff to tell you." I warmed at the possibility of a new friendship, then laughed.

"I look forward to it," she replied, smiling so big her left cheek dimpled. Then she turned and went out the door.

I watched as she went down the steps and off across the lawn to her own home, to where Mitra stood on their front porch. Dunya gave me a single wave and then she called to her grandmother, motioning for her to go in. The door shut, and I smiled; for the visit, for the words, and for all the things *not* yet said.

Chapter 19

It was 2:00 p.m. now in Miami, which meant it was 12 noon in Calgary and a perfect time to call Alison.

I got myself comfortable on the couch again and I dialed her number. On the third ring, the call connected. "Spooky, whatcha got?" Alison said, ready for the scoop as usual.

"You… will not… believe… what I'm about to tell you." I replied, slowing the words intentionally for effect.

"Oh man, I love it—what's happened since yesterday?" Her enthusiasm shot through the phone and she gave me her usual Alison giggle, putting me at ease and making me laugh right back.

"Remember Mom's journal—the one she never filled?" It was more a statement than a question, but still I paused for a reaction.

"Uhm yaaaaaa," she squeezed out.

"It wasn't empty after all," I said, pausing, giving her time to have a conniption.

"Get ouuuut—Tell me!" she shot back, begging for more.

I filled the next hour recalling the details from the journal, pausing only to answer her steady stream of questions. She was a free-thinker who *loved* a good plot twist, and just as Luc had done, she focused on all the similarities and coincidences.

"That's some wild stuff, Spook," Alison said, then took in a breath. "But get this—my mother told me a similar story about this *balance* stuff. About four angels, Archangels specifically. Something about them risking their lives in heaven to help keep the balance on Earth. When Mom had told me the story, I'd figured it was the ramblings of a sick woman—because it was right around the time she'd been diagnosed with breast cancer—the first time in 1990. When she'd made it through, I'd asked her about the story again, but she denied ever mentioning it." Pausing she gave a long-drawn-out breath. "Coincidence? Both your mom and my mom tell a similar story—and both sick with cancer?"

She paused again, giving me an opening to say something, anything. I didn't know what to make of it all. These things resembled something made up—like a dream or a fairytale—a nasty fairytale, but just as fantastic. "What about the stuff Louise told me? Mothers and daughters and more about the balance," I finally said. "Three sick women all saying the same things—or at least recalling similar stories. Could it be the illness, the medication? What about this sacrificing of their lives stuff? Mom and Joan both mentioned it? And keeping *what* secret?" I questioned, letting out a "*Huff,*" that faded out to a sigh.

"Reminds me of stories when people have near-death experiences. They all seem to recall the same occurrence—not the same, but similar. Makes you wonder, eh?" Alison added. It had a similar ring to near-death, especially in similarity of retelling, I mentally agreed. "This would make a great mystery novel," she proposed, lightening the mood.

"Oh my God, I forgot to tell you about the man at my door last night—the one looking for my neighbors."

"What man? Wasn't Luc over last night with his doggie? What's with the neighbors—more butterfly talk again?" she joked.

"Ya-ya. Luc and Raven were here. Also forgot to tell you about the lights going out while I was reading the journal—just my house, the rest of the street was still lit," I said, the memory provoking a little shiver.

"Blackout—were ya dying or what? When'd the guy come ta'the door?" she asked, her words distorting as if she had the phone pressed to her face.

"Luckily, my guardians had arrived before the visitor at the door, but we'd been pretty freaked out already from sitting in the dark talking about the journal and the other stuff. Then we get this knock at the door. I should have been more scared, even the dog was growling. But when I opened the door, there was this hot guy standing there. Almost lost the power to speak," I admitted. I tried to hold back a laugh even though Alison was already giggling at me.

"Where was Luc?" she chuckled out.

"Beside me—watching me act like a spaz." I rolled my eyes at myself. "Anyway, the guy says he's looking for the neighbors—the grandmother, actually. He asked to leave a message—a note, since they weren't home." I paused to flip over the big note pad with all the crazy stuff on it.

"What did the note say? Don't leave me hanging—*Hello*—you still there?" Her voice rose through the phone, practically a shout.

"Sorry sorry—trying to find what I wrote about it. He wrote his name—the last name was in Arabic. Dunya told me it said, Shamsiel *Watcher*."

"His name—that's it?" She sounded as disappointed as I had been.

"Did you ever read the Book of Enoch?" I tossed out.

"Pfff, yaaauuh of course," She guffawed, all smarty-pants-avid-reader-like. "Fallen angels, all the different heavens and—oh man, WATCHERS!" she finished with glaring acknowledgment.

"Exactly! And Dunya said her grandmother told her Shamsiel was here—even before I'd given her the note. He's supposed to be one of the leaders of these 200 fallen angels mentioned in the book," I said. "And the old gal thinks this guy was at my door last night—an angel—at my door!" I laughed, but only because I was nervous about her reaction, *plus* the delirium was building in my brain.

My laughter was followed by a long pause from her. Then in a serious voice, she said, "Spook…," She paused again. "Yer freaking me out—I love it!" From serious to complete elation she added, "Spook—I have to write this stuff down."

"Oh, I have it *all* written in a long list of weird—bizarre—uncanny, and creepy. May have to write a book myself," I mused.

"I'd love to read the journal, Lynn. Read me the part you mentioned earlier, about *The Cipher*," she urged. "But first, let me go get something to drink—I'm parched after all this creepiness." Her giggle muffled as if she'd put down the phone.

I leaned way over and grab the journal off the coffee table. I sniffed it again. It still had a strong smell of smoke even after sitting out. I wished it smelled like Mom and not her stupid cigarettes. Near the end of her illness I'd wanted to be closer to her, sit with her on the couch and be near her, but those damn cigarettes were always in the way. I swear she would have slept with one in her hand if we'd have let her. It was comical now how stubborn she could be. Despite being adopted, I'd known where I'd gotten my stubbornness. Leaning back into the couch again, I flipped open the journal scanning for the pages Alison wanted me to read out to her. They were near the end, the ones with the scratchy printing.

"Spook—you there?" I said into the phone, pausing to flip more pages, searching for *my girl Friday*.

"Right here, Spookarela," she garbled, responding through a big gulp of whatever beverage she'd found for herself. "Lay it on me, sister."

Setting it up I said, "It was August 30th, just days before she died." I took in a deep breath and read my mother's words for her. Nearer to the end of the section, I read slower, "*... it'll be a chance meeting that turns into a great friendship. He will be quick to knowledge and problem solving.*"

"Sound like anyone you know—this Cipher person?" Alison asked letting out a long breath. She'd probably been holding it the whole time I'd been reading to her.

"Sounds like... well, it makes me think of Shortcut."

"Your buddy, Derek—from South Carolina?"

"Yup, Derek *Shortcut* Jones." I'd coined the nickname when he'd shown to be the fastest IT trouble shooter I knew. "I told him about the photo of me with the wings. He was all over it—looking stuff up on the internet. Even sent me a link with similar photos." I paused and rubbed the top of my head again. It was still tender. "But seriously, how could Mom be talking about him? I didn't even know him before she had died. Not to mention—it would make all this other stuff real.... could it be real, Spook?" Before she could answer I added, "My mom wasn't into this fantasy/paranormal stuff. Even the books she read were only about realistic things. She believed in God—to what extent I'm not sure. She did love that *footprints in the sand* poem. You know the one?" I posed, knowing she would.

"I love it too. The one about the guy dreaming he's walking on the beach with God—sees footprints in the sand from both of them," she recalled. "Sometimes only seeing one set—the prints representing different times in his life. He asks God why he left him during the hardest times of his life, and God tells him during those terrible times, when there was only one set of prints, God says, *it was then that I carried you.*"

"Oh, I love that last part." I sighed.

"What are you going to do, Lynn?"

"About?" I let the memory of Mom fade.

"All this—this stuff, these stories I guess," Alison said, sounding perplexed and anxious at the same time.

"Am I supposed to do something with all this? I don't even know what it means. I'm starting to think I'm losing my mind. It hasn't even been a year since Mom passed and all this—all these weird stories and coincidences, are making losing her even worse. Reading her journal—reading about her last days, it's agonizing... and now, all the stuff about secrets and angels, keeping what balance. And who are these four women? What does it have to do with me?" I spouted. My energy was drained from all the recapping and rehashing. I imagined a tiny crack forming on my skull from building pressure.

"Have you told Will about all this?" Alison asked, continuing her questions, providing me no answers.

"He's not back until Sunday night. He'd think this was totally nuts anyway." I laughed at the memory of him trying to keep a straight face while I'd relayed what I considered *serious things*. "Plus, I promised Louise I wouldn't say anything about what she'd told me. Without her particular tidbits, the journal would sound like ramblings written by a sick woman, and the others a bunch of coincidences. Not sure what he'd think about all this angel stuff either—might commit me."

"Do you have to tell him—I mean—right away that is?" Alison asked.

"I guess not."

"Are you going to tell anyone else—what about Derek, will you tell him?" she probed, sending out yet another question.

"Hmmm, that would be a tough conversation. I've told you what a skeptic he can be. He would love being called *The Cipher*." I chuckled. "I need to call Vicki. We email daily, but this warrants a phone call. It's hard to email all this without missing something too."

"I would have died trying to make sense of all this in an email. Still struggling to make sense of it now," she added, giving an unexpected giggle. "Gawd, wish I could be there decoding all this. You'll let me know if anything else happens, right? I mean I'm not gonna be able to let this go myself. Oh hey—I'm seeing Dad later today, I'll ask him about the story Mom told me—check if he'd ever heard her talk about it."

"Wish you were here too, Spook. Too many coincidences I'd have to say. So much for a normal day in the new house." I snickered.

Alison took another deep breath. "This would make for an excellent screenplay, a fantastic mystery," she said. Her voice changed to something a little more mischievous. "Thing is… I don't know who done it!" she said adding a big "*Hoot,*" and laughing at her own joke.

I laughed again, grateful for the comical relief. "Let's say when we find out *who done it*, you can write the screen play. That's if I don't end up in the loony-bin in the meantime, yeesh." Throwing that back at her, I ended with, "Love you, Spook. I'll email ya if anything new happens. Stand by."

"Standing by!" she countered. "Love you too."

When I ended the call, I noted the time was just past 7 p.m.. "Sorry," I told my stomach, giving it a gentle rub.

To ease my poor belly past the late dinner, I tossed together a big salad; baby spinach, strawberries and walnuts, goat cheese and leftover grilled chicken with a splash of homemade balsamic vinaigrette—yum, and then I plunked myself back on the couch.

I made ready to send Vicki a quick email as I ate my salad. I wanted to see if she was home first before I tried to call her. Figured I'd lead in with something like, *hey got an interesting story to tell you* or *guess what I found in Mom's journal*, to spark her interest. Vicki was another realist, but if you gave her facts, she could be open-minded, but if you give her hearsay, she'd lose interest fast. I had the facts, but it was the story itself that might leave her in inquiry-mode, and right now—I didn't have any answers. I hit *send* on the email and got up to put my bowl in the dishwasher. Room for just my dish, I closed it up and flipped the switch. "Ahhh background noise in an empty house—gotta love it," I said aloud.

The lights flickered. And my brain flipped into action expectant of another blackout. I grabbed the candles off the kitchen island and darted to the living room to steal a look out the window to see if any of the other houses were being affected, but nothing was amiss.

Across the street I spotted a man facing in the direction of my house. Not just facing my house, but looking at the house, looking my way, at me—*right at me*. I shivered, but a calmness followed. I wasn't afraid, but I should have been with some stranger—some man watching me. I couldn't clearly see his eyes, but I knew he was looking... right... at me. I sensed no threat, felt only serenity, peaceful—abnormally peaceful if there was such a thing. I guess there must be—because I was feeling it, and I couldn't look away. He was beautifully dressed in a white suit. A white suit like... *Shamsiel*—but not Shamsiel. He had to see me looking back at him, but he didn't seem bothered by it. But then his composure suddenly changed to one of shock. Maybe he hadn't known I could see him. The sound of my cell phone rang behind me and I shot a look in its direction. When I glanced back the man was gone. Despite the phone still ringing behind me, I pressed against the window looking up one side of the street and back down the other. *Nothing*. That peacefulness I'd felt was gone too and replaced by irritation from the ringing phone.

I moved back to the couch and exchanged the candles for the phone. Quick glance, it was Vicki. "Hey," I said, walking back over to the window.

"Hola, Chica. Que pasa?" she said, giving me a dose of Spanish.

"You got my email—I take it?" I paused, checking out the *nothing* up and down my street.

"Lynn? You there—what's going on?" she said, with a tinge of alarm.

"I'm here, good-good—nothing... well something... uhm... this guy...."

"What guy—where are you?"

"I'm... at the house... I'm fine." I tried to sound reassuring. I mean I was fine, just a little baffled.

"What guy? Does this have anything to do with this story you have to tell me?"

"Where do I begin?" Always the questions, never the answers.

I hadn't expected an answer, but she gave me one. "Let's try midway through and go backward from there—the beginning of course," Vicki said, bathed in sarcasm. I could always count on Vicki for a good dose of cynicism. "Wait, let me tell you something first before you get into it. I'm taking *Chinese*—yup you bet—adding another language to the pot. What do you think of that?"

"What—you're having Chinese... for dinner?" I'd missed the last part, I was still looking up and down the street and not keeping up with the pace of her dialog.

"No, ya goof—I'm taking Chinese, not eating it."

"That's pretty cool... but isn't it super hard?" I refocused when I found nothing on my street again.

"Ya, but I can do it. You know me, I like a challenge. Besides maybe it will come in handy someday—new job across the waters, or maybe a cruise. William takes care of China, doesn't he?" she finished, slowing her pace.

"Ya-Ya, all of Asia—you could master a whole horde of languages." She could do it too.

"It's a tough one, but the writing part is amazing, nicer characters than the English language." Changing gears as quickly as she speaks, she said, "What's the exclusive on the journal?"

"Well," I said, tucking away my confusion over the disappearing man. Then I dove into everything, same as I had with Alison, telling her about the writing deeper into the journal. Caressing the leather cover of the journal, I recapped its contents again. I explained how Mom's handwriting had changed and how as she had gotten sicker and closer to her death the words seemed distraught. "Her frame of mind had changed too, but I could still hear her voice in the words," I said.

I paused, and Vicki cut in. "Do you think your mom was losing it near the end? I mean, she was a pretty-sharp cookie, but those last few pages sound off—don't you think? I loved your mom because she was such a character, but aren't you wondering, Lynn?" Vicki asked, soft and slow as if trying not to offend.

But I wasn't offended, I'd wondered it myself, and Mom wouldn't have been offended either, she was fond of Vicki. "Well, I told Alison the same thing. I'm not sure what to make of it. It was shocking to find more of her writing. Haven't digested it all yet." I paused. I would save the rest for a face to face, to avoid sounding crazy. "I'll tell you more when I see you, okay… you know me—always the weird stuff." I gave another pause. "Think I'll visit again in September—once I get this house set up. Last visit was too quick. And I'll be by myself next time. I wanna spend more time with friends. Will can enjoy time in the new house by himself."

"More weird Lynn stuff—excellent, can't wait. Hey, don't read too much into the journal. Who knows what really happens to the mind when dealing with your own mortality," she said, supportive despite her skepticism. There was some truth in her assessment of things, and I had to remind myself of that. "You okay, Lynn?"

"Ya, long day is all…," I took an exhausted breath. "… and I hate when Will travels. But he'll be back tomorrow. I'm fine really—weird stuff—big house, I'm fine," I said, finishing, giving her my best *happy* voice. "I'll let you know when I'm coming up for sure though."

"Okay… if you say so. Call me if you—I don't know… sometimes I get wigged-out in my place by myself too. You really should get a dog."

"Was thinking the same thing this morning," I said, smiling, reflecting on my morning conversation with Raven. "Later, Vick."

"Later, Weirdo," she closed off, chuckling as she hung up.

My skeptic, how was she going to react when I told her… *the rest?* A nervous laugh escaped me as I stared at the unpacked moving bins and boxes.

Chapter 20

I'd gotten through the night in the house alone, but I'd had to sleep on the couch again. It wasn't the house freaking me out, in fact I felt safe here, it was just… the man I saw and, well, didn't see. Not that he scared me either… it just left me with a restlessness.

Will's flight was due to arrive anytime. It wouldn't be long before I got the *I've landed* call, and I'd be able to breathe again.

Like clockwork he arrived, I got my call, and I took a proper breath. Less than an hour later he was in our home, and while he told me all about his trip, I pulled dirty laundry from his suitcase. And y hoobk or by crook, he'd found *another* bottle of rum on this journey, one we currently didn't have, adding to our *now* twenty-three bottles of the stuff. Every one of them was different. Not to mention we have seven different types of tequila along with numerous other bottles of booze from around the world. The bottles came from either Will's tour operators bringing them on visits to the Miami office or from Will dragging them back from one of his trips. And just what I needed, another reminder of his trips and time away from our life. Each one a reminder of the places I'd not been able to visit with him.

In an attempt at being the happy supportive housewife, I'd assembled a snazzy bar area to display the more decorative bottles, some bottles were pretty, though most of it I wouldn't touch with a ten-foot-pole. My favorite bottle was from Venice. I'd picked that one up a few years back on my birthday, on one of the few trips I'd been on. The

Grappa came in a small clear teardrop shaped bottle with a red blown glass heart in the center. Venice is all about the glass.

On the lower shelf I found the perfect spot for the new rum, right between two other bottles, one taller and one slightly shorter and stouter. I'd arrange them all by height, having the taller ones in the back, leaving the squattier ones up front. Standing back, I admired my work, but still, I shook my head. For a couple who rarely drank, we sure had a lot of *hooch*.

When I turned around, there was Will, standing right behind me grinning. "What? Not enough selection for ya?" He knew why I was shaking my head, but he darted around me to get a better look at the spoils.

Rolling my eyes, I said, "Well, there's an uneven number of rum bottles now. Way-to-go." The number didn't matter at this point, but I still had to tease him.

"I'm sure I can make it an even number on my next trip," he said, all matter-of-factly.

The words *next trip* rang painfully in my ears. "Please don't. I'm running out of room in the cabinet as it is," I said, opening the doors wide to show him the tight fit. "We need to have a party soon, put it all to good use. Then you can add back to it, okay?" I laughed but was serious about getting rid of some.

Will laughed and continued to poke around in the cabinet trying to recall what was what, where he'd gotten what, or who had given it to him.

When he'd finished his booze-remembrance, I switched the subject. I didn't need more reminders of his travels without me. "I want to go home again in September to see the girls—just me this time," I said.

"You do need more time with your friends," he acknowledged. "September is a busy time for me at work. I wouldn't be able to go anyway. It'll be good for you—time with the girls. I suspect you'll stay at Olivia's, so you can hug Rachel and Katherine ten times a day?"

"You know it," I said, the thought making me smile. "Hey, you never asked me about how myyyyyy weekend went."

"Well, I half expected to see Luc and Raven here when I got home. Figured they were coming to stay for your time alone in the new house?" he said, glancing around at the boxes from Ottawa. "I'm surprised you don't have all those boxes unpacked and everything in its new place. Not like you to leave things undone. What I miss? Did something keep you from your usual super-speedy unpacking?"

I walked over to the boxes, and said, "I unpacked most of the stuff. These are empty except for the Christmas tree box and the decorations. Haven't figured out where to put those yet. No basement, they'll have to go into a spare bedroom closet I imagine." I lifted the closest empty box. "I had hoped you'd take care of the empty ones for me, put them out on recycle day." I gave him an exaggerated *smart-ass* smile. He thought I'd shirked my end of the deal. He grabbed the box from me and gave me the, *you-are-a-smart-ass* look of confirmation. But he was right, sort-of, *something* had kept me from doing it all.

"Give me the scoop—lay it on me. What strange shit happened while I was gone?"

"What makes you think it was *strange shit*?" I scrunched my eyebrows together as if I didn't already know the answer. "Does everything or every story I tell you have to be strange? Normal stuff happens to me too ya know," I protested, putting my hands on my hips to emphasize the empty statement.

He simply kept folding up the cardboard boxes, staring at me with that *ya right* face he gives me when he knows something weirdly *Lynnie* happened.

I stared back now with my hands in the air questioning. He knew full well I'd give in and tell him some of the *strange shit,* but for now I went with something more normal, the parts about cooking the pasta dinner etc., giving him the play-by-play on the events while he broke down the boxes for recycle. Then I went on with the strange, the Angel Movers, through to the stranger at the door asking for the neighbor, my talk with the PI, and ending with the journal having more in it. I'd left out my conversation with Dunya, and about her grandmother's behavior, figuring the journal was weird enough for him.

"First night in the house alone and the lights go out. Could only happen to you, Lynn. Has been a few weird electrical things going on.

I'll have to get someone in to check it. Maybe pick up a generator—hurricanes and all," he said in response to my *softened* version on the list-of-weird. Typical.

"Uhm... no comment on the other happenings or Mom's journal?" I asked.

"I'm a reality guy. Not sure what to make of all that. The world of strange seems to be your thing. What do you think?" he questioned, not expecting an answer.

He was always like this when it came to *my* stuff. Never delving too deep. I'd get the occasional *'cool'* or *'creepy'* comment from him and the conversation would end there, unless I dwelled on things. I'm the one who reads the books on scary things, paranormal things, fantasy stuff. He reads about real history or real people. He watches scary movies with me, but he never gets scared. I have an overactive well-fed imagination, but when stuff happens to you—like it does to me, the imagination gets fed often.

"I told Alison and Vicki. They think it's cool. Alison, of course, thinks it would make a great screenplay. And they both want to read the journal. I told Vicki I'd bring it with me when I visit," I said, trying not to sound put off by his lack of interest.

"Your friends always love your strange stuff, Lynnie. I'm used to the fact weird stuff happens around you, and well—it's part of who you are." He grinned and piled up the last bin, shoving the last flattened box into it. "What do you want me to say? Based on what the PI found, sounds like your birthmom had a touch of the strange too. That must be cool for you, no?"

When I said nothing and just stood there, he walked over and placed his hands on my shoulders. He rubbed them as if to comfort me, but then he ruffled his fingers behind my ears going for the tickle and trying to make me laugh. And I did, always did, couldn't help it. Damn it.

"You take yourself too serious, Lynn. Not everything has a hidden meaning," he said.

Hidden? Took all I had to smile back at him and not to let my mouth gape. Not as though I wanted to point out the obvious, but how could he not wonder about the things I'd told him.

He turned then and went through the kitchen and out to the garage to dispose of the boxes for recycling. Maybe it was best he didn't know how wacky and *real* these things could be. Hell, I didn't know what was real or not myself. Instead of pushing the subject, I went in hunt of space in one of the spare closets for Mom's Christmas tree and ornaments.

* * *

The next few weeks passed by uneventfully and I was partially relieved, though still hoping for more.

Will and I had gone to our jobs as usual and on the weekends, we'd worked together on new home projects. We'd painted the walls, halls, and doorways, put up a ceiling fan in the master bedroom, hung shelves, and put out all the treasures from Will's trips.

And today, last but not least to paint, was the double front doors. The evidence was clear how often someone had *hoofed* the bottom of the door to force its heavy weight open, the wear displaying its desperate need of a new paint job. I stood outside the front doors examining the wear when a familiar sound came from the side of the house.

My sweaty husband came from around the corner, grinning from ear to ear and showing off his new *eco-friendly* lawn-cutting machine. "Hi handsome, nice machine you got there!" I called out, trying to yell over the rumble of the lawn mower. I waved and tried to keep a straight face. He waved back proud as a peacock and continued down the other side of our half-moon shaped driveway.

The August heat was at its worst, so I turned and went back into the house where the A/C pumped away and where I would feel the cold tile floor on my bare feet again. Then I walked from room to room, making a list of things to get on our 50th visit to the hardware store. Stopping in the kitchen, I heard the lawnmower shut off.

Will came through the back door and then opened the fridge, rummaging around for refreshment. I figured it's the reason guys like to do yard work or work in the garage, it gives them an excuse to have a cold one. *"Fffitht,"* came the popping of the beer cap. Will tipped the bottle back and inhaled two thirds of its frosty contents. "Aahhhawwwhh!" he gave me, then grinned.

"I take it you enjoyed your beer, sir?" I grinned back at him, my eyebrows raised for emphasis.

After tipping the bottle back to finish the beer, he said, "Hey we should go to Fairchild. Get those memorial bricks ordered for Mom, Sal, and Kay. What do you think?" He wiped his face with the edge of his sleeve. "I'm not sure how long it'll take to get them. It's Mom's 10th year in August, I'd like to have them put in by then."

He'd must have been thinking about it during his mowing, but I agreed it was time. "We should scout out where to put them," I said, grabbing myself a beer. "What time are they open till?"

"Can you check online while I cool off?" he said, telling me more than asking and heading towards the sliding glass doors to the patio.

"Sure, sure. I'm all over it," I said, but apparently to myself since he was already through the door and out of earshot. And into the pool no doubt. When it comes to water, there is no wading-in for Will. He takes one step off the pool deck and straight in—down he goes. For me, even when the pool is 85 degrees, I have to ease myself in. I truly think he might be *Aquaman*. Not the 1977 *Patrick Duffy Man from Atlantis* version, with the webbed hands and feet, but more like the original, the DC comic, orange and green wetsuit wearing underwater superhero version. I also think if he couldn't be near or in water regularly, he wouldn't be able to breathe.

I stood at the patio door watching him swim for a few seconds before grabbing my laptop off the coffee table. Bringing up an internet browser window I googled *Fairchild*. While the page loaded, I checked my email inbox. As usual there was my *Saturday AM* titled email from Vicki, which would later be followed up by a *Saturday PM* email, and again on Sunday with the same.

Her email read,

> *Hey there, happy weekend!*
> *You said you're coming home soon, right? How soon? Not like I need to see your goofy face, but I'm sure I could tolerate a few visits with my pen pal.*

Hope you don't mind, I told my mom about the journal. Not all the details, but a summary of what your mom wrote. I asked her if she'd ever kept a journal of any kind. When I'd asked her, she'd looked at me as if I had asked her if she'd ever murdered someone. I don't get her sometimes. After a long mouth gaping pause and a head shake, she'd asked, "Do you still have your grandmother's hope chest?" Nice segue, eh? I told her I still have it and I keep blankets in it now. All she'd said was, "Good," and walked back into her kitchen. Sometimes she says the strangest things. It must be an old-age thing. Shoot me if I get that way.

Anyway, let me know when you're planning to come up. Bring the journal with you, would love to see it.

I'm off for my morning bike ride, Later gator
Vicki

If Will was Aquaman, Vicki was *Beryl Burton*. Vicki would live on her bike if it didn't snow back home. She already milked the no-snow season for as long as she could, riding near into November.

Back at the browser window I found the posted times for visiting the garden. I got up then and made my way outside to where Aquaman was finishing what I assumed to be his 100th flip and turn lap of the pool. "Hey, fish-boy. The garden is open 9:30 a.m. to 4:30 p.m., daily," I yelled, when his head popped above the water.

He flipped his goggles to his forehead and gave me a big grin. "Good job!" he said, splashing me. He flipped his goggles back down and continued for his 101st lap.

"Nice!" Ungrateful water-dweller. I went back inside, dried off my legs and got on with my own day. And first thing first, was to write Vicki back.

Hey backatcha,
Day is going well, lots done, yard work, painting and going to try some of that relaxing stuff I hear so much about.

We're going to go order the memorial bricks at Fairchild for the ladies. Remember that amazing garden I told you about? The money we pay for the bricks goes back into the gardens. It helps with the conservation and preservation of cultivated and endangered plants. I'll take photos of where we want to put the bricks, so you can see the beautiful area we choose. We have a good idea where they should go.

The place just had their Annual International Mango Festival. It's really cool. They had the International Chocolate Festival in January, better weather then for that kind of thing. You should come down for it, you being a chocoholic and all.

As for coming home, I'm thinking late August or early September. Need to see what Will's schedule is. And no worries about the journal, I'll bring it with me. Not sure I understand your mom's reaction though. What's this big old wooden trunk/chest? What's the deal, is it worth something?

Okay, talk to you later.

Lynn

Send.

After the trip to the hardware store, Will and I set off to *Fairchild Tropical Botanical Gardens*, as it was just a short ten-minute drive from our new place. We parked and as usual, we headed for the gift shop and main entrance.

The shop was beautiful with tons of gorgeous gifts and keepsakes representing the gardens. At the information desk we showed our pass and obtained our members stickers for walking around the grounds.

"Who do we need to speak to about the memorial path bricks?" Will asked the lady behind the desk.

This volunteer, as many of them were, was in her mid-70s. She had brilliant white close-cut hair, and she grinned as she spoke. Everyone seemed to love working here, and she was no exception. She gave Will the name of the man who orders and puts in the bricks, and a map for the walkway. She told us to mark on the map where we wanted the bricks to go, and then when we were ready, to give this guy a call. Will thanked the woman and then we went on in search of the perfect spot.

"I know a good spot. I remember a nice shady area under a big tree," I said, hurrying along, watching as Will fiddled with his camera. "It's where the path circles the tree. And there's a bench right there."

"The big tree near the start of the path," Will confirmed. "Was thinking of the same spot. Didn't remember there being a bench, but that's cool—perfect."

We wandered the path towards our destination all the while admiring the bricks from so many others. Some of them were in honor of good deeds, some for weddings or births, and others like ours, were in memory of loved ones lost. Then I saw it.

Approaching the tree, I said, "See, I told you there was a bench." I pointed at the shade covered wooden seat. "Find three bricks next to each other, but not touching anyone else's bricks, okay?" I sat on the bench. "Other bricks will get filled in around them, but for now, let's try to find a spot for just them to exist together."

"Got it," he said, waiting for the other people to move on down the path. Then he knelt to examine the bricks in the area.

"There, over to the right. Just before the path merges around the tree, there—see it?" I gestured. From where I was sitting, I could see three blank bricks with nothing around them.

Will moved from his spot to where I was aiming. "Good job. Think that's the spot. Come over and see," he said, waving me over and kneeling down again. "Look. No others touching, and they'll be visible from the bench," he added. "I'll mark the location on the map and reference the other labeled bricks close by. I'd like to be here when the guy puts them in—wouldn't you?"

He glanced up at me probably because I hadn't said a word since pointing the area out. I was staring at the spot, and I knew I was grinning like a fool. Backing up, I took another look from the bench perspective. I nodded and kept smiling. "The perfect bricks, in the perfect spot, under the perfect tree… near the perfect bench," I whispered to the universe.

Later at home, Will called the number he'd been given and left a message about ordering our bricks. The man called back after dinner giving us a fax number to where we could send the names, dates, and any message we wanted to accompany them. Will told him we wanted to be present when the bricks are put in, and the man confirmed it was possible, but would have to be early and done outside garden hours. Will assured the man we would be available anytime that worked for him. After finishing the call, Will faxed the information along with the 'In loving memory' phrase we wanted with each of them.

Then we waited.

Chapter 21

Another week passed and just as the weekend arrived, the brick-guy called, and we had agreed to meet him early Sunday at 8 a.m..

While Will got ready, I sat in the backyard under the shady part created by the big oak tree. The Butterflies too were fond of this perfect spot, but mainly because I had planted *Mona Lavender,* a butterfly plant under and around it. As like friends and family, butterflies and flowers have a symbiotic relationship, depending on each other for survival. Plants give butterflies food and shelter while butterflies pollinate flowering plants. This interdependence is the most important part of the relationship, losing an individual species can have devastating impacts on an entire ecosystem.

Mixed emotion tugged at my heart as I watched the butterflies flutter around. Losing these three women had severely impacted *our* little ecosystem.

"Ready!" Will called from the back door.

"Yup," I called. I bid goodbye to the butterflies and set off for another potentially emotional day.

When we came to the bend just before the entrance I said, "End of July. The bricks arrived in time for Joan's 10ᵗʰ year of remembrance for August. We lost Aunt Kay last August. Mom's birthday is in August. Kind of perfect, eh?" Will grinned, but he knew I carried a heavy weight in my heart. All I could do was nod back at him for fear of bursting into tears.

We stood out front of the now closed gift shop as a man came from around the corner. Like most of the volunteers he appeared to be in his 70s. He approached carrying a shovel in one hand, a box of what I assumed were our bricks in the other. He waved the shovel, and we both waved back.

At reaching us, he leaned the shovel against the wall, brushed his hand on his pants and then extended the hand. "Will and Lynn I presume. I'm Shawn," he said.

"You got it," Will confirmed, cheerfully shaking the man's hand.

On the release, Shawn turned and extended his arm out to the side, motioning us towards the back entrance. He explained that since all the other entrances were closed until 9:30 a.m., we had to head through the back gate.

"We think we've picked a good spot," Will assured him.

"Good-Good," Shawn said as he turned to follow my eager husband. "Shouldn't take long. Glad you two could make it so early too. Gets hot out here fast now that it's summer."

"Oh, I hear ya on that one," Will replied. "The spot's over here under the tree—in the shade."

Shawn followed Will towards our spot while I walked in silence trailing behind them.

When Will stopped at the location, Shawn put down the box next to the area. "Good spot all year round I'd say," Shawn said, seeing the bench and its proximity.

I watched the process from the bench while Will stood to the side as the man pulled the blank bricks out from the path. Then he turned the box towards Will. "Whose first?" Shawn asked.

After taking a review of the bricks, Will handed him the first one, Joan's. Aunt Kay's followed next and then Mom's, ending the process of laying them down in order of first to last lost. With neither one less important than the other, *chronologically* seemed the best way to go. Shawn placed the final brick in its place and used a small brush to sweep the last bit of dirt off the tops, pushing it into the crevices.

When Shawn went to stand back, Will asked for him to stay for a photo, and conveyed how much we appreciated having this time before the opening. Just before it was time to go, Shawn offered to take a photo of Will and I, kneeling by the bricks.

"Lynn—look, butterflies," Will said, giving a little cheer of delight as a few beauties fluttered by.

I smiled for the photos just as one landed on my shoulder. "Think I got it!" Shawn remarked, his joyful smile gleaming. "You folks have a fantastic day," he followed up, handing the camera back to Will. Smiling again, he grabbed the box and the shovel, and was off to continue with his other duties.

For a few moments the butterflies lingered in the shade, but quickly withdrew as the morning visitors came from around the building's main entrance.

"Ready to go, Lynn?" Will asked, reaching for my hand. Again, I nodded and took his hand. "Can you get the photos ready when we get home—so I can send them to the rest of the family?"

"Of course—easy-peazy," I said, a little more chipper, a lot more actually. A lightening of my heart had spread through me when the old guy had taken that picture. Maybe it was the butterflies. When butterflies are around, it's usually the only time my heart doesn't ache when thinking about Mom.

Back at the house, while sitting at the big kitchen island as Will made breakfast, I took the camera's memory card out and slid it into my laptop. My stomach was already growling in response to the smell of fresh bagels toasting. I let the photos load and grabbed a plate to create a bagel masterpiece with cream cheese, smoked salmon, and tomatoes, oh and a few onion slices and capers.

It was magic to my mouth and medicine for my grumbling tummy. "Thanks—I'll clean up since you made all the fix'ns," I said, shoving more bagel into my mouth.

Will gave me a thumbs-up, and then headed out towards the patio doors.

Turning my attention back to the photo gallery loading, I spotted a nice one of Shawn and his shovel. Next were various photos of the path, the bench, and tree, and shots of the bricks at different angles and different distances. The last was the photo of us, and I double-clicked on the thumbnail to get a better look. He'd done it, Shawn had caught the butterfly landing on my shoulder. "Cool," I said to nobody. But who the heck was that in in the background—over my right shoulder?

It was that guy; the same one I'd seen from the living room window. But how could it be? Thought we were the only ones there. I didn't remember seeing anyone else, and there definitely wasn't anyone standing behind us... or had there been? The idea bounced around my brain like a silver ball in a pinball game. I would have seen him—I should have seen him. I had faced that direction the whole time, right up until... I posed for the photo that is. Maybe Will had seen him. What was he doing there? And what had he been doing on my street? I enlarged the photo... no suit this time, just white pants and a white shirt. Another weird coincidence? I enlarged the photo further and realized that the direction the man had been looking wasn't at the camera. He'd been looking at me... smiling... a fabulous smile, to go with his handsome face.

"How are you making out with the photos?" Will said, startling me as he came back through the patio doors.

"Uhm good, good. They're all ready to go." I stared back at the photo again. "I picked out the best of the bunch. But the picture of the two of us... is well—strange." I tried not to sound all suspicious since I hadn't told him about the guy outside our house. "Do you remember anyone being there—other than Shawn?"

"No, it was just us. Why? The garden hadn't even opened yet, remember?"

"Check out the photo." I pointed at the obvious other person in the image. "I didn't see him, but there he is," I said, conveying the facts and not its mysterious nature.

"Couldn't you cut him out? You know—crop the photo or something like that?" Will suggested, clearly missing my point. "He must work there, got caught in the photo when he walked up the path. What's the big deal?"

I stopped right there. I knew full well he'd think I was nuts if I told him my thoughts on the guy, how he was the same one I'd seen watching me from across the road—how he'd disappeared when I turned away for a second. Will would think it was me seeing something in nothing, or my overactive imagination again. Wasn't worth it. And clearly it was of no concern to him since he'd left the kitchen again. I'd keep this one to myself, or at a minimum I'd tell the girls, and Luc… and maybe Derek. Derek would find an explanation and put my mind at ease. If something messed with my mind, Derek could and would find a way to disprove what I saw and keep the crazy away. I hoped.

Pretending to let it go, I sent the photo off to Derek in an email stating the circumstances of the photo and a brief explanation about the man across the street. He could deduce what he wanted from it. Then I uploaded the remaining photos to the printing service at the local drugstore and moved on to my emails.

I read my Sunday AM email from Vicki, then responded by attaching the photo, telling her about the trip to Fairchild and my observations on the guy in it. Next, I sent the photo to Alison, which would surely stir her creative writing juices again. Both Olivia and Mac would need a face to face for all this weird Lynnie stuff, but that would have to wait until my visit. I still had more to tell Vicki too.

Grabbing my notepad, I added this latest oddity to my list of weirdness. I'd take the list with me on my visit to Ottawa. It would help to avoid leaving anything out, and then they could all be as freaked out as I was. Or possibly they'd think it was a bunch of crap or more of the same unexplained stuff that happened to me. Maybe—just maybe, the list would make it seem less… creepy… and more interesting… even *plausible*. For now, what I wanted was to try some of that relaxing I'd heard so much about, and I took my laptop with me to stretch out on the couch. Setting my computer on the coffee table, I assumed the relax posture.

The sound of my email notification, "*Bing*" woke me from my relaxing. When I turned a glace to my computer, there was a sticky-note on the screen from Will.

> *Got a call from work on a legal issue. Have to go to the office to get the files.*
> *I'll be back soon, and I'll bring something yummy for dinner.*
> *Will xo*

Work—seriously? At least he had let me rest, and he would be bringing dinner back. Guilt recovery dinner, but still dinner.

My computer displayed it was 2 p.m., and that there were two new emails waiting for me.

The first was from Vicki,

> Hi Lynn,
>
> Sounds like a great, although emotional, morning. Nice shot of you and Will, but you've got to Photoshop the guy out of the picture. Who stops behind people while they're taking a photo, hello? Great butterfly though, nice catch on the old guy's part.
>
> You think the man in the photo is the same one you saw standing across the street? You said you only saw him for a minute. Funny coincidence maybe? I'm confused, what's this other stuff you wrote about someone looking for your neighbor? And what's with the guys in white clothing? Is there a convention in town or is it a Miami thing, because that would make three guys in white, right? Now if they were in black suits, I might worry. Kidding LOL. Try not to make too much out of it, but also get rid of the extra person in the photo. Cut him out and send him to me, he's hot.
>
> You said you had more to tell me. Keeping me in suspense?
>
> Did you book your flights yet?
>
> Well, I'm off to make something worthy for dinner and have some well-deserved me time with a new book. Later,
>
> Vicki

It made me laugh that she wanted me to cut the guy out and send him to her. She was a single mom, one of my few single friends, and had been raising her ex-husband's son alone since even before the split. Talk about earning your wings. Her son was away at college and she had her place to herself, and it would be a great time for her to meet someone new. *Try not to make too much of this?* she'd written. Wait until I give her the full story on the guy at my door *and* the story Dunya told me.

The second email was from Derek, and his email I was sure would be filled with a complete rejection of anything mysterious. He'd have a calculated explanation to clear this all up for me, but part of me wished for a more entertaining explanation. "Okay Derek, explain away," I said to the computer, clicking to open his email.

> Hey Lynn,

First, you watch way too many sci-fi shows. I love a good fantasy flick myself, but the point is they're fantasy not reality. I must admit strange things do happen around you a lot, but don't let your imagination mess with you.

Second, I love the butterfly, it's a Monarch, like the ones that go north to Canada. They migrate right through Ottawa. Did you know the migration spans the life of three to four generations? Definitely looks female, no black patch of scales on the hind wings, and veins on the wing are narrower too. I enlarged the photo of course. Ever hear of Point Pelee National Park in Ontario, you're from Ontario, right? Yes, I know it's a province—not a city, and it's the size of four states. Anyway, it's just north of the Canada–United States border in Lake Erie. There's a major archeological site there. They think it was occupied between 700 and 900 AD, so kind of cool. They estimated more than 15,000 Monarchs were there last September. The migration depends a lot on weather and is very unpredictable. Luck of the weather—now you see them, now you don't. Well anyway, great photo. Not as cool as the one of you with the wings, but only because some stupid poser got caught in the shot. Did you want help to fix the photo? I can work some magic on it and when I say magic, I mean software effects, not maaagick.

Last, what guy across the street from your house? What does it matter if it's the same guy? Do you live near the gardens? Could he be someone from a local event, maybe a musician? He's holding a long horn. I saw it when I enlarged the photo. Let me know if you want me to do some photo-magic for ya.

Shortcut out

Paranoia deflected — check. I hadn't told him about the guy in the white suit, the one asking for the neighbor, though I should. I guess part of me wants to believe it's *something,* and Derek usually makes me feel like a bonehead when I go the way of the weird. One of these days I'll have the proof of something real and rock his scientific world, the whole *people thought the world was flat* sort of thing.

I sighed. Did I really want this *whatever* to be real? What if it is? It's not up to me to make it real. What if there is a bunch of guys out there in white suits? *What Lynn, conspiring against you or watching you, Watchers?* Right. I gave my head a shake and deviated from my dwelling on things I had no answer to.

I enlarged the photo as Derek had done and examined the mysterious man more thoroughly. Then I closed it, to pull up an internet browser to google the Monarch butterfly. The front door opened as I did, and in walked Will with his *please forgive me for going to work dinner.*

I smiled at him but not because he was home or because he had dinner, but because of the amazing butterflies on my computer screen. Perhaps I would see them… some—one maybe, when I went north to Ottawa. But the migration *and* my trip were still a month away.

Chapter 22

On Monday mornings, 5 a.m. comes way too early when you've been awake most of the night thinking about crazy weird shit.

Will set off for his morning swim practice while I tried for more sleep before getting ready for work. But instead of more rest, my brain was restless with things like these mysterious men in white. I was confident it was only two, not three men as Derek had suggested. The two were different, but they both wore white clothing, both had stunning hair, clean-shaven, and strong yet elegant masculine features. One dark, one fair. The man in the photo had long blond shoulder-length hair with strands of flax around his face. His eyes were blueish grey circled in dark full lashes much like the other man. But what was with the trumpet? I didn't know. What I did know was I'd be calling Spooky later, she'd help keep my brain from exploding.

At work now, sitting behind my desk, I pondered what was coming at the end of the month. After 20 years in the IT world I was looking forward to redirecting myself into something new. What exactly, I didn't know yet. Maybe travelling with Will, capitalizing on exotic trips instead of home watching the *Travel Channel*. At the end of the month I'd be done with work *and* I'd be going to Ottawa to see my friends again.

It was a slow morning, and I was grateful for once because at 11 — 9 a.m. Calgary time, my phone was ringing and knew who'd be calling. Picking up, I whispered, "Spooky."

"Spooky," Alison whispered back on cue. We both laughed—always did, always will, but still can't remember why we called each other that. "What's with these guys in white?" she asked.

Shaking my head as if she could see me, I said, "I have no frig'n idea. Has to be a coincidence, doesn't it?" I took a fast glance out the door of my office to see if anyone could hear my conversation. Coast was clear. "I don't have a clue what's going on, or if any of this is connected. Don't know what to do next."

"You have to admit, it's pretty cool," Alison responded. "Did you tell Derek—what did he say?"

"Ya, I told him—not the part about the Cipher—not yet, but I told him the stuff about seeing the man on the street. I sent him the photo too," I said, sighing a little. "He totally debunked it."

"Of course he debunked it. You only gave him part of the story. Give him the whole thing. Then tell him to debunk it," she said. I imagined her scrunching up her face and crossing her arms over her chest in protest.

"I'll call him later tonight. Can't talk to him about it here—too many ears." I paused, changing to a happier topic. "Gave notice today. Said I'd help find a replacement. Hate the job but I like my boss, and I hate to leave him without a standby."

"Good for you, Spook. You need time off and a new focus. How about writing a mystery?" she said half joking—half not.

"Me, write a book? Have you lost your mind—wait that's me." Both of us laughed again. "I'm gonna go walk to the bookstore—clear my head. I'll let ya know how it goes with Derek—but I'm not telling him about the Cipher stuff yet."

"Cool beans. Later, Spook," she countered.

"Later."

My brain hadn't exploded, but I was sure the inside of my head resembled oatmeal. To save my sanity, I sent Luc a text asking him to join me for a walk and a quick *powwow*. He wrote back saying he needed the latest info on my wacky world, then ten seconds later he rounded the corner by my office.

Once clear of the office building and crossing the walkway to the bookstore, Luc said. "Soooo what's up?" He gave me a shove, knocking me into the wall as if we were fourth graders.

I shoved him back. "Oooh, just your typical Lynnie stuff—strangers at my door—lost journal pages—mysterious men in white—nothing new. You?"

"Ah, is that all? Seriously—what have I missed? Wait—don't tell me. Do I want to know?" he questioned, a little leery of my response.

I laughed, and as we continued to walk, I rolled out the events from the weekend. But unlike my skeptic Derek, Luc went to the same mind space I did—the *creepy* space.

He rubbed his hands together and took in a deep breath as if he were about to hold it for a deep dive or burst into song. Then he said, "Another guy in white—possibly a third guy or the same guy in a white outfit—same as the guy who came to the door? Different guy, right?" he questioned. But I wasn't sure he wanted me to answer.

"Same suit—similar, a different guy for sure. Same guy in the photo as from the street though. Derek thinks it's a coincidence. Told me the guy was holding a horn or a trumpet. Suggested they were musicians or something. But I haven't told him about the guy at the door," I relayed.

Luc cleared his throat, then whispered, "Well... there are these stories." He paused. "...Stories about spirits... and angels—messengers, which I've heard about—from the older Colombians I've met." He glanced over at me.

"Aaaand?" I questioned, giving my arms a wave.

"Well... they mention different accounts—but all the men wear white. And that horn, they call it Gabriel's trumpet. He's the angel who blows the horn to announce Judgment Day."

Confused, I said nothing and kept pace with him as we approached the mall.

"In Abrahamic religions like, Judaism, Christianity, and Islam, Gabriel is believed to be an angel who performs as a messenger from God. In the Gospel of Luke—it's a biblical text." He grinned.

This was our way with religion; he spoke, and I listened and learned. As Luc continued with the theology class, I continued in silence following his steady pace through the walkway, but this had not been the reaction I'd expected from him.

"Gabriel predicted the births of both John the Baptist and Jesus. Catholics refer to him as *Gabriel the Archangel*. He's mentioned in the Qur'an as well, also as a messenger. In biblical verses which refer to him, he always appears as a man. In the book of Daniel—that's a Hebrew text, it talks about a being that resembles a man, but appears as a prophet. It's something about how he gave Daniel the skills to understand visions," Luc said, stopping me in my tracks—literally. He held both my arms at the elbows to keep me from walking further.

We'd talked about religion before, more matter of fact, but the way he was speaking it sounded like he was stating fact—facts he believed. At first all I could do was stare at him, but then I let it out, "Are you shit'n me? After all this weird unexplained stuff—you lay this on me? Archangels? Man, Derek thinks I'm overreacting and you're giving me stats on some angel messenger. Holy crap Luc, seriously?" I broke free of his grip. "Holy crap! Holy Crap!" I shouted, finishing my outburst. I put my hands to my face.

"Holy Crap is right, Lynn!" he shot back at me.

Dropping my hands, I burst into gut-splitting laughter. I was overwhelmed, but I couldn't help it. Luc quickly followed suit. The two of us stood in the middle of the overpass walkway, gutting ourselves. I caught my breath. "Where did you get all this jargon, you got a secret religion database in your head or something? Man!"

"Hey, I may be all shaved head and tatts, but I know my religion, lady. I go to church—and ya, I read about other religions a lot too," he protested, taking in a long breath to control his own laughter.

"You just happened to know the stats on this particular angel? And you think he's the guy in my photo—the guy who was standing across the street—really?" I asked, half believing his words, half losing it, losing it because I might believe his words. "How did you put these guys in white suits together with angels?"

"I see—I'm the crazy one. After all this talk about angels and Watchers, that journal, and now, these two guys in white—one with a horn, and you think my ideas sound crazy?" Pissed-off it seemed, he started again towards the bookstore, without me.

I quickened my pace to catch up to him. "Whoa! Whoa, Luc, I didn't say you were crazy." I cleared my throat trying to release some of my guilt. "You know I believe in all the spiritual stuff, but when it's presented to you—in your face, it sounds crazy. Sometimes I think I am going crazy with all this stuff. What if the journal, is just a journal—full of words written by a sick woman? What if the stories are just stories and the men in white are just men in suits? And well—I do have an overactive imagination."

Luc stopped again and slowly turned to look at me. "What if... they're not just stories... what if they aren't just men? What then?" He sighed, turning again to keep walking.

"I don't know—how could I?" I pleaded, catching up again.

Luc said nothing more, and the two of us continued our walk towards the bookstore... *in silence.*

At the store we split off as usual, Luc to the *sci-fi* and me to the *paranormal romance* area to see the latest delicious novel about vampires, immortals, or whatever. To give Luc time to cool off, I checked out my new favorite authors, *Moning, Gabaldon,* and oh there was a new one out by *JR Ward,* excellent. I'll take that thank-you-very-much. Then I was off to hunt for Luc.

Whipping around the aisle at the end of the sci-fi section I expected to find him sitting on a bench reading the back of some random book. But no Luc. "Magazines," I said to the empty bench. He'd be scoping out music magazines I figured and headed back across the store. I cut through the section for the fitness and cooking magazines, and when I came around the end of the aisle. Nothing—no Luc.

I stepped out onto the main lane checking to see if I could see him walking between sections, but still couldn't find him. Then it dawned on me. *Religious Studies.* The little devil, he'd be in that section trying to find something on angels, something to prove these were not just coincidences. Heading to the far corner of the store I made my way to the back. When I came around the end of the shelves, there he was, on his knees trying to read the spines of the books under the section labeled, *Theology.*

He knew I was there because he turned his head to look at my feet and then up to my face. "What?" Saying nothing else, he went back to reading the spines.

"Been looking all over for you," I threw back, holding in a giggle. "On your knees in the religion section?" I followed with a burst of laughter. It was a bookstore not a library after all—no need to be quiet.

"Shut-up. I know you think I'm nuts, but this is what I believe in— maybe not every word, but there has to be some truth in it, especially if angels are mentioned in all these different religions." He paused and shifted to sit back on the bench. "Tell me you don't think there's a hint of truth here?"

I sat down on the bench next to him and whispered, "Not that I don't believe—I just don't know what the hell is happening around me. I've told you before I believe there's a higher being—presence or deity whatever, associated to our world. What that-it-he-she is—I don't know." I glanced at all the texts lining the religions section. "Or who or what works for this absolute being—I don't know either, okay. But I know I'm kind of losing it here. You're supposed to give me clarity with religion, not attack me with it." Luc had stared up at me mid-rant, but then returned to reading the book titles when I appeared to be done. I let out a loud breath. "Show me," I said, "Teach me… explain it in terms a non-religious-type-person can understand."

"Look, I'll send you a few links to some stuff on the web," he said, turning to look at me again. "You can read it and if you still don't understand something—ask me. But I don't think whatever is happening—whatever *this* is, has anything to do with one specific religion. I'm not saying I know what's happening, just that there might be something big going on here. You are witness to something major, Lynn," he stated. Like a fourth-grader again, he kicked my foot.

"I don't want to go back to work," I whined, redirecting the conversation.

"Me neither."

"I gave notice today?" I said with a little chuckle. Luc knew it was long overdue, both the notice *and* my laughter.

We continued browsing the shelves, taking a few more precious minutes of bookstore refuge, before we set back to work for a few more hours of torture.

At 4 p.m. I passed by his desk before heading out. He still had another hour left of his day, but it was home time for me. "Later, Preacher," I teased, pushing his mouse, causing him to screw up whatever he was working on.

"Nice. Don't call me that... and you're lucky I wasn't working on something important." He pretended to kick me in the shin, keeping in tune with the same little kid routine. "I'll email you the stuff I told you about later, okay?"

I pretended to kick him back. "Ya-ya sure-sure—send away." I laughed again at poor Luc, stuck in detention for another hour. "Later man," I said, flashing him the peace-sign and giving him an innocent grin.

"Later." He shook his head, but still smiled as he returned to his work.

Thirty minutes later, I was pulling into the driveway and scarcely clearing the over-extended branch of the *Bougainvillea* tree. The tree is about 10 by 10 feet and sits just right of the driveway's entrance. It's got huge fuchsia-pinky-purple flowers, but the branches have spiky thorns. Beautiful and dangerous, and probably why I liked it.

I walked through the front door and my tote bag vibrated. Pulling my cell free, I saw it was Will.

"Hi."

"Hey, what are you doing?" he asked, but he knew full well I'd just be getting home.

"Entertaining the queen," I said, using one of my mom's sarcastic responses. "What's up?"

"Don't get mad...," he said. Gotta love a statement that starts with *Don't get mad*.

"What?" I asked, holding in a sigh.

"The boss needs me to finish some stuff before he leaves for Hong Kong tomorrow, so I'll be late coming home. Sorry."

"That's fine." It *was* fine because I wanted time to check out the links Luc was sending me. "Okay call me when you are on your way — drive safe. Love you."

"Okay, love you too — won't be too late."

I changed out of work clothes and into shorts and a t-shirt, then headed back out to the living room to get my laptop. While the thing booted, I got water and the half-eaten bag of pretzels I'd left on the counter from the weekend. Returning, I checked my emails.

The one from Luc had four links with short explanations for each. He'd also written *'sorry for getting all crusty today'*. But we'd both been crusty. I clicked on the first link and it brought up a page with *Religion* as the title. It was education time for me.

As I read, I learned that Islam was the second largest religion in the world after Christianity. It's a monotheistic faith meaning *one God*, originating in the Middle East. The site stated, *Islam embraces many beliefs and practices in common with both Judaism and Christianity. Judaism, Islam and Christianity are known as Abrahamic religions, the history can be traced back to the pledge God made with Abraham in the Hebrew Bible.* Blah blah blah, over my head. I paused and shook my head. Further down on the same page there was an oversimplified table containing similarities and differences of Islam, Judaism, and Christianity. It compared the statistics, origins, history, and beliefs, and was much more my speed.

The second link from Luc's email took me to a web page titled, *Angel*, with the definition; *A supernatural being empowered as a celestial messenger, for divine justice, guidance and/or protection.* It presented the origin of the English word, *angel*, being a combination of the Old English word *engel* and the Old French *angele*. Both stemming from the Latin word *angelus* or Greek *angelos*. It noted the earliest form of the word can be found in something called *Mycenaean, the most ancient form of Greek, a syllabic script pre-dating even the Greek alphabet by several centuries, as early as 17th century BC.* Blah, blah, blah, whatever, my brain is a sponge. The site mentioned how angels are linked to Buddhism, Judaism, Christianity, and Islamic religions and their associated religious texts. And *Non-Abrahamic* traditions such as Zoroastrianism. *What?* In Indian religions, Sikhism and Brahma

Kumaris... again, what? This should have been titled *How to feel like an idiot*. Last it stated, that in Hinduism, even though they are not referred to as angels, mentioned different spirit beings who can regulate karma. "Bring on the good karma," I said out loud, to any potential spirit nearby.

The third link had the term *Names of God* as a title, with its main page explaining about how many religions have names for God, Abrahamic religion or not. And this list was long; Hinduism, Sikhism, Judaism, Christianity, Islam. African Religions, Baha'i Faith, Brahma Kumaris, Jehovah's Witnesses, Mormonism, Japanese religions, and that *Zoroastrianism*, which, based on what I read had 101 names for God. Wowsers.

Fourth and last, was a link reflecting similar to what I'd read about The Watchers, titled, *Sons of God*. The site compared religious text with ancient stories about the existence of angels. Apparently, there are references to *Sons of God* in the Bible, Torah, Koran, Apocrypha, the Dead Sea Scrolls, and in the legends of the Babylonians and Sumerians. The site referenced different portrayals of their existence and meaning.

It was more blah, blah, blah, but what got me was how the same theme repeated in stories and texts, *and* how none of which were related to one another because of different religions, different cultures, and even different parts of the world. In *Genesis*—a word I knew only because of *Star Trek*—not the proper context obviously, there is a reference about how God seemed to be talking to others around him about the *fate of man* and the whole *eating fruit from the Garden of Eden*, and it implied there were other *beings* with him. In the *Book of Ezekiel*, it mentions the *Servants of God*, having human form, but sporting wings. And in the story of the *Sumerians* it told the *flood story* and how mystical beings, who were on the Earth at the time, ascended back up into the sky to avoid drowning. The Ancient Egyptians' creation myths, gives details of a flood story too, stating the *gods climbed back up into heaven* to escape the flood. The Norse and Hebrew stories tell of *The Watcher*.

The similarities continued on and on, and it was no wonder Luc was so adamant about it. God, angels and their existence crossed many religions and cultures, but I had known none of it before. Possibly I had a sense of it, believing it or not, though I knew it had nothing to do with what one religion says over another. "Okay Luc, I get it now," I remarked aloud to him and perhaps to the karma spirits.

Where did this leave me? Maybe I believe something was happening, and it was bigger than my little world. Information keeps coming at me from every direction. I like the stories and religious stuff, but it seems the same story is trying to come through over and over. Am I supposed to know about or understand this stuff, this story about the four women, those men in white, *Angels*?

I noticed then an email from Derek had come in as I'd been surfing the sites, but it was nothing major, just a *'Hey how's it going?'* one-liner. I needed to tell him the full deal about the men in white, the stories from Louise and Mom, and all the crazy stuff going on, but the Cipher idea I'd set that one aside. He may think I'm nuts, *or* he may find the facts required to figure it out. I hoped he might find answers to what the hell was going on. I wrote him back a quick response asking if he had time to talk, saying I had more fantastical stuff to tell him.

A minute later I got an email back from him saying, *'Call me now, I'm just fixing dinner, can't wait.'* Before I could make the call, my phone chimed. It was Will with a text saying he was leaving soon. It would be awhile before Will arrived, so I continued with making the call to Derek.

I did my best to squeeze everything, and I mean ev-er-y-thing — well, practically everything, about the past few months into a 40-minute conversation before Will arrived home and before Derek starved to death trying to eat his own dinner.

Derek had been resistant at first, but as I'd gotten deeper into it, he just listened. Not that he believed, not yet anyway. He had questioned why I hadn't told him everything in the first place. I reminded him he's the man who always needs concrete proof and all the facts. But, now he had the facts and some proof, or at least my account of the facts. He'd said, *"I'll take a metaphysical approach to this."* I wasn't sure what he meant, but I agreed just the same, and I was happy the *weird* cat was out of the bag. Whatever he found couldn't hurt or change what I believed or felt about the events. I did however, have to look up the word, *Metaphysical*. It was the most *unclear* definition I had read today. But basically, it's a branch of philosophy dealing with *being* and how stuff exists, what things *really* are, what it means *to be* something or as anything outside the explanation of practical science. I figured it meant Derek would take a non-scientific approach to this, or at least he would try.

To end my crazy day on a tranquil note, Will walked through the door with *pizza,* and the best thing for lateness.

Pizza and talking with my husband about *his* day was what I needed, *normalcy,* well—if normalcy was keeping something like this from your skeptical husband. Though with all this religious info floating around in my head, I'd be sure to sleep better tonight with a belly full of pizza. And as well, it calmed my racing mind knowing Derek had the info too.

Off to bed, sleepyhead.

Chapter 23

Each day I watched and waited for something weird to happen. But nothing did. I'd been ready for it—something, ready for whatever, but still I got nothing. And as the week continued, so did the nothingness.

Well, right up until Friday after work, when I got home and found *theeeee* email from my disbelieving friend Derek.

It read,

> Hey Lynn,
> I checked into all you told me, and you wouldn't believe the information I found.
> First, I looked at the religion links Luc had sent you. From there I found numerous references relating to what you'd described. I hit on a cool site that lets you search multiple religious texts at the same time for references on an individual topic, and it had more of the same that Luc had told you. Sorry I took so long to get back to you, but you can get lost on the web reading this stuff. You start with one article, it leads you to another and another, but it all loops back to angels.
> There was also info on texts about Apocrypha or Pseudepigrapha. Great words. Apocrypha refers to secret texts of wisdom found in Gnostic and Christian sects. These Pseudepigrapha, or texts of uncertain authenticity, are considered falsely accredited works where the person who wrote them says the words are from someone from the past or ancient times. Apocrypha refers to things like scriptural texts outside of the Biblical. Lots of texts mention 'the flood' and 'angels', but what I found amazing was the consistency of

the same events found in so many cultures and religions, just as you had said.

Did you know there's a theological study of angels, it's called angelology? The term 'angel' covers a variety of concepts of spiritual beings found in many religious traditions. I read a ton of info on Watchers, Men in White, Angels in White, Grigori, not to mention the pages just on Angels and Archangels. I even searched angel sightings and came across a few links which focused on Gabriel and his trumpet. There's a cool story about 'ground zero' too. Also found references to Shamsiel as a Watcher, but no sightings on him. The coolest site I found referencing guys in white was about 'guardians in white'. It read more like a sci-fi type report on what sounded like aliens, it didn't call them aliens, but seemed like that's what they were getting at, unlike the religious references it was a more modern account of the men in white.

However, when I cross-referenced these accounts, they were much like biblical ones, so much so that the implications made the hairs on the back of my neck tingle. Now I don't conclude this as proof of anything, but it's interesting how often the same story and same angel references are mentioned. And the number of sites dedicated to angels, is unreal.

I stopped and rechecked the *from* on the email to make sure this really was the doubter known as Derek Shortcut Jones who had written this information. I was stunned, a bit confused, and maybe even a little happy, but mostly stunned at what I'd read. And there was more...

Unfortunately, I found no references to the story about the four women, death from secrets, or the passing of information from mother to daughter. Not in anything supernatural or spiritual, just lots of mushy stuff about their relationships.

On the big picture of it all, I don't know what to tell you. It sure is some weird shit, but I'd feel better with some scientific proof, especially for what's been happening around you, to prove it's real, I mean. But, I can't prove it's NOT real either.

You know your friend Alison is right; it would make a great book. Keep me posted if anything else happens and if you need to know ANYTHING about Angels, and like you often joke about yourself, 'I'm full of useless information'.

Shortcut out

That… is not… the message I expected to read. But what had I expected? *Proof*? Proof I'm not crazy… or proof that these stories are real? Those were my choices? Real or crazy? Great.

Luc doesn't think I'm crazy, nor did Alison. Vicki might when I tell her the rest, but perhaps not. Mac would love this. Olivia would too, but she'd be weirded-out at first, I'm sure. And like me, Derek doesn't *not* believe—he just doesn't know what it all means… yet.

"Aaahh why *doesn't* he know what it all means?" I said to the surrounding nothingness. "He always knows the answers."

Luc will say something like, *Maybe we don't have to know all the answers?* or perhaps *Why do you need proof?* or something along those lines. Whatever. I forwarded off the email to Luc anyway. He could see what *logical* info Derek had to say.

Alison would want me to fill her in on the latest developments too, or the lack thereof. I hit the speed dial for Spooky.

Two rings. "Friday-Friday my little friend. How goes it, Spooky?" Alison's happy voice pushed through the phone, ending with a kissy noise. "Muwah!"

"Wow, happy much? What's going on there? Did you find a secret stash of fat-free, sugar-free cookie-dough ice-cream that tastes like the real thing? Tell me," I blurted out, laughing along with her. Nothing like a good dose of Spooky-to-Spooky to end my week.

"My due date is April 7th," she said, leaving me with nothing else but a long pause.

"Oh—man I knew it. I knew this time would be it—3rd time's the charm. Fan-f'n-tasktic!" I threw back at her. "When did you hear back?"

"I was supposed to hear twoooo days ago, and I left two veeeerrry nasty messages—don't these people know my hormones are already a mess?" she said, ending in a giggle.

"Tell me more," I laughed.

"Was gonna say—I can't believe you called right after I got the news, but you always know shit—don't you?" She stopped and took a few breaths. "You're the first person I told—well, Ken first—then you." She giggled again.

"Wow—a baby. Oh my gawd—it could be four babies, right?" Happy and excited, it was my turn to take some breaths. They'd been going through fertility treatments and were down to the last four eggs, and *all* had been implanted on the last appointment. This was their last kick-at-the-can so to speak.

"No—shit, sister!" she shouted through the phone. "The ultrasound will tell us more next week. Not sure what to wish for," she said, letting out a huge gasping noise followed by another laugh.

"Ahuuughh, more waiting, eh?" I knew all too well about waiting—not baby stuff, but other stuff.

"Yup. Okay, now you—what's shak'n in your world today?"

"Wait, tell me more about yours." My world could wait, this needed to be about her, and I needed the normalcy of *real* life and its stories.

"Okay," she said, then continued at length about what was next, how she was feeling, and how cute Ken was about everything.

As she went on with the details, I was more than aware of how much I hated being so far away, farther than any of my other friends in Canada. I'd figured she and Ken would come down here to see the new place, but it looked more like we'd be going out there now. Pregnant meant limited travel. But I loved Calgary anyway, and I loved them. They deserved this baby or babies as it may very well be.

"Spook…," she said.

"What Spook?" I asked, puzzled. My face was hurting from all the smiling and laughing.

"Tell me…."

"Tell you what?" My puzzlement turned to confusion.

"What did the Cipher say? Haaahaaaa haaaaauuuhhhh," she said, laughing at throwing out Derek's supposed title.

"Oh, shut-up."

"Okay, no—I'm serious now…" She cleared her throat. "…what did Derek say—did he respond? Please tell me he responded."

"Yup," I managed, "he responded all right."

"What—are you going to make me beat it out of you?" she demanded, giggling louder.

"Let me read you the email, you can make your own assessment," I said, then led her through the email, trying to keep the context of his words relatable, comparing his notes to my own. "So... what do *you*... think of that?" I ended.

"Well...." Alison made a smacking sound with her lips. "Uhm... he seems enthusiastic about the whole thing." She paused. "...Aahh... he'll make a good point of reference if you have questions." Another pause. "Would make a good call-a-friend if you're ever on a gameshow," she added. I could practically hear the grin stretch across her face as she said it.

"Ya, he's enthusiastic all right," I said. "But if he's this Cipher— isn't he supposed to come up with the answers? Or maybe he's not the Cipher. I don't know—am I truly considering he's this helper from Mom's journal? Could this stuff be real?" I glanced at my laptop as if to find inspiration and shook my head. Been a lot of head shaking lately—mainly mine, but maybe it would shake the crazy loose.

"Look, Spook, maybe he needs more clues," she stated, as if sensing my lack of enthusiasm. "You can't put a puzzle together without all the pieces, right?"

"Maybe... maybe you're right... ya you're right—definitely, he just needs more pieces," I assured her, nodding my head like a fool. "But what if there are no more pieces? Nothing's happened all week— what if that's it?"

"You can't possibly think that's it?" She made a huffing sound. "Go about your days like you have been. Stop looking for the clues— or pieces. Go back to living your life the way you always have. Let things just happen. I don't think this is something you can force, whatever it is," she said in her talented *Alison-way*, loving and optimistic.

"You rock, Spook."

"I know." She giggled a little more.

We chatted and laughed some more, then exchanged our *see-ya-laters* and hung up.

There it was. I would live my life as if nothing has, is, or would happen. Things would fall into place, the answers would eventually show themselves, and I would have something for Derek to piece together for answers. Live my life, let things flow. I could do that.

A half hour later, Will was through the door from work, with his cellphone to his ear. He was frowning. Kept saying, "Uhm," and, "ya," a lot. I knew he was talking to his dad, but I couldn't make out much else. After a few moments he ended the call, only to stand there giving me a blank stare.

"What?" I prodded, trying to think happy thoughts, living life, letting things flow, la la la la laaaaaa.

"Louise…." He ran his hand over his face as if trying for a clearer expression, but his disbelief registered. "…has *cancer*…," he said, his voice trailing off.

Louise… cancer… I didn't get it. But there it was when I checked my email again, an update from Louise letting me know what was going on. She'd been diagnosed with Large Cell Carcinoma. The nasty stuff is usually reserved for people having lung cancer. Her lungs were full of fluid, as was her abdomen, and she'd had tubes put in to drain the fluid, but they couldn't find the source, couldn't find a tumor. Her email said they'd been testing her for weeks now, but she hadn't said she'd been sick. They have her starting treatment in a week, but they needed her to build her strength up first. The doctors are expecting she'll need twelve treatments, so a full year of chemo was ahead. They told her they would shoot for six treatments and then reassess before moving forward from there *if possible*.

It wasn't a very promising situation as this bastard is one of the deadliest cancers, and with a high rate of recurrence. How could she have gotten cancer with her super clean life? It would be like a vampire getting skin cancer—impossible. But what I was realizing now, was anything is possible.

After trying to digest the information Louise had sent, I wrote her back telling her I'd be home in the next few weeks, no quick visit this time, but also no Will this time. Having no reason to wait, I booked my flight home for the end of August. Done.

I composed a second email to send to Luc, telling him the horrible news.

I didn't understand cancer, the human body… *life*. Stuff like this shouldn't happen to good people. Louise was another butterfly in my ecosystem… and I've lost too many butterflies already.

My cell phone rang. It was Luc.

"Hey, Preacher."

"Hey, Lynn. Shitty news. How ya doing?" His voice was sad and hushed.

"Not so good. I figured I'd be coasting a while before I got any more bad news—at least this type of news." I spoke quietly, trying not to disturb Will, who was doing work on his computer in the kitchen. I moved out of the kitchen and headed off to my bedroom.

"Uhm… yer going to think I'm crazy," Luc said.

"That would make two of us. What?" I asked, sitting down on the bed.

"Now let me get this part straight first—okay?" He cleared his throat. "Louise is your friend from Ottawa, right—the one who lives next door to Will's Dad?"

"Yup."

"Uhm… she's the one who has you over for dinner whenever you stay at Will's Dad's place, right?"

"Yes. What?" His questions were making me anxious. I was confused enough about everything as it was.

"I'm getting there—wanted to make sure I had the right person." He paused. "And she's the same one who told you the story about Will's mom?"

"Yes, the same person—point please." I had one nerve left, and he was dangling from it.

He cleared his throat again, and I had a feeling the *crazy* was next. "The one where Will's mom said, *You can't tell anyone I told you… sharing the secret will make you sick?*" Luc said.

His slow recall of words made me suck in air and hold my breath. "I… didn't think… about that," I said, letting the words out with my breath. "I always aligned the story to the mothers and daughter stuff, and how she kept trying to get Will and me together. Both she and Mom mentioned the same thing about *sharing* the secret. How did you even remember that?" My head was reeling. How could I have forgotten it? Of all the messages trying to come through—this part, I didn't want to be true.

"That—and the other weird shit you've told me, kind of stuck with me. I know it sounds out there, but do you think she could be sick because she told you the story?" he asked. There was a hint of uneasiness in his voice, not about the facts, but more in relaying them.

"Gawd, I hope *she* doesn't think so. Makes you wonder if there aren't more secrets out there being told—more and more people getting sick and for no good reason. Cancer sort of works like that, eh? You expect someone who smokes two packs a day to get something, but when someone who lives a super healthy lifestyle, gets cancer— you have to wonder how the hell it happens," I considered. It made my brain and my heart ache.

"It's scary shit, Lynn. I'm really sorry about your friend. Maybe you shouldn't visit her. What if talking about this makes her worse?" he said, giving way to a hint of panic.

"I can't not go see her, and I *won't* be bringing this up. She's got way more important things to deal with—like stupid chemo, losing her hair and puking up her favorite foods for the next six months." Saying the words out loud made me sick, made my head pound and my chest tighten.

"I know." He let out a long-muffled moan.

"If any of this is true—any of it, I have to see her. Especially if there is a chance we could lose her!" I was angry now, pissed, fuming at the whole goddamn mess.

"Okay—Okay Lynn," he said, his voice lifting slightly. "I didn't mean to upset you—made me think is all... and wonder. Could be just one of those things—random things that happen to people—good people." His voice softened as if realizing his own emotions.

"Sorry—this stuff is getting to me... sorry," I said, feeling guilty now for shouting. "Look, I know what you're saying, and well, at this point who knows what's possible. But I don't want to think about it, okay?" I took another long shuddering breath to calm myself.

"You're going home in a couple weeks—you'll feel better once you see your friends. But I'm here if you need to talk though, about anything."

"Ya… thanks, Luc. I'll see you at work Monday."

"Later," he whispered, ending the call.

* * *

I'd gotten through the next two weeks with no *bizzaro-world* episodes and I'd tried my best not to think too hard about anything otherworldly. I'd stopped looking on the web for answers as well. But what had helped best, were the updates from Louise's end saying she was feeling a bit better, she'd started treatment, that her sons were home with her for this first part of her journey, and that she was surrounded by those who loved her. She was a tough cookie, if anyone could beat this, she could.

Friday had been my final day at work, *forever*—well at this job. The gang had surprised me with a farewell breakfast, homemade and brought in by the girls—thank heavens, and not by my guy friends. Computers were their thing, not cooking. It had been more emotional than I'd expected too. I'd had to hold back tears more than a few times, but the dumb comments from the guys helped keep the tears back. I was definitely *not* going to miss the place—but I'd miss the camaraderie and the faces of my friends.

Saturday night, I'd packed for my trip while watching Will pack for his. He wouldn't be leaving until Monday, but since we'd gotten suitcases out, he'd happily packed along with me. *"You're off to Taiwan and I'm off to glamorous Ottawa, the world is clearly off balance,"* I'd stated, admiring the pile of clothes that awaited being stuffed into my bag.

"Your trip will be better than mine—you'll be with your friends. I'll be journeying with strangers, eating weird food—and once again not understanding the language," he'd pointed out, trying to comfort me. "And now that you're done with work—we'll have more time to travel together. Go—have fun on this trip. We'll plan something when you get back."

"It'll be good I know… I just hate when you travel. It'll be the first time we're away at the same time—but not together," I'd said, whining a teensy bit.

I'd put the journal aside last night to pack as well, but this morning I chose instead to carry it in my tote for today's travels.

At 8 a.m., we pulled into the airport. Then we did our usual hug and rock we do when we don't want to see the other's sad face. "I'm only gone for a short time. I'll be home before you even get back. Don't worry about anything, okay," Will whispered into my ear.

I gave a muffled, "Okay," as I nuzzled into his shoulder, trying to memorize his scent.

Two kisses and an, "*I love you,*" later, my rolling suitcase and I were off into the airport crowd.

Chapter 24

Angel of Grief Sculpture – Sunday, September 16th, 2001,
Protestant Cemetery, Rome

Vretil admired the figure of the kneeling angel. He touched its outstretched hand as if to stir it from its rest. The statue was a depiction of no angel in particular, but with this angel's position and bowed head, Vretil sympathized with the sentiment of the pose. *Kneeling from exhaustion,* Vretil assumed. He wondered what the angel had been thinking, what had caused him to collapse with such sorrow before his image was cast in stone. "I know you're there, Uriel," Vretil acknowledged, in a voice louder than was typical of him.

Uriel stepped up next to his longtime friend and brethren, then said. "Why are we here? Why did you ask me to meet you at this place—here, far away from the others, far away from where we should be?"

Vretil continued to gaze at the statue. "I think the book is missing," he stated, not answering Uriel's queries. "My Charge went to see Michael's Charge, but I don't know why. It was before she moved out West to be with her daughter. Though the book was not among her things."

"Does Michael know—not where the book is, but that she made contact, I mean?" Uriel asked, glancing at the statue of the grief-stricken angel.

Vretil turned to look at Uriel. Once again not responding to his friend's query, he said, "It's been 70 generations. They had all worried about this *Y2K business* on the millennium, but what they should have been worrying about was the stroke of midnight for this past new year's, 2001, not 2000."

"I'm not sure what will happen now that Shamsiel and the other leaders can have influence over their descendants. Can you imagine, all this time—watching over people like *Hitler, Pol Pot, Saddam Hussein,* or *Idi Amin, Genghis Kahn, Mengele,* and not being able to interfere, only watch? I know not all of whom they watched were bad, such as *Siddhartha Gautama, Gandhi,* the *Supreme Buddha* some call him. You know him, short-guy-no pants, glasses." Uriel laughed a little at his own words. "There's also the *14th Dalai Lama,* a man with no motives other than world peace. *Mother Theresa* is another, thin lady—petite… and *Michelangelo.* And we mustn't forget *Thomas Alva Edison,*" he conveyed, turning back to admire the statue.

Bothered, Vretil shook his head at how easily Uriel could make light of things. "We both know the flood didn't eliminate the 200 or their offspring, not all of them anyway," Vretil said, his voice rising. "And since they are no longer bound—what's to keep them from becoming involved now. What if their involvements are harmful? What if they have encouraged bad behavior out of spite for having been held down for so long? Look at this year so far; 300 elderly Bosnian Muslims were beaten and stoned by Serb nationalists at the reconstruction ceremony of the Ferhadija mosque in Banja Luka, Bosnia."

"What is your point?" Uriel questioned, turning back to his friend.

With more frustration surging, Vretil said, "The victims weren't soldiers, they were old people!" He sighed. "In June, there was the Nepalese royal massacre. The Crown Prince of Nepal, prince-what's-his-name, *Dipendra,* killed his father the King. He killed his mother and other members of the royal family, then shot himself. I can't bear to think about any of the other incidences."

Desperate to ease his friend's sorrow and anxiety, Uriel said, "Vretil, my friend, *Arch of Karma*, you are the wisest of all. As record keeper, you know karma is the universal law of cause and effect, and that the path and the way they walk upon that path has an impact not only on themselves but also on the environment around them."

"Exactly my point," Uriel replied. "What about the natural disasters that have happened. That 7.6 magnitude earthquake hit El Salvador, 800 people are dead, and thousands are now homeless. The earthquake in Gujarat, India, it killed more than 12,000 people. Another, a 6.6 hit El Salvador again, killing at least 400, and Peru had a 7.9 earthquake. And you know that's not the end." He crossed his arms over his chest trying to get a hold of his anger. "These obstacles and challenges they encounter on their journey are supposed to help teach lessons of compassion and love. How am I supposed to guide and instruct them—show them, that what they give, eventually they receive—good or bad? How are they supposed to deal with these things?" His voice faded as he turned away from Uriel to face the statue. Reaching out, he touched the statue's hand again. "Why wasn't Shamsiel or one of the other leaders watching Bin Laden?" he blurted.

"Oh Vretil, he was… he just wasn't watching the man's followers," he empathized. "I sense something else has happened—what is it? Has something happened to your Charge?"

Vretil's arms tightened across his chest and he let out a long exhale. "Not my Charge—her mother."

"Thought you believed things were fine since the *first* book incident, and the bout with breast cancer that followed?" Uriel questioned.

Vretil grimaced. "That was a close one. She'd taken the book out from where she'd hidden it—to look at it I guess, but she'd left it out unprotected. That act had brought on her cancer. When she'd been sick from the chemo, she'd started to tell her daughter about the balance. Her daughter had asked her more about it when she was better, but she'd denied ever mentioning it. I figured that little slip-up had put the fear of… well… *death* in her." Grimacing again, he took in a breath to go on. "I'm afraid her actions from the past and whatever she's done now with the book have caused her more harm."

"Please my friend—tell me what's happened." Uriel was growing impatient. "Is this why we're here—the book?"

Looking away, he said, "The chemo and radiation has caused her Type 2 diabetes. She's developed this *fibromyalgia* thing too, and by the time she moved to be with her daughter, she'd already shown signs of COPD." Pained, Vretil placed the palms of his hands against his face.

"Do you think she's done something with the book—something that has caused these illnesses?" he asked, grasping his friend's arm.

Pulling free of Uriel's hands, Vretil said, "She's showing signs of dementia now too—and I sense she's scared, but... I don't know what she did with the book. She may have told someone where it is, but I fear she may lose her memory before her daughter knows her role. The book may be lost... forever." Vretil turned back again to his friend. He knew his faced resembled that of someone who had not slept in weeks. "What Uriel?" he asked, when he caught a glimmer of hope flash in his friend's eyes.

"Well...," Uriel pondered, "...if the Watchers are no longer bound—do you know what this means?" He grinned. "Neither are we!"

Acknowledgment softened Vretil's worried face. "Clever, *Arch of Peace, Harmony, and Balance*. Very clever."

Chapter 25

At 12 noon, my carry-on and I rolled off the plane. Direct flights were the best, and to my delight, I was through immigration and through the baggage claim area in record time, and I headed for the main doors.

A dark swipe of something moving, caught my attention, and I turned towards the far corner of the walkway near the exit. When I tried to focus on whatever had dashed by, there was nothing in my view of the area. Then the back of my neck tingled, each tiny hair along my hairline rose as though a cold breeze had brushed across it. There'd been no air movement inside the building and no person rushing past to create it. What the...?

Nausea struck me so hard I doubled over. Clutching at my stomach, sweat beaded on my forehead as I tried to drag my luggage towards the exit and the fresh air. Then I saw it—*him*. A large man dressed all in black. Dark hair and eyes matched with an equally dark goatee that surrounded a grin from right out of a nightmare, like a hungry wolf who'd been starved for months. Handsome yet evil, the man stood flush against the far wall near the sliding doors to the outside. And he stared in my direction. No, not in my direction—right at me.

I stopped and brushed the edge of my sleeve over my forehead. When I glanced back towards the dark figure—he was gone. And just like that, the overwhelming need to toss my cookies was also gone.

Again, what the...? I straightened then and pushed through the revolving door, moving quickly to the fresh air.

I was relieved to find the smiling faces of Olivia and her daughters waiting for me. I shrugged off the sickly sensations, along with any thoughts of that unnerving smile the stranger had given me. Wiping my forehead again, I rolled my luggage towards my happy greeters.

After hugging Olivia first, I moved on to the closest *cherub*. "What's happened to you girls? You've both grown a foot since I saw you last." I hugged the second angel-face, and then I wrapped an arm around each of them as we walked.

"They're even taller than their Mom," Olivia noted. "Get going you two. Your father is circling the pickup area waiting for us."

The two broke free of my clutches and took off to find their dad. I put my arm around Olivia, and we watched as the two girls flagged down the family car.

"I'm sure he'll slow down, so we can jump in when the doors swing open," I yelled to them. The girls smiled back at me knowing their dad would curse if we took too long and made him circle more than once. When a residual shiver travelled the length of my spine, I took a quick glance back over my shoulder. *Nothing*, but still my senses were on high alert.

"We'll be lucky if he slows at all," Olivia joked, laughing hugging me tighter, and pulling back my attention.

The drive from the airport had its usual entertainment with, *"Daaad don't drive so fast."* and, *"Daaad turn up the music."* And Mike's, *"Giiirls, your mother is trying to talk"* with me wedged between the two little—now big, pixies. But I relished the normalcy of the family banter and the comedy of the family dynamic. This was where I needed to be. And all thoughts of the strange encounter at the airport had vanished by the time we reached the house.

Mike dragged my bag out of the car and up to the spare bedroom, while Olivia and I went to the kitchen for—what else, *wine*.

"Soooo?" she questioned, "I can tell you have stuff on your mind — what gives?" She was giving me the *tell-your-mother-the-truth* expression she typically reserved for her girls.

"You mean besides the fact I already told you I had stuff to tell you?" I giggled. But she had me.

"Don't you get smart with meeee—missy," she countered. "Let's have it." She took a long sip of her wine and crossed her arms over her chest holding firm to her glass *and* her fervor.

She was such the mother, and I loved her for it, but I wasn't ready to spill yet. "Can it wait until after lunch? When the rest of the gang is off doing their thing?"

"Well… all right. Mike's taking the girls to riding later and they'll be there all afternoon," she assured me, "But don't make me wait any longer than that." She cocked her head towards the noise of the family in the other room, then gave me a sideways glance followed by a little smirk.

"I promise—I'll give ya the whole deal once we're alone." I gave her my best sneaky face, darting my eyes back and forth. I took a suspicious peek over my shoulder for effect. Then changing the subject, I asked, "What's for lunch, Mom?" I bumped her ribs with my elbow.

"Mike and the girls already ate. They wanted to get going after we picked you up, but weeee are having leftover lasagna from last night. Shhhh—they think it's all gone." Her voice trailed off to a whisper as she peeked around the side of the kitchen, checking to see if anyone was coming.

As expected, the girls came through the kitchen for their *goodbye kisses* before taking off to the barn. Next to being with their mom, the barn with all the beautiful horses, was one of their favorite places to be. And less than five minutes after we heard the garage door close, Olivia had the secret stash of lasagna out of its hiding place, and into the microwave for a reheat.

Two minutes later, we were savoring man-size portions, along with our afternoon wine. Not our normal time for a glass of wine, but it worked. Especially when you didn't have to be anywhere other than right where you were. Not knowing how to start the *weird Lynnie stuff* conversation, I asked, "So what's new?" Still avoiding a little, I chewed the last mouthful of my lunch.

"I'm back at the NICU," she tossed out.

"Uhm… what?" Was all I could manage, that and scrunching my eyebrows together in confusion.

"At the hospital. I got a job at the children's hospital neonatal intensive care unit. I had enough of the regular office. It's fulltime — better pay. I'm happier there too, but it's a longer drive to this location." She followed her statement with a long *sigh*.

"I'm glad… it's a better fit," I assured her. "Any other news you've left out?"

She shook her head. "Your turn." Smiling slyly, she sipped her wine again.

I put my fork down and picked up my half-full glass of wine and took a long sip. "Well, let me think where to start…."

Olivia reached over for the bottle and topped up our glasses. "Sounds like this is going to be a *long* story."

"You have no idea." I took another sip of my now *full* glass. "You know how weird stuff happens to me — around me, right?"

"That's an understatement." She rolled her eyes and took another sip of her wine.

"And you know how my mom had that journal, right? Well…," I said. "Did I tell you about the Angel Movers?" She shook her head *no*, and I led in with the details about movers instead of the journal. I continued on to the stranger at the door and to all the other angel — watcher weirdness. Then I asked, "Did your mom keep a journal?"

Olivia didn't respond, she just stared at me. One sip, two, and then a *third* — more like a gulp, almost finishing her wine. Taking a breath, she said, "I have to say… I have not come across anything in Mum's things. I still have her roll-top desk to go through, but Lynn — what the bajeezes?" She took another sip.

I laughed — couldn't help it, considering the absurdity of the information I had conveyed. "There's more…." I paused, giving her ample time to react as I knew she would.

"More? *Christ!*" she belted out, almost spitting out her wine. She stood from her seat, then crossed the kitchen to grab another bottle. "This is going to be a two-bottle story I can tell." Laughing, she topped up my glass with the remainder, and then opened the second bottle.

"How about we go sit on the couch—get more comfortable for this... saga?"

I nodded, and we moved to the living room. I rested onto the big couch while Olivia took her favorite chair facing out towards the backyard. Settled, I said, "You know the guy I just mentioned—the one who came to the door for the neighbor?" I took a small sip.

"Right, forgot all about him—not." She snorted. "The angel guy Shhhammy—watcher, 200 angels—think I got it, go on," she prompted, tipping back her glass again.

"Well, the next morning after he came to the door...," I started, carrying through to tell her about the man across the street and in the photo at the garden. I went on further telling her everything, the journal, the PI's stuff, all about Luc and his take on things, and about the stuff Derek had found. I explained Alison already knew everything, and that Vicki had most of the story, but I still hadn't told Mac. "Still haven't told Derek about the whole Cipher thing—not ready to lay it on him yet. Plus, it's more of a hunch than fact, and him—well—he likes facts," I reminded her, as she sat quietly, her stare intense.

Blink-blink went her big blue eyes... sip... blink, and sip again. She pressed her lips together creating a tight line with her mouth... then the head nodding started. She pushed her lips out in a sort of *fish mouth*, followed by a deep breath in, stopping the head nods. And then when I figured she might speak, she let out the breath, and then took another sip of wine. And the head nodding started again.

"Liv... say something...." Pleading with her, I sat up in my seat. "You have to say something." I laughed the words out still nervous for her response.

She took another deep breath in and out, then took another sip of her wine. "You know...," she said, before taking a second sip. "You know how I always say the two blue jays in the backyard are Mum and Nan?"

"Ya, I love that."

"Well, I say it because my Nan told me a story about the blue jays—about how they are watching over the daughters of mothers." She followed with more of the head nodding, but faster this time. "She told me the daughters of mothers had to keep the balance and the birds would watch over them. It was a little story she used to tell me—to make me feel better, safe." She took another sip of her nearly empty wine glass. "It's not as huge as the stories you were told—but you have to admit the similarities are uncanny," she finished, taking the last sip of wine, which thankfully stopped the nodding.

I took another sip of wine. We both stared out the big living room window, watching the blue jays... watching them—watching us.

Oliva said very little the rest of the evening, and definitely nothing on anything I'd shared with her. She may have been in shock, I thought and felt it better to let the topic go for now. We'd finished the second bottle of wine and were tidying up the kitchen when Mike and the girls arrived home. After a quick update for their mom, the girls went off to clean up and get ready for bed. Mike had gone off to his office to do whatever.

"Time for me to get ready for bed," I said, tucking the dish towel through the handle of the dishwasher.

"Me too," Olivia responded, placing the rinsed-out wine bottles in the recycle bin.

"Night-night," I said, leaving the kitchen, checking over my shoulder and making sure Olivia was okay. She was wiping down the counter for the third time. It was typical of her. I wasn't sure she was truly okay, but I left her to her cleaning routine.

I was sitting on the bed with my latest paranormal novel in hand, when Olivia came into my bedroom, already in her pajamas and slippers. Shutting the door behind her, she then climbed up beside me like a little kid. Staring at me, she crossed her legs Indian-style, and then started with the head-bobbing thing again.

"What's with all the up and down with the head thing, Liv? You trying to shake up all this info, so it makes sense?" I asked, smacking the side of her arm with my book.

"Yup," she replied, still nodding.

"Okay—stop. I'm pretty sure I can hear your brain rattling in there now," I smacked her arm again lightly. "You must have questions—comments, or possibly even *answers*?" I said, shrugging and putting my book on the side table. Reaching down, I grabbed the journal from my purse and handed it to her.

She stared at the journal for a second and slowly she put both hands around it like it was fragile. Then she flipped through the pages. After skimming the last page of messy printing, she said, "Well, that's everything right? You told me all of it—I mean even the stuff you figured would flip me out? Because you gotta know I am flipping out, right? It's cool and all, but it's really-really bizarre—you know that, right? I'm not sure what to do with it all. My first thought was—*ya right*—but your face went all serious, and I knew in my gut this was something—something possibly real—but totally out there." She patted the journal. "What are you going to do? Are you supposed to do something? How are you supposed to know what to do—or if there's even something to do, I mean?" she said, rambling off in a tangent, ready to go over the edge.

The floodgates were open, I thought, grabbing her shoulders with both hands. I gave her a good shake to stop her. "I don't have any answers, Liv. All I have is a bunch of questions and stuff—weird stuff and a major gut feeling that something is happening, something big. Too many things are connected. Too many things can't be coincidence. Right now, I'm moving forward letting things unfold, waiting to see when and if anything else happens, or leads me to more information. I wanted you to know what was happening. I didn't mean for it to mess with your head. Telling you—is just better. This way if more happens, I can easily fill you in—without having to relay the back story, right?" I said, finishing my own little rant. I let go of her shoulders.

She smiled, took a deep breath, then reached out and hugged me. Letting go, she got off the bed, and she said, "Promise me, that you will tell me everything—even if you think I'll lose it." She placed a hand on the doorknob.

"Promise," I said, smiling, trying to assure her. "Night, Liv."

"Night. Deep breath in… exhale… deep breath in… exhale," she said out loud as she retreated from the room. And as if leaving the room of a sleeping baby she shut the door without a sound.

I didn't bother with trying to read my book, I couldn't focus. Instead I lay in bed thinking about the two blue jays in the yard, watching over. It reminded me of the butterflies in my yard and it gave me some peace, as my mind and body… finally… dozed… off.

Chapter 26

In the morning the gang was up with a clatter, running around readying themselves for work and school. I sauntered down in my pajamas, poured myself some coffee, and stood back to watch all the coordinated chaos. Hugs all round, Olivia was out the door first, Mike next, and then the girls.

Aware that Olivia had to work most of the week, Vicki had taken today off to hang with me, *babysitting* me for the day. She'd be coming to get me around 11 a.m., so I could take my time getting ready.

Today was *Vicki and Lynn* Day, and like always, she was punctual, arriving at 11 a.m. on the nose. On the drive I did my best to fill her in on the remaining stuff I hadn't shared yet.

Vicki's a rational person, so I'd gotten a lot of, *"okay,"* type responses from her, but when I'd finished, she'd given me a similar but shorter version of the confusion-rant Olivia had given me the night before. "I should have told you sooner. Hard to explain in email. You and I rarely get on the phone considering we chat so much via email," I explained.

"Ya, it's cool. It's a lot to digest," she said as she pulled into her parking spot.

"I have something to show you when we get up to your place." I grinned.

Inside, we did our typical exchange of ideas about life and all its challenges. And while Vicki created something wonderfully healthy for our lunches, I placed Mom's journal on the dining room table next to her laptop.

Vicki came in and placed my lunch in front of me. Before even putting her plate down, she stopped and turned to look at me and smiled. "Is that it?" Slowly, she eased into her seat, still staring at the journal, plate still in her hand.

"That's it," I said. I knew she would enjoy reviewing Mom's words.

She picked up the book and gave it a little sniff. "I can still smell the smoke on it from her cigarettes." She crinkled her nose.

"Ya, I put dryer-sheets between some pages hoping the smoky smell would go away. It's not near as bad as when I first got it."

Just then her home phone rang. She grabbed the cordless from the side shelf next to the table, and said, "It's my mom—just a sec." She put up her index finger, then answered the call.

"Hi, Mom...."

"Yes, Mom...."

"No, Mom... Lynn's here."

"Yes, Mom—for a while this time... she brought her mom's journal, the one I told you about."

"The trunk?"

"I told you I still had the trunk, why, what...?"

"Okay, Mom...." Putting her hand over the phone, she said, "She wants to know if you'll come visit while you're here."

"Tell her, *Yes, Mom.*" I rolled my eyes, laughing at their dialog.

"Yes, Mom, she'll come by and say hi...."

"Okay, I'll talk to you later... Bye, Mom." She hung up and put the phone back in the cradle. "What is with her and that trunk?" she threw out, chuckling a little.

"Show me—show me the trunk," I said. My senses were a tingle, I needed to see this illusive item.

"After lunch," she said.

I agreed, but my tingle-meter was in red alert.

Vicki flipped through the journal as we ate, and I watched her as she savored the words. Having savored my *meal* too quickly, I went into the kitchen for seconds. When I came out, Vicki was gone. I set my plate on the table, glancing around the small apartment. I moved forward when an urging sensation directed me towards the back of the apartment.

There I found Vicki standing in her bedroom, staring down at something against the wall. Stepping through the bedroom doorway, I realized what it was... *the trunk*. "That the infamous trunk?" I snickered.

"What is it with her and this trunk?" she said again. "I mean it's just an old wooden chest. Well, it's the hope chest, my maternal grandfather made for my grandma. There's nothing special about it—he wasn't primarily a carpenter," she confirmed, bending to open the lid. "I store blankets in it now—see."

"Well, take the blankets out—let's have a look. Arrr," I responded, using a lame pirate imitation.

Vicki rolled her eyes and let out a cackle.

As we lifted blankets out, my fingers tingled, my palms prickled adding to my already active spidy-senses. When the last quilt was out, it revealed a large but expectedly plain interior.

"Seeee, I told you, nothing," Vicki confirmed.

Kneeling, I rubbed my hands inside along the bottom and against the walls. "Seems shorter on the inside—don't you think?" I said, knocking each side with my knuckles. "You hear that... the hollow sound?" On each end, there were shallow two-inch cubbies for smaller items. I tapped on the top of each end, a hollow sound came again but only from the one side.

Vicki knelt beside me and knocked as I had done. "Hollow?"

"Hold on, I have an idea," I said dashing out of the room. Returning with my cell phone, I quickly texted Derek, asking him about this type of chest and if it had hidden compartments. This would be like a game for him. He wouldn't ask why, at least not right away.

A minute later came his response, he wrote,

Is it a seaman's chest?

I wrote back explaining that it was a hope chest, big like a seaman's chest, and sounded like there was a hollow part.

A second text came requesting a photo. I sent one, and we waited patiently for my faithful troubleshooter.

Two minutes later he wrote back.

The right side has a hidden compartment.

"There's a hidden compartment," I said, putting my phone down beside the trunk. Then I tried moving the inner wall, but nothing budged.

"Maybe there's a latch," Vicki said, checking the bottom, only to find it was as smooth as the sides.

Texting again, I told Derek we couldn't find how to open it.

When his next response arrived, I read it aloud. "Pull out the tiny divider piece... in the small shelf like area... then push the interior wall of the shelf towards the open area of the trunk." Vicki performed the instructions as I read them, pulling out the divider piece and pushing the shelf inward. As she finished pushing the inside panel over, my phone rang in my hand. "It's Derek?" I said, more a question than a statement.

I hit answer, but before I could even say hello, he said, "Shortcut here. You guys on a pirate ship?" His voice shot through the phone full of laughter.

"It's a map!" Vicki yelled. "There's a freak'n map in this old freak'n chest!"

"Did she say map—you guys arrrrre on a pirate ship, aren't you?" he said, this time more serious, but still laughing.

"No, ya bonehead, it's an old trunk in Vicki's bedroom—no pirate ship. Really—Derek, a pirate ship?" It was my turn to laugh.

"What are you guys doing? Seriously, maps and old trunks," he asked before I could explain further, laughing even harder now.

"It's nothing major," I told him, and that I hoped he could help—and he did. End of story.

"Alright, contact me if you need another mystery solved," he ended, hanging up.

"He's loving this—is all," I said when Vicki gave me a curious look. Switching up, I said, "Whatcha got?"

She flattened out the paper on the floor in front of both of us. We sat staring at it saying nothing. Her phone rang again, and up she got, running from the room to get it. I followed.

Answering it without looking to see who it was, she said, "Hello!"

"Mom...?"

"What's the deal with the trunk?"

"I'm not shouting...."

"Don't change the subject...."

"Mom... we found a map in the trunk...."

"No, Mom... an old map...."

"In a secret compartment...."

"In the trunk... Mom!"

"Tell me about the map...."

"You can't pretend you don't know...."

"You asked meee about the trunk...."

"I'm not trying to be rude, Mom...."

"Fine. Go make Dad his lunch... I'm not done talking about this... Mom?" She pulled the phone away from her ear to look at it and then looked at me. "She hung up on me."

Bringing the phone with us this time, we returned and plunked back down on the floor.

I spit out a laugh. "What was that all about?" I prodded, flipping the map over to check out the other side. Vicki and her mom always had this *interesting* back and forth to their conversations.

"She's acting like she doesn't know what I'm talking about. Like she doesn't know what trunk I mean. She kept trying to change the subject—the woman called me, didn't even tell me what she was calling about." Vicki stared at the map. She blew out a breath and tried to refocus on the find. "Map looks old, not pirate ship old, but still old. Says *Ottawa* on the back." she pointed out. She turned the map back over. "It's a map for the old streetcar."

"What's the big deal? Why would someone want to hide a map of that?" I scrunched my face in question.

"Hell, if I know—wait. Mom told me that when she first came to Ottawa, the streetcar ran as far as Britannia Bay—it's Britannia *Beach* now. She told me she used to go there in the summers to swim and that it had a big family picnic area," Vicki recalled.

"What's the writing here, in the lower left-hand corner?" I pointed at the scribbles.

"Mom's handwriting." Vicki read the words aloud, "'*I had to hide it somewhere, so I chose here.*'"

"Hide what?" I asked, bringing the map closer to read.

Vicki snatched the map from my hands and stood. "Let's go!"

"Go where?"

"Here." Holding up the map, she pointed at the words *Britannia Bay*. She turned and headed out of the bedroom, and I followed again. Grabbing her keys and purse off the side shelf, she started for the door. "You coming or what?" she called, looking back quick to see if I was with her. I grabbed my tote and was off after her before she could close the door and lock me in.

"Treasure hunt!" I called, racing down the three flights of her apartment building to the car. "Holy crap, lady, wait up would ya." I managed to get in the car before she pulled away.

She drove out of the parking area and up the road towards Britannia. As I examined the map more closely, she sped around the corner heading south to the water. "Easy there *Andretti*! Let's make it alive... watch those turns. Or do you want me to throw-up in your car?"

"I'm going to kill her you know." The car tilted as she took another sharp turn.

"Who? Your mom... not before you kill us—slooooow down!" I hollered, gripping the *holy-shit* handle as we went around the corner that led onto Britannia Road. She slowed when the sign for the Britannia Bay Yacht Club came into view. Then she turned onto the final stretch and drove to the end.

I pointed out the main clubhouse, the dock area, and a smaller building that resembled an info booth as Vicki searched for a parking space. When she found a good one, she pulled in.

She shut off the ignition and then turned in her seat towards me. "Okay, did you find anything else on the map?" she asked

"You mean all that valuable intel I got while reading the map during the wild drive over here?" I said, displaying my *you've got to be kidding I almost threw up* look.

"Give me that," she demanded jokingly, grabbing the map. "What's this?" Pointing, she indicated a tiny symbol on the map. It was a box with an X through it. "That has to be it."

"It what... has to be it because what—X marks the spot?" I laughed out. "Hold on, I'll text Derek on this one—hold up."

My text read,

Yo, Shortcut... need help.

Obviously, he couldn't resist because in less than thirty seconds, he wrote back.

Shortcut here, what's my mission? LOL

I grinned even though I knew he'd be off on the pirate idea again, but I wrote back.

Map, symbol, square box with an X in the middle, what is it?

Another thirty seconds later he had the answer, and again I read it aloud. "He wrote, '*Too easy... it's not a box with an X... it's a diamond with a cross. You really do think you're pirates. LOL it's a symbol for a historical site.*'" Both of us glanced around, panning the area. "You see anything resembling a historical site?" I asked.

"There!" Vicki announced. "The information booth—we'll ask there." She shot out of the car but at least this time she didn't run.

The two of us walked to the far corner of the property to the little white hut with the lovely blue nautical sign that read *Grounds Keeper – Information*. Stepping up, Vicki asked the old guy behind the booth if there were any historical sites on the grounds.

He pointed to the old bell set up right near the water. "That's all that's left," he said, though his grin seemed to say more, mischievous like a child with a secret.

We thanked the man and continued our quest over to the bell.

The yard-tall bell hung off a large metal frame, supported by an old wooden base. The base rose about two feet and was surrounded by overgrown grass.

"Maybe that's not it. Any other symbols on the map?" Vicki inquired, a bit discouraged.

The hairs on my arms tingled as though a frosty wind had passed over my skin. "This has to be it. I know it… but don't ask me how, Vick—I just do."

"Okay—Okay, I get the whole feeling thing. Let's peek around—but remember this is all that's left of whatever was here," Vicki said.

I bent to examine the wooden base. "More wood—maybe more secrets?" I gave her a couple eyebrow raises and turned back to examine the base.

"Whatever," Vicki said, focusing back on the map.

I poked at the old wooden frame and traced a hand over the sign plate. My hands prickled again. "Plaque says, *'Here she stands to watch over us'*. The date reads *1937*. The building—or whatever, must have been demolished shortly before. Based on the date, the bell was like this even before your mom had come here," I concluded.

"Could it be it wasn't my mother—perhaps my grandmother? It was *her* chest," Vicki proposed. Still unconvinced, Vicki moved from the bell to wander along the water's edge.

Not giving up, I moved my hands along the back of the base. There was a ridge there, nothing big, about two inches from the bottom. I ran my finger along the ridge to where it ended, a few inches shy of a foot. I slipped my forefinger into it. When I pulled it out, a wedge of rotted wood came with it, crumbling as I pulled it free. "Oh my gawd, Vicki, look!" I yelled, giving her a wave-over.

She rushed over and dropped to her knees. "What, an old piece of wood?" She picked it up, and it fell apart even more.

"Noooo, look—It's another hidden space." I bent down closer to the opening, my face at grass-level. "There's something in there," I said. Reaching in carefully, I grabbed on to a solid something. I eased it out, hoping *it* wouldn't fall apart like the wood had. Sitting up with it now, I turned to show Vicki. It was a long narrow box with a ship painted on its lid.

She took the box and turned it over several times. "It's definitely hollow, but where's the stupid opening?" she cried in frustration.

"Hold on—let me text Derek again." I laughed. I knew he'd howl when he read this next message, but still I believed we had something here.

> *No pirates, just a wooden box 9 x 2 x 2 with a ship on it with big*
> *white & red sails. Can't find how to open it.*

Not as if he were sitting around waiting for a puzzle to solve, but his response seemed to take longer this time.

"Anything yet?" Vick asked.

"Nothing… wait—incoming," I shouted, feeling the vibration of the text. "Here we go, instructions. I read—you follow." Refocusing on the text again, I read, "'*Okay, you're going to have to call later and tell me what the hell this is all about. Sorry for the long text, but here goes. It's a pencil box, I believe*'." I smiled at Vicki, and continued, "*The ship picture is most likely what they call marquetry work.*"

"Whatever?" Vicki shot out.

"Hold on… '*To open it, look for a finger notch on top to slide it back*' there Vick—right there, the worn area," I said, pointing at the obvious wear spot. "Wait—don't pull it back all the way, he says, '*slide the top back about two inches, the top of the box needs to swivel to the right.*' There's a lower compartment," I ended, laughing at his playfulness, he'd ended the text with, '*SC out*'.

Finishing the steps, Vicky swiveled the top of the box open and we both peered in.

There was another folded piece of paper inside it. Vicki lifted it out handing me the box, then she unfolded the paper. It had a rough edge along one side as if torn from a note pad. Vicky turned the page upright and read. She let out a small gasp and stared at me.

"What?"

"This handwriting—I recognize it… it's my mother's," she said, continuing to stare at me.

"Whadsit-say, what… does… it… saaaay," I pleaded. My heart pounded in my chest because I knew it was something, *big*.

Looking down again, Vicki spread the paper out wider. She took in a deep breath, letting it out slow as she smoothed the edges. After a few moments, she looked up at me.

"Go on—read it out. What is it—a love letter?" I prodded, but she only stared at me. "It is—isn't it?" I grinned.

"Nope." Saying nothing else, Vicki handed me the letter.

I took the paper and scanned it. It had a rough looking symbol—star shaped, in the upper left-hand corner near the beginning of what I viewed as hurried handwriting. I took my turn to read it fully.

> *To my daughter,*
>
> *Last night a beautiful man approached me in the park near the house. He was in a white suit, and he called himself Michael. His voice put me at ease. I listened to this man, and I believed everything he told me. He told me to write this down and hide it, in hopes you would be directed to this place, and find what you needed to know to keep the balance.*
>
> *The balance must be kept by the four, The Sorceress, The Healer, The Scribe and The Linguist. It must be handed down from mother to daughter, although the message cannot be passed freely, as the daughter must seek out the knowledge, find the message, and then and only then, can she ask the mother for the truth. All other roads lead to illness or death.*
>
> *I only knew the description of one, but I have no name. She is of Irish descent and from an original line. She grew up on a farm, but later lived across the water with the men who fly. She and her mate met there while dancing, and it was there she lost a baby. She has existed with her mate longer than her time alone.*
>
> *She's a mother of four children, two boys and two girls. She is a great listener, a fantastic baker, mother, homemaker, and caretaker. Though she has her share of emotions and trials, she functions more at a universal level than at a personal one. This means her sadness is not just from her personal vested concern, but also the suffering of nature and humankind around her. She possesses deep faith in the elements of nature and therefore has an aura for psychic clarity allowing a pure connection with the Goddess. Her spirit unites with air through meditation and determination, and she may have been born with some or all of these aptitudes. She is the Sorceress, The Witch, and she holds the Grimoire of Nature, the Tree of Life will be in plain sight.*
>
> *This is all I have to share with you. I pray you find this message in time.*

"WHOOOAAA?" I shouted, my head shooting up. Vicki was still looking at me, but her expression held more intensity. I was sure my eyes bulged with that same intensity.

"No—shit, Lynn," she threw back at me. "You know we'll be paying my mother a little visit now." That intensity of hers shifted to something more like suspicion.

At the second she made her comments, a *repulsive* premonition flared in me, the kind I get when I *shouldn't* do something, but I couldn't tell her I was having one over the idea of ambushing her mother. "First, I think we need to go over everything—I mean everything I've put in my list-of-weird, then add this new stuff." I held up the letter. "Can you hold off grilling your mom for a day or two?" I asked, trying to appeal to her calmer side.

"I hate when you're right, Lynn. *If* I went over there right now, demanding answers she might deny everything. But the letter says I can come to her, now that I found this—this whatever."

"I know—just give it a few days. Give us a few days to get what we know in order, well—some kind of order," I pleaded, looking the letter over again. "It must have been put here a long time ago, so you need to make sure she's ready to tell you." We needed to take more time with this, I needed more time.

"Aren't you curious—you of all people, with all the fantastic things you've already been told—shown? Don't you want answers?" Vicki asked as she got up and turned to head back to the car. I followed, keeping up with her quick pace.

"Of course I do—but if this is something real—really real, I want to understand all of it. I want to know who these four are, what your mom has to do with all this—not to mention why I'm even involved."

"I have to admit, besides the fact that this is absolutely out there—it really is fun," she roared, grabbing my arm and pulling me along to the car.

Back at the apartment, Vicki asked, "Can you leave the journal, so I can read everything?" She played with the zipper of her cycling jacket like she didn't know what to do with her hands.

"Ya that's why I brought it. Let me make some quick notes on the letter for my list first. This way you can keep them both for your *analysis*," I said, half-teasing, half-serious.

Before the two of us headed out the door again, she said, "Here!" and tossed me a bag full of cookies. "Healthy cookies for the girls—but don't tell them they're *good for you*, they won't eat them. They taste like something wickedly bad for you—but without the calories." She winked. "Oh, you can have some too."

Gripping the bag like it was filled with treasure, I followed her down the three flights again and out to the car. "Olivia will love you for this—these—them—the cookie bootie, arrrr," I said, keeping with the theme of the treasure hunt. Vicki rolled her eyes at me again and we got in the car.

We did our best to talk about other things, but we kept falling back to the conversation of today's quest. When we pulled into Liv's driveway, Vicki put the car in park. Turning towards each other, we gave up one of those front-seat-awkward hugs. Laughing, I reached back over the seat and grabbed my little bag of goodies and then got out. I gave her a quick wave and shut the car door. She gave a *honk-honk* as she pulled away. I waved again and headed to the front door. I was grateful how easily my friends accepted the bizarre, the strange, the weird and wacky—the out-of-this-world of *me*. Just wish I could.

Dinner at The Whites played out as usual, Mike cooked, and Olivia cleaned up. Olivia does some cooking, but she seems to be more the cleanup-person in the family. The girls take their turns washing dishes and hate every minute, but from what I could see, it was a well-oiled machine. I've tried to help, but Olivia rarely lets me do much.

After dinner, the family members went their own ways, Mike to the TV and his laptop, while the girls went to their bedrooms for homework, making it a perfect time to catch Olivia up on the day's events.

The two of us hauled baskets of clean laundry from the basement to the second floor. Then as we folded the laundry on her bed, I brought her up to speed. "Vicki will wait to talk to her mother," I told her, "Until I get this stuff better organized. You just can't go at Claudette with guns blazing if you want answers."

"My mom would have been the same. I don't think that generation does well with the ambush approach," Olivia noted. "The four? What do you make of that? Sorceress—Witch, Healer, Scribe and… Linguist, right?"

"Give me a second?" I put down the socks I was trying to match, then I left to get the list from my room. Returning, I flipped open the notepad, and said, "Something... somethiiiiing Mom wrote—there—from the journal. Cathy's mom mentions *The Witch,* and Sorceress, but I guess they're sort of the same thing, like Mage or Sorcerer, but the other titles are the same. The journal has some similarities to the letter. The letter also mentions a man—the one who came to her, similar to what my birthmother described."

Olivia shook her head and started with the head nodding again, but this time it was more like she'd remembered something. "Didn't Louise say something like that about Joan's story... *that a man came to her?"* Head still nodding.

"Yes—oh geez, I'm gonna have to organize all this into comparable facts like Luc suggested. I wonder if it's the same man." I skimmed the list.

"Could be different men," Olivia added, folding the last t-shirt from the load.

As she moved from room to room dropping off clothes and towels, I followed her to their intended targets. Heading back towards her room I asked, "Do you remember your mom saying anything remotely like this before she died." I was curious about the *secret* and *illness* parts of the stories, it seemed they were shared during a sickness or a person's last days.

Olivia stopped in the hallway, the empty laundry basket still in her arms. I swore I smelled wood burning, like her brain struck a match to her memories. "Only thing I can remember," she began, "was how adamant Mum was about me getting Nan's roll-top desk." Olivia continued to her bedroom. "The woman's dying, and she was more concerned with a desk. I'd wanted to have it before she'd even mentioned it—but she knew that. My sister wouldn't care about something like an old desk. So there was no doubt I'd get it. But still, I didn't understand her sense of urgency." I trailed in behind her as she strolled back into her room.

"Nothing in that desk I assume?" I asked, desperate for something.

"Nah, I've been through it from top to bottom. Mostly paperwork and a few knick-knacks of Nan's."

"I know I'm reaching, but you never know—can't ignore any avenue." I turned and headed back to my room.

"I'm with ya on that one. Hey, what's on for tomorrow—more treasure hunting?"

"Today was Vicky and Lynn Day. Tomorrow is *Mac and Lynn Day*," I called back from my room.

"I know you're staying here with me, but when is *Olivia and Lynn Day?*" she asked, standing in my doorway, lower lip pushed out in a fake pout.

"Hey—you know they have to babysit me while you're at work. You're off Wednesday so Wednesday is *our* day!"

Her pout changed to a smile. "Perfect. Now go get some sleep, detective." She put her hands on her hips giving me her best *mom's in charge* routine.

"Yes Ma'am," I threw back at her as I slowly shut the door.

Chapter 27

Sitting at the kitchen table, I witnessed the same dance as performed the morning before, this time Mike was out the door first, then a repeat of the hugs from the girls before they set off for school.

I carried my coffee with me as I walked Olivia to the front door. "Keep me in the loop," Olivia said, heading out the door, and setting off for her day.

"Of course," I said, through a sip of my morning coffee, waving to her from the front door.

Unlike Vicki, Mac was, well, a little less organized. And as expected, the minivan swung into the laneway at 10:15 a.m., fifteen minutes past our scheduled pickup. Not surprising though, she has a household to keep, two small boys to run after, not to mention she runs a business from her home, *and* she's taking on those homeopathy courses. I didn't care she was late, I was thrilled to see her big grin through the van window. She gave me the *hurry-up* honk, like I was the one who should get a move on. Funny-girl.

"Hold your horses," I shouted, using one of my mother's familiar sayings. I locked the front door and ran to climb into the passenger side of the van.

"Where to, Magoo?" Mac asked, still grinning.

"Aren't we going over to see yer mom this morning?" I asked, noting the first thing on our to-do list.

"Visit Monica—check," she said. With a, "Weeeeehh," sound of delight, she pulled out of the drive.

Mothers and daughters sure can be a funny twosome, I reflected. One minute fighting and the next minute laughing and hugging, usually followed by some crying and more laughing, and Mackenzie and Monica were no exception. Mac and I have known each other since long before we grew *boobs,* and despite the fact that Mrs. M. was an amazing cook and baker, visits with her are always enjoyable, and she always had a good story to share with us.

"What time is it?" Mac asked, "Forgot my watch." She gave me a big toothy grin.

"Ten-twenty-five." I grinned back, knowing she rarely wore one.

"Nice," she said, giving the van a little more gas.

"Why?" I asked, turning to face her while she drove, noticing she was smiling bigger than usual.

Cutting a quick glance my way, she said, "Ms. Monica will be making something super-stupendous at this very moment and I'm sure it will be piping hot and gooey by the time we get there." She punched the gas a second time.

"Hey, slow down. I have something to tell you and I want it all out before we get to yer mom's."

She slowed the van and said, "Holy shit, Lynnie—what's up? You never want to pass on Mom's food."

"I still don't, but... I have some wild stuff to tell you. I think you should pull over to the gas station," I added, pointing to the station's opening in the road. She conceded, turning in as I had suggested, but I'm sure only because I had my serious face on. It was probably best not to be in motion for what I had to tell her.

Parked, she turned towards me. "Okay, lay it on me."

To make this last info session easier on me, well—on both of us, I reached into my purse for my list-of-weird. I'd taken time last night to arrange the events in chronological order and connect the similarities. I smiled at her first to reassure her it wasn't something awful and then took a deep breath. "We've known each other a loooong time, Mac... and you have an open mind and heart, but the stuff I'm gonna tell you... it will seem reeeeally out there." Mac waited as I took another deep breath. "I've already told Alison, Vicki and Olivia, and I wanted to tell you face to face. That way you knew I was serious." I paused a few seconds for her to get ready.

"Yer not going to tell me you're moving to France or something are you? Because Miami is way too far already," she shot out.

"Noooo, I'm not moving." No one understood the distance more than I did.

"Okay, go ahead," she said, wriggling a little in her seat.

For the next twenty minutes, I gave her the full deal, pointing out all the similarities, coincidences or whatever, as I went. She sat quietly gawking back at me, and like Liv had, she did a few head nods, and even a few mouth and facial contortions, but she kept quiet and let me get it all out. When I finished, I handed her the list.

She took a quick scan of my notes and then closed the notepad. "Now what?" she asked.

"I must be getting better at the telling because you questioned none of it," I said, relieved yet mildly puzzled.

"It's out there for sure, but when does weird stuff *not* happen in your life?" Giving me a couple blink-blinks of her big brown eyes, she went on. "Okay-okay, I have to admit this is major weird—and I'm not saying I'm not in what-the-fak-mode, but you know me—my mind's waaaaay open for this stuff. Way open," she finished, turning forward again in her seat. "How's about we go get some Monica-munchies, and talk about it more after—good?" She handed me back the list and got the minivan moving again. I figured this was her try at assuring me she didn't think I was nuts.

Arriving, we found a visitor's spot out front of her parents' garden-home. Fred, Mac's dad, already had the door swung open, letting their two little dogs out after us.

"Weeeeeell, look what the dogs dragged in," Fred joked, as we slid passed him through the front door. "Moooniiicaaa, the girls are heeeere!" he called out to his wife, before calling after the dogs.

"She's in the kitchen I take it?" I said, smiling at him. And already knowing the answer, I ran up the stairs to the kitchen following the amazing smell of what I assumed were cinnamon rolls.

As I hit the top of the stairs, I saw her through the open kitchen doorway. She turned, already sporting a big grin. "Oeewwww look at you. Come give me a hug. Are you hungry?" she asked even before ending the hug. Funny, *Are you hungry* was almost always the first thing out of her mouth when friends visited. She was always cooking or baking something, and she seemed to get pleasure from feeding everyone. This was another hard thing about being far away… *no Monica food.*

"No way—those look gross," I said, faking a grimace and pointing at the cinnamon rolls. "What is that horrible smell?" She made a cranky face and swatted me on the butt. "Aaaahhh Mum, like Mac says—I'm a walking stomach, feed me—feed me," I pleaded, trying to affirm my love for her, *and* her cooking.

"Forget it," she said, giving me another swat with the dishtowel. "Out you go… at least until they cool."

I scooted out the door and into the living room where Mac sat looking amused by our behavior. "Where's Fred?" I asked, looking over the banister and down the stairs.

"He's off on errands. Mom gave him a list of things to get at the grocery store and such. He always runs into someone he knows, so he'll be gone for a while," she said. "And not as though he needs another cinnamon bun." She winked at me, holding in a laugh.

Monica came out of the kitchen, this time without her apron, carrying her always-present cup of tea, and followed by her little poodle. She and the dog settled into her favorite spot near the window. The other little dog had found a spot stretched out on the couch next to my thigh, squirming like he couldn't get close enough. But that was fine by me, it made me feel good.

"Lynn, how are things," Monica asked, sipping her tea gingerly as if testing the temperature.

"Tell her about the journal," Mac prompted, eyebrows raising up and down.

I turned and gave Mac the face—the *what-do-you-mean-tell-her-about-the-journal* face—but too late.

"What journal?" Monica enquired, this time taking a generous sip of her tea.

I gave in and shared the info, only because Mac would want to hear Monica's perspective on it. I told her how I'd thought it only had the one line of writing, but that there was more. I told her about my birthmom and even the stuff about the four women being mentioned. She said little, only let out a few gasps when I mentioned the four. It was only when I was done that she spoke.

"Well, Lynn that's an interesting story," she said. Then she quickly rose from her chair and headed back to the kitchen, so fast that she knocked the poor little dog off the chair. Mac and I looked at each other, both making a *WTF* face. Then we both got up and went to the kitchen.

"Mom… what's up?" Mac asked, as if we'd missed something in the conversation.

"Did I say something to upset you, Mrs. M?" I asked fearing I had, wanting to fix it.

"No…. Nooo… I have to tend to these cinnamon rolls that's all." She kept her back to us as she leaned over and picked up the spoon she'd been using to ice the rolls. "Mackenzie, do you still have your great-great-grandmother's cookbook?" she asked, changing the subject.

Possibly my hunger was getting the best of me—or then again maybe not, but that sensation was back again, the same tickling I'd felt at Vicki's about the trunk.

"It's on the shelf in my kitchen with all the other cookbooks I don't use," Mac scoffed, giving me a baffled look.

Monica turned and handed me the dripping spoon. "I'm going to go lie down for a bit. I think all this baking has tuckered me out. Excuse me girls." She turned to leave the kitchen. "Oh, Lynn—please take some cinnamon rolls with you." Her voice had a dazed quality, and her expression was blank as she left the kitchen.

"Sure… thank you," I said, worried watching as she left the kitchen.

"Okee-dokee then, I guess we're out of here," Mac prompted. "Grab a few of those rolls would ya."

Still puzzled, I packed a dozen rolls in an already waiting plastic container Monica had set out for us. Then we headed out the door and back over to Mac's place.

"Do you think I did something to upset her?" I asked Mac as she drove.

She gave her head a tilt and a shake. "Lynn—I don't know what that was. She's getting older, and she tires easier now, but you know she's never like that with you. She'd sit and talk with you for hours if you let her." She frowned. "But why was she asking me about that old—and I mean *old,* cookbook?"

"She's always cooking—maybe she wants to borrow it back. Who knows?" But I didn't believe it was nothing. Changing things up I said, "Hey can we swing by the car rental place? I need wheels for the rest of the week. Hate making you guys cart me around everywhere."

"Sure-sure, works for me—but you know none of us mind."

The rental place had me on file from previous visits, and as a result, I'd gotten a little compact car and was out the door again in no time. I followed the *NASCAR* minivan-driver through the backroads of her neighborhood and when she pulled in the driveway, I pulled up alongside on the road out front.

Up the stairs and through the front door, I followed Mac straight into the kitchen. I set the container of rolls on the counter. Looking around the kitchen, I said, "Show me the book—the old cookbook." Something about the mention of it at Monica's had tickled my senses. Mentioning it now, further pushed that feeling to a crest, and I knew it had meaning. What, I wasn't sure, but it had my curiosity up.

Mac drug out a little footstool. "It's up here, with all the other cookbooks people have given me I never use," she said, pointing at the top open shelf over the stove. "I've never even cracked the old thing open." Still on the stool, she leaned down and handed me the cookbook. "Here you go—fill yer boots," she teased.

I grabbed it. "Thanks," I said. It had to be another one of those *things*—I knew it, that or my circulation was on the fritz, because while my fingertips felt frozen, my palms were ablaze from the first touch of that book. And while I examined the book, Mac got out two plates and two rolls.

The old cookbook was leather-bound like a journal. It was about 6 x 9 inches in size and much different from the larger more modern cookbooks you see today. The front had an image of a tree with long outstretched branches, twisted and knotted, with leafy foliage hovering over the trunk. It reminded me of Celtic knot drawings and tattoos I'd seen. The trunk of the tree added to the ancient appearance with its deep roots spreading out and down into another design of similar knots.

"Hey," Mac said, motioning me over to the table to sit and eat.

"Sorry—thanks," I said and sat down. I took a big bite of the roll and then wiped off my hand before opening the book.

The first page was blank, but the paper wasn't *paper*, it was more like cotton fabric meshed with fibers from plants or something organic. Judging by the books thickness, it had at least 100 pages, all of which were stitched into the binding.

"When I saw the tree on the front, I figured it was homeopathic *earthy* stuff," Mac said, picking at her cinnamon bun. "Was going to pull it down and check it out again, since I've been taking those courses."

I didn't respond, only flipped to the next page to find a handwritten table of contents.

"Well?" she questioned.

Without looking up, I read out the first three chapters titles in the list, "Chapter One, *The Healing Circle.* Two, *Understanding Holistic Healing,* and three, *Herbology and the Symbology of Herbs....*"

"See, I told you—homeopathy stuff," she confirmed, taking the last bite of her gooey roll.

My senses prickled more, as did the fine hairs at the base of my neck "Four...," I continued, "*Metaphysics 101... The Law of Balance, Universal Law & Chaos, The Law of Accountability,* and *The Basics of Karma & The Chakra System....*" I glanced at her, but this time she said nothing, only stared back at me. I went on. "Five... *Witchcraft & Sorcery, The Laws of Magical Rites, The Do's and Don'ts.*" I stopped again, and she grabbed the book from my hands.

She took her turn now, continuing from where I'd left off. "*Basic Wiccan Philosophy. What is Magic, Spell Construction, Wiccan Symbols, Scrying... Tools for Ceremony and Ritual*—what the...?" she shouted, "Are you shit'n me here, Mom?"

Snatching it back, I flipped forward and read the next written page. *"Holistic Healing... all living things, join all things, and bond us to the Divine Awareness. Magic is a process of the direction and use of psychic energy, natural and unseen forces which encircle all...."* Keeping it out of her reach, I flipped further ahead. "There's even a section for the Beginners Guide to Rituals." Flipping again, I stopped at something even weirder. "All the handwriting under the spells section looks like foreign writing — looks backward sort of. That's weird." My brain tried to make sense of it, but it was out of my reach of clarity. I glanced up at Mac.

At that, Mac's open mind slammed shut. "That's weird? The backward text is weird — that's all you think is weird in there — seriously?" she rambled out. "Lynn, it's a...."

"Grimoire — oh my gawd, it's the *Grimoire of Nature!*" I said, cutting her off. Jumping up, I carried the book with me to get my purse.

"What the hell are you talking about?" she screamed after me.

I ran back to her, flipping open my notepad to where I'd recorded the message that Vicki and I'd found yesterday. "Here, from the letter — the one we think Vicki's Mom wrote, *She is the Sorceress, and she holds the Grimoire of Nature, the Tree of Life will be in plain sight.* This is the grimoire, Mac — the tree... it wasn't hidden... it was in plain sight," I explained, giddy.

"You're telling me my great-great-grandmother was a Sorceress? A Witch?" As if fully understanding, a calm smile spread across her face. "How cool is that?" she shot out.

On a squeal she got up out of her chair, but I eased her back into it. I was worried she was about ready to take a header over the crazy edge. Smiling back at her I said, "You realize you're connected to all this — your family that is. Vicki's Mom — whom you've never met, wrote a description about...," I paused. "...wait — it's not your great-great-gran — it's... your mother — it's Monica." I stared at her again. "Holy crap Mac!" I turned my notepad around to show her the description.

Mac read aloud the description, *"She is of Irish descent,* check... *She grew up on a farm,* check... *later lived across the water with the men who fly* — Dad was in the air force in France — check... *It was there she lost a baby...* check." She sighed a little but continued going, "She met him when she was 18 at a dance… check. Children… check. *Great listener, a fantastic baker, mother, homemaker, caretaker*… it's all her." She looked up at me as if hoping I had something brilliant to say, but when I gave her nothing, she said, "Holy crap is right—the little witch never said a thing while we were there… *little witch*," she added, snorting a laugh at her own pun.

"I'm seeing more than a pattern here. Mothers, daughters, the whole *can't tell you* thing. All the stories mention something about *illness* or even *death* if the secret is told. The letter said, *it must be handed down from mother to daughter although the message cannot be passed freely as the daughter must seek out the knowledge.* No wonder your mom was weirded-out by the journal. She knows, Mac… she knows, like Vicki's Mom knows."

"What do they know—what?" she questioned, her smile fading.

Taking the grimoire from her again, I flipped back and forth through the pages, only to stop at the last page. On it I found a symbol, a *sword* with a *snake* wrapped around it. It was medieval in appearance and took up most of the page. Turning the last page to see the back of it, I found more writing, but this was different, written by someone else.

"*Dear Daughter…*," I read aloud, stopping to show Mac the faded handwriting. She straightened in her chair and leaned in as I tilted the page her way.

"That's Mom's handwriting, Lynn. What's that symbol next to the writing?" She pointed at the rough star-like marking, making a face that mirrored her confusion.

"It's the same symbol we found on the letter," I told her. I moved my chair to sit beside her, so we could both read.

> Dear Daughter,
>
> My instructions were to write down what I've been told. I hope you find it in time. You need to know about everything, you need to know about the balance.
>
> A few days ago, a man approached me as I sat by the lake near the cottage. He was a handsome man, and he wore a white suit. He said his name was Uriel, and he had the most calming voice. His scent

reminded me of fresh baked bread. I listened to his words and I knew he spoke the truth.

The balance must be kept by the four, The Healer, The Scribe, The Linguist and The Witch. We must hand down the responsibility from mother to daughter. These responsibilities cannot be passed openly as the daughter must find the truth on her own. Then and only then may they ask the mother. This responsibility comes with a heavy burden of illness or death if spoken or written otherwise.

I was given the description of one other. She comes from a strong line of women although some more maternal than others. Her grandmother had been married to a surgeon, whom she later abandoned leaving her child behind. He remarried and had two additional daughters. The first daughter, once grown, worked for a physician. Her daughter grew up to become a nurse, and eventually became part of parish nursing, and whose role reclaims the historic line of health and healing found in many religious traditions. The spiritual element is central to her practice. Her belief is that all people are sacred and must be treated with respect and dignity. She knows health is a dynamic process which symbolizes the spiritual, psychological, physical, and social dimensions of a person, and challenges traditional health care to provide whole-person-care. After the birth of her own two daughters, and knowing the experience was an emotional and spiritual experience with long-term impact on a woman's personal wellbeing, she changed her focus to assisting in the childbirths of others. Mothering the mother, she would call it, giving the necessary support, care, and advice during pregnancy, labor and the postpartum journey.

The healing comes from within and is not something one can hold. She is the Mother Goddess, The Healer, and she carries the Caduceus of Healing.

I cannot reveal any more, but I am here, as I have always been.

We sat there for a long time, both of us taking in long steady breaths, exhaling as if breathing was something we had to concentrate on. I think I even forced myself to blink a few times too.

"I gotta call Vicki," I said handing her the notepad. "Write that out while I call." My list-of-weird continues. I dialed anyway but got no answer at Vick's. I left a brief message outlining the events at Monica's and item we found in Mac's kitchen. I also mentioned I got my rental, and I'd be heading out soon back to Olivia's for the night.

Just as I ended the message, a car pulled into the drive; Mac's husband and kids. Mac hurried back up the stool to put the grimoire back in its place... for now.

Through the front door came the kids running straight for Mom and asking for something to eat. Following them was Mac's cheerful husband, Don. "Hey Lynn," he said.

"Hey," I said, then turned to Mac. "I'm heading out. We'll continue this later, agreed?" I turned towards the door and I closed the distance for one of Don's typical *Ultimate Fighter* wrestler hugs. He lifted me up and crushed me until I couldn't breathe. "Don you're gonna break a rib one of these days, I tell ya!" I pushed out of his grip, still gasping for air. "Later kids," I said directing it at Mac and Don and not the *ankle biters*. A quick peace-sign and out the door I went.

Pulling away, I smiled thinking about Mac and how she'd be flipping out over things, though still loving every minute—like I was. "Vicki's Mom is one. Mac's Mom is two," I reviewed aloud. "But who were the others of this foursome?" I'd considered for a second that the description in Mac's book could be my mom, but she'd never done *parish* nursing and she definitely did not have *two* daughters. Considering Mom's journal, I guess I believed she'd be part of this. Maybe she was a conduit, the receiver of information—like I seemed to be, and her part was getting this all started. "I don't understand this," I shouted as if there was someone listening, huffing with frustration at my lack of insight. "What are you trying to tell me? Am I leading my friends into disaster, is it a good path—the right path?" I banged my palms on the steering wheel.

There were no other cars at Olivia's when I pulled into the driveway. Probably best, as I needed to call Vicki again. But before that I needed to call Derek, get him to find out about the tree-book-thingy *and* that sword and snake symbol.

Up in my room I dialed his number, it rang, and Derek answered. "Hey," he said.

"Hey man, ready for more puzzle solving?" I asked, softening him up before I laid the rest on him. I still hadn't digested the new info myself, but I wanted to make sure I relayed it clearly. I didn't want to sound off my rocker despite the fact my balance on the earth was rocking a little.

"First, tell me what you guys were doing. Come'on," he said, pausing then, leaving me with dead air.

"Not sure you'll like what I have to tell you." I gave him the dead air this time.

"Lynn, you can tell me anything—you know that. I won't judge. Is it something to do with all this angel business?"

"Not exactly—I'm not sure—maybe...." Pausing, I considered his question again. "How long you got?"

"Right now—not much. Can I call you back in half an hour?" he said. "Give me the puzzle stuff for now and we'll talk-talk later, cool?"

"Cool. Okay, well… first is an old leather book," I said, going with the gentle intro. Next, I went with the *Band-Aid* approach. "Possibly a grimoire." Riiiiip.

"A what?"

"Bear with me, man. It has a big old tree on the cover. Search Tree of Life. Shush…," I said before he could interrupt. "...lots of branches and roots all woven together." I paused giving him time to get it all. "Second, is a symbol with a sword and snake. Got it?"

"Grimooore… Treeeee roots and branches. Snake and sword—got it. I'll call you in thirty."

"Deal. Later, Derek." I ended the call.

I'd gotten that out without a million questions from *Mr. Skeptic*. Although waiting was painful, it was better than the question brigade. How was I going to tell him this new stuff? I'd given him all the other things from my list-of-weird, and he'd handled it, but he may need time adjusting to this new info. Telling Derek, or any scientific person this, is like telling a little kid there's no *Santa Claus…* it's like shattering their whole belief system, and I was about to shatter his. He likes facts, not faith, and now I had… facts? What did I have—was it actually something?

Thirty minutes on the dot, the phone rang, and I answered, but before I could say anything, he started in. "Okay, from what I can find based on the description you gave, The Tree of Life, is also known as the *tree of knowledge*. Representing the concept that all life on Earth is connected. It's used in science, religion, philosophy, mythology, and a bunch of other areas like that."

"Uhm, alright," was all I could manage.

Jumping back in, he said, "Some believe it connects the heavens to the underworld and all forms of creation. Branches up to heaven — roots down to the lower world. The tree itself represents the earthly plane. The *Celtic* Tree of Life depicts the different forces of nature uniting to create harmony. It's interpreted as wisdom, strength, and longevity. Oh ya, and as birth, death, and rebirth."

"Cool." I responded, still waiting for something I could use. It *was* cool though.

"Thought you'd like that part. It's also associated with spiritual growth, like with the *glyph* — that's a diagram of the tree of life in the *Kabbalah*. It's supposed to be a magical symbol representing the path to God and how he created the world."

"Magical?" I asked in a breathy whisper.

"Just wait — it also refers to an old magical saying, *As above, so below*. Saw this phrase repeated throughout the occult and magical groups I found. It originated from *Hermetic* texts — also used in the Wiccan religion, and it's where you get the term grimoire."

"Did you say Wiccan — as in Witch?" Was this more of his sarcasm or was he starting to believe?

"Yes — as in witchcraft," he said. Swear I heard him stick his tongue out at me. "I also found a connection with the *Kabbalist* Tree of Life," he continued, "relating to *chakras*, which led to karma in the Hindu religions. The internet can be an informative *and* scary place," he finished, chuckling a little.

"Explain the *as above — so below* part." I wanted the info but was still stalling, trying to gather my thoughts on how to explain the messages we'd found. Leaning back against the bedframe I readied myself for more.

Heard him take in a deep breath, then he started again. "The saying led me to *The Emerald Tablet,* which is said to have secrets to magical stuff like *alchemy.* This brought me to the word, *Hermeticism,* a set of philosophical and religious beliefs. It mentions three parts of the wisdom regarding the whole universe again, *Alchemy, Astrology and Theurgy...."*

He stopped with a yawn, giving me a second to interject. "Theurgy?" I asked.

"Believe it or not, I had to look that one up. It refers to *the operations of the stars* and the fact that there are two different types of magic— complete opposites to each other. You've heard of the first I'm sure— *black magic,* relating to evil spirits. Theurgy, divine magic, relates to a union with divine spirits. It's also referred to as *The Science of Divine Works."*

"Well, at least it mentions science," I said as a timid effort for his acceptance. He was right though; the internet was an informative and scary place.

"Right—wait for it...." He laughed. "... it also subscribes to the concept that beings—gods and angels, and mythological beings, actually exist in the universe."

"That's uhm—wow."

"And the snake-sword thing, it's a *caduceus.* It's a *Hermeticism* symbol used in alchemy among other things, aaaand—that's all I got," he said finishing.

"Don't ask," I shot out before he started with the questions. "I'm gonna tell you now, what this is all about—as long as you listen. I know you won't judge, but there's some wild shit going on here, Derek— wild."

"Go ahead—shoot, I'm ready." I could hear shuffling noises like he was settling in for a long story.

"Uhm... on top of all the other stuff I told you...," I started. Then I led him through the path from Vicki's Mom, *her* reaction, the trunk, the map, the hunt, and the letter, reciting it for him word-for-word. Further I told him about Mac's mom, *her* reaction, the book, and the second description, reading it word-for-word.

"Hmmm?"

"Hmmm? That's all I get, hmmm?" I said. I'd been ready for all sorts of balking like I usually got from him.

"I'm surprised at how much information is out there about this stuff," he said. "I mean it sounds like a great story, but Lynn... I'm finding stuff that's well... *real*." My mouth hung wide open, and I almost dropped my phone when I checked the screen to see if it was him I was talking to. He continued, "There are tons of secret societies out there, *Freemasons* being the most famous. Who's saying you haven't stumbled upon another one—a matriarchal one perchance."

"You... you believe this might be real... *you*?" I questioned, making sure he wasn't about to *punk* me.

"Yeeees me, Lynn. Your IT guru, scientific geek, fact-or-nothing-friend, Derek. And yes, I believe this could be something real."

His little shot of sarcasm caused me to pause again, because I realized, he was ready.

"Lynn? Did you faint?" He laughed.

"Ha—nope. Okay, Derek...," I said, still holding back. "... I have one more thing to tell you."

Chapter 28

**Confederation Square – Thursday, August 14ᵗʰ,
The Northeast Blackout of 2003, Ottawa**

Standing on the topmost step at the Canadian National War Memorial, Raphael glanced around the triangle shaped area of the monument to the Valiants Memorial at its edge. Then he gazed down the steps to find Michael sitting on the corner of the bottom step facing the Chateau Laurier hotel.

"It's beautiful here, central — perfect," Raphael acknowledged. Michael giving no response Raphael said, "I love how it's framed by all the landmark buildings. I can see the Rideau Canal from here too. It's a National Historic Site of Canada you know, a World Heritage Site as well."

"Hmfff," Michael grumbled, still looking down.

Raphael descended the steps to peer over Michael's shoulder. "A laptop? How do you have internet during a blackout?"

"Magic," he responded, holding one hand over his head, rubbing his fingertips together like a magician.

"You're not?" Raphael scoffed, still leaning over to see.

"Nooo… air-card." He tilted the laptop, so Raphael could see. "Magic is Uriel's department," he reminded, before going back to what he'd been doing.

"Did you know this is the second most widespread blackout in their history—after the *1999 Southern Brazil* blackout of course?" Raphael said. "This current one affects about 10 million people in the province of Ontario alone, aaaand 45 million people in the U.S." Pausing, he glanced around again. "Why are *you* here—do you like this place?"

"Central—like you said. Good reception, but the internet keeps dropping as they bring the grids up and down," Michael answered, still not turning to look at his friend. "I'm the Arch of peace, harmony and balance remember?"

"Riiiiiiiight like you didn't lead our brethren of light in a battle against the legion of those of darkness. You being all warrior-like, and that symbol of yours—what is it again… Right a sword," he taunted, brimming over with sarcasm.

Michael turned and stared up at Raphael. "Are you done?" Then he turned back to his computer. "This is Gabriel's favorite spot, he's the war fanatic. He brought us here for that ceremony—if you recall?"

Sitting down beside him now, Raphael glanced over at the 12-foot long, dark Caledonia granite sarcophagus, *The Canadian Tomb of the Unknown Soldier*. "I remember… it was the morning of May 28, the year was 2000, and the body of this soldier was transported from Parliament Hill," he stated, pointing to *The Hill*, "… brought here on a horse-drawn gun carriage from the RCMP. Governor General Clarkson and Prime Minister Chretien were both in attendance… veterans, Canadian Forces and RCMP personnel were in the funeral procession." Raphael got up and walked over to the tomb. Again, Michael kept his gaze lowered. "Gabriel had said, '*The unidentified soldier had been selected from a cemetery near Vimy Ridge*'. That's the site of a famous Canadian battle in their First World War. They created it to honor the Canadians who were navy, army, air force, and merchant marine—for those who died… or who *may* die for their country." He sighed. "Past, present, and future."

"They moved him from the Cabaret-Rouge British Cemetery in Souchez, France, near the memorial at *Vimy Ridge*," Michael said. "The soldier was selected from the 1,603 graves of unknown-Canadians buried there." He paused. "I like that they put a grave marker on the now empty grave to show that his first resting place was just as important," he added.

"It's sad, but it's a good place—a place of honor. No wonder Gabriel likes it so much," Raphael surmised. "What are you looking at?"

"Disasters," Michael said.

"Pleasant topic," Raphael said, walking back over, again peering over Michael's shoulder at the screen.

Michael shifted so his friend could see. "Here, look. Since 9/11, a list of all the man-made and natural disasters." He turned the screen towards Raphael. "Looks like it's getting worse. We're not having any impact."

Raphael took over, reading the words on the screen aloud. "A large section of the Antarctic Larsen Ice Shelf disintegrated consuming about 3,250 km over 35 days, and it continues... Floods ravage *Central Europe*. There was an eruption on the volcanic island *Stromboli*—that's off the coast of Sicily. It caused a flank failure and tsunami, and the island had to be evacuated. There was a major weather eruption, producing more tornadoes than any single week in the U.S. history—393 tornadoes reported in 19 states. Across the sea, all of Italy except Sardinia was affected by a power failure which cut service to more than 56 million people." He glanced up at the calm skies, then back down to the screen again. "It goes on," he said. "Massive earthquake devastates southeastern Iran, over 40,000 people reported killed. The Cedar Fire, which started in San Diego County, burned 280,000 acres, 2,232 homes, and killed 14 people." Stopping, he turned away from the list, shaking his head slowly as if his neck were stiff and it pained him.

"That's just the tip," Michael said. "Look at the human disasters...." Michael pointed at each item on the list and read. "In Egypt, a fire on a train injured over 65, killing at least 370. There were a series of riots after 59 Hindu pilgrims died on a train, burned by a Muslim mob in India—the riots left hundreds dead. And see here—this train disaster in Tanzania, 281 people killed, it was the worst rail accident in African history. Here, look—more of them killing each other. India's worst Hindu-Muslim violence in a decade, more than 1,000 died in the bloodshed."

Raphael scrolled the list to a final few that were regrettably no less tragic. "These are the ones which affect me the deepest—the preventable ones." He paused. "That woman in Texas, *Andrea Yates*, drowned her four children—*preventable*. She'll spend life in prison for that sickness. There's the Russian passenger jet, which collided with the cargo plane over a town in Germany, 72 people died—*preventable*. The air show in the Ukraine, a Sukhoi Su-27 fighter crashed killing 85 and injuring more than 100. Worst air show disaster in history. And this one, the Station Nightclub fire—100 people dead. Terrible. Preventable. Dumb," he said, shaking his head again.

Michael took his turn and scrolled the list. "Oh, here's a beauty. You remember that archbishop from Boston, *Cardinal Bernard Law*...," he asked, "... he finally resigned. Allegedly because of the Catholic Church's sexual abuse scandals and cover-up of the priest-child molestation." Pausing, he drew the palm of his hand across his face, like somehow that would cleanse him of the horrid thoughts. "There is nothing I loathe more than when someone makes money from someone else's tragedy. See here—Peter Paul Rubens' painting, the first version of *The Massacre of the Innocents*, sold at a Sotheby's auction for the equivalent of $76.2 million U.S. dollars. Apparently, the buyer was the *2nd Baron Thomson of Fleet*, whatever that means." Disgusted again, he rubbed both hands over his face. "I hastened to even glance at the list of terrorist bombings. Some of those suicide bombers were women. *Times—they are a changing*, they say."

"Michael, you know Gabriel spoke with Vretil. The *Water-bearer* and Gabriel's Charge are back in contact," Raphael stated.

"Is that supposed to make me feel better?" Michael asked, moving back the computer to his lap.

"Back on course and able to bring the four together," Raphael added. "And you know Azariel watches over him."

"How will Gabriel's Charge do that—bring them together? He keeps saying '*You'll see*', but... well, his Charge is only in touch with one—mine," Michael reminded him. "Hasn't even met yours yet."

"That's where the Water-bearer comes in," he countered, taking the laptop from Michael again.

"So, because another Arch—one who governs the waters of Earth, has been *watching over the water-bearer*, I'm supposed to think this is a done deal?" Michael scoffed.

"Awhh, Michael, you know our fellow Arch is more than that—he also protects the inner emotional waters of those he watches over... reflecting the love that is irrefutably theirs and always, always available to them from the universe. He's an important part in their dreams and their intuitive wisdom." Raphael paused again, gazing around at the surrounding splendor.

"I didn't mean to—I mean—it's not as if...." Regretful, Michael lowered his head.

Raphael finished for him, "... not as if Azariel made the same sacrifices we have, or our Charges have. I know." He patted his friend's shoulder.

"In the meantime, things are falling apart all around us. Unless they show *Him*, they give a damn—He won't give a damn. The Watchers are free to influence their descendants any way they choose. It's obvious most are still angry with *Him*," Michael said, a poor try at redirecting the conversation.

Raphael searched the internet. "Not all," Raphael said. "Some only watch over their descendants—even the bad ones, and they don't influence them into evil. They believe in free will, the will to choose good over evil. Gabriel told us—if needed, the four could gather to show *Him* they believe in what their mothers had done before them. It's not enough they each passed the secret and the burden to their daughters—not anymore. A gathering is needed to prove they believe in humanity. Gabriel assured us."

His words had been an attempt at convincing Michael, but he needed them too. The leaders of the 200 would wait to see if the Charges failed. He knew if their Charges failed, that those leaders who watched over the evil of the world, might nudge that free will in the wrong direction, create chaos on Earth, showing *Him* that man was not worth the effort, humanity was not worth sparing. Some of his brethren understood their penance for their crimes, while others, their anger has only festered through the generations of men. Without proof that humankind—these women, are worthy in His eyes, what or who will hold evil back from destroying the Earth?

"How can Gabriel be sure? I know why I chose whom I chose—why *we* chose whom we chose, but that was also 5000 years ago. He only made his choice 35 years ago. What makes his choice the right one—what makes it so special?" Michael challenged.

Having no good answer, Raphael said, "Here's a good one. Last February, the global protests against the Iraq War—remember? Over 10 million people protested in over 600 cities worldwide. It was the largest protest to take place before a war occurred. He turned the laptop towards his friend.

"But you forget." Michael paused. "In March, a month later, the Iraq War began with the invasion of Iraq by the U.S. and allied forces—their protests did nothing," Michael reminded, sounding hopeless.

After an exhaustive search, Raphael paused and said, "What about this one? *Yusuf Hamied* and his India-based company *Cipla*... they broke the alliance of those multinational drug companies. They created a generic AIDS drug costing one tenth the price of the brand name. They run a free cancer hospital in India. Even launched the world's first once-a-day AIDS treatment and offer free doses of nevirapine if needed—it prevents babies from being infected when they are born to an HIV positive mother. The owner was quoted as saying he, *didn't want to make money from AIDS* and that he, *makes enough on other things*." Raphael smiled at his friend. "There, one person helping many—like our four have always done," he finished, hopeful in easing his friend's pain, and perhaps his own.

Michael turned to his friend and in a calm voice he said, "It's not enough. The balance is still off... and getting worse. HE doesn't see... HE does not care."

Chapter 29

"Cipher eeehhh?" Derek said, tossing out the title with a jokey Canadian accent, followed up by a laugh. "Read it again."

Laughing a little with him, I reread the description noted from Mom's journal. *"He won't know he's the one. He will reveal himself. But while everyone can see him, only you will hear him and he, you. They speak the same language... he will be spiritual, but of no specific religion, it'll be a chance meeting that turns into a great friendship. He will be quick to knowledge and problem solving."*

"Have to admit—sounds a lot like when you and I met, sounds a lot like *moi!*" he gloated.

"Yup," I said, then heard the front door open, followed by a gaggle of voices. I covered the phone. "I'm up here, down in a sec!" I called out, even though my car was in the driveway showing I was home. My words were chased with a quick shout back from Olivia.

"Come get dinner," she yelled.

My stomach growled as I refocused back on Derek. "Well geeze, I saw you do a *Rubik's cube* in like under five minutes. You're not only book-smart—you're common-sense smart, well—most of the time." I smiled into the phone. "You don't just state the problem, you immediately come up with a solution. Remember when you told me about your discussion regarding the governments in Iraq? You'd said, *Just buy them all a TV. In no time at all they'll be more worried about who's winning Dancing with the Stars than trying to bomb Americans.* Your coworker agreed it was brilliant too."

We both laughed.

"First, it was under two minutes, not five. Second, this is a huge simplification of my Middle East reformation plan/joke—but the premise holds," he assured me, following with another laugh. "As for puzzles, I have a collection of wood and metal brainteasers and at work—they know me as the one who can do that stuff. My business partner has a small metal puzzle on his desk—I'm one of only two who've gotten the pieces out, but I'm the only one who can consistently do it, aaand who can get the pieces back in—which is harder by the way." His voice continued to energize as he spoke. "I love puzzles and brainteasers. I particularly like those requiring digital manipulation and patterns. I also use phrases like *digital manipulation* because, well— I'm a geek."

"Is that all," I joked.

"Well, in college I invented a language with a coworker. We could talk about people at meetings without them knowing—it was more of a joke. I also like the challenge of puzzles where you have to decode an encoded phrase using simple letter substitution. I have all the techy toys too, have them all hooked up at home. I can watch my TV on my phone anywhere I can get a signal—and I can also monitor my security cameras from my phone. Did all the wiring and installation of the security cameras. Wired my entire house for phone, cable, and network—all by myself. I prefer to do things by myself. Ever try to fish a cable from an attic to a crawlspace—super hard to do alone," he added, ending his puzzle affections on an informative note.

"Not to mention, intelligent, perceptive—likes his toys, but doesn't play games. Musically and artistically creative...," I tossed out, adding subtle bits of sarcasm.

Missing my sarcasm, he said, "I could do any work as long as the work challenges me creatively. I'm levelheaded—but I can be prone to frustration I'm told."

Upping the sarcasm, I added, "Don't forget, extremely loyal, a strong sense of responsibility, is sound, and healthy."

"Now you're making me sound like a pet dog." We both laughed again. Switching gears, he said, "Lynn, for religion I used to think my views were *Agnostic theism,* but now I'm more *Deism*—but I kind of go back and forth."

Head shake. What? "Uhm—no—explain please—I no understand dayiiizzzm or theeeizzzm," I drew out, making sure I came off as stupid as I felt.

"Oops sorry. Agnostic theism—believes in the existence of at least one god, but believe the existence is unknown. Deism is also a belief in a god. Also, that the universe is a creation, and it has a creator, but is a belief that the god doesn't interfere in the affairs of humans or and I quote, *suspend the natural laws of the universe.* But Deists will also reject paranormal events like prediction and miracles. How's that?"

"Hello, hello, hello," came Olivia's voice from bottom of the stairs.

"Sounds like yer needed," Derek said, obviously hearing her voice.

"Ya, dinner is probably ready."

"Should let you go—but keep me in the loop. If you need *The Cipher*—just call." He hung up, but his laughter still rang in my ear. Then I caught the sound of double footsteps racing up the stairs.

Bursting through the open bedroom door, the girls toppled in onto my bed. Outsmarting them I circled around off the bed to the doorway and darted out into the hall. But they were after me in hot pursuit. Descending the stairs, I could hear Olivia's voice thundering from the kitchen.

"No running! One of you is going to wipe-out-down-those-stairs and I'm not going to help pick you up—do you hear me?!"

"Yes, Mom," I mocked, sock-sliding across the linoleum into the kitchen followed by my pursuers, all three of us slamming into the counter. "What's for dinner?" I asked for the collective, already aware of the pizza aroma in the air.

"Don't any of you touch that pizza—until you wash your hands. Lynn yours are clean, but those two just got back from the barn," Olivia said, placing her hands on her hips. "Both of you go." She waved them off attempting to keep a straight face. Then pulling plates from the cupboards, she asked, "How was your day?" When she turned back to see my eyebrows raised so high they practically reached my hairline, she froze. She lowered the plates onto the countertop without breaking her gaze on me. "Quick tell me before the girls come back," she whispered, turning her head to the side as if listening for the pitter-patter of eavesdroppers.

"Can't—too much, but Mac and I found another clue—ssshhhh." I placed a finger to my lips and leaned back to peek down the hall. "Mac's Mom—like Vicki's, is involved." The girls picked that moment to come scurrying around the corner to the kitchen, clean and ready for pizza. "I'll tell ya after dinner." I winked.

"What-What? Tell you what?" asked little Miss Nosey, Rachel—Liv's youngest.

"None of your bees-wax," her mom told her. "Eat your dinner."

I almost choked on my pizza hearing her *momminess* again, but I managed a smile and continued to devour my dinner.

They were the fastest pieces of pizza I think we've both ever ate. We left the girls sitting at the table to finish while the two of us headed out for a walk and private talk.

"Just going to go walk off the pizza, girls. Your dad will be home soon, leave him some pizza please. Back soon," Olivia called out as she closed the front door behind us.

We circled the block a few times, enough that I could get everything out and Liv could ask her bazillion questions. "Mac's mom indirectly led you to this old cookbook—a grimoire you called it, a magic cookbook? And it has a description of another one of the four? What are the chances of having both Mac and Vicki's moms involved?" she questioned me. Not like I had any flipp'n answer for her. Questions, questions, questions—mystery, mystery, mystery—whoosh.

"Ya, well, I called Derek to find out about the tree on the cover and I told him about the Cipher stuff—finally," I said, as we rounded the sidewalk to the front door. "I also asked him to find out more about the other symbol too—the sword and snake thing from the book."

"You mean a *caduceus*?" Olivia threw at me as she opened the front door.

The downy hairs on my arms spiked. I grabbed her hand, pulling on her and keeping her from entering the house. A slight electrical shock travel from my hand up the length of my arms straight to the back of my neck. Tingle. "What did you say?"

"Oh, let me show you." She took my hand off her arm and yanked me forward through the door, then down the hall into the office. In the room there were boxes upon boxes overflowing with contents. "There...," she said, pointing at a small pile. "... see, it's a medical symbol. It's on tons of Mum's things—from her nursing days." I stared at the stack of stuff, at the symbol, then turned my head to stare at her. "What... WHAT?!" she shrieked, already flipping out.

I pulled free of her grip, pivoted and headed back out of the office, and ran up the stairs to my room. I was feeling it, whatever *it* was—I was definitely feeling it again, that knowing sensation that screamed *you're on to something*. The same something I'd had about the trunk and the cookbook. "Hold on!" I called down to her.

I was back with my notepad and the description of the woman. I grinned as I held up the pad for her to see. "Olivia—the last page has the caduceus on it and the description that followed ended with, *She is the Mother Goddess, The Healer, and she carries the Caduceus of Healing.*"

"Give me that," she screeched, snatching the notepad from my hands. As she read her eyes became glassy and her eyebrows rose. "Uuhhhmmm, this is Mum—this description... it's my mother." Her voice trailed to a whisper as she glanced up at me and then back down at the paper again.

"Olivia... you're sure—really sure?" I asked, uncertain what to do at this point. It had to be true. I slid into the office chair, I needed to sit down, needed to fully grasp and get a grip.

"Every word—it's her, right down to her grandmother abandoning the husband and daughter. That daughter is Mum's mom—my Nan," she responded, slumping down on to a box next to me.

"How about we review everything here with the medical symbols on it, okay?" I said, getting up and stepping towards the stack of her mom's nursing things.

Olivia got up too and together we went through each item. We examined key chains, papers, a mouse pad, and everything that had some rendition of the symbol, but we found nothing helpful. Nothing to indicate something like what was found with the others, and nothing that gave me the *tingles* either.

"Are you sure there isn't anything else of your mom's with this symbol somewhere—anywhere?" I asked. My frustration was hitting a new high. Someone or something was pointing the way, but at the same time throwing down roadblocks.

"That's everything," she countered, exhausted, dropping herself back down on a nearby box.

And then the words came. "The desk—show me the desk!" I demanded, practically dragging her from the room. "Where is it?"

Not saying a thing, Olivia moved to lead the way into the basement. At the bottom step, she pointed to the far end of the room, to a very, very old roll-top desk. Without hesitation, we were on it, going through all the drawers and cabinets.

"I've never been able to open this part," Olivia said, pointing to a small shallow drawer in the roll-top part. "It looks like a drawer, but there's no handle or knob." She stood back glaring at the desk with similar frustration you associate to that of a flat tire.

"Let me call Derek back," I said, dashing off to get my phone.

I bounded up the two flights of stairs, cornered the doorway and grabbed my phone off the bedside table. I dialed and two rings in he answered.

"I haven't done anymore looking into the snake and sword thing...," he tried to say, but I cut him off.

"It's a medical symbol—but I need your help with something else."

"Cipher to the rescue—whatcha got for me?"

Still out of breath from scaling the stairs, I panted out, "It's a desk, roll-top—super old. There's a small drawer—or what looks like a drawer, but it doesn't have a visible way to open it—no handle or anything." I grabbed my notepad from off my tote. Listening now, I ran back down the stairs to where Olivia and the desk were waiting.

As Derek clacked away on his keyboard and I waited for his findings, Olivia tried to pry the thing open with a butter knife.

"Got it," he said in my ear. "The drawer has a pressure point. Press up-under and forward to get it to slide out."

"Olivia stop," I said, still holding the phone to my ear. I used my free hand to pull Olivia's knifed hand away from the desk. "Derek says you have to push up on the bottom of the drawer and at the same time slide the thing forward." I tapped the underside of the drawer to make sure she got what I was saying.

Without a word, Olivia put down the small knife, and then followed the instructions. Olivia *gasped* as she maneuvered the drawer out of its slot.

"She's got it open," I told him.

Olivia glanced at me and smiled, but then she kicked the side of the desk, pissed-off possibly because it hadn't shown her the way sooner. With the drawer open now, we both peered in. "There's a key," we said in unison.

"Key?" Derek asked through the phone.

Olivia reached in and took out the key. "There's no keyhole... for that type of key... in this desk," Olivia said, pressing her lips together in disappointment. Blowing out a burst of air, she shook her head frustrated.

I was worried she'd start with the head-bobbing again, but she'd only continued the shaking—no nodding this time, not that it was better.

"Derek. Olivia says the key won't fit any of the keyholes on this thing," I said, holding back my confusion and frustration.

"What year is the desk?" he queried, sounding as though he might already have an answer.

I bumped Olivia with my elbow to get her attention. "He wants to know what year the desk is—any idea?"

As if feeding the memory fire in her head, she said, "Well... it's Nan's desk. Must be late 1800s I figure." She started with her head-bobbing routine again.

Good grief. With an eye-roll, I relayed the info back to Derek hoping to move this quest along.

With barely a pause, he said, "Okay...." I overheard more clacking noise, fingers on a keyboard. "Can you see the right side of the desk?" I could hear the excitement building in his voice.

"No—side is against the wall, why?" I asked.

"There's a hidden compartment," he tossed back. "There should be a small door on the side panel of the desk. Can you move the desk away from the wall?"

"Hold on—I have to put the phone down...." I set the phone aside but put him on speaker. "...Can you still hear me?"

"Roger!" he bellowed, his enthusiasm breaching the speaker.

"Olivia." She stared at me. "We have to move the desk away from the corner. Derek said there should be a small door on the side panel," I told her.

Her head-bobbing stopped and with only a slight hesitancy she followed my lead. Getting a good grip, we then yanked the desk away from the wall, moving it from the corner. We knelt to examine the side panel. "There's a small door in the panel. It's about four inches high and eight across," I called out to the Cipher waiting like a genie for a wish request.

"Do you see a keyhole?" he asked, before I could say anything else.

"Uhm—yes." I watched as Olivia placed the key in the slot and turned. "Key's in.... Open!" I announced.

Olivia reached into the opening, then pulled free a small box that bore of course—a caduceus, on the lid. She tried to open it. "Are you kidding me?" she shot out, failing miserably. "Don't tell me this is another trick-puzzle-box-thing." She sat back on the carpet, box in her lap. Crossing her arms over her chest, she looked to me for a reprieve.

Again, I turned in the direction of the phone. "We've got another box... it's smooth on all sides and it has the caduceus symbol carved on it," I said, passing on details, presenting the next challenge.

"Carved on it or into it?" he said, right away.

"Into—deep in." I ran a hand over the grooves of the image, a sensation like static cling fuzzed against my palm. *Tingle-tingle.*

"Oh, I know this one—it's a puzzle key lock," he shot back full of smugness.

"Aaaaand?" I asked, better understanding Olivia and her head actions, wanting to shake mine along with her. Olivia smiled in relief, giving a few more head-bobs.

"The caduceus itself is a key in this case. Pull it up to remove it and slide the top off the box." Confidence not lacking, Derek let out a big sigh as if in relief he had the answer.

Our relief tripled as Olivia manipulated the box and pulled out the caduceus shaped piece of wood, then slid the top of the box forward. In doing so she revealed an inner compartment lined in dark burgundy-coloured velvet.

"Well—what's in it?" he called out through the speaker, the anticipation killing him.

"Paper... a piece of folded paper," I told the anxious voice. "More paper...."

"Aaaaand?" Derek mocked, sounding more anxious now.

Olivia took out the paper and put the wooden box on the floor. Slow and careful, she opened the folded document. It had the same medical symbol watermarked on the upper right-hand corner of the page and appeared to be stationery possibly torn from a pad because the top end rolled inward. There was handwriting on it and it presented the same strange symbol the other messages had, the star-like, the black inked shape reminding me of a squashed spider.

The expression on Olivia's face changed from relief to shock... and I knew what it was. "Derek—I'll call you back."

"You're killing me here, Lynn," he said, hanging up—no questions asked.

I maneuvered myself and sank down right next to her to examine the paper together. "That's the same symbol the other messages had. Looks like a squished bug," I whispered.

Olivia laughed a nervous laugh, then pressed her lips tight together again. She followed with a deep breath in, blowing it out in a shudder. "That's Mum's handwriting... she had excellent handwriting, always perfect." I gave her a little grin. She grinned back, but her eyes got a little teary as she nodded at what was another *big thing*.

"You ready to read it?" I asked, knowing this stirred her emotions. Being it was her mom's handwriting, and like the others, it was most certainly a message for her.

"Yup." She nodded again. Then slowly and softly, in that little pixie voice of hers, she read,

To my Daughter,

Please believe me, I wanted so much to tell you everything.

Yesterday afternoon, while sitting out back of the church, a man wearing all white approached me. He told me his name was Raphael. Although it wasn't odd to find such a well-dressed man here, it wasn't a Sunday, but I listened to all he had to say. I know the words he spoke to be the truth. I am writing as he instructed me and will find a place to hide this where you will find it. Please trust the words I share, I wish I could say more.

The balance is what we trust, it must be kept, and by the four who know, The Scribe, The Linguist, The Sorceress, and The Healer. It is the mother's role to hand down the duty to the daughter. These responsibilities unless absolutely necessary, must not be handed down directly, the daughters must find the truth themselves and then they may ask for the rest. I believe strongly in upholding these responsibilities, but they come with a weighty burden if broken, one of illness or death.

I was told to reveal the description of the individual, the one I knew of. The original ancestral line recently broken, she is the 5th generation in this new line. She is the daughter of a strong French woman, the second eldest between two sisters, and has a younger brother. She once lived as a single mother out West, but later found her soul mate through the aid of her first daughter. Finding her Knight, she later gave birth to two other children; a daughter and then a son. Together the family moved East.

Although, she grew up in a small town, she loved big cities and their festivals. A gentle, but formidable force she faces adversity straight on, leaving anyone in the dirt who tried to harm her nearest-and-dearest. Her life's path meant that she called many places home. As a planner of weddings and writer of bridal etiquette, as a scribe documenting historical records, and even in her administrative duties, her career choices were always a creative outlet for her amazing energy. She lives by the belief if you learn you grow.

As is found in all literate cultures, in some form or another, she is The Storyteller, The Scribe, and she carries the Codex of Balance.

Should you not find this in time, I fear I may have to make the sacrifice for the balance.

I am here when you are ready.

Olivia's voice caught as she read the end of the message. She tilted her head, her gaze drifting off as if her mind wandered.

"Did you want to read the other messages? I have them written out," I reminded her, trying to snap her out of her daydream.

"Uhm ya... that might be a good idea... sort of fuzzy on this... it's strange to see her handwriting... conveying this... this type of message... to me," she said, gasping a little as her voice trailed off to follow her unfocused gaze again.

I gave her a nudge, showing her the notepad. "Here's the first... and there's the second one," I said, flipping the pages back and forth from the two entries I'd transcribed.

"It brings it all home when it's your own mom that's involved— felt different when it was a story about other people," she noted, flipping through the rest of the notepad.

I knew what she meant, I'd felt the same when I'd read mom's journal. Life is easier when the stories are at a distance, but when it's your story, it takes on a whole new perspective.

"You said the same weird symbol was on all the messages?" Olivia asked. She held up her mother's message and traced the symbol with her finger. "Looks stamped on, official in a way."

"Ya, haven't even looked into that part yet. Other than the titles of the four, and the idea of balance and sacrifice, it's the only other thing linking the messages, oh and the man—men, they all claim to have met." I checked my watch.

"What Lynn?" Even in her daze, she'd noticed I was slightly off my emotional game.

"Just checking the date. I've only been here 2 1/2 days and look at the stuff that's happened." I glanced again at my watch, this time checking the time. "Should hear from Will soon, maybe tonight. With the time difference, it's hard to coordinate a call from *Taiwan*...." I paused. "Hey, I'm surprised we haven't heard from Vicki yet." To say my thoughts and emotions were all over the place was an understatement. Even though we'd found so much, I felt lost. It seemed as though none of this had to do with my mom. It had started with her journal, but now each clue or find, lead away from it, her—from me.

"Does Will know about all this stuff?" Olivia cut in, rousing me from my musing.

"Hell no—you know how he is. He'd have committed me. And this stuff—it's not about me, not mine to tell." *Not even close*, my brain said despite it all being revealed to *me*—to us. "He goes with the flow where my weirdness is concerned. Doesn't waste much thought over it." Doesn't waste much thought with anything in *my* life lately it seemed. "But he doesn't need to be involved—not his thing, ya know," I said, rationalizing, trying to convince myself of my own words.

"He can be on a need to know basis," she said, laughing.

"Oh, yer funny," I said, giving her a tiny shove. Clueless together, we sat on the floor looking back and forth from the notepad to the newly discovered letter. "Sheeshh—I haven't even emailed Alison about all this stuff yet—or Luc." The hairs on my arm prickled.... "ALISON!!!" I belted out, jumping up and heading for the stairs.

"What? Alison what?" Liv cried out, grabbing the box and its contents, following me up the stairs.

Heading back into the office again, I said, "Let me borrow your computer. Mine's packed in my tote upstairs—and yours is already up." Sliding into the office chair I shook the mouse back and forth to clear the family dog screen saver.

"What about Alison?" Olivia asked me again, hovering over the chair to watch what I was doing.

I logged into Facebook and went straight to Alison's homepage. Clicking on her notes area, I found what I needed. "Here. The letter's description reminded me of something—something Alison wrote." I scrolled past the photos to find the paragraph. Pointing at the exact words I wanted her to see, I said, "It's about her mom."

"What? Where?" Olivia squinted at the small writing.

"Alison wrote it—it's her mom's obit... *Beautiful Claudie took her place in God's House*," I recited. Stopping, I reached for the letter in Olivia's hand. "It says the same stuff—not the exact words, but it's the same." Olivia moved in closer for a better look. "Alison's writing says, *You Learn, You Grow* and so does your mom's letter... *She lives by the belief if you learn you grow.* And see here, *finding her Knight, she later gave birth to other children; a daughter and a son. Then the family moved East.*

And Alison's words, *the man who became their Knight. When Alison and Adam arrived.* After Alison and her brother were born, they all moved from Victoria, BC, out east to Ottawa." I stopped to reread both the obit and letter again, searching for more similarities.

Olivia picked up the notepad from the desk. "Vicki's mom knew about Mac's mom—well a description of her at least," she said. "Mac's mom wrote about my mum, and mine wrote about Alison's mom. That makes four," she pointed out, picking up the letter again.

"You're right—was thinking there would be one more, but we have the four." Taking the notepad back and then a pen off the desk, I wrote out the connections, saying them aloud as I went. "Monica is the *Sorceress—Witch*. Pamela is the *Mother Goddess—Healer*. Claudette is the *Storyteller—Scribe*, and Jeanette, Vicki's Mom, must be the *Scholar—Linguist*." The clarity short lived, I said, "But where's the description for the Scribe? Let me see the letter again."

Olivia handed back the letter, and I went straight to the bottom of the message.

"Here at the end—like all the others, As is found in all literate cultures in some form or another, *she is The Storyteller, The Scribe, and she carries the Codex of Balance.* It always ends with the description—and what they carry. The information about Vicki's Mom must be in this codex thing. Any idea what a codex is?" Again, less clarity and more confusion settled in.

"Look it up," Olivia said, playing the smarty-pants. "Internet, hello."

Right she was. Search.

"Okay, here we go…. A codex… Latin for… trunk of a tree or block of wood."

"She's carrying a tree?" Olivia snorted, followed by a giggle.

Laughing with her I said, "Hold on... is a book in the format used for modern books, with multiple quires or gatherings blah blah blaaah... sheets of paper or vellum in groups of two folded and stitched through blah blah blaaah... typically bound together and given a cover."

Olivia scrunched up her face and said, "So it's… a book? And this helps us how?"

"I have to call Spoo—what time is it?" I said, glancing at my watch again.

"Almost nine o'clock—why?"

"Perfect, it'll be near seven o'clock in Calgary. She'll be home now," I said, rubbing my palms together.

Together, we headed up to my bedroom, shutting the door behind us to keep out of earshot. It surprised me that none of the family had bothered to see what all the up and down the stairs had been about, but I was glad we hadn't had to explain it.

As if reading my mind, Olivia said, "Homework, and Mike's watching the game." She shrugged and laid out all the mystery items on the bed for my call to Spook.

"It's ringing," I beamed. It wasn't always easy to get Alison on the phone with the time-change thing.

Three rings in she answered. "Spooky, how's Ottawa?"

I smiled as I always did when I heard her voice, then I put her on speakerphone. "Hey, Spook. Ottawa—well, it's interesting." I giggled a little in anticipation of what I was about to tell her. "Olivia's here with me—got you on speaker so we can all talk." I took the next 20 minutes to get her up to speed, but I left out the piece about her mom until the very last. "Alison... as I told you, the latest thing we found was in Olivia's Mom's desk, but the description is something you need to hear... ready?"

"Ready. But is this one different from the rest? You're going to have to read all the messages to me," Alison said, her voice suddenly serious.

"Of course," I said. But when I looked to Olivia for input, she only stared back at me, shifting her gaze to the phone and back at me again.

"Hi," Olivia managed, going back to glancing at me, at the phone and then back to me again.

Alison giggled out a, "Hey, Liv," and waited for the rest of the story.

I picked up Olivia's letter. "Let me read Liv's Mom's letter to you first. Then I'll read the others, okay?"

"Sure-Sure—You know I need it all, Spook, but go ahead, read away girl." I pictured her bouncing a little in her seat, ready to burst if I didn't get on with it.

"Okay, here goes...." I read the letter word-for-word, pausing only at the end, as I knew the realization of the words would be clear to her, they were practically her words after all—or pretty damn close to it. When I finished, I waited anxiously for a response, but there was only silence. "Alison?"

"Interesting," Alison gave me, followed more silence.

"Ouch, Spook—interesting?" I threw back at her, stopping, hoping for more from her.

She made a sound like throat clearing. "Normally—maybe not so normal, but normally, I feel like Mom's here—I've told you that before. And that letter... it sounds... well, the letter sounds so much like... how I would have described her—but I guess I had described her that way, hadn't I?" Another long silence chased her befuddled words.

"It's like her obituary, the one you posted—parts of it anyway," I said. "What about the rest? Am I wrong to think it's about your mom?" I kept my words gentle. Like with Olivia, she wouldn't be able to talk to her mother about this. But neither could I with my mother.

"Wow," Alison said, going with the short answer again.

Then Olivia spoke. "I know—seems like a fun story until you realize you're involved, eh?" She smiled at me.

"Ya," Alison shot back, sticking with the one-word answers.

"We—you and I, are in the same boat, Alison. Both our moms are gone—no one to ask about this," Olivia responded, showing her usual compassion, "but we're going to go talk to the other two moms—don't worry. We'll find out as much as we can." Olivia's worried-mom face was clear, she was ready to leap through the phone to hug the girl.

"Spook?" I said, taking my turn, though I'd been unexpectedly left out of the *we*.

"Ya, Spook?" she responded, giving me a two-word answer this time.

"You okay?"

"Totally okay—sorry... just a lot to take in. To be honest... I'm kind of fixated on this whole codex thing now."

Taking a leap, I said, "Do you remember anything like that—a book, an old journal type thing—something your mom may have had?"

"Hmmm... I'm going to have to ask my dad about this. If she had anything like it, he would know." Her tone brightened at the mention of her father and she sounded more like her cheerful self. "Let me call you back, I'll check with Dad."

"Deal. Gotta call Vicki anyway. Need her in the loop on the latest," I told her. "Call if you find out anything. We'll call if anything new crops up at our end."

"Spook," Alison said again.

"Ya, Spook?"

"This... really would make a cool book," she shot out, laughing loud and hard this time. "Stand by Spooky!"

Laughter all around, I ended the call. Giving Olivia a big grin, I said, "She'll be juuuust fine."

Olivia laughed again. "Let me check on the girls while you call Vicki. I'll be right back," she said. Then she hopped off the bed and scooted out the door.

As Olivia ran to do her mom-duties, I grabbed up the letter ready to read it out for Vicki this time.

The phone rang only once before Vicki jumped on the line. "Been waiting for you to call—got your message about Mac and her mom. How crazy is that? How are we going to figure out who the other description is about? I read your mom's journal by the way—wild."

Oh my gosh, I'd forgotten she'd only had the short version of the Mac's story, and now I had Olivia and Alison parts to give her too. "Vick... we figured out who it is."

"What? Who? You did—how?" she shouted, cutting me off.

"Hold up there, sister. Let me get this all out—hold all questions until I'm done, okay? It'll be easier." It made me laugh to hear the eagerness of my skeptical friend. Coupled with laughter, I went through all the new details. I ended with the last letter describing Alison's Mom, telling her how Alison was checking with her dad for more info, and that if any existed, she'd get back to us.

As if digesting well the new bizarre info, Vicki led with, "In the meantime, we need to go see my mother. She was the first—first letter found that is. We can grill Mac's mom after. You mentioned she was sort of out of it near the end of your visit. Let's hope she's ready to talk, now that we have the grimoire," she said coolly. "I'll call Mom now. Let her know you're coming for *a visit*. Is Olivia available?"

"Actually, she's off tomorrow—works out perfect," I told her. "Let me know what time, and we'll come get you. Wait—don't you have to work?"

Vicki let out a high-spirited laugh. "It seems I have a migraine coming on and by morning I won't be able to go to work." I could hear the grin in her voice. She followed with, "The game's afoot, Westlake. Work can wait."

"You got it, Sherlock—call me back." Chuckling again, I ended the call.

The day had been one hell of an adventure and information overload for all. But I had a *prickling* sensation there was an information avalanche coming our way, especially once we talked to the mothers. I wondered what Mom would have thought of us on this adventure. She'd loved mysteries, though she'd had no real-life mysteries of her own, unless you considered dying a mystery.

My heart panged with a hint of sadness, but I tried to distract myself with eavesdropping on the mother-daughter banter. I could hear Olivia out in the hall giving the girls instructions on tidying their rooms and how, "*Money doesn't grow on trees, so pick up your clothes so they don't get damaged.*" I smiled at the normalcy despite the list of crazy in my hand. It helped.

My phone rang then. It was Alison calling back. "Yo, Spook. Whatcha find out?" I chimed, pushing away my grief.

Giggling like her usual self again, she said, "Well, Dad said he remembered her writing in a big old book he assumed might have been a journal. Was back around the time she was first diagnosed with breast cancer. When he'd asked her about it—she'd said nothing. He said he never pushed the topic either. Told me the last time he'd saw the book was just before they'd moved out here to Calgary."

"Wow, does he know where it could be now?" I asked, cutting her off, anticipation screaming through me.

Just as excited, she said, "Here's the thing. He thought it was weird because she'd said she'd needed to go see some woman before they'd left—took the book with her. He has no idea who the woman was. When they flew from Ottawa to Calgary, he'd asked her if she'd packed her journal for the shippers or if she'd be bringing it with her on the plane. She'd said—he quoted, *It's not a journal,* and told him it was in a safe place and gave him the *don't ask me anymore about it* look. So, he didn't."

"Went to see some woman?" More mystery, but possibly one of the moms.

"I wonder if it was one of the four," Alison added, in line with my thinking.

"The letters say they each only know the description of one though. But based on the connections, your mom would have known the description of Vicki's Mom. It's the only description missing," I said. "It has to be her—she's the only one left," I paused. "We're going to see Vicki's mom tomorrow—actually. She's arranging it. But I'll check with Olivia too, see if she has ever come across anything like the book your dad described. Can't hurt to check all the bases."

"Lynn, call me if you find anything, or if you get anything from the moms, please," she pleaded.

"When I know—you'll know. I'm just... well, here to help you find out whatever it is. Don't worry, we'll figure all this out, okay?" My voice softened as I tried to reassure her.

"Love you, Spook."

"Love you too, Spook. Stand by." I hung up and set my cell phone on the bed just as Olivia came through the bedroom door. "I talked to Alison," I said, before she could ask.

"Anything?" She rocked back and forth from one foot to the other like a little kid who had to pee.

"Her father remembers a book—an old one, but he hasn't seen it since before they'd moved out there. One curious thing though, before they moved, she'd gone to see some woman. Her dad didn't know who it was, but said she'd taken the book with her when she did."

"Some woman?" Olivia repeated, still bouncing on her toes.

"Has to be Vicki's mom don't you think? She's the only one left. Alison's mom had her description," I said.

"Who says the woman has anything to do with this? Should we make that assumption? Could be a friend of hers." Stopping her foot to foot dance, she sat down on the edge of the bed looking perplexed.

"Get this, when Alison's dad had asked her mom about the journal, she'd said she wasn't bringing it to Calgary. Said it was in a *safe place*. What the hell do you think that means?" It was my turn to throw out a question, mystified over another hidden item. What was with all the hiding?

"Lynn, it makes sense. All the other stuff was hidden."

"But why hide it before she left for Calgary? If Alison needed to find it—how the hell would she?" I threw at her.

"Things seem to be unraveling, but still nothing makes much sense. And why is my mum part of this whole thing? What is this whole thing?" she tossed back, just as confused.

On a hunch I asked, "You haven't seen anything like a journal in your mom's stuff, eh? No big old books in any of those boxes?"

Deflating my hunch, she said, "No—nothing like that, only a few old medical books."

"Was worth asking. Process of elimination," I said, hopeful things would become clearer soon.

Chapter 30

Vicki had called back last night, saying *"everything was a go"* for the visit with her mom, telling us to come by her place for 9 a.m..

After the family took off for the day, Olivia and I readied ourselves for the next adventure. Olivia finished cleaning the breakfast dishes, and I gathered my notepad and the letter we'd found in the desk. Then we were on our way. And as Olivia drove, I called Mac.

Putting her on speaker, I relayed to her the latest in the details on our little mystery. "How crazy is that?" I said, finishing.

"Can't believe my mom wrote about your mom, Liv. I haven't even talked to her since Lynn and I were over there. She doesn't even know we looked at the cookbook—uh sorry—grimoire, yet," Mac said. "But I'd like to hear what Vicki's Mom has to say first before I approach her again."

"Ya, don't blame you. Your mom seemed shaken when I told her about the journal." I said. "I'll call you after, okay?"

"Cool. I've got my hands full this morning with the boys and a bake sale at the school. Not sure my healthy organic carrot muffins will go over too well though." Mac snorted, causing Olivia to snort back with the mom-knowingness.

"Save them for me, I'll eat'm," I chuckled, "as long as they taste good."

Mac cackled, and said, "Okay, Little-miss-stomach, the leftovers are yours. Later, Liv—later, Lynnie."

"Bye," Olivia said.

"Later, Mac." I said, ending the call and just as we pulled onto Vicki's street. I was still giggling a little as we pulled into the back of Vicki's building.

Vicki was on the back steps bouncing on her heels raring to go — *go grill her mother*, that is. Spotting us, she headed towards the car. She was already talking before I rolled down the window to greet her. "What are you rambling about?" I threw at her, only half hearing her rant.

Swinging open the car door to the back seat, Vicki said, "Had to go back up to get the journal—almost forgot it. I wanted to show Mom, ask if she knew anything about your mom's involvement in all this."

I hadn't allowed myself to revisit the idea of my mom having *anything* to do with this, and I held little stock in it now.

"Okay, Vick—where to?" Olivia asked, her hands at 10 and 2 on the steering wheel.

"Make your way towards Island Park Drive and over the Champlain Bridge," Vicki said, giving out the first of many instructions that would lead us in the pursuit to our destination.

"Oh, I know that route across the bridge—it goes over the Alexander Island. You can get off the bridge halfway and drive around on it," Olivia recalled.

I fiddled with the car's radio, trying to find a decent station that wasn't all chatter.

"Ya, the area's beautiful," Vicki added. "Okay, once we get across, head west on to Lower Road towards Aylmer."

After crossing the bridge, we drove through the smaller towns towards Vicki's parents' place. We took turns recapping the different elements of the story and the clues we had uncovered. Vicki had told us *"first things first"*, recommending we find out what her mom knew, before telling her what we'd discovered. I was nervous, not just about confronting Vicki's mom, but about what else we might find out. The more we unraveled the mystery, the more questions we seemed to have.

We turned the last corner and pulled onto the street. Halfway down I could see the house, the one with the garage in the basement, half in and half out of the ground. Olivia pulled into the driveway, and I spotted Vicki's Mom through the living room window. She was wringing her hands. Not a positive sign.

Shutting the car door, Vicki announced, "Theeeere sheeee iiiis," and then turned to look at Olivia and me. "All these small towns are part of the same big city now—did you know?" Vicki paused. "She hates that." Her smile widened as she waved to her mom in the window. "Okay girls, here we go," she said, as we walked up the steps.

The front door creaked open, and we followed Vicki into the front hall. As I closed the door behind me, Jeanette came around from the living room and stared directly at me, past even her daughter. She smiled wide and let out a huge air-filled sigh that sounded much like relief. From behind Vicki, I raised my hand and gave her mom a little bending one-finger-wave.

"Well, Miss Lynn, it's been a while since you were out here visiting us. Come in—come in," Jeanette said, as she ushered us all in. "You must be Olivia." She smiled at Olivia. "Victoria can you get the tea, it's in the kitchen," she said, not looking at her daughter, gesturing the way for Vicki as if she didn't know where the kitchen was. "Come girls, have a seat," she continued, directing us to the seating area in the living room.

The look on Vicki's face had me holding back a laugh, and not a little one but the kind that starts at your gut and pushes its way passed your tonsils trying to get out. Her mom had a way of pushing Vicki's buttons, and the woman knew it too. It's a long-played game for both, I think.

But like a good daughter, Vicki went to tend to the tea while Olivia and I went and sat quietly. We'd found a seat on the long couch facing inwards under the large living room window. Jeanette, *Mrs. Quinn*, sat in a small-upholstered stiff-back chair, leaving the well-worn recliner for Vicki—and no doubt, *Mr. Quinn's* favorite chair.

Vicki returned from the kitchen with the tea, a counter move for her mother already in the works I was sure, then she set down the tray with the teapot and… *three* teacups. "Oh, did you want teeeea?" she asked her mother, smiling one of those *smart-ass* smiles of hers.

"No Dear, thank you. I had some before you arrived," Jeanette countered, smiling back as if she'd announced *check* in a game of chess.

Hiding her defeat, Vicki grabbed her tea and sat back in the recliner. It tipped ever so slightly to one side. The off-kilter likely from her father's attempt to read the newspaper, straining to one side to get enough light from the small table lamp. Accustomed to the tilt, Vicki steadied her tea on her knee and began. "Mom, the chest—Great-gran's hope chest." Pausing, she took a sip of her tea and glared at her mother over the rim. Before Jeanette could respond, Vicki interrupted by swiftly taking the journal from her oversized purse and setting it on the coffee table next to the tea tray.

"What's that?" Jeanette asked, straightening in her already rigid chair. Folding her hands in her lap, she leaned forward to look at the journal.

"That's my mom's journal—Vicki mentioned it to you," I answered, knowing full well she had, yet still trying to be polite. I leaned forward and turned the journal such that it faced her.

Vicki moved forward, and her chair tilted back to center. "Remember, I told you about the story from the journal, Mom? You brushed it off—changed the subject by asking me about the chest— remember?" Vicki gritted out, as if she'd declared *checkmate*.

Olivia sat in silence watching the strategic movements of the players, looking from Vicki to her mother in anticipation of a response. When no one said anything, she turned to me, eyes opening wide as if to say, *do something quick.*

In response to her plea, I said, "Mrs. Quinn—we found the map in the chest…." I cleared my throat, I hadn't expected to speak, "… and we found the letter, the one you hid in the pencil box near the bell." I wasn't sure what else to say. Vicki should have been running this show, *drilling her mom* as she'd said, but instead she leaned back in her chair, tilt and all, saying nothing more.

Jeanette looked back to the journal and then down at her lap. As if nervous, she smoothed the fabric of her skirt where her folded hands had lain. "What a relief," she finally said. Straightening again, she sucked in a long breath through her nose, then blew it out through her mouth. "It's been hard, keeping this to myself for so long." She took in another long breath, this time letting it out in a loud sigh.

But before she could continue, Vicki cut in. "Mom—there's more, we have two more letters."

Jeanette's mouth hung open as she stared at her daughter. As if realizing her unladylike expression, she raised a hand to cover her mouth. She remained silent as Vicki explained the details of all the things we'd found. Then when Vicki presented her the list-of-weird I'd created, she remained motionless, uttering only the occasional, *"oh,"* or, *"I see,"* as the facts and finds were relayed to her.

"Can you tell us what you know, Mrs. Quinn?" Olivia asked, her tolerance for the situation escaping her. "Who was the man, the one who came to you?"

Shaking her head, Jeanette said, "There isn't much more I can tell you, you already have more than I had to give."

"Mom, some guy tells you to write a letter about this story, about four women and some secret for keeping the balance—to hide the information, hoping I'll find it someday? Are you kidding?" Vicki's voice rose as she went on. "Who was this guy and *why* did you believe what he told you?" Vicki leaned forward as if pushing her mom even more.

Based on the blank eye-bulging stare Olivia was giving Vicki, she was as shocked as I was by Vicki's forcefulness... but these were the questions, and we needed the answers. "Who was the man, Mrs. Quinn?" Olivia asked a second time.

Again, Jeanette shook her head. She put her hand to the side of her face and let out a soft whimper. "Oh, I don't know... I mean—I'm not even sure he was human... but he looked like a man. He was beautiful... he wore an exquisitely tailored suit—all white... there was something about him...." A soft blissful smile crossed her face. "... it was magical... he spoke, and I couldn't help but listen... and believed what he was telling me. There was a power in his words, but his voice and his expression remained gentle." Leaning her head to the side, she passed her hand over her ear as if remembering the man's voice.

"Mom?" Vicki said, startling her mother.

Jeanette sat up straight again glancing back to each of us. "You don't have to believe me, but I believe. My mother had told me before she died, that this was my burden and secret to keep now, and I would someday pass it on to my daughter." She sighed. "When you didn't have a child of your own—a daughter I mean, I believed your sister to be *the one*. But when this man came, he told me it was you. His visit, it confirmed my suspicions that the balance was off. He told me, of the four, only one had daughters, and that the other lines were breaking. He confirmed what my mother had told me—that I was, *the Linguist*. I was, my mother was before me, and her mother before she, and so on."

"When did Grandma tell you this?" Vicki questioned, setting her teacup on the tray.

Looking straight at her daughter, Jeanette said, "You have the gift, Victoria, the gift of language, it comes easy to you too. He said he watches over us, our line of women, and that you were the next. He also told me something had happened, something he could not explain, but he allowed me to write part of what I knew—without harm. I wrote the description of the Scribe as it had been told to me." She lowered her eyes to her lap and once again folded her hands there.

Now I shook my head. "I thought the mothers couldn't tell the daughter anything unless they asked. How was your mother able to tell you?" I asked, even before Vicki could.

Jeanette lifted her gaze to my now confused face and in a soft voice, said, "She chose to tell me. She sacrificed her own life because I had not come to her." She placed her hand over her heart as if in pain. "I was too self-absorbed in my own little life to see what I needed to see. How much alike she and I were, but I didn't want to admit it. Stubborn, I should have addressed it—should have talked to her about it… she would not have had to sacrifice her life for me, for the balance." She sighed out the last words and turned to her daughter. "Vicki, you remember?" The pain and sadness were clear in her expression. "Your grandmother died in this house. She was visiting, staying in the bedroom in the basement. Everyone assumed she'd suffered a stroke in her sleep." Her expression was pleading now. "When your sister was born, you moved into that bedroom at first, before the addition was complete—do you remember?"

Vicki nodded in recognition. "It'd been a few years after she died, when I'd woken in the middle of the night... I'd felt her presence. It was as though she'd been touching the pillow next to me on the bed. I wasn't afraid, I was happy she was there—protecting me." Vicki got up from the recliner and stepped forward to kneel in front of her mother. Vicki covered her mother's hands with her own and gazed up into her mother's face.

"It's real, Victoria... it's real," she said in a loving voice, smiling at her daughter.

Clearing her throat as politely as she could, Olivia said, "I'm sorry to interrupt, but my mother never told me anything like this before she died—not one word."

Jeanette turned towards Olivia and gave her that knowing motherly smile. "Perhaps you didn't see, maybe she tried, but you didn't hear her... was she often sick, your mother?"

Olivia gasped, putting both her hands up to cover her mouth. Through them she whispered, "Yes... oh my God... after my youngest daughter was born, she'd had a stroke around the same time. She'd retired from nursing afterwards. Before her cancer diagnosis she'd been complaining all the time about discomfort, had wanted me to come visit her in Kingston." Olivia sighed. "It's two hours away—and I had a fulltime job and the two girls to watch over. My husband was working out of town at the time. I'd refused to go... my sister lived in the same city, but Mum wouldn't ask her to come... I couldn't understand...." Olivia covered her face as the tears came. "Why—why didn't she tell me?"

"Why didn't you ask her? So much alike and you refused to admit it... you are your own person, yes?" Jeanette added, giving us the sense of how she had felt with her own mother.

I wrapped my arm around Olivia and whispered in her ear. "It's okay, we're here—we're all here. Yer Mum's message got through, Liv—we found it, sshhhh." I rubbed the side of her arm and gave her a little squeeze before loosening my grip. Leaning forward I put down my teacup. I hadn't drunk any, only held it to be polite. I grabbed the tissue box from the side table and handed it to Olivia.

Patting her mom's hand, Vicki said, "The message has been passed from mother to daughter for centuries—but now, for some reason this man—theeeese men, have changed things. There has to be a reason for all of this. I'm not sure what we do now, but I believe this is something big. I also believe we will find the answers, together." She smiled at Olivia.

Olivia dabbed her eyes clean of mascara and turned her head my way. "I agree with Vicki," she said, "I believe this is real too—how about you, Lynn?"

"Me? Have you forgotten?" I joked, "I'm the one who brought all this weirdness into your lives in the first place." Chuckling a little I picked up the journal from the table and turned to Vicki's Mom. "Jeanette, what does this have to do with the four? Did you know my mother—did you know Sally?" I held up the journal with both hands, still looking for my own selfish clarity.

"My dear, Lynn. I am sorry, but I did not know your mother. I don't know why she was given this information. She mentions your birthmother as the one who told her, correct?" Reaching forward, she put her hand around the journal.

Relinquishing the journal to her, I said. "Yes, but I don't understand my birthmother's involvement either—neither are one of the four."

Leaning back, Jeanette flipped through the journal and read the passages swiftly—a speed-reader like her daughter, the Linguist as she'd said. "It says a man came to her—your birthmother, says the man's name was Gabriel. Perhaps she was a conduit through which the information needed to pass—from her to your mother, so you… could gather the others—the four. The daughters are all friends of yours, are they not? Possibly this was the change Michael spoke of." She set the journal back on the coffee table.

"Mom, do you remember ever seeing an old book? A big journal— a codex?" Vicki asked, tossing out yet another part of the story, a part we still needed solved.

"Uhm…." Jeanette paused, biting the side of her lip.

"Mom, what is it?"

Jeanette turned to look at me again. "Lynn, your friend Alison, does she live in Calgary?" As if assuming the answer to come, she chewed the other side of her lip raising her eyebrows in question.

I looked to Vicki, to Olivia, and then back to Jeanette, and spoke the answer the others already knew, "Yes."

"What do you know, Mom... the book? Do you have the book? Tell us."

"Mrs. Quinn?" Olivia questioned. "What about Alison?" Olivia was usually the quiet one, but now she was impatient. I wasn't far behind her.

We all leaned closer as Jeanette took in a ragged drag of air, readying her answer. "Uhm, it's been a while since I thought about the woman, Alison's mother I mean. We were never told the names of the other women, only the description of one." She paused. "It was in the spring when she came to my door. The spring of 2000, I remember because it was after all that Y2K mumbo-jumbo nonsense with computers or whatever."

"Mom," Vicki pushed.

Jeanette shot her daughter a look that screamed *give me a moment please*. Shifting, she repositioned herself on the chair. "Anyhow... I'd been home alone when an unexpected knock had come from the front door. I'd peered out through the front window." She pointed to the window behind where Olivia and I sat. "There was a woman on the front step. She kept looking around and over her shoulder, like as if afraid someone was watching or following her or something. She'd seemed harmless enough, around my age—you know. I'd opened the door to greet her, but she'd pushed past me into the front foyer." Jeanette shook her head as if remembering the abruptness. "First thing out of her mouth she'd said, '*I'm one of the four, I'm the Scribe.*' It'd taken me a second to grasp what she'd said—since no one had ever spoken about these things other than my mother. Then she'd held out a book, an old book—thick, leather-bound, and said, '*I've written everything down*', then she'd pulled the book back against her chest, wrapping her arms around it as if protecting it. I'd asked her how she'd found me. She said she'd known about me—all of us, from the codex. Said she could trace our ancestries from the information in the book, through the lineages recorded there. She'd known she wasn't supposed to write more than her own history, about her role with the balance, but said she had to write what she'd discovered from reading it, so it was clear for her daughter. *And* she'd said she needed to hide it, hide the book somewhere in Ottawa—couldn't take it with her. She'd told me she was moving to Calgary, to be closer to her daughter, but was afraid someone would discover the book going through security at the airport, or that she might lose it in the move."

"Mom, did she give you the book? Where is it?" Vicki asked, interrupting her story.

Turning, Jeanette looked at me again, ignoring her impatient daughter. "She'd told me she had two daughters—that the youngest was the *chosen*—but had no daughters of her own yet. She'd been worried about the balance, and she'd known contacting me would put her health and possibly even her life in danger, but she'd needed to take the risk. That's all she said... well, all she said the first time."

"First time?" I questioned wearily, my patience wearing thin.

Jeanette rubbed her arm as if it pained her suddenly. "She didn't tell me her name—and I didn't really know who she was until now—just her role—The Scribe, but she contacted me again," Jeanette said, still rubbing her arm, "... about four years ago—this time by phone. She'd wanted me to know the location of the book, because she'd said her mental faculties were failing her, and she'd been afraid she may not remember where it was when the time came... so she told me." She continued to rub her arm, the arm Vicki had told me about a few years prior, the one with the limited mobility.

"Are you okay—your arm?" I asked. I could tell she had more to share when she turned to Vicki. She had never given her daughter a clear answer as to how she'd hurt it or why she never pursued treatment to fix it.

Turning back again, she said, "I was told—I guess we were all told, never to write out anything having to do with the secret... but... I figured that since this wasn't the information I'd been given initially it would be fine to write it down... and I did." There was a collective gasp as we all leaned a little closer. "I wrote it on my personal stationery... but something happened... to my arm. The doctor called it *frozen shoulder*, but I knew what it was. Out of fear I burned the paper thinking it would fix my arm—but it didn't." Pausing, she rubbed her shoulder and turned a glance to the teapot.

Impatient, Olivia spoke again. "Do you remember where it is—where it's hidden?"

Jeanette put her hand to the side of her face, the palm covering the corner of her mouth. "No," she said.

We all gasped.

"All I remember is she hid it near a monument downtown. I'm sorry, it was four years ago, and my memory is not what it used to be—but don't tell your father I said so," she aimed at Vicki. Jeanette leaned forward and grabbed the handle of the teapot. "More tea anyone?"

Vicki took the teapot from her and set it back on the tray. Settling back in the tippy chair, Vicki said, "Mom...." Then reaching into her big purse, she pulled out the letter. "What about this? You told us you were not supposed to write things down."

Jeanette glanced at her daughter, then to me, and then to Olivia. "I told you, Michael said I could write it, he told me no harm would come to me. We—the four, as I understood his words, were all told to write what we knew. I never asked my mother how she knew who the Scribe was. It changed with each generation and I only knew about the one from my own." She turned to look at her daughter again. "You're the Linguist now," she pointed out. "And you know who the Scribe is for your generation. I guess you know all of them now." As if to show she was done, Jeanette got up from her chair. "Well, ladies, I'm sorry to say, but this old gal is exhausted. I need a rest now." She turned away and headed down the long hallway towards the back of the house.

We sat silent, glancing back and forth at each other for a moment before Vicki gathered up the teacups and took the lot back to the kitchen. Olivia, the *good mother* that she was, followed, insisting she help Vicki tidy. I remained on the couch trying to piece things together. It was time to call Mac I knew, and I took my cell phone out of my purse to do so.

When the phone picked up, even before Mac said hello, I could hear her youngest calling to her. *"Moaam..."* then, "Hey, sup-Lynnie?" came Mac's hurried voice.

"Over at Vicki's Mom's place—getting ready to take off again. Thought I'd call to update you—but you sound a little preoccupied at the moment."

"Give me 30 minutes and I'm all yours. I'm just getting him off to JK, then my afternoon is free," she said, excited through her distracted. *"Booo, put your shoes back on pleeease....* Sorry Lynn—kid has to change his shoes like five times before we can go out the door. See you guys soon. *Last pair...,"* she said, words trailing off as she hung up.

I laughed picturing her and her son and their *clothing struggle.* He had to dress himself it seemed, and he loved clothes. Gee, wonder where he gets that? I was still chuckling when the two came back from their tidy-tasks.

"Was that Mac on the phone?" Olivia asked, still drying her hands on a dishtowel. She stepped back to the kitchen doorway and tossed the towel on the counter. "Did you get her up to speed?"

Before I could get an answer out, Vicki grabbed the journal and handed it to me. "I've read it ten times already—think I'm good," Vicki said. She gave me a quick smile.

I took the journal and wedged it into my tote. "Ya, it was Mac—and no I just told her we were here, but we're leaving soon. She had her hands full getting her youngest off to junior kindergarten. Said she'd be free in thirty."

"Back in a sec," Vicki said, heading down the hall to the bedrooms.

Olivia came and sat with me on the couch while Vicki went to check on her mother. Neither of us knew what to say nor what to think at this point—at least I didn't. A few minutes later Vicki came back.

"Sound asleep. Guess this could wear a person out, but it's obvious Mom was relieved to get it all out though, finally," Vicki said, turning, glancing back down the hall, then back at us. "I'm ready when you're," she said, grabbing up her things.

"Yup, one sec," I told her, adding more notes in my notepad. I wrote out the names of the four women. Who knew whom, knew their descriptions at least, their daughters' names, and then the names of the men who'd visited them. But there wasn't a man's name to put with Alison, at least not yet. We needed to find that codex, but until then, I wrote *monument downtown,* next to her name. We knew who the four were—are, but I didn't know where or if I fit in. Did I fit in—and into what exactly? I chose to keep those questions to myself, and I flipped the pad shut.

Chapter 31

"A monument, surely they jest? I can think of ten off the top of my head *and* in the downtown area alone. Great help this was," Michael shouted, dissatisfied. "Vretil—what happened? Your Charge—what was she thinking?" Aggravated, Michael turned and paced while the others continued to stare at the house.

Addressing no one in particular, Vretil said, "I was with my Charge, while the rest of you went to yours, to tell them to write the descriptions. But I did *not* ask her to write the description that she knew, because she'd already made the visit—I was there," he confessed. "And alas, her doing such brought more illness on herself, *Dementia* this time. And because of it, she could no longer recall the hiding place," he said, turning away from the house, watching as the women came out the front door. "With the book hidden, leaving her daughter the description would have been useless—they need the book." Again, he stated the obvious. "I'm leaving now to watch over my Charge. Perhaps her father knows something. Anything would be helpful now." Then he was gone.

"The mother of Michael's Charge does not remember the details. She'd written it down not thinking it would be of any harm, but when the function of her arm became limited—she burned the note. She figured she would regain the full use of her arm... she did not, and the message was lost," Raphael recapped, watching as the women got into the car to leave.

"My Charge will help," Gabriel declared, appearing at their flank. He kept his expression calm, observing as Michael raised his arms and continued to walk in a circle. Although his heart too raced with anxiety, he said, "They are close."

Waving his arms, Michael said, "Why can't we find it for them—give it to them? It would be faster for us to search all the monuments. It could take forever for them to find it." Frustration taking over, Michael placed his hands on the top of his head, then slid them down over his face, messing his long curly hair.

Gabriel shook his head. "It's only been three days and see how far they have come. With my Charge's help, they will find the book of Balance."

Raphael removed Michael's hands from his face. "I agree with Michael," he said, turning to look at Gabriel. "Wouldn't it be easier if we stepped in, got them what they need?" He turned back to stare at his distraught friend.

"Both of you—enough!" Gabriel shouted. The two said nothing, only waited to see what else was coming. "How would stepping in prove anything to Him? You believe He will think it a great sacrifice on our part? They have to do the hard part themselves—they have to find their way. They—it's the only way, have to figure it all out. Once they have the book, they will understand. They will know what to do next," he said, ending the plea with a winded sigh.

Raphael let go of Michael's hands and stared at Gabriel.

Michael stepped away from Raphael towards their furious friend. "Gabriel," Michael said, "you better be right."

"Again—I agree with Michael. You better be right," Raphael said, running his hands over his own hair, his fiery red brush-cut reflecting the sun. "You better be right," he repeated in a whisper.

Smiling in response, Gabriel disappeared.

Gabriel reappeared behind Uriel, who stood alone watching Mackenzie's home. Gabriel said nothing, only stood there staring straight ahead like his friend.

Without turning, Uriel spoke. "I feel something—someone... someone watches—besides us. Do you feel it, the stillness?"

"Shamsiel?" Gabriel asked.

"No... but yes I believe it's a Fallen. Something evil lurks... malevolent... they lay in wait." Restless, Uriel panned the length of the house and yard and then up to the rooftops. Anxious, not wanting to leave, he said, "Where are the other Charges?"

"On their way now, won't be long. Michael and Raphael are with them," Gabriel said, taking a step closer to his friend, though only to comfort his own unease.

"Where is Vretil?" Uriel questioned, turning now to look at Gabriel.

"Out West, with his Charge," he said, pretending to be unconcerned. "He wants to see if she'll find out anything from her father." Giving him a reassuring smile, Gabriel then turned back to the house, continuing to watch Uriel's Charge through the window.

"What's the problem now, Gabriel?" Uriel asked, calling his bluff.

"Oh look—here they come. Good!" Evading the question, Gabriel unwrapped his arms he'd had tightly crossed over his chest, then pointed down the street to the oncoming car. "Do you still sense the *other*?"

"Yes—maybe—I'm not sure." Uriel watched as the car pulled up along the roadside next to the house. He scanned the immediate area again. "No—they're gone... for now."

Michael and Raphael appeared, joining them.

"Who's gone?" Michael asked, leaning around Gabriel, addressing Uriel directly.

"Who indeed?" Raphael pondered, "who... in... deed?" He shivered a little though it wasn't cold out... and even so, he never felt the cold.

Chapter 32

Vicki had sat up front this time with Olivia as she'd driven us back across the bridge and on to Mac's place. The two of them had chatted about what we'd learned about their mothers and all the other stuff that bound them together now. I'd sat in the back running the information over in my mind and trying to rationalize what it all meant.

I'd become less a part of these things, even more now than before. I'd needed connection myself and had chosen to make a call to Derek. I'd wanted to update him on the latest even though he wasn't involved really either.

He was more a *conduit* like me, but evidently, he was more useful. And as the car rounded into Mac's neighborhood, Derek picked up. "Hey man," he said, answering the bat-phone—or Cipher-phone as it were, "Ready to fill me in, or is there another puzzle for me to solve?"

He was as eager as the rest of us, so I gave him the play-by-play of who knew whom, what Vicki's Mom had told us, and summed up the questions we still had. "We're almost at Mac's place now," I told him. "She needs to be brought up to speed too."

"You okay, Lynn?" he asked as if sensing my lack of enthusiasm. "You don't sound thrilled about this adventure anymore—what happened?"

That's one of the many things I loved about him, he always had a genuine concern for his friends. I let out a big sigh of recognition, and said, "Can't say—not right now. Too many questions. Figured I'd find out more — more about why my mom was involved, or at least why my birthmom was." I let my voice trail off, keeping it low so the others couldn't hear, but it didn't matter, they were too busy going on about their own involvement, to be concerned about what I was doing.

"Lynn, at the pace you guys are uncovering stuff, I'm sure you'll find more answers — and soon. Don't sweat it," he said, making it his priority to cheer me up. "You have to admit it's pretty cool how this brings all of your favorite people together — me being one of them." He snickered.

It made me smile even though I tried to fight it. "Yer right, it is cool — super-cool. We'll find more stuff I'm sure... thanks for that."

Derek continued with his *cheering up*, as I watched out the side window of the car as the long stretch of houses sped by. Then the car turned the corner onto Mac's street. "Hey, I got more info for you — about matriarchal societies," Derek added.

The car came to a stop, and I cut him off mid-explanation. "We just got to Mac's — can I call you back once we talk to her?"

"Ya, of course, pretty cool stuff I found — call me as soon as you can. Shortcut Out," he ended, then hung up the call. Vicki already had the door open for me, so I slid over to get out of the car.

As I got out, I noticed our friendly watch-doggie, Cooper scampering across the front lawn. Then he halted about 10 yards from us, sat down, and then cranked his head to the side. He stared at something next to the house, but there wasn't anything there. Well, nothing I could see, but dogs seemed to have a sense about things humans overlook. Ignoring us, he lowered his big body to the ground, still staring at the *something* near the house. It wasn't like him to be preoccupied *and* not wanting to greet guests. I scanned the property, and a prickling swept over my skin — followed by an itchy-breeze. Then the sensation was gone, just like that.

Not all my sensations turned out to be something. I shrugged it off and continued across the lawn and up the steps to the front door. Following a step behind me were my two chatting friends, oblivious to their surroundings and to what I and possibly Cooper, were sensing. I stopped at the top of the stairs and pulled open the screen door. I took a quick glance back over my shoulder and both Vicki and Olivia slammed into the back of me like bumper-cars. I turned back to find Monica and Mac standing in the kitchen. They stared back at me as if I'd interrupted something.

Surprised, Mackenzie said, "Holy crap, Lynnie, how did you get past Cooper without him seeing you?" She noticed the other two smashed up behind me. "Not that he'd attack—but he's sort of my alarm system, or at least he usually lets me know when someone's coming."

"He's out there, watching something. Didn't pay any attention to us," I said, thumbing over my shoulder in Cooper's direction.

"Okay," Mac said, a little skeptical, peering passed the three of us out the front door.

"Hi, Mrs. M," I said crossing the expanse of the kitchen to Monica's already open arms. "Glad you're feeling better."

"Much... much better now this is all out. It's a challenging secret to keep, especially when one feels something is not right with the world," Monica shared, loosening her hug-hold on me. She smiled at me, putting her palm to my cheek. Lowering her hand, she glanced over at the others. "You girls must be hungry, have you had anything to eat?" Typical Monica, always eager to feed the world.

I was thankful she was back to her usual self again, and it was one less thing I had to worry about. I peeked over Monica's shoulder to spy a huge stack of homemade muffins plus a few large loaves of bread. The smell alone was mind-altering, and I felt even better with breathing it in. "Mrs. M, this is Vicki, and Olivia—the others," I said, stepping back to introduce my friends who stood in the doorway.

Olivia spoke first. "It was my Mum you wrote about," she said, giving Monica a huge smile. A little sparkle of tears dampened the corners of her eyes.

Monica stepped forward and put both her palms to Olivia's face, smiling at her like she'd just done with me. Gazing deep into Olivia's big blue eyes, she said, "It's a pleasure to meet *The Healer*. Are you ready?"

"Ready?" Olivia questioned, placing her palms atop of Monica's, staring back at her with a slightly panicked expression.

"Mom, don't freak her out, geez—we're all still trying to get a grip here," Mac cut in. "C'mon in—all of you. Let's sit in the living room." Mac swept her arm in a big circle directing us towards the living room. "Go ahead Vick, give us the update. Tell me what you got."

Mac led the crew into the living room and then rested down into the sofa chair. Vicki followed next, sitting on the couch at the side nearest to Mac's chair. With an arm wrapped around Olivia's shoulder all protective-like Monica led Olivia to the remaining space on the couch. Must be a mom-thing, and funny considering Olivia was usually the mom in most situations. Entering last, I grabbed the footstool and made myself comfortable for the swap of information. Incoming, avalanche warning, hold on tight.

We all sat silent as Vicki recalled the morning's events and the new information we'd gotten from her mother. I'd added that Alison was checking into things with her dad at her end regarding the codex. I also jotted down the info I decided either needed recording or further research. Then I gave Monica the list of things I'd been recording since this adventure had become, then showed her the letters. Lastly, I showed her Mom's journal.

Sitting up in her seat now, Monica removed her arm from around Olivia's shoulder. She'd been holding on to my friend through the whole discussion. "Well, girls," Monica said, "it's fascinating to hear all of this, having only ever known, well… what I knew. I never considered I'd be hearing the stories about the others—let alone sitting in the same room with their daughters." She turned. "Lynn dear, you are not directly involved—not one of the four, but you were needed to bring the girls together." She said the words as praise, her love wrapping around me, approval twinkling in her eyes.

"Still trying to figure that one out myself," I said, hiding my disappointment on the matter, and taking in the kindness she offered.

Monica turned to Olivia next before panning the other faces. "Something or someone has directed the lines of these women to this exact place. The fact—well, Alison aside, that all of you are here in this city—and that Alison had lived here, is quite remarkable. I never knew where The Healer lived, I never imagined she was in Ottawa, or even on this continent for that matter. I assumed we were all spread out—there were only four I mean, to keep the balance."

"Tell them what you told me, Mom," Mac prompted, getting up from her chair and hurrying to the kitchen. Mac clattered around in the kitchen as we waited for more.

"The balance between good and evil...," Monica said, stopping as her daughter returned to the room.

Mac carried with her a tray of homemade bumpy muffins with bits of red berries peeking out of them. She also had a stack of plastic cups and a pitcher of ice water.

"Aaaahhh Miller muffins," I swooned, grabbing two off the top of the pile.

The others followed suit, and Olivia filled the glasses with water, handing one to each of us.

Monica smiled at me, big, shaking her head. She always wondered where I stashed the food I ate, but she also knew I was a good customer to feed. I smiled back at her. "Hollow leg," I said, tapping my right as if revealing the secret.

She laughed and shook her head again. Then she glanced around the room at the waiting faces. "Well...," Monica began again, "...the balance was kept for generations. We proved our love, making sacrifices to show our strength as humans, as women. As you have gathered from Vicki's mother... if we told anyone, our health would be impacted. Keeping the secret was how we could prove we believed—that we understood the importance, even if we didn't know... everything. It wasn't so much about faith in what we had been told, but more about having faith in each other, and ourselves." She picked up her cup, took a long sip, and then continued. "We all have free will, and it was—and is, our choice to make the sacrifice to keep the balance, to make sure the secret is passed on. It meant we were willing to sacrifice our lives for the truth." Her relief was clearer, even as she spoke the words of sacrifice. She wouldn't have to make that horrible sacrifice, now that her daughter had found what she needed. She took in a deep breath.

"Who are these men—the ones who told you what to do?" I asked. "You said your mother gave you some insight into your role, but it wasn't until these men, or man—I'm not clear about that part yet, approached you, that you could write stuff out—without harm I mean."

Monica nodded at me, understanding my jumbled words and my uncertainty. "I'm sure it must seem confusing," she said. "It was easier for me when I found the grimoire and approached my mother. She told me the secret—just our part of course, it's all she knew. From there I studied the grimoire, but I also moved forward with my life, waiting until it was my turn to pass it on. I'd known something was off regarding the balance, but it wasn't until this man came to me that I knew for sure. But all he'd told me was that the four were instructed to write what they knew, to hide it in such a way it could be found—but only by each daughter." She let out a long exhalation and seemed to search for what to say next. "I thought it would be Mackenzie's older sister who would come to me—she already had a daughter. But the man told me you were the one." She glanced at Mac. "When you didn't have any daughters, I wasn't sure what it would mean." Her voice trailed off as if the recollection hit on past fears.

"What does this all mean," I asked, expressing my earlier thoughts. "Of the current four, one has a son through marriage." I turned to look at Vicki. "One has two sons." I looked towards Mac, and then to Olivia. "Olivia is the only one with daughters." I turned back to Monica. "Alison is pregnant, but I don't know the sex of the baby—won't know until the baby's born," I said, pointing out the glitches in this mother-to-daughter transfer of things. If this is how things had always been, and even with what little information we had, I understood that something was seriously wrong now.

"Only one daughter is chosen if two exist in the line… and yes, the balance is in extreme danger," Mac stated, handing her mother the grimoire she'd brought in with the tray.

"All we know right now, is that you were all helped by Lynn it seems. Somehow, through her birthmother, to Sally—to her," Monica said, turning to smile at me again. "They… these men, found a way to unite the four… for what—I'm not aware of, but it's something to help keep the balance, I am sure."

Mac sat forward pointing at the grimoire. "I've read that thing back to front at least five times—well the parts I understood that is. Some of the recipes—uhm spells, are in a different language, looks backward. I don't know, I'm new to this stuff—brand-new."

"Can I see?" Vicki asked, "Maybe I can read it... The Linguist remember?" She grinned as if she already had the answers and reached out for the grimoire.

"I've been through it many times before myself," Monica noted, "and I cannot read the spells, the ones Mackenzie mentioned." Graciously she handed Vicki the grimoire. "Many involved in the goddess movement regard the Earth as a living goddess. I represented the Sorceress, but it's Mackenzie's role now. For some, this role may have been figurative, but for others like my grandmother, it was more literal. She's the one who wrote these backward-spells. Over the years I'd looked into such things and read many books, but I settled into more of the Kitchen Witch role like my mother, and not of a full sorceress, witch or such, like my grandmother. I'd concerned myself more with my environment, ecology—the goddess movement as I mentioned, or *ecofeminism* as it's sometimes referred. Most humans misuse the Earth or nature, and due to their lack of respect for such things, it too is now in crisis." Monica stopped to glance over to Vicki. "Anything dear?"

Vicki shook her head. "Am I supposed to know how to read this? Looks more like a puzzle than a language. Like you both said, it looks backward. But there are other spells here in plain English—have you tried any of those yet?"

Reaching for the book, Monica said, "Yes, some... but they're minor. Let me show you." She flipped through the pages, stopping only briefly to squint at one of the unreadable spells. "I believe the use of this other language was lost generations ago." She continued to flip through the pages only to pause again. "Here—this one." She handed the book to Vicki pointing to the spell on the page. Monica sat silent as both Vicki and Olivia reviewed the spell she'd pointed out. Then she said, "There isn't much I can give you... you have each other now, more than any of us had before." She took a long breath in and then slapped her lap with her palms. "Mackenzie—girls, I must be going."

Looking at her daughter she said, "You know your father will be all a tizzy wondering where I've run off to." She stood then and took the time to look at each of us, giving each a smile specific and unique to our own needs.

Mac stood, and I followed, walking with both of them to the front door. Olivia and Vicki called out their goodbyes from the couch, their noses now buried in the pages of the grimoire.

"Lynn, you'll come over again, won't you?" Monica requested. "I'm sorry about the last visit—but you understand now." She wrapped her arms around me and squeezed as if trying to pull out the pain and loss of my past year.

"Of course, I will—someone has to taste-test your cooking. It's a tough job, but I'm just the woman for it," I replied, squeezing a laugh out of her.

Releasing me she turned to go out the door, then she took a quick glance back at her daughter. "Mackenzie dear, you'll call me if you need anything—if you hear anything more, yes?" She turned back and proceeded down the steps.

Cooper was fast at her side near the bottom of the steps, escorting her to the car and standing guard as she got in. With a quick wave, Monica pulled out of the drive and was off.

Mac and I stood in the doorway watching the car roll up the street and disappear out of sight. "Wanna try a spell?" I asked, smiling so big my cheeks pinched. I turned to see Mac's smile bigger than usual.

"Yup," she gave me through an over-stretched smile. We both laughed, and she shut the door. She gave me a little shove back towards the living room where the other two were finishing their review of the pages.

Vicki had opened the book wide on the coffee table to the spot Monica had shown her. "We have to try this—but I still need to figure out the others," Vicki said.

"What one did Mom pick?" Mac asked, leaning into the page and turning it so the words faced her.

"We could call Derek—he might have an idea about the language—or I could email him," I suggested, adding a quick change in direction. "Mac can you scan a page of the weird stuff, so I can send it to him?"

"Weird stuff?" Mac said, glancing up from the page. "That would be the whole book, skeeeuuwsss me—the whole grimoire, if you want me to scan just the weird stuff." She cackled again, and stood, taking the book with her up the stairs to her home-office.

"All of this is weird stuff—take your pick," I responded, waving my arms out over the different items we'd found like a gameshow host. The other two laughed. I took out my laptop while Mac scanned some pages. And as my computer came to life, Vicki stood and walked over to the living room window, peering out to the front yard. "What's Cooper doing?" I asked her.

"Not sure. He's standing near the end of the lawn, facing the house—no, he's looking to the side—wait, he's looking back at the house—and to the side again. He's wagging his tale a lot. If dogs could talk, I'd swear he was talking to someone—well acknowledging someone... or something." Vicki put her hands on her hips and leaned into peer farther up the street, turning her head side to side as if searching for Cooper's *something*.

"Done!" Mac announced as she bounded down the steps, jumping to skip the last one. "Anyone need anything?" she called out as she passed through to the kitchen. Returning she cradled a large bag of sweet-potato tortilla chips, along with a plastic container. "Homemade hummus, anyone?" Making room, she put the container on the now cluttered coffee table. She busted open the bag and then extended an arm my way. She let the bag hang off the end of her fingers. "Lynnie?" She shook the bag letting the smell of the goodness waft closer.

I leaned across the table, reached in and grabbed a handful. "Never met a chip I didn't like," I exclaimed, laughing and taking a bite of one. "Thanks."

Then Olivia gathered the tray and empty water pitcher and took them to the kitchen, making even more room for the new goodies.

Mac placed the bag on the now clearer coffee table and cracked open the hummus container. Dipping a chip first, she then grabbed the grimoire and sat back in her chair. "Now let's see the spell Mom picked." Bringing the page closer to her face, she read, "*Periwinkle Protection Spell....*"

"I love the colour periwinkle. Mac, you got any dried periwinkle in that kitchen of yours?" I asked, letting out a childish laugh. I crunched down on another chip, letting the end of it stick out from between my teeth, and I smiled.

Mac giggled. "Kitchen's stocked, girlfriend—thanks to Monica. She brought me all sorts of cool stuff." Giving me a wink, she shoved a hummus loaded chip into her mouth.

Vicki, done with her observations of Cooper, returned to the couch and snatched up the bag of tortillas. Reading the side of the bag she said, "Nice pick... love a healthy chip." She reached in for a handful and then passed the bag to Olivia.

Taking the bag, Olivia sat forward in her seat. "Protection—that's a good one. Kind of creeped-out at the moment." She paused. "Oh… did I tell you I found this amazing book of Mum's? It's all about natural healing and chakras. Very cool. Would be a good pairing for your stuff, Mac. Sorry, go ahead—keep reading," she finished, doing her head-nod thing and letting out a nervous giggle.

As Mac read the spell aloud, I sent off an email to Derek summarizing the latest along with explaining the attachment. Among my emails was a response from Luc saying he wished he could be there for the adventure and that he couldn't wait to hear all about it when I got home. There were a couple from Will that he'd sent much earlier, it being the middle of the night where he was now. One of them had photos of a tour he'd been on that day, temples and gardens, typical of Asia.

Turning my attention back to Mac's reading, I asked, "How will we know if the spell works?"

Making her own questioning face, Mac glanced back down and skimmed the writings again. "Here…," she said. "If you feel any malevolence around you now, you should feel a sense of calmness and peace when it's completed and are surrounded by the protection." She read it out a second time as if she hadn't quite grasp it the first time.

"So, no big explosion, sparks or fancy colours then?" I joked, scrunching my mouth up like I'd eaten something sour. The others laughed though Olivia's laugh sounded more nervous than the rest. Comic relief, *Check*.

"Well for your information, *missy*, Mom told me periwinkle was a powerful magical herb. Has to be gathered under the strictest conditions, *and* it's good for a few things," Mac said. "Protects against the evil-eye…." She squinted an eye at me. "… shadows and spirits. Good for love and passion and even brings back lost memories." Scrunching her face, she gave a little witchy-cackle as if mocking me.

"*Bing*," went the loud email notification on my laptop, causing all eyes to turn my way.

"Email. It's from Derek." I lowered the sound on the laptop, hoping that he'd provided us more clarity.

"Read it aloud," Vicki said.

"Okay. He titled it *Matriarchy*. He wrote; In case you are not familiar with this, it's a female society where mothers in particular, have the central position. Makes sense," I mused. "*There's a system used to trace the lineage from the mother through maternal ancestors called Matrilineality. The actual line of descent from a female ancestor where the children in all the current generations are mothers is called a Matriline.*" Pausing, I reread the lines again to myself, making sure I understood it.

"Man, he really is the facts-guy," Vicki let out, laughing, waving a hand for me to continue.

Glancing around at the others, I smiled, then refocused back on the email. "He writes; *It's a fact, that in some cultures, the more ancient ones, association to their groups was and for some still is, inherited matrilineally.* Everyone catch that?" I chuckled a little. "He mentions, Cherokee, Iroquois and Navajo in North America and others from Indonesia, Northern India, China, Spain, France, West and North Africa, and the list goes on. They are considered women-centered societies, centered on—same as what Mac's Mom called Mother Goddess worship and referred to by feminist scholars and archeologists as *Maristic*."

"Wait till you tell Derek about Monica's comments on that— coincidence my fanny," Vicki added, the skeptic now becoming a believer. "What else does he have?"

I looked back to the screen again. "He's got a reference here that goes back to even before the USA became a nation. There was this *Iroquois League composed of five to six Indian tribes,* he noted as *the Great Binding Law of Peace.* He explains that it was the *groundwork where women took part in the decision-making.* This included things like whether they went to war or not. He wrote, *the time of reference was not known, but was passed verbally until the late 1800s. They guesstimated its origin to be somewhere around 1000-1450 AD and it still exists."* I stopped there and said, "That's cool, eh?"

"It is cool. Any other cultures mentioned?" Olivia spouted, appearing a little less *creeped-out* now.

I skimmed ahead on the page. "Yup, he states—what he calls *the obvious, the Amazon society, found in Greek and Roman mythology.* But he also says there are not a lot of facts on this one. He mentions that the *Sarmatians were descendants of Amazons* and *Scythians,* that *they dressed like men of their time and hunted alongside their husbands."*

"Where the hell is Sarmatia?" Mac asked, making a little laugh-grunt sound.

Putting a hand in the air, I followed with, "The Cipher covers all his bases. *Sarmatians, from the Iron Age, were an Iranian culture. They lived in an area now Southern Russia, Ukraine, and the Eastern Balkans. They flourished during the 5th century BC to 4th AD."* In defense of Shortcut, I stuck my tongue out at Mac. "Man knows his stuff—or how to find it."

"Anything else?" Mac asked, sticking out her tongue in reprisal, following it with another big laugh.

"Here's one for ya, Mac, your family being Irish'n all. Celtic myth... he writes; *There's lots of evidence about these ancient societies where females held superior power, more than many of the societies today. Some studies indicated that this power was not in myth alone, but was in legal proceedings associated to marriage, divorces, property rights and ruling rights.* How about that?" Pausing, I shoved two chips into my mouth for good measure.

"Niiiiiiiice," Mac slid out. "Should have more of that now I say." Sitting up, she leaned in to dip another tortilla in the rapidly disappearing hummus.

"There's a little summary at the end of the email." I read ahead. "He says in finding these facts, he believes it relates to what is going on. But he can't find anything like this mother-daughter setup we have—not even a hint. He put; *There are tons of matriarchal societies in different cultures throughout history, but no record of anything like this.* He figures since we know of some members and have a type of *proof* that it must be an established secret society of some sort. That there are *always conspiracy theories or rumors of secret-types, past and present.* He'll keep looking he said."

What about the spell stuff? Vicki questioned, giving a loud "*Smack*" to her thighs with both hands. "Didn't you send him the pages?" She pushed. "This is interesting and all, but how about the language?" She rubbed her thighs.

"Holy crap—he wrote back so fast I forgot." Scrolling the email past the secret society part, I spotted his last blurb. "Uhm, oh—he wrote; *It would take a little more time... have faith Har Har-har, no pun intended.* Nice," I said, giggling.

Mac gave another little witch-cackle for emphasis.

Vicki seized the bag of chips from Olivia's loose grip, scaring the crap out of her.

I laughed again at all of them, and said, "I'll send a few other tidbits for him to solve in the meantime. How about the names of the men in white? I can't be the only one curious about them?" I glanced up at the others to see if they agreed.

"Uriel," Mac responded.

"Michael," Vicki reminded.

"Don't forget Ralphy-boy," Olivia noted, perking up again.

"Raphael aaaand Gabriel. Oh, and we better add Shamsiel to be safe," I finished, adding him to the short list of characters. The others let out a collective sigh as if they'd all run out of energy at the same time. I hit send and sat back to survey the room. What was that noise? Something... something coming from outside.

Oblivious, Mac opened the grimoire again and extended her left index finger up into the air as if to start the spell. The sound grew louder. Whatever it was—was coming closer, getting louder... stomping... more stomping... *closer*... it was up the stairs, at the front door…. "Okay troops, here's what we need…." Mac said, as the front door swung open.

I screamed, making Olivia scream, causing Vicki to toss the tortilla chips into the air.

Through the door burst Mac's husband and kids, scaring the bajeezes out of all of us. Mac slammed the book shut and sat up with a look on her face like she'd been caught doing something she shouldn't. "Honey, you're home… already." Handing the book to Vicki, she gathered herself and got up, scooting to the front door to greet her husband. The kids skidded past their Mom, and ignoring us, they dashed up the stairs to their rooms. *Boys*.

Checking his watch, Don said, "Early—it's 5:30? We're late, but who's counting." He grinned, giving his wife a little peck on the cheek.

Mac peered through the doorway of the kitchen to the clock and then back at us. "Where the hell did the afternoon go?" Mac questioned wearily. "Guess time does fly when you're having fun—eh girls?"

We all smiled back, guilty, nodding in agreement. Olivia gathered up the coffee table mess and both she and Vicki went into the kitchen. Vicki hid the book among the other cookbooks on the shelf. I shut my laptop, then gathering up the other *weirdness* items hoping to avoid detection from any prying eyes. And while Mac kept Don occupied by listening to stories about his day, I packed everything into my computer tote with none the wiser.

"Don't let me interrupt you girls," Don said, wrapping a big arm around Mac's shoulder, flicking her earlobe with his thumb, making her giggle nervously.

Simultaneously we all, Mac excluded, being she was glued to her husband's side, moved towards the front door. We exchanged our goodbyes when Don released his wife to wander off to the rear family room to watch TV. *Boys*.

"We'll regroup tomorrow. Call me in the morning," I whispered, leaning in to give a squeaky-kiss on Mac's cheek.

Olivia scooted around me. "Gosh, my husband will wonder what the hell happened to us too." She pushed open the front door. "Thanks, Mac. I take it we'll see you… tomorrow?" She turned. "Come on, Vicki we'll drop you off on our way."

Vicki gave Mac a nudge, then a nod as she pushed through the front door. "See you later *Witchiepoo*," she kidded in a not so quiet voice, making us all laugh again.

"Nice *Pufnstuf* reference. Got anything from this decade?" I teased, following her out the door.

At our descent, Cooper was up the stairs and in the house in a flash. I turned to wave at Mac before getting to the car. She stood in the doorway holding the screen door wide, waving and giving me a big toothy grin.

A sudden gust of wind caused the screen door to fly loose from her hand and slam against the side of the railing. Winds from all directions pushed in on us and we scrambled to the car. The strength of the wind caused even the car doors to *slam* shut. Leaves flew wild around the yard, and as we pulled away from the pocketed gale winds, I watched as Mac retreated inside to her little family and to safety.

Chapter 33

Dark skies had threatened rain, and the sun had hidden behind the clouds giving an appearance of time much later in the day. Gabriel and the other three had remained near the side of the house watching as their Charges had disappeared inside the house. Not a soul had been present on the street—not a human soul that is.

"Cooper old boy, how are you?" Raphael patted the dog's flank. Cooper lay at his feet still watching the house.

"He senses something too," Uriel said. "They always know when good or evil is around. Some even know when a storm approaches." Looking up, Uriel scanned the skies for any signs of a storm. "Humans would be wise to watch their pets for signs of change, good or bad — but they don't, most don't."

"Michael, there's your Charge at the window," Gabriel noted. "What do you suppose they are doing in there?"

"Talking." Michael grunted. "Laughing, what else?" Michael pulled his long wavy hair back from his face, securing it with a leather string at his nape. "Why? Do you think they're in there solving the mystery of how to save the world, Gabriel?"

Gabriel gripped his side in a mocking wince. "Ouch!" he voiced. "You give them little credit. Look how far they have come in these few days." Reaching to pat Cooper, he bent to look the dog in the eyes. "Even Cooper here has more faith in his master than you. Don't you buddy?" He rubbed him behind his ears and scratched under his chin. "Gooood boy."

"Could you two please stop bickering?" Uriel shook his head and moved away from the others. Cooper got up and followed alongside him as he walked the perimeter of the property. Around back of the house, the two peered deep into the shadows made by the intense thickness of the trees.

Cooper gave a low, "*Growl,*" as he approached the back edge of the yard.

"You feel it too, eh boy?" Uriel said. Cooper leaned into him. Uriel patted the dog's head. "Come! To the front yard, I hear them leaving." Turning together, they moved back around to the front.

"It's the family—the boys, they've just arrived home," Raphael shared, as the pair came from around the side of the house. Raphael noted a hint—but only a hint, of something in his fellow Arch's expression. "What is it Uriel? What did you find? Is something out there?" He moved to stand next to his friends once again.

"Something or someone is here, yes?" Looking around, Uriel scanned the neighboring homes and up to the rooftops. "But where exactly I don't know." Uriel stroked the top of the dog's head.

Cooper stood facing the house panting contently. He watched as his family stepped inside the home, safe and sound.

Tight to Uriel's right, Raphael stood with his arms crossed in discontent at the notion that an *unknown* presence was watching them. At Raphael's right, stood Michael. And next to him stood Gabriel. In lowered voices, Michael and Gabriel still bickered, though Gabriel had one side of his shoulder-length blond hair tucked back behind his ear, *listening*.

The front door cracked open, but it was just the girls exiting from inside the house. Cooper was up and bounding for the front door.

In Cooper's place appeared a dark-haired figure.

Uriel turned at an unfathomable speed towards the new arrival, causing the others to scatter. Uriel's auburn hair blew back in streams as he called forth the North winds, his energy fierce with protection for his Charge—for their Charges. "What in the name of Heaven and Hell are you doing here?" he shouted, booming like thunder, arms splayed out to the sides in full command of his grace.

Gabriel quick to Uriel's side, restrained him from a lethal engagement, yet still Gabriel brought in additional winds from the West.

Michael and Raphael bordered their brethren. Michael to the left conveying the winds from the South, Raphael to the right pulling winds from the East. Together they commanded a whirling vortex of energy and power surpassing.

"Control yourselves, please. I come as a friend!" Shamsiel bellowed through the blast of air and energy. "It's not me you should worry about. I'm on your side—always have been!" He held up both his hands as a sign of peace. Lowering his arms now to waist level he turned his hands palms up to expose his vulnerable heart. He stepped forward with no sign of apprehension in his movements, expressing *his* trust in them.

Gabriel released Uriel when a fraction of calm brushed over his friend, the North winds dying down and Uriel's hair settled back behind his shoulders.

Gabriel commanded the West winds to cease, and then Raphael followed suit from the East.

The South winds still dancing around Michael's feet betrayed his calmness, revealing his distrust. "Who is it we should worry about— my courageous friend?" Michael questioned, his wavy waist-length hair still lifting from the winds.

Shamsiel spoke only one word, a name, "Armaros."

"Armaros!" Uriel spat out. "Why?"

Shamsiel took another step closer to Uriel, closer to all of them. "He was here—outside the house, when it was just you, Uriel—just you."

"The *Cursed One* was here, I sensed it—him. Someone had been watching," Raphael confirmed. "Why are you here... and why are you wearing white?"

Maintaining his calm, Shamsiel took in a deep breath. "I have a stake in all of this too, you know. I watch over both my good and evil descendants, but I want them *all* to choose the path of good. They are presented with the right choices, but they have to decide for themselves. I cannot make them choose." He took a small step forward. "Armaros, on the other hand, wants them to destroy the Earth—each other... themselves. He craves evil—evil men, and the evil they make. And he wants your Charges to fail," he said, explaining and defending in unison. "And Armaros wears black—not me. Suits his shoddy blue-black hair," he threw out, still upholding an openhearted stance.

Breaking away from his friends, Uriel stepped forward to greet his brethren. Placing both his palms over those of Shamsiel, he gazed into his eyes, his soul... that soul which was once the Guardian of Eden. "How did he know where they were?" Uriel asked, revealing his own fears.

Moving forward and placing him at the center of their protection, Uriel along with Michael, Raphael, and Gabriel encircled Shamsiel, awaiting his answer.

Shamsiel relaxed, sensing their grace from all sides. Focusing, he stared deeper into Uriel's eyes, then asked, "What draws out evil like no other?"

"*Magic*," Uriel said in a whisper, closing tight his eyes as Shamsiel grasped his hands to steady him.

Chapter 34

Glancing back through the rear window, I watched as leaves and street debris swirled, the trees bending from the force, and then... nothing. The air stilled as we drove further up the street.

"Did you guys feel that wind? What the hell was that?" I asked as the car turned the corner at the end of Mac's street. I shivered, shifting to gaze through the side window of the car. A rushing sensation hit me and the world outside the car sped faster than normal. But when I looked down at my hands, my movements appeared as if in slow motion. Trying to calm my thoughts, I closed my eyes. I hadn't felt this strange sensation since I was a kid. Blindly moving my hands from my lap to my face, I pictured the movements the way they felt, *normal*. I opened my eyes again, but the images outside the car still rushed by, faster than the actual speed we were driving. Watching my hands again, though there was no resistance, the movement appeared slow and forced like being underwater. Panic swept over me and I sucked in short gasps as if the surrounding air was thinning. The movements of the girls in the front seat seemed normal, but nothing was... *normal*. Light-headed, I shut my eyes again and put my hands up to cover my face, blocking out any of the light.

"You okay, Lynn?" came Vicki's voice.

I opened my eyes again. Vicki had turned back in her seat, peering around the headrest, eyes opened wide as she stared back at me.

"Ya," I replied. *Normal...* the world had returned to normal, "Just got dust or something in my eyes... wind—all good."

"She okay?" Olivia asked, watching me in the rearview mirror.

Vicki turned to face front again. "Dust... in her eyes," Vicki told her.

Olivia still glanced at me through the mirror—always the Mom. It made me smile a little, but I was swiftly pulled back to the memory of the last few minutes. My smile was lost, and I rubbed my eyes, and the car abruptly came to a stop.

We'd already arrived at Vicki's place? So fast—what the hell?

Vicki got out. Then I got out from the back seat of the car and moved into the front, my legs a little unsteady as if navigating from a rocking boat to a dock.

"Okay troops," Vicki called out. "Call me tomorrow morning. I'll be home with another migraine," she informed us, leaning a hand against her forehead and smiling.

I mimicked the motion adding a mock faint, but it was easy to do considering. Waving back at her, I shut the car door.

The rest of the ride seemed fine. *Thankfully.* We drove past the farmers' fields where in the distance, there were deer feeding on the remnants of the summer corn harvest. I tried to focus on other things but couldn't help the occasional glance at my hand, checking for any unusual movement.

Once at the house while Olivia went to talk to her husband, I took time to myself up in my room. I sat on the bed running through everything, the weirdness with the car in particular. It'd been years since I'd had anything like this happen. Why now—why a repeat of that bizarre state? What did it mean—what did it mean back when I was a child? I'd never mentioned it to anyone... because it was weird, dreamlike and hard to explain. I hadn't a clue what it meant when I was a kid, buy it had gone away. Why was it happening now? As an adult I was just as lost.

Shaking it off, I grabbed my cell phone from my tote. As I was plugging my cell in to recharge, Olivia came through the bedroom door.

"I know—silly question, but are you hungry?" she asked. "Mike made dinner, it's still warming on the stove. He's off now to the barn with the girls," she informed me, giving me one of her inquisitive yet gleeful smiles.

"Are the girls going to be pissed you're not going? I mean you've missed a few barn trips already." I slid myself to the edge of the bed to get up, but then waited for her response.

"Naaa, Mike seems to like it and the girls enjoy showing off for their dad. The girls would live at the barn if we'd let them." She grinned again. "Plus, how often do I get *Lynnie-time*? They understand." She reached out a hand and pulled me to my feet.

The house phone rang, and she was out the door again running after the ringing phone. I waited and sat back on the bed. She returned to the open door of my room, cordless phone in hand. "It's a friend from work." Covering the phone, she whispered, "She's pregnant, 38 weeks. Doula's out of town for two days—knows I'm good with this stuff. Give me two secs...." She held up two fingers and backed out of the room.

Pre-labor pains I was betting, and she'd be more than *two secs* helping this one out I was sure. But it made for the perfect time for me to call Spooky and give her the latest.

My phone rang four times before going to voicemail. I shot a glance at the clock. It was too early; she'd still be at work or about ready to leave. For now, a detailed message outlining the latest info would have to do. She's the *fourth* after all, and they needed to find that damn codex, perhaps the last missing piece. I ended the message asking if she'd spoken to her dad about the book again, *and* that I wished she was here for all this.

Food was next on my agenda, and through a plate and a half later, I watched Olivia as she coached her pregnant friend. Stubborn, the pregnant woman wouldn't get off the phone to call for medical help, and she didn't want to leave her home, it being her original birth-plan. Here you have this nervous first-timer, alone in the house, doesn't drive, husband's four hours away stuck in traffic on the highway, and her *birth companion*—they're sometimes called, is out of town for the first time in 38 weeks, helping with another birth. But that's the thing though, not all women live in or even have close-knit communities where their sisters, mothers, aunts, or even friends are available to support them through pregnancy, etc. It would be scary to experience it alone and a Doula is supposed to help fill that gap, but this time Olivia was the one who had to fill it.

Olivia herself had had two babies, never officially trained in childbirth, but she had the knack like her Mum, and it was amazing to watch, *The Healer* in action. Her intent was clear, help the woman have a safe and satisfying experience despite the fact she couldn't be right there with her. Olivia had told me *labor Doulas* rely on techniques like massage and positive positioning, but all she could do was guide the woman, offer emotional support, encouragement, and nurture her through.

It was evident she'd had a powerful impact on this woman's labor, because short of an hour later the *self-delivery* was over. Mother and baby were happily on their way to the hospital for a check-over, and Olivia sat at the dinner table finally eating her reheated dinner.

It was a spectacular ending to yet another adventurous day.

* * *

Olivia and I sat at the kitchen table, sipping our coffee and watching the morning activities as the rest of the family scrambled to get ready and head out for their day. Kisses all round and then it was just the two of us.

"So," I said, pausing, letting Olivia figure out what I meant. I took the last sip of my coffee, ate the last corner of my toast, and then rose to tidy my dishes. Padding around the kitchen still in my pajamas, I waited for her response. My 'so' hadn't been for anything specific, there was too much to choose from and it had been just an opener for dialog, because I didn't know where to start.

"Mom and baby are fine. Spoke with her and her OB this morning," Olivia said in response, picking the most recent of events. She refilled her coffee cup and went to sit in the family room off the kitchen.

Following suit minus the coffee, I trailed after her and picked my usual spot on the big couch across from her. "That was amazing by the way," I said, grabbing one of the decorative couch pillows and giving it a teddy-bear-like hug. "Was awesome to see you focused and fearless."

"Fearless—ha! I was scared shitless the whole time—well, not the whole time—but most of it. I figure the illusion of calmness was better than none, eh?" She giggled a little and sipped her coffee.

"Whatever it was—you were incredible. Don't sell yourself short, Liv—end of story," I told her, not letting her deny her just dues.

"No blue jays today," she redirected, glancing out the large window behind me. "Do you think they're watching?"

"The blue jays?"

"No... the moms. Do you think they're watching us? Or over us?" she explained.

I took a deep breath in knowing where this was going. Letting it out, I said, "I like to think so. I don't know if the signs are real or we want them to be real, but either way it helps me cope... helps me accept that Mom is gone... gets a little less excruciating every day." My heart ached a little after the admission. *She really was gone.*

Olivia shifted in her chair. "Only Thursday, Lynn, and look where we are. I keep telling myself it's like uncovering a missing branch of a family tree, but it isn't—is it? These aren't lost relatives, not really." She paused. "It must be what it's like to find out you're related to royalty or a famous person," she said. As if confused, she scrunched up her face.

"I would imagine it's more like what archeologists must feel when they discover a lost race or missing link to some society or culture," I said. Running the idea through my head again I glanced her way.

"Glad we're not alone in this—whatever this is," she said, placing her coffee cup on the side table. Bringing her legs up, she wrapped her arms around her shins and rested her chin to her knee. Staring at the floor, she sat fixated somewhere lost in her thoughts.

To shake her from her musing, I said, "Someone must be watching us." Her head popped up off her knees. "I feel it—felt it, yesterday at Vicki's Mom's, and after at Mac's place."

She pulled her knees in closer, wrapping her arms a little tighter, knees to chest. "Why didn't you say anything then?" she asked, mouth hanging slack in anticipation of my response.

"Just used to not saying stuff, I guess. Tends to freak people out. Know anyone like that?" I gave her the all-knowing eyebrows up and down gesture.

"Who, me?" Mockingly she pointed a hand to her chest. "Who am I kidding, right? I'm a little freaked right now hearing it. Sorry, you're right—hate when you're right." She giggled at her own silliness.

I smiled and leaned back against the couch. I ran my hands through my hair and along my scalp in hope to generate the perfect answer. "No—don't say sorry, it's all freaky. You're not alone—freaks me out too." Though it wasn't the idea of someone or something watching, I was used to the weird feelings. It was not knowing the *who* or *what* watched us that was getting to me. "Phone's gonna ring," I tossed at her, the words just coming out.

The phone rang, and Olivia stared at me. With her mouth hanging open once more she let the thing ring again. After the third ring, the old-school answering machine clicked and played the family recording. Two beeps sounded, and we both turned towards the machine on the kitchen counter. Then a voice came. "Hey, Chicas— Vicki here. Everyone up and at'em? Call me," the voice said, trailed by a third beep ending the recording.

"Oooohhhh creeeeepy," I said, following up with a laugh, cracking the mood. Olivia shook her head and laughed with me. Though her laugh sounded a tad nervous as if trying to grasp the not-so-profound premonition I'd just thrown at her. "See, look at that, I throw a small prem your way and you practically have a coronary. And you think you can handle me telling you I sensed something or someone watching us—while we were all talking about that strange stuff with the moms? Right." I scoffed, crossing my arms over my chest.

"Okay-Okay," she said, sitting up and beginning her defense. "I'm a little skittish, but I'd rather know. Just say it. It'll give me a chance to get used to your *feelings*, then I'll be less distressed about it, okay?"

"Oookaaaay," I responded, "Whatever you want." I gave her a crafty smile and tried my best not to laugh.

"Well, I don't mean throw it at me all at once for heaven sakes. Let a girl eeeease into the realm of your mystical ways," she countered, forcing a laugh out of me, followed by her own.

"Suppose I should call Vick back, eh?" I laughed again.

"Don't tell her why we didn't pick up—she'll think I'm a big sissy." A further plea was clear in her expression as she tried to smile through her embarrassment.

We had no plan of action to give her, but I grabbed the cordless from its kitchen cradle and dialed Vicki back.

She answered on the second ring. "Hola."

"We're up, breakfast is down, but we're still in our PJs. You?" My hope was she had more to offer than we did.

"Same," she countered, "but I'm showered and dressed—been up since 5 a.m.. I've been on the computer for a couple of hours looking at the things Derek told us. The Matriarch stuff, you know." She paused. "What's the plan?"

"Find anything more?" I asked. So much information, yet too many pieces from our discoveries ran through my head.

"Nope. I tried a slew of different searches, but Derek pretty much covered it," she said. She'd obviously been feeling the loss the same as we were. "We didn't get to try that spell—the protection one."

"Maybe we can try again today, but we gotta make sure we're not interrupted this time," I said, letting out the tiniest of giggles, remembering our shock when the family had bolted through the door.

"I take it you haven't heard from our Witch yet this morning?" Vicki asked, then laughed. She rarely scares that easy.

"She'll call once she gets the gang out the door," I assured her. "And she'll be dying to get back at it—if I know my Mac. Stand by, I'll ring you back when she contacts us," I said, preparing her for the delay. "Gotta get cleaned up too."

"I'll be waiting," Vicki said, and hung up.

Olivia sat tapping the side of her coffee cup as if lost in thought again. Then she said, "You know," followed by a pause, and possibly another inner deliberation.

"Normally, I would say, ya—but I need a little more here, Liv." I waited for her to unscramble her thoughts and set the phone on the coffee table.

"You know...," she began again. "...hear me out—what if... what if these men are part of this secret society? I mean they have to be part of it somehow—right? How could they know about things? I mean not even Derek could find stuff." She paused and stared at me as if hoping for clarity.

"Okay Liv, it's freaky-time." I paused, assessing her readiness. She didn't flinch. "What gets me... is how all the moms say the same stuff. Like, *'well I think he was a man'*. What does that mean? It's usually followed with, *'he looked like a man'*. From the descriptions they sound like *men*—not women, and similarly gorgeous in their appearance or manifestation—or whatever."

"What's your point?" Olivia took a sip of coffee.

"So, what—there's a bunch of gorgeous model-like men assisting mothers in passing on the secrets associated to their lineage. Really?" I questioned, stating the obvious fallacies first "Are we ignoring the blatant inaccuracy here? Are we afraid to consider them as anything other than men? We have accepted aaaall the other stuff; the secret, the sickness, this whole keeping the balance, but what about who or what these messengers are. What about these *Watchers* my neighbor spoke about?" I paused and panned the room stopping at the big living room window, but I couldn't sense anything, and this time I was trying to. "What are we afraid of, saying it out loud?" Though protesting my thoughts, I was still uneasy, and a tad scared... that I might be right.

"What are you talking about?" Olivia asked, glancing in the same direction I was.

I didn't have all the answers, but one of us had to be brave enough to say it, so I did. *"Angels,"* I whispered. The phone rang, and we both jolted as the thing vibrated on the coffee table.

This time Olivia grabbed it to see who was calling. "It's Mac," she said, clicking the call button. "Hey, Mac—what's up?" she said, faking calm, cool, and collected. "Sure-Sure, we'll see you then—bye."

"Over to Mac's we go," I confirmed, getting up and heading off to go get ready.

"Angels?" Olivia shouted after me. I stopped on the staircase. "Angels," she repeated in a softer voice as if warming to the idea. She continued to follow me up the stairs.

In 15 minutes flat, I was in and out of the shower. Another 15 minutes after that I was dressed and down the stairs with my computer tote in hand and ready for whatever the day threw at us. At least that's what I told myself. Another 15 minutes later, Olivia descended the stairs wearing jeans, runners, and a long-sleeved t-shirt, emulating *my* usual garb. She did however don earrings and a matching pendant letting her habitually polished self shine through. And lipstick—she couldn't go anywhere without her lipstick.

"Think I like the idea," she said, stopping as she hit the last step before the landing. "The angel thing I mean. I just hope they're not aliens or something scarier." She snorted a laugh, grabbed her purse and headed to the door. "See—I can handle it," she assured me as she went out the door... without her keys.

"Ah, Liv?" I called after her. She stopped and turned to see me holding her keys up by my index finger.

"Right, keys—need those, right." She giggled, snatched the keys, and continued down the walkway to the car.

"Ah, Liv?" I said a second time.

"What—did I forget my head?" she laughed out, turning back again.

I pointed at the front door. "Ya might wanna try locking the door with those first, before you start the car. Want me to drive? Rental's right there." I pointed at the little car parked on the street while still pointing at the front door with my other hand.

She rushed past me with a groan and locked the door. "I'm fine—just fine," she countered. "Get in the car, Miss Smarty-pants." She pressed the car door button on the key-fob a few times showing me she had it under control. "I drive better under pressure," she announced, giving me a big silly grin and sliding into the driver side.

On the drive I called Vicki to let her know we were on our way. She'd said she was, *"Ready-ready,"* but that she would meet us there since she was too restless to wait.

Phone tucked away, I turned in my seat and stared at Miss Good Under-pressure. She was good under pressure with the important stuff, just don't rely on her to remember her keys, tie her shoes or zip her fly. I grinned. She gave me a sideways glance, sensing I was staring I guessed.

"What now?" she squeaked. "What—did I put on mismatched earrings or something?" She touched each of her ears a few times and checked her pendant.

"Nope." Was all I gave her.

"Okay—maybe I'm not cooompleeeetly in control, but I'm doing my best here," she said, smiling and not looking at me again. She continued driving in silence for the last stretch to our destination.

As we turned on to Mac's street, I gave a little fake cough. "So, you're happy I'm not considering aliens or something scary for these men?" I paused. "What makes you sure all angels are good?" I knew this would mess with her a bit and I tried not to smile.

"Oh—no. Don't you start. I'm only just beginning to accept that theeeese men might be something other than just men. Don't give me stuff about good angels—bad angels." Her face scrunched up, and she slammed on the brakes. Though she'd only been going about five kilometers an hour as we pulled up to Mac's place.

"C'mon, Olivia—you have to be open to the idea that anything is possible. Be prepared." I raised my eyebrows, giving her a few up'n downs for emphasis. I grinned, couldn't hold back any longer.

Olivia scowled at me, hiding a smile as she got out of the car. She gave me the finger—not *that* finger, but the one your mom gives you when she doesn't want you to say one more word.

I said nothing and shut the car door, noting that anxious Vicki and her racecar were already here. On the far left of the lawn sat Cooper, no bark, no rushing to greet us, just contentment and tail wagging.

Up the stairs and through the front door after Olivia, I spied Mac and Vicki in the kitchen. They were going through large plastic bags of what resembled dried flowers. The time on the wall-clock read 11 a.m., *and* I noticed there were no small humans running around. "Where are the monsters?" I asked, passing through the lower part of the house and looking towards the stairs to the upper level.

"My lovely husband took the kids to the cottage early. I've got a *jewelry* party to get ready for—or at least that's what I told him. I'll just tell him they cancelled last minute and join them at the cottage Saturday morning." She made a pouty-mouth, faking a *poor me* face.

"Nice one," I said, giving her an encouraging nod. "What's do'n?" I strolled over to the counter full of dried *somethings*.

"Spell stuff," Mac said.

"Smells good in here," Olivia spouted out as she passed by the kitchen to the living room.

Vicki and I followed as Mac carried her large tray of *spell stuff*, instead of food this time, out to Olivia and our gathering space. Mac lowered the tray to the empty coffee table, then sat down in her usual spot.

Olivia had already taken her place on the couch at Mac's right. Vicki went to Olivia's right, and I maneuvered to sit on the footstool near the end of the coffee table. One by one we presented our contributions filling the remaining table area. Vicki had her map, letter, and pencil box. Olivia had her caduceus box, letter, and key, and I had Mom's journal. Mac already had the grimoire out and had bookmarked the spell with a lavender coloured ribbon. We glanced back and forth to one another, waiting... for something... or someone to speak.

I went with the obvious question. "What is all this?" I said, pointing to the tray full of its accoutrement. I made a big circling motion around the lot, yet knew it were pieces for the spell.

Mac scooped up the grimoire and cleared her throat. "I went through the list of things I needed for the spell, and the preparation required before doing *any* spell. You can't just ramble off stuff and presto you have harmless magic. You need to prepare the space—bless stuff, you know."

"You're the Witch, you tell us," I said.

"There's a whole list of do's and don'ts in the book and even a beginner's guide to rituals," Vicki informed us. "Go ahead, Mac—read a couple."

Mac wiggled her butt in her chair and cleared her throat a second time. "Do's... *All actions should be of positive intent. Only perform a spell with joy, love, and kindness. Give respect to all living things. Accept the responsibility for your actions...."* Stopping, she glanced around at us. When no one said anything, she continued. "Don'ts... *Never cast a spell out of anger, jealousy, or greed. Never cast a spell for harm or to endanger another living thing or force someone into following your will and want, like a love spell.* Even a healing spell is manipulation it says—best to get permission first or *Soul Permission* it's called." She paused and glanced around at us again. "I give you guys permission, just so you know. If I need healing—just do it."

"Me too," I confirmed, glancing over at Olivia.

"Yes—me too. As long as it doesn't hurt," she added, giving us a nervous grin. "Vicki?"

"I'm in—heal away," Vicki said, completing the permissions and waving a *continue* hand at our Witch. "Keep going, Mac."

Taking another quick look around at everyone, Mac started again. *"What to Wear...* everyone wearing comfortable clothes? Says we need to be in what we feel most comfortable in."

Nods all around.

"Check. Next, *What You Will Require...* We need a representation of the *Goddess.*" She pointed to the flowers in the vase on the tray and continued. *"The God...."* She pointed to the twigs in the same vase. "Needs to be oak, in case you're wondering. The stone is for Earth, incense for Air, white candle for Fire and the little tiny bowl of water is for, well—Water. These elements also represent North, East, South, and West, respectively."

Olivia reached for the tray and from it she lifted a bundle of dried herbs and took a sniff. "Sage?" She pointed the herbs in Mac's direction, then set it back on the tray.

"A sage smudge stick. You light it to sweep away all the negativity—cleanses the circle," Mac clarified. "And before you ask— yes, this is my wand. It was a wooden chopstick, but it's a wand now. It says *tools are tools, and the power comes from within*—so don't laugh," she finished, but laughed herself. "Vicki," she called out, more a command than not.

"Crap, almost forgot," Vicki said, getting to her feet and sprinting to the kitchen. She quickly returned with a bottle of wine, four plastic stacked cups, and from the smell of it, banana bread. "We need *cake and ale, or wine* the book says." Smiling, she handed each of us a cup. She poured a little into each glass in our now outstretched arms. "I've already set up the candle placements using a compass to mark the four corners," Vicki said, *two-finger* pointing at all the candles, doing her best flight attendant imitation.

Mac leaned in and picked up the sage stick of the tray. Taking the matches next, she struck the first one and lit the sage, allowing it only to smoke rather than burn. She stood then and began walking the area, sweeping the sage through the air, and circling the space three times. When completed she wet the end and extinguished the smoke, returning both items to the tray. "Everyone ready?" she asked. She flipped over a square piece of parchment from the tray, revealing a hand-drawn five-pointed star in a circle. A pentacle, with the words *Earth, Air, Fire, Water,* and *Spirit* written at each point.

Olivia leaned in to take a better look. Her eyes bulging, she said, "I'm as ready as I'll ever be." She leaned back, giving us that nervous grin again.

"Okay," Mac said, "I did my herbal bath before you all got here. Need a clean witch, a ritual cleansing of the body and relaxing of the mind," she assured us, chuckling a little.

The rest of us giggled nervously.

"As well...." Pausing, Mac pointed to the perimeter. "...there is a white chalk line on the floor circling the seats—so stay in the circle." She moved the items from the tray into position. With the pentacle in the middle, she placed the small white candle on South, the stone at North, the dish of water at West, and the incense at East. She lit the candle first, then used it to light the incense, and then placed the candle back at its spot.

"Now what?" Olivia asked, anxiety seeping out.

Mac took the chopstick—*wand* in her right hand and lifted it into the air. "I consecrate this wand to be used for purposes of good in the practice of my craft. I change this wand by the elements of Earth...." She touched the tip of the wand to the pentacle.... "By the element of Air...." She waved it through the smoke of the incense. "By the element of Fire...." She passed it through the flame of the candle. "And by the element of Water," she said, dipping it into the little bowl. "This tool is now—by these powers that bind it, to aid me in my efforts."

"Aren't you supposed to protect your circle with something like small gargoyle-type figures?" Vicki asked, glancing at the far corners to where she'd placed the candles. "It mentions something about that in the book."

Mac grinned as she reached under her chair and pulled out a plastic bin. Standing again, she popped the lid and walked to the first corner. She placed a figure beside the candle and continued such for the three other corners. Returning to her seat, she placed the bin back under her chair.

I tried desperately not to laugh, but I couldn't help myself. The others joined in as we all glanced around the room at our protectors. There in our protection corners, compliments of Mac's boys, stood a six-inch tall *Spider-Man* at North, *Batman* at South, *Superman* at East, and at West… *Wolverine*.

"West is my favorite," I blurted. "Wolverine's Canadian after all—just say'n." The others shrugged. I guessed comic books had never been their thing.

"Right," Mac said. Then she raised both her arms high in a V shape over her head and began the chant. "The circle is not only around us, it is also above and below us. I call to the corners, the four elements, to bear witness to this rite taking place and to guard this circle and those within it." Mac waved her arms in and out in representation of all of us. "North—element of Earth and Winter." She touched the stone and pointed the wand to the North candle. "East—element of Air and Spring." She passed the wand through the incense smoke again and pointed East. "South—element of Fire and Summer." She swished it through the flame of the white candle and then pointed to the South candle. Ending she said, "West—element of Water and Autumn." She dipped the wand in the water bowl and pointed West to… *Wolverine*. "I cast this circle in a place that is not a place, where time is not time, and in itself parts of the whole."

Vicki snatched up the other pieces of paper from the tray and handed one to Olivia and one to me. Keeping one for herself Vicki said, "These eight words on the paper are the witches' Rede."

"Repeat after me," Mac said, "An ye harm none. Do what ye will."

We followed her lead, repeating the phrase three times over. When Mac finally lowered her arms you could, well—I could, feel the power in the room, in the space around us.

"Do you feel it?" I asked, not expecting anyone in particular to answer.

"I do—I really do," Olivia uttered in a soft voice. "I spoke the words from my heart, and I feel it all around me—energy... peace... love." Glancing to Vicki and then Mac, she said, "What about you two—anything?"

Vicki put her hands in the air. "Holy crap. Something—it's there."

"Cool," Mac said. Even after everything she'd just recited it seemed it was all she could muster.

"Mac, you did it—you really did it," I said. Mac grinned. "The circle is cast right—what now?" I rubbed my hands together eager for more. "Ready for that protection...?" Thunder boomed stopping short my words.

Lightening followed with a crackle and Vicki brought down her hands from touching the air. When the lights flickered, Vicki stood, but Mac reached out and grabbed her hand before she could move. "Don't!" Mac shouted. "Don't move, I mean—outside the circle." Tugging a little, she motioned for Vicki to sit back down. Then slowly, starting with behind Vicki, Mac's gaze followed the edges of the room, around Olivia and then ending at a space near me.

All eyes on me now, I scanned the room feeling for those things *unseen*. Chill air danced at the perimeter of the circle with the lights flickering every few seconds. "Do you feel it, Mac... circling?" I whispered. The tiny hairs at the back of my neck bristled as my heightened senses went into overdrive.

"I feel it, Lynn—what is it?" Mac questioned, staring at me as if I possessed the answer. "Nobody move—stay in the circle," she commanded.

Nobody moved. I said nothing, only kept my senses tuned to whatever was with us. Whatever it was, still circled.

Picking up the grimoire, Mac flipped directly to the bookmark of the protection spell. With little hesitation, Mac said, "Vicki—the jar," and reached a hand out in Vicki's direction.

Vicki grabbed the clear jar from the back of the tray just as lightning splintered in full view of the front living room window. Startled, yet not saying a word, Vicki removed the lid and handed the jar to Mac.

"Vicki, put those small vines and blue flowers inside," Mac instructed, pointing to the baggie of dried flowers. "It's the periwinkle from Mom's garden."

Vicki placed the items in the jar. Outside now, rain rushed down in grey sheets.

"Olivia," Mac continued, holding the mouth of the mason jar out towards Liv. "Place the photo in the jar."

Olivia picked up the photo, taking a quick glance at it. "It's a picture of this house?" she questioned. But then grasping the concept, she put it in the jar.

"And the paper with the address written on it," Mac prompted, pointing at the paper that had been under the photo.

Olivia shoved the paper in atop the photo.

"A pinch of salt to break up the negativity being generated around us," Mac said, adding the salt. "Storms create all kinds of energy, some negative—some positive." She took a hastened glance out the window, then she picked up a small dark pouch from the tray. Handing it my way, she said, "It's vervain—makes the spell move quicker."

"Are you shitt'n me here, Mac," I shot out. "What—are we warding off vampires now?" I laughed a little in disbelief, still taking the pouch.

Mac ignored my comments and went on. "Quickly—place about a tablespoon of the stuff in the jar," she said.

I tugged the tiny drawstrings to open the top of the bag and then tipped a guesstimated amount into the jar.

With the jar gripped firm in her left hand, Mac threw out her right hand to Vicki again. "Lid!" Vicki handed her the lid and Mac topped the jar and screwed it tight.

The only item that remained on the tray unused was a black *magic-marker*, seriously—no pun intended. Mac took it and drew a pentacle on the lid. She held out the jar with both hands. "Okay, girls, let's load this spell with our positive intentions," she said. "Visualize the protection of this property—its people and belongings within and cast off this negative—whatever. Concentrate." Then she chanted again, this time something about *tiny flowers and white stars... power placed into this jar*. But I was too focused on positive thoughts to catch all the rhyming parts. Ending Mac said, "Guard well my home, evil's touch is over, no more will they roam." The lights stopped their flickering, and the sky made no noise.

We watched out the window as the rain dissipated and as the clouds splintered as a thin ribbon of sun attempted to escape its dark hold. Whatever had crept around our little gathering was now gone, replaced by a clean sense of peace and safety. The safety stretched out from us, from this room, this home and farther. How far, I didn't know, but the sun was out—that I knew.

Vicki put her hands up again and smiled. "Holy crap," Vicki spouted again.

We all smiled, even Olivia, and I was glad because she'd seemed like she might pee her pants for a second there. Then creepily on cue my cell phone went off and Muse's *Supermassive Black Hole's* dark and heavy corded ringtone filled the air with eerie song lyrics blasting from the tiny speaker.

"Holy crap is right," I said, singing along with it. Doing a few head-bang moves, I grabbed my tote and did my best air-guitar. I can't sing to save my life, but at this point it made for well-needed comical relief.

"Nice," Mac said, laughing at my smooth moves.

"It's Spook—perfect." I grinned big. "Hellooooo," I answered, stretching out the *o* for emphasis. "What shak'ith?"

"Oh man—we just had the biggest thunderstorm here—right over my house," Alison threw out. "Only clearing up now—was crazy, snapping and crackling all around us." She let out a heavy breath. "I'm by myself, Ken's still at work. Freaked me out I guess, ya know?"

"Oh, do I," I shot back. Been a lot of freak, freaked and freaking-me-out going around it seemed. "We had the same thing happen here—like you said, *just clearing up now*." Turning the phone away from my face I put it on speaker, letting the others in on her end of things.

"You guys just had a storm too—what are the chances?" Alison said, adding a little giggle.

"Wait until I tell you what we did. You might not think it chance afterward." Nodding my head like she could see me, I looked to the others knowingly. Then I continued to tell her the *what's-what*, as Mac circled the room performing a closing chant to close out the circle. It would make it safe for us to leave it, still *fully protected*. I was good for now, right where I was, drinking the rest of my wine and eating the banana bread.

"Oh Spook, I have to come home," she said, thrilled to hear about what we'd been doing, but a little pissed at missing out and all. "I need to be there for this—I'm missing all the good stuff. I need to check for flights—anyone got room for me?" she tossed out.

"My son's away at school so I have a spare room. Come on over girl," Vicki offered to the rescue.

"Girls...," Alison started again, "...I've got more stuff from my dad... and based on the message you left me, Lynn—it could be relevant. You guys ready?"

"Shoot, Spook," I said, giving her the *we're ready when you're ready* command.

"Hear ye. Hear ye—just kidding," she joked, followed by a little giggle of nerves. Then she started again. "Okay, I asked my dad about the book again, well—not about the book, but more about what they did on their last days before moving. Dad told me Mom had made him drive downtown—twice. The first time had been to sell her writing desk. Apparently, there'd been a lady interested in it, but Mom wouldn't let Dad go with her to the shop, had made him drive then park while she went."

"Did you tell your dad about her visit to Vicki's mom's place?" I asked.

"No, why?" Alison asked back.

"I didn't get a chance to tell you yet, but your mom called Vicki's Mom, four years ago."

"Wait—what? She called, why—what for?"

"Told her the location where she'd hid the book. Said something about her mental faculties failing her and how she was afraid she wouldn't be able to remember where it was—when the time came." Whatever that meant.

Alison let out a tiny gasp. "Four years ago? That was around the same time the dementia had started. Holy moly." Alison took a few deep breaths. "Where is it?"

"Well—that's the problem." I hadn't told her the bad part yet. My turn to take the deep breath. "Vick's Mom can't remember exactly, but it's in or near a monument downtown—vague I know, but better than nothing—right?" I said, awaiting her response.

"Spook," Alison said.

"Spook?"

"You're not going to believe this," Alison said, "but the second time dad took her downtown… was to see a monument, the one near to where she'd sold the desk. She'd been adamant about going to the Human Rights monument before they left. He told me he'd driven her there, but again she'd wanted to do it alone. And knowing my mom's way—Dad hadn't pushed the matter. He said she'd had a satchel with her, with something big and heavy in it, but he hadn't bothered asking. Said when she'd come back to the car ten minutes later, the satchel had looked empty—and again he hadn't asked about it. My mom could be a tough nut to crack," she noted, giving another little giggle as if remembering the strength of her mom.

"Oh my gawd," I said, and reached into my tote. Sliding out my laptop, I booted it up in record speed.

"WHAT?" they all yelled in unison with Alison.

"It must be there, yes?" Alison said. "Is there something else, Spook?"

"Alison, don't you remember the photo I sent you—the one of me at the monument?"

"Oh my gawd is right, Spook," Alison said. "Have the others seen it?"

"No—just Liv. I'm bringing it up for the others now, but this has to be it." I clicked into the photos folder. Finding the image, I double-clicked on the icon to open it in its full glory. Mac, Vicki, and Olivia gathered in around my computer screen as I enlarged the photo, showing them the point I'd wanted to make... *Angels*. There it was, the image of me standing in the opening of the monument—me... with wings.

A tiny, "*Bing*," sounded from the computer.

"Email," I confirmed as the others gawked at the photo. A small email pop-up notification appeared in the lower right-hand corner of the screen. I read the notification aloud for Alison. "The email sender, *Derek Jones*. The topic header, *Conjuring Angels*...."

Chapter 35

Outside the house on the front lawn, the five stood. Michael and Gabriel stood to the left of Shamsiel, Uriel and Raphael to his right. The sky was quiet, the air unruffled showing no sign of anyone or anything malevolent.

"They did it," Shamsiel announced. "Your Charge did it, Uriel. She cast her first spell, and a good one at that. Her intentions were admirable and all of them possess positive intent. Armaros may have taught the first humans how to cast spells, but he never cared about their intent. And it's why he's known as the *accursed one,* you know."

"He was one of yours, was he not?" Michael questioned.

Mournful, Shamsiel unable to deny the truth, shook his head in disgust. "Yes, he was—or is rather, the 11th leader of the 20 of us who led the original 200. I learned soon after our fall that his intentions were not that of helping the human race, but were to influence, and watch their destruction." Shamsiel released a held breath.

"Listen!" Gabriel interrupted. "They know where the codex is."

Vretil appeared then, standing behind Uriel. "You are the one who works with nature, Uriel," Vretil said, stepping forward to place a hand on his friend's shoulder. "You oversee the divine origin of alchemy—not Armaros. You hold authority over Earth as does your Charge... for now."

Breaking the line, Gabriel stepped ahead and turned to face the others. "Aren't you listening to what is happening? The Cipher—he is starting to believe. He searches for the knowledge to help the others. He has found one of the keys. They need only to obtain the codex to find the answers. They are close now — so close."

"They'll still need the other key, the code to the divine script," Raphael pointed out. He stepped closer to the house to peer in through the window.

"What the...?" Alison hollered through the phone's speaker, following my reading the subject line of Derek's email. "Keep reading, Spook."

"Hold on — give me a sec," I said switching from the photo to my email. "Ready?" I asked, glancing around at the others as they took their seats again. They were all nods and smiles.

"Ready," Alison said through the phone.

Then I began. "He wrote,"

> *Okay Ladies,*
>
> *I do love a puzzle, riddle, or brainteaser, but the stuff you're sending me is stretching my brain way out there and the scientific side of me is getting stomped on. That being said, let me start with those pages you sent, since they were the most like brainteasers and were also where I found the most concrete facts.*
>
> *I researched different writing systems and alphabets at first, but then I had to add a third option to the search... and yes, I added the word magic to the mix. Bam — there it was. Every time I did the search I came up with the same results.*
>
> *What you have there in that recipe book is what's called 'The Theban alphabet'. Its origin is unknown, but it's sometimes referred to as 'The Runes of Honorius' after the alleged inventor 'Honorius of Thebes' in the early 1500's. Some references state it started as a Latin cipher sometime before the 11th century and possibly used it as an early alchemical code alphabet.*

I paused and shrugged my shoulders. But when no one interjected, I read on,

> *You'll like this part, it's also known as the 'Witch Alphabet', 'Witch Writing', or 'Witches' Runes'. It's like a code or cipher used to hide magic writing and has an almost one-to-one correspondence from Theban to the old Latin alphabet. Letters we use like J, U, and*

W, are not unique in this. The letters for 'I' and 'J' are one symbol, and 'U, V, and W' are also represented by one character. Another thing, it's not backward, it's written left to right like English, and it's the slant of the letters that make it look backward. Also, it seems to be just an alphabet, with no spoken language associated to it.

Stopping again, I said, "He attached the alphabet for us to use. I'll print a copy for Vicki to help translate the stuff in Mac's book. Mac, can you or someone grab it from your office printer?"

"It's a *Cuneiform* script," Vicki noted, leaning in to see the attachment. "Now that I have the letters, I'll be able to translate it without a problem — all I needed was the key."

I nodded at Vicki, but I hadn't really grasped what she'd said. I refocused back on the email, scanning to where I'd left off. "He says,"

There are two reasons a person would use a unique alphabet; first is for concealment, to hide it from the average person, the second is to increase the strength of a spell. It gives greater power to the words than writing them in ordinary letters. The two reasons working together.

Pausing, I gave a thought to what he'd written, the reasoning for the use.

"Makes total sense when you think about it," Mac said, returning with the printout. "What else?" she asked, handing Vicki the paper with the alphabet.

"He also found religious and magical references to letters," I said in response, and continued to read aloud,

Hebrew letters were viewed as magical by Jewish people. The Kabbalah system is based on the principle that each Hebrew letter is considered a 'living spirit or angel'. Though Hebrew and Ancient Greek have pretty much been removed from everyday language use, the two alphabets were used by magicians to symbolize words or names of great power.

I halted reading aloud and skipped past the other quotes he'd added on ancient alphabets and language, to find the part we needed. "Here we go," I stated, and read on,

From the two pages you sent, I found the first one was about 'Scrying', or more commonly called, 'Seeing'. It's a magical technique used to see things, but in a psychic way, like in a vision. You can use crystals, glass, water, or smoke, etc., or anything with a reflective quality. It's used for seeing past, present, and future, like in fortune telling, most using a crystal ball. A lot of different cultures and different belief structures use it, but it's not supported in the scientific community as a valid method for prediction or seeing things not seen by the human eye.

"He mentions the *Magic 8 Ball*—you guys remember that thing?" I remembered. "It was that black plastic ball that mimicked the 8 ball from a pool game, but bigger. It had a little window where you could see the dark blue liquid inside, had a thing bobbing around in it with different answers on each of the sides. When you flipped it upright — one of the sides would float in the window to give you the answer to your question—only yes and no questions, remember?"

No one said anything, they only sat there staring at me.

"Sorry—got off track." I regained my focus, only to be thrown off by Alison giggling again. It being infectious, it made the other serious faces break into their own laughter. "Where was I?" I said. Smiling, I found the spot and went on with Derek's words,

The method on the scanned page outlines using water. I looked that up as well. The term is called 'hydromancy', where visions can come from the colours, or ripples in the water when magical words are said over it. The purpose is to gain insight using this foresight. Says this is a big part of witchcraft for interpreting signs, events, or omens. Usually through contact with supernatural beings, often described as gods, angels, sometimes fallen, and even demons. I liked the definition, 'A systematic method used to organize things that appear to be disjoined or random information into order for problem solving', but then again, those in the scientific realm dismiss it.

Here is the bizarre part, not that the other stuff wasn't bizarre in my opinion, but this page is about invoking spirits or conjuring angels. I've tried to translate the spell, but not very well. Vicki may have a better chance at it, but it involves lighting a candle or incense that has been cleansed and charged up with positive intentions. The spell is spoken over a flame or smoke to conjure or summon the spirit, to ask for a favor or knowledge from them, while making your intentions clear.

"Okee-dokee. Shall I go on?" I asked, glancing at Mac, noting her keen expression. She was clearly onboard with the whole *conjuring* idea, but Olivia's expression showed doubt, or it could have been anxiety, it was hard to tell with her. But I figured no objections meant keep going, so I did,

> *Here's the kicker; those names you gave me for the men seemed familiar, but when I searched them individually, pairing each with the white suits or clothing, I got nothing. But when I searched the names together with or without the white suits, I got results. Consistent results every time, and I also realized why they were so familiar. I'd seen the names before when I searched stuff for you Lynn. Uriel, Michael, Raphael, and Gabriel are collectively known as Archangels.*

"Whoaaah!?" Alison shouted through the phone. "Oh man I love this!" Her words made everyone giggle again.

My heart pounded so hard that I wondered if the others could hear it. "Continue?" I questioned again. They said nothing through their giggles, and I trudged on,

> *They are most commonly referred to as the messengers and are angels who have authority over human affairs.*
> *It seems as though you are dealing with men named after the high-ranking angels, or if you believe in the stuff, possibly the angels themselves, your pick. Below, I outlined the most common facts about each.*

My brain was about to explode, not from the information but from who it was coming from. "I'm a little stunned at Derek delivering this info, he's a major non-believer, but I think we may have converted him," I chuckled out.

"This will be interesting," Vicki said, still doubtful.

"Yup," Olivia said through nervous giggles.

"More magic—I hope," Mac added.

Luc had driven it home in our last conversations, and I knew what was coming or what I *felt* was possible, this idea of angels. I was open to the idea. The others, I wasn't so sure what they thought, and chose to paraphrase the info Derek had compiled. "Let's see what we've got here...," I began. "Gabriel—his name means *God is my strength*, known as the Archangel of revelation, creativity, and faith. He commands the West winds, his element is Water, his season is Winter, and his symbol is the *trumpet*." Pausing, I recalled the other times his name had been mentioned before all this. Turning to Vicki I read, "Michael—his name means *Who is as God*, known as the Archangel of peace, harmony, and balance. He commands the winds of the South, his element is Fire, his season is Autumn, and his symbol is the *sword*."

Vicki nodded her understanding, taking it all in.

"Raphael," I said next. "His name means *God has healed*, known to be the angel of science and knowledge. He commands the East wind, his element is Air, his season is Spring, and his symbol is *a vial of ointment and an arrow*." At those words, we all turned to look at Olivia. Alison couldn't see us, so I said, "Spook, Mike is Vicki's and Ralph is Olivia's. The next one is Mac's. You catch that?"

"Roger," Alison confirmed.

"Uriel, his name means *Light or Fire of God*, known as the Archangel of enlightenment, physical order, and ecology. He commands the North winds, his element is Earth, his season is Summer, and his symbol is *an open hand holding a flame*." I glanced over to Mac. Her face scrunched in a way that implied annoyance. "Mac?"

"Wait—does that mean... Gabriel is Alison's guy?" Mac asked. "Isn't he the one from the journal and that other story you told us about, Lynn? Has to be, no?"

I shrugged, and Mac looked to the others perhaps to see if they had made the same assumption.

"What about the other guy who came to Lynn's door—Shamsiel?" Vicki questioned. "Could be he's Alison's guy? We don't have the information Alison's mother would have written, not like the others— not yet anyway."

"Has to be in the codex," I said. "We have to get that book—go downtown to that monument." It was my turn to look for confirmation.

"Does he say anything else... about Shamsiel?" Olivia asked, finally speaking up.

Glancing back at the computer screen, I searched the last part to Derek's email. "Yup, he's got one more piece," I said and continued,

> *This Shamsiel guy, he's something different. He's an angel all right, and it seems he was once the guardian angel of Eden, but he is now considered a fallen angel. He's stated as being the 16th Watcher of the 20 leaders of the 200 fallen angels mentioned in a text called the Book of Enoch, and he was sent to Earth by God. His name means 'Mighty sun of God' and he's the one who taught humans the mysteries of the sun. A few references also say that in the Kabbalah, he helped the other guy, Uriel, during the angelic wars. One reference says he commands 365 angelic legions, while another reference lists him as an angel to invoke during spellbinding.*

"That's all he wrote," I finished. His words were reminiscent of Dunya's from when she'd told me about Shamsiel, and of what I'd found in similar accounts when I'd searched it myself. Regardless, as someone who seemed to have selective insight for other people, I was lost to my own lack of knowing in this regard.

"Uhmmm," came Alison's voice from the cell phone. "Is this Shamsiel guy supposed to be good or bad? Because if he's bad—I'm rooting for Gabriel to be my guy." Pausing, she let out a big puff of air. "And I agree with Lynn, we need the book—I need the book. Spook?"

"We'll find it—don't you worry, okay?" I assured her, being she was the only one of us not able to go on the hunts.

Alison gave another long pause and then she said, "I think we should keep this to ourselves—the letters and the book, and well—everything. Just between us and the mothers." Letting out a loud breath, she added, "For now."

Everyone nodded in agreement.

"We're with you on that, Spook. Just those who know, or need to know, like Derek," I reminded. He would need to stay in the loop, to help if we needed him. We wouldn't be able to keep him away from this mystery now even if we wanted. I noted the time again, 5 p.m.. Six hours had passed since our arrival, but it still hadn't gotten dark outside. And it was lucky for us because there was no way we could put this off another day. "Who's ready to find that book?" I asked, panning the waiting faces of my friends.

Surprisingly, Olivia spoke first. "I'm ready. Let's go get that book—the codex thing, and get to the bottom of all this."

Both The Witch and The Linguist followed up with enthusiasm and agreement to that of The Healer. The only response left was that of The Scribe.

"Spook, you okay with us going ahead? I'll call you back if-and-or-when we find something—you cool with that?" I said, hoping for a positive answer.

Alison's heavy sigh was followed by, "Sure-sure, what can I say? But call me as soon as you find anything. You hear me—anything," she said.

"You know I will—stand by," I told her.

"Standing by," she confirmed, letting out another sigh, then hanging up.

I frowned and put away my phone. She should be here for this. It was her part, her mom's part, and she was stuck all the way across the country. I knew firsthand it wasn't remotely the same getting updates fed to you through the phone. Poor Spook. She'd be here soonest, but in the meantime, we'd have to find this piece for her.

As I scanned for more emails—just in case, Mac gathered up all the *witchy* items. The others helped by packing away the pieces to the quest in a large wicker basket that Mac had foraged from the basement.

Mac tied the lid securely closed. "I'll hide this in my office. No one ever goes in there—too much girly stuff from my business, repels the boys like bug-repellant," Mac shared as she proceeded up the stair to hide the treasures.

I shut down my laptop and tucked it into my tote and set it under the coffee table. Totes and purses were also repellants for boys and men, but no one would be home to touch it tonight, anyway.

Ten minutes later, we piled into Olivia's car and were off to continue our quest. Olivia had insisted on driving, stating again that she was best under pressure. Vicki had taken the spot as copilot. Mac and I sat in the rear performing as backseat drivers, but since Vicki worked downtown, she had been better at giving Olivia the best option for parking up-close and personal to the monument.

In line with our intended target, Olivia parked near the corner of Elgin and Lisgar. We all got out and collectively stared over to *the monument*.

Leaving the others, I walked to stand at the northeast corner immediately adjacent to the monument, to get a different perspective. The Ottawa City Hall Heritage Building loomed up in the wake of the monument a few yards behind. Turning my back on the place, I assessed the businesses of downtown Ottawa on a Thursday evening. Straight in front of me was 200 Elgin with a bank on the main level rising to the now dark office high-rise. To the right was the office building where Vicki worked. At the southwest corner was a busy coffee shop, and at the southeast corner was the Presbyterian Church showing no action for this hour. The City Hall being down-wind of the Parliament Precinct, there wasn't usually a ton of action at this juncture, but tonight there seemed to be groups of people gathering at the far side, though no one as far over as where we were.

My friends came to meet me where I studied the city. I turned, and we all faced the monument, then together we began the walk towards our target.

Approaching the monument from the south, we passed by the totem-like figures known as *The House of Canada* part of the monument. We circled around to the north side where there were six large concrete riser-steps leading up to the front of the monument and its archway entrance. It sat on the lawn in front of that beautiful 19th century heritage building, bizarre and in high contrast.

We split up then, taking turns looking at all the bases of the statues, all the plaques, every edge, and every curve. Nothing seemed to stick out. Nothing called to us—to me... nothing... *nothing*.

"Call Derek," Olivia suggested. "Maybe he'll be able to help us with this one. I know he's not from Ottawa, but I bet he can find something on the internet that could help. I'm at a loss here—you?"

"Was thinking the same thing, Liv," I said, taking out my cell phone. As the phone dialed, I panned the area again looking for something... anything.

"Cipher here," Derek's voice shot out following the first ring.

"You're liking the handle, eh?" I laughed a little at his continued enthusiasm.

"Whatcha got for me, L?" he said, sounding all serious and *007ish*.

I turned back to the full view of the monument. "Here it is, Shortcut. We're all at the Human Rights monument, we think the codex is hidden somewhere here. We have no idea where exactly, but things seem to point us here—to the monument."

The sound of clicking computer keys was followed by, "Let me seeee... here we go—got an aerial shot of the place, plus a street view. Checking for the city write-up—hold on," he said, chased by the sound of more key clicks. "The totem figures—the ones which look like large *Lego* people, how are they secured to the base?"

Leaning over, I inspected a totem. "Looks like concrete posts," I told him, pocketing my cell phone and going with my *Bluetooth* earpiece and hands free for the hunt.

"Do they swivel?" he asked.

Knowing better, but still, I wrapped my arms around the closest base and tried to turn it to the left. "They must weigh a thousand pounds each at least," I grunted, trying to turn the pillar the other way, having no effect and feeling completely ridiculous.

"Right, let me check the monument design." There was a short pause. "Looks like the guy who created or designed the monument didn't design the base. It was a company that used to be located in the east end of the city, but they're out of business now. They specialized in decorative flooring for office buildings with areas of high traffic. Says they also made floor safes and conduit casings for utility wires and piping. Maybe the book is in the base?"

"Ya think?" I shot out, throwing a little sarcasm at him. "We figured it could be here, but not sure how to open or where it opens."

"Hold on, Snarky-Snarkerson, I'm looking," he huffed into the phone, keyboard keys clacking away. "How about this? One design was for encasing utility wiring and pipes in the floor, but with a hidden panel for access to do maintenance when needed. The panel, hidden in plain sight, was under a swiveling concrete pillar—decorative—no real function. Requires two people to open it... as pressure to move the pillar must be equal on all sides. Guess it kept the average person from leaning on it and accidentally opening it." He clacked away on the keys some more. "Get this, the material used to assemble the monument was donated from materials previously used in the testing of this conduit floor design… one of those pillars must move," he suggested.

I paused, eyeing the 20-foot-tall statues, and then checked on the others. Vicki was standing inside the monument reading the different plaques, most of which were in different native languages. Mac was walking around the outside trying to find a hot or cold spot, possibly indicating something beneath the surface, *Witch* stuff I assumed. Olivia stood near me waiting for a miracle to come from Derek, much like our other hunts before this. Turning to face her I said, "Derek wants us to try turning one of the totems." Knowing it sounded absurd, I smiled at her, but I was still willing to try it.

"Oookaaaay," she hesitantly agreed, moving towards the nearest pillar. "Now what?"

"Now what?" I said into the phone. "Liv and I are at one of the pillars."

Right away Derek said, "Try applying pressure to all four sides, each of you using your hands and at the same time, try to turn it to the left."

Repeating the instruction to Olivia, the two of us placed our hands on the rough surface of the totem's base. "One, two—threeeee." With combined pressure, we attempted to turn the thousand-pound column, but, "No good," I told him.

"Try the next one—maybe it's only one of them that moves."

He seemed optimistic, his excitement growing with the new puzzle, so we stepped to the right and tried the next totem. This one carried the sign inscribed with the words *Rights* on one side and the French, *Droite* on the other. Mid-grunt I realized what the problem was with this plan. If it took two people to turn a pillar for this puzzle, how the hell did Alison's Mom do it, alone? "Derek—this isn't it," I sighed. "Has to be something where one person can do it—and an older person at that."

"Oh ya, forgot about that part—was good though, eh? Almost worked," he laughed. "Could totally picture the two of you trying to move those monstrous statues." He was laughing a little harder now.

"Funny—ha—got any other ideas?" I laughed a little, knowing he was right about the way we must have looked. Anyone glancing our way would have thought we were *hugging* the enormous things. I've seen stranger things, no harm. Laughing a little more, I smiled at Olivia who was now shaking her head and trying not to laugh.

"What else do you see in the area—buildings, gardens, anything?" Derek asked.

"What used to be the Ottawa Teacher's College—is right next to it. It's just a heritage building now and part of Ottawa City Hall," I said, scanning for anything else of interest. "Let us check out the area. I'll call you back."

"I'll keep checking at my end—over'n out," he said.

The phone went silent, and I made for the nearest entrance to the heritage building.

Out front, there was a sandwich board sign showing that tonight was the *'AIDS Walk for Life'* event and that the sign-up area was around to the left at the *Marion Dewar Plaza* entrance. Mystery solved—that was why all the people were gathering over that way. Checking my watch, I informed the others the race would start soon, scheduled to begin at 7 p.m.. I also noted that although this building's official hours were usually Saturday and Sunday, the facility was open for the event. Good thing for us because it meant we could go inside and snoop around while the crowd's attention was on the race.

My friends followed as I walked up the two large stone steps. Then I stopped, glancing upward surveying the entranceway which lay before the main door. It was at least 15 feet high, but the front part of the building stretched up over two stories. It had a diverse roofline with a central pointed belfry, gables, and assorted turrets. I stepped forward through the archway to grab hold of the hefty ornate handle. Pressing down on the lever and anticipating the weight of the enormous wooden door, I gave it my full strength and yanked to open it. With both hands I pressed the door wide and held it until my friends could pass through.

Inside was a long rectangular central pavilion defining the main block of the building and a typical format for this type of academic institution of its time. The interior, even with the boring grey stone, gave off a gutsy eclectic vibe. It had different architectural details such as Roman style columns, and Gothic-style flat-headed and semi-circular windows. Based on the info board next to the entrance, it had been built in 1875, but had still been connected to the newer modern wing of the City Hall. The info board also stated that the building contained the Mayor and Council members' offices, along with a bunch of other offices and committee rooms. One of the committee rooms had the description; *The former library for the teacher's college*, alongside its title.

I continued forward, walking the stretch of the hall and observing the historical documents and memorabilia from the earlier years displayed along the gallery-style walls. I stopped to glance around the expanse of the building's main hall, just as my phone vibrated in the side pocket of my cargo pants.

"Incoming!" I announced, tapping the answer-button on my earpiece. "Secret agent, Westlake here...." I said, then cringed and sucked in a quick breath, hoping it wasn't a morning call from Will. I wasn't ready to explain that little title I'd just given myself.

"Agent 99 checking in Secret-Spook," Alison responded, letting out a boisterous laugh.

"Nice, Spook—primo counter," I gave her, complimenting her brilliant use of nostalgic pop culture. But she was always fast like that, it was one of the many things I adored about her.

"Well...," I let out, trying to figure out which details to give her first. "No luck with the monument." It was basic info, but I had little else I could say.

"What do you mean *no luck*?" I could hear the grumble in her voice.

"No luck—meaning, no way is there a hiding place in the public monument." Emphasis on *public*. "But we are investigating other options. I'm standing in the main gallery of the old City Hall, behind the monument. Figured we'd peek in and see if anything—you know, spoke to us."

"Uh, Spook," she said, "My mom took courses at that college."

"Hold on," I said, waving the others over. "It hasn't been a college since 1974—when was that?"

"Well, she took courses there a few months after we moved to Ottawa—I was just little then, but she told me way later that she'd taken courses in literature and library studies."

"Oh man—with the monument being a bust, we wondered if the building was the hiding place. But this building is massive—wouldn't know where to start. The place isn't normally open now either," I told her. "Only reason we're inside is because there's a special event on in the main building. Place is wide open for spectators though," I clarified, then heard a *beep* on the line. "Give me a sec, Spook—got another call coming in—hold on." I swapped calls.

"Ciph," Derek started, but I cut him off.

"We're in the building and Alison is on the other line—her mom used to take courses here when it was still a teacher's college, *literature, and library studies.*"

"Did you check the library?" he asked, sounding a little too smug for my current mood. Cutting me off this time, he said, "Based on the floor plan diagrams I found, the library was in the far-left side at the back of the building. The most recent floor plan shows the same space as being used as a conference room, and the diagram indicates symbols for rows of shelves."

"Library it is—I'll call you back." Clicking back to Alison, I gave her the info Derek had just relayed. "I'll call you back too, in case I need Derek for something else—okay?"

"No prob—99 out," Alison confirmed, ending the call.

Turning, I met the faces of my three friends, then I looked directly at Vicki. "We'll go to the library," I said. Then I looked to Mac and Olivia. "You two take watch. Anyone heads our way—let us know." They all nodded, and we spread out.

Mac and Olivia split off to watch the front and back entrances while Vicki and I headed to what used to be the old library. I noted that the odd person or two still passed through the connection from the new to old parts of the building. I realized we needed to be stealthier in our actions because once the race started, there would be an influx of people coming back into the building. That gave us less than 15 minutes before we no longer had the place to ourselves.

Hurrying to the end of the lengthy hall, we found a room plaque that displayed we'd reached committee room 9B, the one designated as being the old library. Stepping towards the door, I took a quick glimpse around at the others. Nods came from all, and I moved forward to peer through the door's glass window. There was a desk lamp on in the room, but no one appeared to be inside. I grabbed the doorknob and turned it slowly to the right. Jackpot—the door was unlocked. Opening it just enough, Vicki and I slipped in, and shut the door behind us.

Something in the room was off. From the outside, the door was near the end of the hall giving you the impression that the room ended there as the hall did. But in fact, the room itself expanded both left and right, revealing that the entrance was in the center, not the end. Over to the left were two long tables set in a slight V shape with chairs tucked in under, four per table, facing towards the center of the room. Behind the seating was an expansive wall of bookcases filled with large binders individually labeled. On the far wall across from the entrance, was the same modern shelving with its sleek lines and streamline design, both obviously put in more recently with the linking of the new and old wings.

To the right, in the other half of the room, were deep ornate antique bookcases lining its wall. In high contrast to the sleek modern-style bookcases, these were more along the same design period of the original building. The dark stained deep wood-grained shelves had handcrafted decorative carved edges. Carved ginger-breading hung from the top frames of the cases, shadowing the deep-set shelves. The shelves themselves were well used and contained old hardcover books of all sizes and thicknesses.

Vicki and I stepped closer to examine them. Some titles I recognized, not because I'd read them, but because I had heard the names before. There was *Little Women, Jane Eyre, Wuthering Heights,* and *Great Expectations* plus countless others. The books had been well cared for; in fact, the covers were beautiful. I stepped back again to study the bookcase.

The shelves comprised five separate units of casings, stretching what I guesstimated to be about 25 feet long. The end cases were different and seemed to frame the other three. They all had the same ornate gingerbread edging on top, but the two end ones were different on the bottom.

Bending down, I saw that the three center cases had elaborately carved legs holding up the cases, whereas the end ones had intricately carved panels that covered and hid the depth of the underside of the bottom shelf. It appeared decorative rather than functional, but I knelt to get a better look and found the legs hidden in behind. On each unit the bottom shelf appeared to be the same height, about ten inches high, though the other shelves above varied in height being adjustable to accommodate the varying book heights.

"Gorgeous," Vicki said, running her hands over the carved wood and across the softened book covers. "Now what?" she questioned, looking over at me.

I reached out and caressed the wood myself. "Man, I don't know — let me take of few pictures. I'll send them to Derek. He's waiting for my call." I took my phone out and snapped a few shots of the shelving and its individual units, including the top and different bottoms. I hit *send* and panned the huge room again.

There was a similar setup of tables and chairs at this end, all facing inward to the center. It was a committee room after all. As I turned back to face the hefty line of shelves, my cell phone *twittered* in my ear. "Hey, Lynn here," I answered, expecting a response from possibly anyone — my husband included.

"I take it you're in the library — amazing woodwork. Don't see stuff like that anymore. Nice they kept it," Derek said. Obviously, he'd searched reference to the inside of the building, and had been waiting anxiously.

"Other side is full of modern shelving — looks totally off, but I'm sure it was economical, whatever." Taking a quick glance over my shoulder, I frowned at the high contrast shelving that didn't blend with the old handcrafted gorgeous wall in front of me. "Got anything for us?"

"You know I do. Wouldn't be the *Cipher* if I didn't," he laughed out, enjoying this a bit too much.

"And...." I had to roll my eyes at that one, but still waited for his brilliant discovery.

"I found a guy online who does reproductions of old furniture—for customers who want the look but don't want to pay the antiques prices. He makes a shelf unit similar to the end sections of that unit—hides the functional legs or posts with the decorative panel. The legs carry the weight of the unit, but the panel gives it that thick heavy exterior of antique pieces. He even has a video on his website—shows how it works."

"What do you mean, *how it works*?" I cut in.

"Well it says the original ones he tried to replicate were similar in that the panels were actually hidden compartments. You could remove the panel to reveal the legs or use them to hide—whatever. Video shows how the panels release."

"Now'd be a good time to tell me how that's done—trespassing here," I scoffed.

"Don't get your panties in a knot. Are you able to see the outer sides of the end units?"

Going to the right side of the end unit, I replied, "Affirmative. It juts forward about four inches from the shelves and has about a two-inch gap between it and the wall." Motioning for Vicki to check the other at the far side, I waited for his next tidbit.

"Four inches, two-inch gap—check," Vicki said, giving me a thumbs-up from the other end of the shelving unit.

"Okay, we have access—now what?" I asked, anxiously staring over at Vicki as she waited.

"Say these magic words—just kidding."

"Derek!" I gritted teeth.

"Chill—*sheesh*. There should be a knot in the wood—it's a fake knot. Do you see it?" he asked, a tad anxious, but still laughing at his own joke.

Sliding my hand along the wood and into the gap there was a change in the wood's texture. "I feel it—at least I think I do. Can't see it—it's further in."

Glancing up at Vicki, I watched as she repeated the actions. "Feel it," she confirmed, giving me a nod.

"Push the center of the knot, it should give way easily," he said, confident. "It's not supposed to be hard, but I'm sure that's why it's hidden—so no one would touch it."

I pressed the textured spot on the wood, and the decorative panel popped forward revealing a one-inch gap along its seam. "It opened," I whispered. Not sure why I whispered.

"Got a gap," Vicki tossed back at me, waiting for our next move.

I ran my hand along the edge that poked out from the bottom shelf and stopped. "Do we pull?"

"Slowly," Derek instructed, "Using both hands, pull the panel forward on the same angle it's leaning out at—an arching motion. This is an old piece—be careful."

You'd think he had us defusing a bomb or something, but I passed the next steps on to Vicki as instructed. Then placing my hands equidistance apart on the panel, I eased the wooden piece forward. As I pulled, I saw the primitive mechanics of the release on the same side to which the pressure point was located.

"Well?" Derek's voice pelted into my ear, startling me.

Damn good thing it wasn't a bomb. Not responding, I glanced down the line of shelves to Vicki again. She shook her head, signifying she'd found nothing behind her panel. I leaned down to the now open space... and there it was... *something*.

"Got something," I said. Smiling in triumph I reached in and then hefted out what appeared to be an antique box. It was inlaid with different pieces of stained wood or more possibly different types of woods set in on its top.

"What is it?" Derek asked, as if pushing for his own triumph.

As much as I wanted to torment Mr. *Smart*-ass, I gave in. "It's about 12 to... 15 inches wide, the same deep, and about half that high. It's got two small drawers in it, but I can't seem to budge them. There's a keyhole on the front—but no key...," I said, only to halt when the door to the room cracked open.

"There're people coming," Olivia said, standing half in and half out of the doorway. "We have to go."

"Call you back—gotta bounce," I told Derek, and hung up before he could reply. Together at our respective ends, Vicki and I pushed closed the shelf panels and then were up and out of the room a split second later. With the wooden box secure under my arm, we took off through the back entrance that led us to the linked walkway joining the old wing to the new.

I snickered when we exited the building because unexpectedly, we were about five yards from where we'd parked the car. Note to self; *when treasure hunting, try back or side doors first.*

My inner giggle cut short, I halted in my tracks about ten feet shy of the car. The little hairs on the back of my neck prickled as nausea travelled my body in a hot flush. Cradling the box against my chest, I turned back towards the door we'd just come out from... but saw nothing. I sucked in a breath and panned the buildings across from us on the side street... *nothing.* I blew out the breath and sucked in another through my nose to ward off the sick sensation, then stared down to the end of the street away from the main drag. The night's sky was darker now, only the occasional lamppost lit the sidewalk, but this time, there was something... *someone.*

A large figure stood near the edge of the apartment building where the street cut off. He stood next to a lamppost, but more in front of as it cast a large looming shadow leaving his face obscured. I squinted, trying to make out the details. Another wave of nausea hit. Straight from my stomach it pushed a foul taste of bile up to touch the back of my throat. Fighting the bitter taste, I took in a deep breath. I held it a second, then let out the air slowly to see a cold mist escape into the night. The air was no longer cool like earlier, but *cold*, frosty, and definitely colder than normal for September. Clouds moved in fast, covering the light of the quarter moon and a shiver ran up my spine to meet my bristling hairs.

"What is it Lynn?" Mac asked, seeing me stop short of the car. The others had their hands on the door handles ready to get in. Everyone's breath puffed into the air now, mine coming quicker than the rest.

I shot a look over to Mac. "Not sure... *something*... someone," I whispered, trying to swallow back the sick feeling that climbed the backside of my throat. Then like a savior, Olivia popped the locks on the car, and lickety-split, I ran to join them. Blinking clear the tears of my frosting vision I climbed in. I glanced back towards the figure, but he was gone. And thankfully, so was that dreadful feeling.

Vicki sat in the back with me this time, examining the find. "Looks old," she noted, "Looks like the top of a small desk."

Peeking over my shoulder and out the back window, I double checked to see that the *someone* was truly gone, and not just hiding in the shadow of the building. But there was, *nothing*. Turning back to Vicki I tried to refocus.

"Could this be the desk Alison told us about? Her mom sold her desk to someone—at least that's what her dad had remembered," Vicki said. "I'd pictured a desk-desk—with four legs, big surface, but this could still be it."

Saying nothing, I shifted the box to get a better look at it.

"It's like one of those lap-pads you get for a laptop computer, instead of it sitting on your legs—it's raised up for more comfort," Vicki added, placing it now on her lap as if to show me.

"So much for her visiting the monument, the sneaky-devil was hiding this—not selling it," Mac added from the front seat.

Vicki tried to pry the edge open, but nothing budged. "It's locked," she said.

"Book's gotta be inside," Olivia added, hopeful, glancing at us via the rearview mirror.

Twisting in my seat again, I peered out the back window one last time. As we drove up the road, I saw someone, no—not someone... *four* someones, stepping forward from the shadows into the glow of the streetlamp. I rubbed my eyes. That first lone figure had pulled me into a foggy place in my mind, one of sickness, anguish, pain, and sorrow. But something had chased off that horrible awareness, replacing it now with lightness, with a sensation of wellbeing, of comfort, and of *safety*. As we stopped at the far end of the street, I continued to peer out the back window. A *fifth* figure appeared under the shaft of light thrown off from the streetlamp. Joy and solace filled me as I watched each of them step forward into the light, fracturing the shadows and collapsing darkness.

"Think you should call Alison—have her confirm what we found," Vicki remarked, shaking me from my inner reflections.

I blinked, and the scene was lost as we rounded on to the main street.

Chapter 36

"Told you they'd find it," Gabriel gloated, staring down the way as the car stopped the end of the street.

"None too soon!" Uriel roared. "Armaros was here—again, he watches them." Furious, he did a quick scan of the area. Michael and Raphael did the same.

Gabriel crossed his arms over his chest, shaking his head disappointed at how the others had reacted to the now forgotten success of their Charges.

Uriel turned to face Gabriel. "Now what?" Uriel questioned, half expecting to hear a series of thunderclaps. Shamsiel appeared next to him.

Shamsiel was close enough that he whispered into his ear. "Now, I will watch him," Shamsiel breathed out, with enough volume that the others could hear.

"Did you see that?" Raphael demanded, followed by a loud gasp. "Gabriel's Charge, she looked right at us." He gasped again. "How could she see us? She wasn't meant to see us—who revealed themselves? Gabriel was it you?" he accused.

The others stood dumbfounded, staring as the car rounded the corner and out of sight.

"Me?" Gabriel deflected, "She doesn't require a reveal to see." They all turned and stared at him now, mouths a gape, *including* Shamsiel.

"What… in heaven's name… is that supposed to mean?" Michael challenged.

A familiar *tweet* sounded in my ear. "Someone's calling now," I said. I answered the phone but suddenly lost my words. "Sup," was all I got out. My mind still lingered on what I'd experienced outside the building, and on what I'd just seen.

"Okay my flight's booked—I'll find that damn book if it kills me," Alison stated, fixed and determined "I'm arriving 10 a.m. your time—meet me out front at the arrivals—okay, Spook."

"Spook." My heart pounded in my throat. "I'm not gonna stop you from coming. I think you should be here, anyway. But we found something…."

"Whaaaaaaat! Why didn't you call me?" she hollered, cutting off my words, and not like her usual serene nature.

"Quiet down there, Mamma-bear," I said, my brain fog clearing due to her volume. "Don't let Ken hear you getting all worked up—he won't let you come. May tie you to a chair to keep you from leaving—plane ticket or not." I could picture it too, Ken wrapping rope around her in a chair, like a villain tying a damsel to the tracks in one of those old black and white silent films.

I heard her take in a few slow deep breaths. "Sorry, Spook…." she breathed out. "Hormones are a bitch," she added with more deep breaths. "Ken's working late tonight—thank gawd."

"Tell me he knows you're coming?" I pleaded.

"Ya-Ya, I've been working on him all week. Doesn't like it much, but he knows the score when it comes to my friends."

"Don't worry, I'll be there to pick you up. And Spook… I think it's your mom's writing desk thing—whatever, that we found." I paused but got no response. "Can you describe it for me?" I had to make sure we had what I hoped we had.

She cleared her throat as if choked-up over, and well, *hormones were a bitch*. "It's uh… uhm, wood… about a foot and a bit wide and deep, and six-inch-high… not really a desk I guess."

"Check," I confirmed, waiting for more.

"It's uhm... inlaid with different wood... oak, walnut and poplar," she added, "all different colours. Was a Christmas gift from my Great-gran to her daughter—my grandmother. My gran gave it to my mom when I was born... has to be at least 130 years old," she said. "Does it have two small drawers, one on each side?"

I nodded at the question though she couldn't see me. "Yup," I said, finding myself once more at a loss for words.

"Please tell me that book was in it," she urged.

I swear I could hear the blood rushing in her ear, right through the phone. Frustrated myself with the book-hunt, I uttered another one-word answer, "Locked."

"Shit!" came from Alison's end, followed up by, "Shit, shit, shiiiiiiit!"

When Alison finished her curse-rant, I said, "Spook, we've got the thing and we're heading back to Mac's. That's all that matters now. You'll be here in the morning and we'll figure this all out. Don't stress. It's not good for the little *Disco-Dancer* you're carrying there," I said, making my attempt to get a chuckle out of her, get her back to her usual composed-self.

It worked. She giggled, making me giggle back.

"Okay," she said. "But if you get the damn thing open—call me." She giggled again. "Meantime—I need to replenish, this dancer's kicking up a storm—making me hungry."

I pictured her rubbing her tummy trying to sooth the junior *Rockette* growing in her belly. "You know I'll call, this is about you now—all of you," I said, giving her more reassurance. It was obvious now, this was not—nor had it ever been, about me or my mom. My gut twinged at the realization of my words. "Take your time, get your stuff ready and I'll see you in the morning, okay?"

"Okay—love you, Spook," she said, sounding much calmer now.

"Love you too." I ended the call.

The car pulled into Mac's driveway and I checked the time again. It was already 10 p.m.. The time keeps racing, how is it I—we, weren't noticing? More strange stuff to add to the mix. Seemed like time moved faster around us while we're mystery hunting or maybe it had something to do with using magic. Was it magic—real magic or something else, or was I seriously losing it? Whatever it was, time was definitely being affected. And we could sure use some magic to get this writing box open.

One by one we piled out of the car and scrambled up the front steps. The calm cool air from earlier was now stale and *staticky* as if a storm was on its way. It made me want to rush inside to avoid the pending onslaught. The others felt it or something like it, because I wasn't the only one sprinting to get inside, but for them it could have been just about the lap desk. Mac sprung the lock and once again we went into the safe sanctity of our Witch's dwelling. Inside the atmosphere was in contrast to the outer, much like fresh air after a rainstorm, with the same tranquility as if everything would be all right now.

I placed the wooden box on the coffee table and took a few quick photos of it for our friend The Cipher. He would need images I assumed to help get it open. "Mac, can't you do a little presto-shizam-abra-capokus here, and crack this puppy open?" I asked, secretly crossing my fingers and making a wish hoping she could.

Olivia and Vicki came and sat on the couch in front of the table between where I stood. Mac walked over and stood at the end of the coffee table directly opposite from me. In a sweeping motion she raised her arms over her head, moving them back and forth over the box. She closed her eyes.

"Alohomora!" Mac commanded, waving her hands over the box, eye still closed.

"Pffft—Did you just *Harry Potter* this box?" Olivia chuckled. "You did—didn't you?" She put her hands on her hips.

Vicki rolled her eyes and mirrored Olivia's hands on hips.

I gawked at each of them, confused.

"What?" Mac asked, letting her arms drop and slap against her sides. "Thought it might work. That kid used it to unlock doors."

"Yaaaa—in a mooovieeeee," Olivia tossed back at her, laughing. Hard enough, *gut-ripping,* that she gripped her side and let out an, "Owwch. Ouch. Ouch."

"Mackenzie, really?" I said. "How about you do a few *Bugs-Bunny* tries like *Pokus-cadabra, Walla-Walla-Washington* or *Newport-News*?" Then just like that we were all ripping a gut, including Mac.

She was now giving a stitch in her side a good rub. "Maybe there's something like it in the grimoire—can't hurt to look," Mac suggested through the pain of her laughter.

"Can't hurt a Witch for trying," I said. "In the meantime, let me send off the photos to Derek—get him back on the job so to speak." I shook my head again at Mac's attempt and then texted the photos. Regaining my seat on the cushy ottoman, I slipped my laptop bag out from under the coffee table and set it up alongside next to the old wooden box. The antique box sat in brilliant silence and dignity in contrast to my computer as it *bleeped* and *twittered* into action. Then I checked my email for, well, *anything.*

Will had sent another email with more photos attached. I clicked on it quick to see a photo of him standing next to the *100-butterfly* vase that I knew represented the *Quing* dynasty. He'd brought home a replica of it for me a few trips back, along with chopsticks etched with butterflies. The replica was beautiful and though I loved it, it also reminded me of how *real* his life was and how *replica* mine had seemed. Even with this mystery, though it was real, it wasn't mine.

Grimoire in hand, Mac returned to the living room and planted herself back on the big couch-chair. She skimmed the grimoire for what I concluded must be for her one-millionth time.

"Could you try scrying—like Derek had mentioned. Maybe you could scry an answer to open the box?" Olivia suggested, apparently board with waiting.

"Not sure that's how it works, Olivia," Mac said. "Think it's more for predictions. And unless I've missed an unlocking spell in here, I believe we need a key."

"Not sure Alison would be okay if we smash the thing open either," I shot out, into their dialog, still staring at Will's smiling face as he stood next to another artifact.

"Bing," went the email notification on my computer announcing a new message.

"It's from Derek," I said, switching to the new email.

"What's he got for us?" Olivia asked, leaning in.

"I'm seriously considering writing a book about your adventure, Lynn, or contracting someone to do it," I said, reading Derek's first line. I glanced up at the others, grinning.

"Not if Alison gets to it first," Vicki added.

I smiled again and continued to read his email aloud,

> If it's the same piece I found referenced to online, it was handmade by some woman's great-grandfather. Says there are two inkwells inside, two small pencil or pen drawers and a hidden compartment. The bottom is false. Says if you pull up the wood-slat on the bottom side, it shows the inlaid delineation of the partition. You need to use the key to open it first, then there is a bunch of maneuvers you have to do to get into the hiding space.

"His instructions say, *First pull...*," I began, only to be abruptly halted by a "*SMACK*" sound and grumbles of annoyance. "What?" I said, looking directly at Vicki.

"Hello, people—we don't haaaaave a keeeeey," Vicki declared, slapping her hands on her thighs a second time in aggravation.

"Crap!" Mac stomped her heel. "Right, bit of a hiccup there." She put her hands to her face in frustration.

The enthusiasm fading along with their earlier optimism, I said, "I'll just write Derek back. He'll find a solution."

Olivia leaned in again as I clacked away on my keyboard. Vicki rubbed her thighs and Mac dropped her hands from her face. Vicki started *dew-dew-dewing* the *Jeopardy* theme song, and I glared back at her, stopping her mid-*dew-dew*.

"Hey, I've only been here four days, and we've come a long way in that short time. A little more patience would be nice, please," I said, hitting send on the quick message. I was trying to help solve the—*their* mystery. Wasn't mine to solve anymore, but you don't see me bitching about it. "Do you think Derek's got nothing better to do than chase around after our wants? He usually responds right away and 99.9% of the time—he's got something for us." Each of them eyeballed me with their own version of the *oh really* expression plastered across their faces. "Sorry," I said, red-faced, still feeling the urge to scream.

"No... you're right, Lynn. I'm sorry," Vicki said, her tone regretful. "I was getting used to the instant gratification Derek's been giving us." She tried to smile through her impatience, but I'm sure based on my expression, she knew I was just as frustrated with everything.

"We're all anxious now... now that things feel so close," Olivia said. "But then we get presented with yet another roadblock." She sighed. "I'm glad Alison is coming, maybe having the four of us in the same city—room—space—whatever, will have some impact." The others nodded like bobble-heads, in agreement with Olivia's theory.

Some impact? I guess four days of impact wasn't enough for them. Regardless, I was also resigned to the idea that, *Alison being here*, was key and would help move things along. The real key was to get that book out of this damn desk thing, but we had no actual *key*.

The book was in there, I knew it. And besides the fact my alarm-tingle-senses were going off like the bell at a fire station, I knew Derek would find a way to help us, *again*. I also knew I needed to finish this one last thing, then I could let it go, or at least I hoped I could let it go. They wouldn't need me after we got the book out. They could stay in touch with Derek on their own if needed. He's the one with the answer—not me, and the last thing I wanted to do was be in the way. It was time for me to hand this mystery off. I glanced around at my friends.

Olivia and Vicki were examining the box and its many coloured woods while Mac scanned through the grimoire again for the billionth time. I watched them, pondering each of their roles. They needed to find their own way, their own solutions. They needed to see that... they *must* see it. This is their legacy and possibly their destiny, and truthfully, I wanted them to get off their butts and find the answers themselves. They'd had it easy having Derek, figuratively by their side. And I know he probably—no not probably—definitely, loved this. From what I'd gathered, this whole thing, all of it, was about *sacrifice...* theirs, *the four*. It's about a belief system, showing that each of them believes in their roles, the roles that have been their ancestors' for generations before them. It's been nearly effortless thus far, though I've also considered what that could mean... that perhaps the tough stuff was yet to come. They need to be ready. It's time for them to work together, without me in the middle, find their own kinship in these new friendships. I was confident now that my journey in this was to get them here—together, in the same place. My next journey was to let them transition forward as a unit without me. It's not my journey, not anymore.

"Lynn, you seem a million miles away. You okay?" Olivia asked.

"Oh, I'm good," I mused, bringing myself back to the here and now, giving her my best *happy* voice. "Just tired that's all." She smiled, but I don't think she believed me. She must have noticed me lost somewhere in my deliberations. I check the time on my computer again. "It's almost midnight," I pointed out, wondering again about the loss in time.

Mac let out a big *"Yaaaawn"*, causing a chain reaction all around our little space.

"Everyone will be in bed at my house," Olivia yawned out. "They don't seem to care what I'm up to. Not one call or text from either of my daughters or my husband... just as well." She shrugged.

"You working tomorrow, Vick?" I asked through my own yawn. She was the only one right now who had responsibilities she'd been shirking.

"Think I'll be working from home," she said, giving me a quick wink. "I'm usually the only one in the office on Fridays—I won't be missed. I'll keep my work laptop handy should any of the *crybabies* I work with need me. I've already finished my work for the week, and I'd normally spend the day emailing you—if you weren't already here," she joked, giving me a tired grin.

"True," I agreed equally sleepy. We lived for those emails to help get us through our days. "Okay troops, lets wrap it up for tonight. We're all tired and this desk will be here in the morning to torment us again." I gathered my laptop and glanced around at the other sleepy faces.

"I'll put the desk in my office with the other items," Mac said. Getting up off her favorite chair, she leaned over the coffee table and lifted the small wooden desk as if it were a newborn, using both arms to cradle the box to her chest.

I got myself up and made ready to leave, then paused. "Doesn't anyone find it strange that not one of us... not one of you, has rejected the idea—the possibility... of angels?" I paused again looking at each one of their tired faces, searching for some semblance of confirmation *or* rejection, or that even speaking the idea aloud might possibly blow their minds. But I got nothing—nothing but a series of half-shut eyes and tired smiles.

Then together we moved towards the front door, drained from our earlier adrenalin-rush of finding the last piece to the puzzle—well, *almost* last piece. One after another we crossed the threshold of our safe-haven and out into the real world. Tomorrow was another day, and tomorrow, Alison would be here.

"So we wait again," Uriel sighed out. He motioned for the dog to go inside, to guard his Charge.

Cooper paused at the top of the stair and took one last glance back. Then he turned and went through the open door to his home. The door shut, and the locks clicked into place.

"They can't stop now," Shamsiel protested, looking to the others for reasons. "They are so close."

Vretil appeared then, and Shamsiel gritted his teeth to halt his protest, acknowledging the sudden appearance of the *Divine Scribe.*

"They wait for The Scribe, and rightly so," Vretil said, hoping to comfort Uriel. Vretil had been on the other end of the country, watching over his Charge while the others had gathered here. "They'll resume in the morning, do not fret." Turning a glance Shamsiel's way, he said, "You—here again, shouldn't you be watching over something, or someone notably evil? Why do you linger here—with us?"

"Vretil," Uriel addressed his friend. "You know Shamsiel came to warn us, and *yes*, he watches over something evil—*Armaros*. The bastard has been trailing our Charges, and Shamsiel has been trailing *him*." Panning the faces of the others, Uriel turned back to Shamsiel. "Tell him."

Shamsiel stood his ground as if the weight of the world rested in his words to come, and perhaps it did. "He was outside the house, then downtown outside the heritage building when they found the lap desk, your Charge's lap desk—her mother's actually. Armaros was there each time—watching."

Vretil sucked in a breath, his expression fierce. "And where is he now?" he questioned. "My Charge will be on her way here soon and I will not risk her safety."

All of them watched as Shamsiel squeezed his eyes shut and bowed his head. Using all his God-given gifts, Shamsiel focused, *searching*.

"Well?" Vretil asked.

As though the word spoken was too thunderous and marred his senses, Shamsiel's hands came up to cover his ears. "I don't know," he said, "But not here... not close... not in the city... and not even this side of the country," he finished, before lowering his hands.

"Noooo!" Vretil shouted, strangling a breath, disappearing before anyone could say another word.

* * *

THIS IS NOT THE END

Printed in Great Britain
by Amazon

15746220R00205